Sailor Home From Sea

A Surf City Mystery

James R. Preston

Sailor Hone From Sea
by James R. Preston

Cover design by Heather Swaim

Rendrag Publishing 12/15/14
ISBN: 978-0-9911516-1-5 (sc)
ISBN: 978-0-9911516-2-2 (hc)

This book is for Carol Comparsi
&
Bill and Louise Hulbrock

This sailor truly came home from sea when you took him in.

I have loved to the point of madness; That which is called madness,
That which to me, is the only sensible way to love.

- Francoise Sagan (1935 – 2004)
French playwright, novelist and screenwriter

Grace Harmony Stillwater Her Book

February 16, the Year of Our Lord 1934

Dear Diary,

My name is Grace Harmony Stillwater. I am nineteen years of age, currently living in the town of Platteville, Texas. Seven months ago I graduated from Daniel Boone High School. I am the first lady of my family to achieve this distinction, although my mother certainly could have if her father, my grandfather Lamentations, had not insisted that she marry.

My mother saw me putting my good dress in my bag. It was after dinner and she came to my room to give me some extra okra that she had saved. Grandfather Lamentations had put it on his plate and then didn't finish it. I made Mama eat some of it. She is so thin and the dust makes her cough. I worry about her. It was a nice Sunday dinner. We each got a potato and some okra and even some nice string beans that Mama got from Mr. Dawkins because she mended his coat and for once Grandfather's prayer was short enough that the food was still hot. Forgive me for saying that, Lord, but it is true and I know You love him because he is a good man even if he is a hard man sometimes. She gave me a cute little book with a real leather cover and a little clasp and said I should write in it every day so my children would know my story. My Mama gave you to me when she saw me with my Sunday dress out.

I write this evening because my mother knows that I am planning to leave home. My youngest sister, dear little Hope, came in and whispered to me, "Mama knows you are fixin' to run away." Mother does not like it, but she will not stop

1

me. Papa is working so hard to make our farm survive that he has not noticed my preparations and of course Grandfather Lamentations does not know.

Tomorrow morning I will set out for California. I will stay with my friend Lou Helen Hodges. Lou Helen was a year ahead of me in school except she quit to go to California after the principal told her she had to work harder or she would not graduate. A week later she just returned the dress of mine she had borrowed -- we have been the same size since the third grade – rode the bus to Lubbock and got on the train. We both worked at the Piggly Wiggly last summer so we both have a little money saved. I don't want to be an old lady working in the Piggly Wiggly and anyway the manager said he didn't know how long he could keep me on. So many people have left. They just abandon their farms and go west. So the Piggly Wiggly isn't selling half of what it used to. I have my High School Diploma and I want to do something. I don't know what, but it's not here in Platteville.

Lou Helen wrote me and said there is work in California. She has a job riding horses in a movie! If I stay here I do not know what will become of me. Nothing beyond marrying, probably one of the Whateley boys, and raising children. I just don't love those boys, not the way I want to love somebody.

I know the moment when I decided with great certainty what I must do. I found my mother very early one morning, reading my history book and she was crying because she didn't know all the words.

Daddy's land is about played out and he doesn't have enough to plant in the spring anyway. We had a dust storm that just about blotted out the sky and they say the dust is blowing all the way to New York but I don't know as I believe that. Last winter was hard and we about froze and they say it doesn't ever snow in Los Angeles.

Dear Lord, please look out for Mama and Papa and my sisters Faith and Hope and brothers Joshua and Deuteronomy and Grandfather Lamentations.

I know of a great job that I can have whenever I want. The pay is outrageous, the offices are spectacular, your co-workers interesting people. The work is challenging, a total rush when you win. The annual Winter Party has a Porsche Carrera as a door prize. I could go back whenever I wanted; I really could.

-- From the Journal of T. R. Macdonald

Chapter One

My gunshot wound was mostly healed so I went surfing.

I woke up, as usual, a little before dawn, and said, "I feel great." I was downstairs sleeping on the couch. I kind of like sleeping there when Kandi's not with me. I leave the blinds open in the family room and the view out over the channel, even in the gray pre-dawn light, always makes me feel good; that, a deep breath of sea air, a cup of freshly ground Kenya AA coffee and a brand-new stand-up paddleboard make life worth living. Like I said, I felt great. It was a fine morning, clear, no wind. Surfline dot com said it was low tide, three to four feet. The cameras showed mid-sized glassy waves. Perfect.

Fortunately I'd slept in board shorts (Kanvas by Katin, of course) and a t-shirt, so all I needed to do after coffee was step into my sandals and grab the car keys, wallet, and cell phone from the beat-up little table in the entryway.

I opened the garage and stood for a moment admiring my new ride. A couple of months ago I'd done a favor for some extremely wealthy people and during the course of the favor I had totaled my car. The hot rod was sort of a thank you. From the outside she looks like a 1955 Chevy Bel Air two-door hardtop, the kind they call "shoebox" or "tri-five" but there's not a stock part on her. It's sky blue with a cream top with a two-door steel body that was built by a company that specializes in replica car bodies.

My feet were getting cold so I quit admiring the car and hoisted the board up onto the roof rack, tossed my wetsuit and the paddle into the back seat, and pushed the button to raise the garage door. I wasn't singing my song, but the Beach Boys would approve anyway.

When the garage door started to rumble up I looked in the rear-view mirror and saw feet. The toes were pointed toward me. They had on green tennis shoes, tight black jeans and as the door moved up to show me shins, the feet turned and ran then the door stopped about three feet from the floor.

Pushing the control in the car did nothing, so I jumped out, dropped to the floor and rolled out under the door, in time to see a skinny kid beating feet down the middle of my street. I ran after him but I was hampered by my sandals and his head start. I was holding my own, maybe gaining a little, when a figure in a dark sweatshirt launched itself out from behind a hedge and tackled me. We both went down, with the other guy on top.

In high school and college I was a wrestler so this was not exactly a new position for me. The thing to do in that situation is to keep rolling, use the momentum to roll over on top of the other guy. It didn't work, at least not the way I hoped. We rolled but before I could get on top he shoved me aside, got to his feet and ran. I stumbled to my feet and chased him, but it was no good. Before I closed half the distance he dove head first into the side door of a van and it accelerated away quickly, too quickly for me to get the license number. For a moment I stood, hands on knees, panting. Then I straightened and walked back to my house. On the way I checked under my shirt and was relieved to see that the little round scar that marked where I'd been shot had not opened up. I groped at the one on my back that matched it and my fingers came away blood-free.

As I walked up the driveway I looked for anything out of the ordinary and found nothing. Then I noticed a small black cylinder, about the size of a tube of lipstick, in the grass next to the driveway, and when I picked it up I saw one end was curved glass and the other had a short wire sticking out. It was a wireless webcam. I was looking at it while it looked at me. I debated with myself for a moment—call the cops or not? I decided not. I had no license number, no real ID on the van or the people, and it looked like nothing was missing. Also, my neighbors have seen police activity at my house a few times in the past, and I didn't want to add another incident unless I had to.

I took the camera into the garage and put it in a metal toolbox, closed the lid. Then I pulled the manual release, rolled the garage door down by hand and went back inside. I went through the house thoroughly and found nothing that didn't belong there. I logged into my security system -- some of those times the police have been at my place convinced me I needed a good one -- and checked the activity log. No breaks. And my cameras covering the driveway only showed a figure in a black hoodie sweatshirt who turned and ran as the door came up. Then I watched myself roll out and sprint away, exit stage right. I thought I looked pretty good for somebody recovering from a gunshot wound.

Now what? The obvious answer: surf.

The garage door opened the way it was supposed to. While I was letting the Chevy's engine warm up I checked messages. My phone showed there were no texts from my Significant Other, Mary Shaw, aka Kandi, which kind of surprised me. As part of a doctoral program in psychology she was interning at a Chicago facility for the seriously nuts called the Usher Clinic. How crazy were some of the people at Usher? Her first patient was a cannibal. He killed his wife, froze her disemboweled body and ate her, or as much of her as he could before the neighbors started to wonder about her absence and he got caught. The competition for the Chicago internship had been fierce, but she beat out the other finalist for the position, a guy named Bernard Sigmund. Okay, nothing from Kandi. But her work was challenging and I knew she didn't have a lot of free time. Time to surf. And I felt great. Kids maybe planting cameras around the house was not enough to ruin the day.

I cranked up the stereo and took Algonquin to Warner and turned left on Pacific Coast Highway to a surf spot known as Seacliff. I watched for anybody following me. Watched carefully. I prefer surfing at the famous Huntington Pier, but they were setting up for a surf contest that started in a couple of days and as a result the beach was crowded with crews setting up bleachers and portapotties.

A week ago, anticipating my recovery from assorted injuries, I had bought myself a new board, a huge, almost ten-foot stand-up paddleboard. On old-style longboards like my dad used, you paddled on your knees, resulting in lumps of cartilage called "surf knots," (a. k. a. "housemaid's knee," but no bitchin' guy ever called it that), bumps on your shins just below your kneecap. Then modern short boards let you lie down and paddle. And now there are SUP, stand-up paddleboards, where you don't lie prone and stroke, you stand up and paddle with what looks like something you would use in a canoe. After I bought it, I had sent Kandi a picture of my new toy and in the email said I couldn't wait to get her out on it since it would float two adults comfortably. Kandi doesn't much like the water, so I thought this might help her get used to it. She hadn't responded, but I knew that was just because she was immersed in work. This one was made to imitate an old 1960's surfboard, blue body with a stripe down the center that was painted to look like a balsa stringer.

I got lucky and found a spot in the small parking lot on the cliff overlooking the beach, fed the meter, put the paddle and my wetsuit under my arm, picked up the board (there's a slot in the middle that provides a way to grab it.) It's not as easy as it looks in the movies, but I made it down the incline to the asphalt bike path, waited as a lifeguard drove by on a four-wheel ATV, and across the cool sand to the waves. There was no waxing necessary -- this baby came with a sure-grip rubber mat for you to stand on, so I was in the water as soon as I zipped up my wetsuit. Of course I watched the break for a few minutes before heading out; if you've surfed for any length of time you know to do that, checking the current, the shape, and where the groups of people were. Once I was in the water it was awesome, stroking along, as stable as if you were standing on a coffee table. I am a natural goofy foot, meaning that I surf with my right foot forward, but this board was so stable you could ride it any way you wanted, so I just stood, faced forward and paddled. The surf was small and the shape medium-to-poor, perfect for somebody like me learning a new form of surfing. There were about a dozen people out that morning, The sun came up over Saddleback Mountain and the early morning light poured through gaps in the clouds, painting bright spots on the slate gray seas, lighted areas that moved, broke up and reformed. Red sky at morning. It was enough to make those of us out for some early-morning tubes stop and watch.

I caught one small wave and rode it straight in. I paddled back out and turned. Outside the break line I stood on the board and looked at the parking lot. A light-colored van had pulled in next to my Chevy. As I watched, a man wearing a baseball cap got out of the van and stood looking out to sea. Then he raised binoculars. Not unusual; watching people surf is a local tourist attraction. When I looked again, the van was gone.

I paddled around for a while, getting used to the board, amazed at the stability. After an hour or so the wind came up and blew out the surf, so I came in. On the way home I checked and there were no messages from Kandi. As I parked the car and dragged the paddleboard off the roof rack I was wondering, not concerned yet, but wondering.

I called her. It went straight to voicemail. That meant her phone was turned off, which she did when she was working with a patient. I told her the surf was up and that she should call me, went out back, peeled out of my wetsuit, carefully rinsed off the zipper -- salt water is hard on almost any form of metal -- turned it inside out, rinsed it, and hung it up to begin drying.

On the kitchen table my laptop chirped. Thinking it might be Kandi, I opened the email program and saw that it was from someone called Tex. I figured "Tex" was Kandi's cousin Chet Shaw; he loves the Wild West so I made the foolish assumption that he had a new screen name. I was wrong.

When I opened the email it showed me a picture of Kandi. I can't say I was alarmed, not yet. She was sitting in a chair at the end of a row of identical seats that looked like they might be in a waiting room somewhere. She was wearing a short denim skirt and a long-sleeved white blouse, unbuttoned, over a pale blue tank top. Her purse was next to her and a small wheelie suitcase was at her feet. Slowly, one at a time, words appeared below the picture:

But I cannot sleep—how can I with the terrible danger hanging over my

darling, and her going out into that awful place....

This wasn't from Chet Shaw.

Kandi had been photographed sitting somewhere. The suitcase made me think it might be an airport. It could be an old snapshot of her travels after she graduated from UCLA, except there were no travels; after she got her bachelors, she immediately entered the doctoral program. And I could tell she was tense, nervous. When you love someone you study them, you want to learn body language, clues to mood and feelings, and I had spent my career interviewing business executives so I had a lot of practice. I zoomed on the picture and studied it. No, not tense. Scared.

Three minutes later I had sent a text to Chet and another one to Kandi.

My phone rang. My HBPD detective friend Tony Genucci said, "Mac, have you been to the stable?" Tony is a good friend and we've been through some interesting stuff together. He likes designer suits, fine dining, and police work.

"What?"

Behind him, I could hear the chatter of a busy police squad room.

"How would you like to do a little investigating? Poke around a little bit, get some information for me? Knowing you, you're going to do it anyway." He paused. "I can make you semi-official."

In the background a voice said, "Hey Tony, GQ called. They want you for the cover."

Another voice said, "He was on last month's"

Tony responded, "Stinman, you know you can't read."

I said, "They never let up, do they?"

"You made me, if not famous, at least well-known. I'll start to worry when they let up."

Tony is on his way up, to either the FBI or Homeland Security, and some of his colleagues on the force give him a hard time about it.

"What's up? What stable? And a strange thing happened a little while ago that I want to tell you about. And I've got an email that worries me."

"Sounds like a typical morning for you. Anybody break into your house or beat you up?"

"How did you know?"

"Lucky guess -- and one of your neighbors has cameras that feed to Harbour Security and they sent us the video. You were doing well until the second perp tackled you."

"Oh."

"So is there anything you would like to tell me?"

"Later. Look, somebody sent me an email --"

He cut me off. "I caught a different case. Beachside Stables. Central Park. They have received threats. They are in the middle of remodeling and they have an artist documenting the process."

"All right, Tony, I'm waiting for a text . . . ."

"The artist is painting scenes of the remodeling. The messages say they need to make him stop."

"Tony, I'm lost. Why are you working this? And why do you want me involved?"

"You really don't know?"

"No. Talk fast; the suspense is killing me."

There was a pause while I listened to more background chatter. Then he said slowly, "The artist doing the painting is Mike Macdonald. Your father."

Now it was my turn to be quiet for a moment. How much to tell Tony? Eventually, all of it, it was that kind of friendship, but now was not the time. The woman I love was still on my laptop screen, looking afraid. "Tony." Deep breath. "What about him?"

"The private stable in Central Park has been receiving threatening notes. Last night there was a small fire. This all started with a grant that funded the remodeling and the artist to create the watercolors. The anonymous donor added a condition. All of the construction work has to be documented in paintings by your father. You know all this."

"I don't know any of this."

Tony paused. The conversations of people in trouble filled the background. "I see," Tony said. "There have been threats to the stable where he's painting. And these threats mention your dad by name." He paused. "Mike Macdonald. Another detective recognized the name and passed the information to me."

"And now you say there are threats. Threats that use his name."

"Correct." I was truly stuck for a response.

"T. R., are you there?"

"My father paints watercolors?"

There was silence on the other end. Even the background chatter had died down. Tony skipped the obvious embarrassing questions and settled for "Yes."

"You said something about a fire? Anything else beside the notes?"

"Vandalism." He paused, then went on, probably reading for a report. "The incidents began a few days after your dad started painting. And last night, the fire. You really don't know?"

"He's not big on staying in touch."

"I see. Things are a bit tight around here, budget-wise. I thought you might like to go out, take a look around the scene. Mac, if this is uncomfortable for you, or awkward in any way, it's all right. You don't have to go."

"I'm a civilian."

"Sort of. Past events have made it unclear exactly what you are, but yes, you will have no official standing."

The email worried me, but there wasn't much more to do now.

"Sure, why not?" Maybe my father's feelings had changed. After all, he was in Huntington Beach. "This is the stable in Central Park?"

"Beachside Stables is a smaller equestrian facility next to the one run by the city. It's been there since the twenties. Caters to high-end horse owners, but definitely needs some work because of its age."

"All right, I'll go over and look around."

I cruised down Warner, turned right on Goldenwest, and parked the Chevy in the shade of a Jacaranda, next to a Ford crew-cab. I killed the engine and sat for a moment. The faded red pick-up had seen better days, but it looked like it was ready for work, with the tailgate down and a stack of 2-by-12s sticking out. The red rag tied to the end of the lumber fluttered in the breeze as I sat in my car, putting off the inevitable. A young guy in a hardhat and a ripped wife-beater top that stretched over a good start on a beer belly, walked up and slid out two of the boards. He looked at me incuriously, settled them on his shoulder, and left. Even through the rolled-up windows I could hear the sounds of construction: somewhere a saw sliced into lumber, diesels chugged, and over it all there was a rhythmic clank-clank of machinery. It was like stepping back in time, to summer days when I'd gone to work with my Dad to watch because I liked it and because we couldn't afford day care. I liked it because my mom was gone and I was with my dad and he was doing neat stuff, driving heavy equipment. I liked it until I figured out how much my dad didn't like it, parking me in the office while he worked. I remember watching the office manager enter tidy rows of numbers into spreadsheets, and eating the extra Tiger Tails and Ding Dongs I'd packed, along with any crew donuts that were left after lunch, stale or not. With a little effort I could revisit the dull resentment at my mother for leaving. It took no effort at all to remember my confusion trying to figure out what I had done to make her go away. It was bad that I didn't know what I had done wrong. It was worse that my dad didn't know either, but in my heart, back then, I believed he was sure it was something I'd done, maybe just the fact that I was there.

We didn't get over it; we grew out of it.

Things were getting better. When I was in ninth grade my dad got a job driving heavy earthmoving equipment doing site prep for a hillside housing development in a new South County development called Aliso Viejo. There was a lot of overtime so he wasn't home much.

One day the assistant principal pulled me out of homeroom and took me to the office. They said an embankment of loose dirt had given way under the water truck my father was moving. He was hurt. Was there somebody they could call?

It was the assistant principal who finally volunteered to drive me to the hospital; my father was still in surgery so I waited. I lied and told the AP I had someone I could call and he left, his relief obvious even to a kid. It was okay. I had my allowance and there was a food machine and it was so long ago that even in a hospital it still had old-fashioneds -- cellophane-wrapped things we called lard bars, three of them leaning against the spiral rack. I bought them all and held them on my lap for what seemed a long time. Then I ate the old-fashioneds, one after another.

A man came out wearing pale green scrubs. He said, "I'm the surgeon who operated on your father."

"Okay."

"You know what the femur is? The big bone in your leg? The femoral shaft—here, look at this." He sketched a drawing on a piece of notepaper from my backpack. "This is the long part, called the femoral shaft. It goes from the hip down almost to the knee. The bone gets wider just before the knee."

"Okay."

"Your dad's injuries are multiple fractures to the femoral shaft, including one down in that wide part before the knee. I'm afraid these are serious injuries."

"He's gonna be okay, isn't he?"

The surgeon patted my arm. "We're doing everything we can."

It was okay. We had insurance. The union helped. At first, of course, it was awful: hospital, surgery, home for a while, then more surgery, then here are your new crutches, Mr. Macdonald, we think you will be able to get around just fine. Just fine until you go to a movie and where do you put the damn things after you've made it to a seat? After the first time he had to collect the sticks, slide his arms into the metal circles and gimp off to the men's room halfway through *Titanic*, we switched exclusively to rented DVDs. We made it a joke. He'd mutter, "Titanic" and I'd hit the Pause button. But we got over it.

Things were getting better. I looked in the mirror one day -- it was summer and there wasn't much to do -- and said, "I'm fat." I pulled the emergency 12-pack of Tiger Tails out from under my bed and ate the three remaining. Then I started running. I gave up Snow-Balls in favor of the wrestling team and surfing. First using one of my dad's dinged longboards, then a used tri-fin. And I found out that I didn't like surfing -- I loved it. Then there was CSULB and Diana in my Health Ed class on the first day with no pen, no book, no note paper and she was late. Love at first sight.

My dad thought Diana was the best thing that ever happened to either of us. At first he was right.

Then I graduated and we got married and I got a job, with a boutique brokerage called Fields, Smith, and Barkman. "Boutique" meaning that we handled a small number of very wealthy clients. All at once canned Dinty Moore beef stew was no longer a diet staple; it was Chanticleer or Five Crowns whenever I had a spare evening. On the evenings I didn't have to spare, she got stoned. My beautiful bride, who I had loved from the moment she first borrowed notepaper and a pen from me in Health Ed, sank into giggling, blank-eyed bliss. Her parents moved into assisted living and we moved into their house in Huntington Harbour. In my own defense I handled all the details and I visited them regularly, always with a new excuse for Diana's absence.

Then I left her, not in the sense that I found another woman, but my job took me to Manhattan; she didn't want to go and then she was killed. And my father hadn't spoken to me since Diana's funeral, when he asked me a question I still couldn't answer.

And here we go again.

Chapter Two

Nobody stopped me so I walked along the path toward the sounds of construction and found him sitting in a canvas-backed folding chair. I stopped and looked.

He was wearing a faded red t-shirt with the diamond-shaped Jacobs logo on the back and plaid board shorts. With a pang I saw that he still had the surf knots. But now his legs were shriveled and dead. His head was slumped forward and his chin rested on his chest. I could hear the snores, more short snorts than long snores and that brought back a memory, too.

I stood for a moment just watching him sleep, not sure of what to do.

There was movement behind me and the guy in the wife-beater shirt stepped around me, holding a finger to his lips. He gently took the paintbrush from my dad's hand and put it in a jelly glass of liquid. For a moment I thought my dad might wake up—he shifted in the chair slightly but a moment later he was back to snoring. The young guy picked up a blanket and spread it over the withered, knotted, legs. I wished I had thought to do that. He gestured and we stepped away.

"You the son?"

"Yeah. T. R. Macdonald."

"Jerry." He stuck out his hand and we shook. "We like the old guy. He don't sleep so good, you know. We let him sleep when he crashes here. Man, he's got some surf stories! You know he surfed Doheney? Before the breakwater ruined it? And he was a top ten finisher in one of the early contests at the pier."

"Yeah."

"Hey, we, me and some of the guys, were thinking we'd take him with us to the contest next week. Bro, you oughta come with, it'll be cool."

"Thanks, Jerry, I will if I can."

Jerry nodded.

As I walked back to my car he said, "Hey, man, I'll tell him you came by." I thought he might say something like, "He talks about you," but he didn't.

As I started the Chevy an old man, late seventies at least, holding a flat-bladed shovel stared at me. He shuffled over to the car, dragging the shovel, and said, "My name is Neville. I take care of things. What's yours?"

"T. R. Macdonald. Call me Mac."

"Hello, Mr. Mac." He shoved his hand in through the window and we shook. "My name is Neville. I take care of things. Acey's the boss. And Jackie works for her. Do you know them?"

"No, I don't."

"Oh. Do you know who my people are?"

"No, I don't, Neville. Who are they?"

His face fell. "I don't know either. But I have a book." He pulled out a paperback copy of *The Wasteland* held together with a rubber band, and showed it to me. "Okee-dokee. Bye-bye." He put the book back in his pocket and walked away, dragging the shovel. A middle-aged woman in jeans stood next to him. He waved. She didn't.

On the way home I picked up a shrimp burrito with a side of rice from Fred's Fine Mexican Food. Back in my family room I spread out lunch. Out of habit I tapped the touchpad. I'm kind of a news junkie so it immediately went to a current events site. It automatically pulled up a story about an artist winning a grant to produce watercolors documenting the reconstruction of Beachside Stables, not because I'm interested in art—I'm not, except as an investment and I do not offer advice on that—but because the painter had my last name.

Local Stable Gets Remodel

Beachside Stables, formerly Stables-by-the-Sea, has been a part of the Orange County equestrian scene since the 1920s. This reconstruction, for expansion and modernization, was funded by an anonymous grant. The donation included funds designated for a series of watercolors to chart the course of construction. Painter Mike Macdonald will produce the art, some of which will be auctioned off at the grand opening. Macdonald, formerly an Irvine resident, is known for his renderings of construction sites throughout Central California.

Now they tell me. I stared for a moment, then shook it off. I couldn't get it out of my head: my father had relocated to my home town and not told me. Looked like nothing had changed.

The burrito was great, as usual. Tiny little shrimp grilled and wrapped in a flour tortilla with just the right amount of green sauce. I looked down at my plate and it was nearly gone. I finished the last bite of rice and, loaded down with a cup of coffee, cell phone, and laptop, I walked out back and sat cross-legged on the dock and looked around. It was early afternoon and the channel in front of me was clear and smooth except for the regular splashes created by one of my neighbors swimming by. She does a mile a day, winter and summer, without a wetsuit.

I live in Huntington Harbour, an upscale part of Huntington Beach, California and no matter what anybody says, we are the real Surf City, USA. The Harbour, always spelled with the British "u," is a development on five islands dredged out of a mud flat back in the sixties, before Environmental Impact Reports, Save the Wetlands and years of lawsuits. Back then it was, "Hey, I got a bunch of bulldozers, let's build a housing development." Diana's parents had bought one of the originals, paying the then-fabulous sum of $50,000 for a two-story, five-bedroom, three-bath waterfront home, complete with boat dock. Diana stayed behind when I took a job offer in the Fields, Smith, and Barkman New York office.

My AP news feed was still up and running. Under Local Headlines the first story was:

UCLA Teaching Assistant's Death Under Investigation

Los Angeles and state police are investigating the hit-and-run death yesterday of Bernard Sigmund, 30. Police declined to provide further details, but would not rule out homicide.

I had scrolled on to the next story before I made the connection. When I did I felt a prickle along my spine, and I have learned not to ignore those prickles. I immediately hit the back button, and as I did I remembered.

Sigmund was one of Mary's colleagues in the Psych Department at UCLA. I had apparently entered his name along with others when I set up the news-monitoring profile, causing the story to pop up. I had never met him, but she had talked about him as one of the people against whom she was competing for the Chicago internship.

Now the prickle was gone, replaced by a little alarm bell ringing in the back of my head. I got a picture of Mary with ominous words as a caption. Somebody wanted to plant a camera at my house. The doctoral candidate who was Kandi's competition for the Chicago internship was killed in a hit-and-run accident.

I tried Kandi's cell again. Straight to voicemail. I called the Usher Clinic and got, "We're sorry, all our lines are busy. We care about your call, and we care about you. If you think you or someone you know has a psychiatric emergency, call 9-1-1. Stay on the line to leave us a message. The Usher Clinic thanks you for your patience." I was thinking about what to say and had settled on casual – something along the lines of, "This message is for Mary Shaw. Hey, Mary, call Mac when you get a chance" – when I heard, "The voice mailbox is full. Please try again later."

Now I was officially concerned

When you need information, call an expert, right? I pushed the speed dial for Kandi's cousin, Chet Shaw. He was in San Francisco, speaking at a computer-security conference. High-level, invitation only. But he'd take my call if he could.

And got his voicemail.

Maybe they were all at a party and I wasn't invited. I left him the message I had planned to leave for Kandi.

Now what?

First things first. I went out back and dried off my board before carefully leaning it against the house, checked my wetsuit and found it still damp so I left it.

My phone chirped. "Chet, I was just about to call you again."

"Then you've heard."

"Yeah, the cops just decided to call it a possible homicide and I thought you could do some digging."

"What? Of course it's a homicide. He shot her three times." My chest constricted and I couldn't breathe. "Mac? Mac, you there, pard? Wait, whoa, whoa, who are you talking about?"

I swallowed. Shot three times. Swallowed again. "Sigmund."

"Who's Sigmund? I'm talking about the murder-suicide at the clinic in Chicago where Mary's interning. Yesterday."

"Mary—"

"Oh, Lordy, sorry, sorry, pard. Mary's fine, fine but there was an incident where she works, a bad one."

After we got our wires uncrossed he sent me a link to the article. It was from *The Chicago Sun Times* and dated two days before.

Bloody Murder-Suicide Shocks Usher Clinic

The apparent murder-suicide today of two psychologists at the Usher Clinic shut down the Chicago mental health center, home to some of the most disturbed individuals in the nation.

Police said there is no evidence of patient involvement. Usher officials were not available for comment.

Responding to an anonymous tip, police discovered the bodies of Jennifer Prewett and Harold Lugard in clinic office. The unidentified caller said there had been shouting and "loud thumping sounds." Police found Prewett already dead, shot multiple times with a small-caliber handgun. Her co-worker Lugard died of an apparently self-inflicted gunshot wound. He was found on the floor next to Prewett.

The 40-year-old Usher Center for Rehabilitation Studies is a well-known Chicago institution, associated with the University of Chicago.

"Chet, I need you to dig into the Chicago thing."

"What are we looking for?"

"I'll know it when I see it. Meanwhile I'm sending you a picture somebody calling themselves 'Tex' sent me."

"Tex?"

"They wanted to make me think it was from you so I'd open it, and it worked."

I forwarded the email. He looked at it and whistled softly. "Mary. Not good."

"Can you ID the sender?"

"Sure, but it will be some Internet cafe. Anonymous. But the snapshot was taken this morning at O'Hare. Probably a waiting room. And before you ask, the picture records latitude and longitude and when it was taken."

"All right. Do the Chicago killings and then Sigmund. Leave the email ID for later."

"What about the quote?"

"Last. Lowest priority."

"On it."

Then I called Tony back. "Tony, Mac."

"Have you been to the stable?"

"I called because the Suit Police want me to make sure you're wearing one." He was able to resist my wit. Tony's a hard case sometimes. "Listen, I have a question."

"Tell me about the stable first."

"I saw my dad, but he was asleep. Met one of the construction workers, a young guy named Jerry, and an old man called Neville. I didn't get their last names."

"Neville doesn't have one. He was a foundling, literally left on the doorstep in 1935."

"You been reading Dickens again?"

"*Bleak House.* Why?"

"Oh, nothing."

"Neville has lived at the stable his whole life. Mentally-challenged. So you just left? That's not like you at all.'"

"I have other things on my mind. Look, I really do have a question."

"Oh, good. I was so afraid I'd have to work today." Somehow he didn't sound too enthusiastic, despite the fact that I have helped him more than once, and had been instrumental in getting him transferred to Crimes Against Persons, which he wanted because my pal is ambitious.

"This is a good one. People will think you're Sherlock Holmes."

"I *am* Sherlock Holmes. Okay, Mac, I really am working here, unlike certain individuals I could name. You got up and went surfing, didn't you?"

"Who, me?"

"I knew it. I'm working."

"You want a homicide? Dude, you came to the right place. It's about that UCLA hit-and-run

"It took place in Westwood."

"I know. Isn't it great? You can get in good with the LAPD."

"State Police have it." There was a pause. I could almost see him, sitting at his perfectly arranged desk, an island of neat in the midst of the bustle of a busy police squad room, straightening the crease in his suit pants as he decided what to say.

The thought of possibly helping the Staties got him, like I knew it would. He said, "Wait one." He turned away from the phone. A moment later he said, "You have my attention for the next three minutes."

"The people investigating it need to look at it very carefully. It might not be the simple hit-and-run it looks like."

There was a pause, then "Why do you say that, Mac?"

"Bernard Sigmund, the guy who was killed, was a colleague of Mary Shaw's and two days ago there was a murder-suicide at the place she's interning in Chicago." I hadn't liked it when I first heard about the accident and the shootings and as I heard myself describe it to Tony G. I liked it even less -- you're not paranoid if they're really after you, right? Or maybe if they're really after you it doesn't matter if you're paranoid. Something like that.

I heard his keyboard clicking. "I see the report. You think this may have something to do with Ms. Shaw?"

"I can't see how, but it's certainly coincidental."

"I'll call you back. Goodbye now."

A moment later I was texting Kandi.

U ok? Heard about recent events. Let me know.

I got up and paced. I checked the Boston Whaler again. I thought about the end of the *Diana*, my Catalina 34. It sank after people who didn't like me shot holes in the hull. But that isn't what finished the job. The end came when I set fire to the boat and burned her down to the waterline. I decided I'd rather do something dumb than do nothing at all. Little alarm bells were going off in my head. In the movies when that happens the hero usually knows what to do, but no clue presented itself and I was not sure I'd recognize one if it did. If I got a flight out of LAX I could be in Chicago by dinner and Kandi would be glad to see me when I turned up at her workplace, maybe. Probably. She was pretty serious about her work and keeping counseling separate from her personal life. Screw it. I could take her to a late dinner at a cool jazz place I knew on Navy Pier. My phone vibrated in my pocket. It was Tony.

"All right, Mr. Macdonald, we need to know everything you know about Bernard Sigmund's death." His use of 'we' and 'Mr. Macdonald' was a warning that people were listening. Answer with care. Probably best to leave out the funny comments about the Suit Police.

"Sigmund worked with Kandi, sorry, with Mary Shaw, at UCLA when she was a teaching assistant. They didn't get along. They were the top two candidates for the Chicago internship. She got the job. He didn't."

"How did Mr. Sigmund feel about that?"

"He was pissed. Your turn, Tony."

Obviously speaking to impress whoever was listening, he said, "Mr. Macdonald, you are not to repeat what I say next to anyone. Your deductions were correct. I spoke to the officer in charge and requested a second look from the ME, which had already been completed. The Medical Examiner concluded that Mr. Sigmund was dead when the car hit him, not long dead, but dead. The body was damaged by the impact, typical pedestrian-versus-car rotation, causing multiple points of impact on the pavement, as well as extensive abdominal bruising, multiple fractures of the tibia and fibia plus a subdermal hematoma caused by a skull fracture. His body was damaged to such an extent that the evidence marks were partially obscured."

"What killed him?"

Another voice said, "Detective, no. He's a civilian."

Tony said, "Yes, no, not exactly. He's not totally a civilian. My responsibility."

The other voice, probably State Police, said "Yes, it is."

"Mr. Macdonald, cause of death was strangulation. Fractured hyoid. Somebody choked him to death; judging by the ligature marks and leather fragments in the wound, probably with some kind of wide strap."

"Belt, maybe?"

"Detective Genucci, once again I caution you." LAPD? Or somebody else, somebody more formal?

Tony ignored him. "The leading thought at the moment is a wide belt, one old enough for it to shed bits of leather."

"Okay, Tony, listen, I—"

He cut me off. "Mr. Macdonald, is it your expectation that I will believe you deduced this, that you made this connection solely on the basis of another crime in Chicago?"

"That's the truth." Even to me it sounded defensive, maybe a little whiney.

"The investigating officers are skeptical. They want to know how you came up with specific information they had not developed yet; they believe you have a source of information other than the news." He paused and I wondered if he was adjusting the creases again or flicking a bit of dust off his polished wingtips. "I helped you. Now you need to tell us everything."

"All I know is it's just too coincidental. Two, no, three, three people connected with Mary killed in the space of 48 hours."

There was silence on the other end. "That's really all?"

"That's really all."

"All right. Information about the belt is being withheld in hopes of making the murderer overconfident. All right, I have to go."

"Tony, wait, wait a minute. Can you talk to Chicago? Find out the details of this murder-suicide?"

He said that he had anticipated my request and already sent the email; the other person on the line grunted and told me to stay available for further interrogation. I said it was something to live for.

After Tony said "Good bye, now" and hung up I stood for a moment, wondering what, if anything, I should do next. Nothing came to mind. LAPD wouldn't like it if, immediately after talking with them, I hopped a flight for Chicago. They'd get over it, I hoped, before they arrested me.

I was saved from having to think too much. My phone chirped again.

When I answered, Chet said, "Mac, I'm trolling for names here, like I always do, and do you know a Mike Macdonald?"

"What about Chicago?"

"Done. I'm sending it."

"Mike Macdonald is my father."

There was a pause, then, "Hey, cool. He's been given a grant. He's painting at a stable in Huntington Beach."

"I saw it."

My relations with my father were great when I was growing up, really. My mother left and he stepped up, raised me the best he could, and if you ask me the man did a damn good job. Then some other bad things happened to him, and he dealt with those problems, too. Then I left my wife. Then she was killed and that was the thing he couldn't deal with. A year ago at her funeral, standing by the open grave on a hillside in San Pedro, looking out over the harbor, he asked, "How could you?" He turned and struggled up the grassy hill to his car. We hadn't spoken since and, yes, if you think that question echoes in my mind when Tokyo's closing and the New York market hasn't opened and the only sound is my breathing and the gentle lap of the water against the dock as I sit crosslegged on the wooden planks and wait for the sun, you would be right. I haven't visited her grave. Sometimes she talks to me, but I haven't visited her grave. I thought my father was living a hundred miles north, in Ventura, but I guess I was wrong. He moved back to Huntington Beach and didn't tell me.

My friend Walter "Snake" Dalrymple arrived and strolled into the back yard. He's in his sixties, short and round and bearded. As usual, he was dressed in jeans, a t-shirt and Birkenstock sandals. Basically, with his hair down to his shoulders, he looks like somebody who fell asleep at Woodstock, just woke up and doesn't like what he sees. Despite a degree in physics from Berkeley, he's a librarian at Cal State Long Beach. I brought him up to speed.

Snake said, "The dead guy from UCLA."

"And a murder-suicide where Kandi works. And I got a picture of her sitting somewhere, like a waiting area in an airport. Chet's digging for information on the sender and the quote." I showed him the picture on my laptop.

"It's Jonathan Harker talking about his wife Mina Harker, née Murray."

"Of course it is. Snake, what are you talking about?"

"*Dracula*. The quote is from *Dracula*." I guess I looked blank. "The epistolary novel published in 1897 by Archibald Constable and Company, written by Bram Stoker, b. 1847, d. 1912. Not in any of the movies." I don't know if Snake has true eidetic memory, but if he doesn't he's damn close. If he reads it, he remembers it.

"Boy, I'm really glad you clarified that. Harker, he's the guy who eats bugs, right?"

Snake looked at me pityingly. "No. Renfield eats bugs in the movies. Harker and Van Helsing are the heroes; Mina is the love of Harker's life and Dracula wants her. Almost gets her, too." He shook his shaggy head. "If Stoker wrote *Dracula* today it would be a collection of emails, texts, and blog articles." He looked out over the water, then down at me. "Get up. I need a beer." I got up and we started back toward the house. "Your life is blog material and it's cranking up again, isn't it?"

Closing the screen door behind me, I said, "Snake, I just don't know." But I was pretty sure that, as Sherlock would say, the game was afoot. See? I have culture, too.

My love's name is Mary Shaw, but she made up 'Kandi' when she went to work in a bar. That's the name she used when we met and I thought of her that way. And it looked like we were once again involved in something unpleasant. The next call proved it was more than just the two of us. Chet said, "Mac, where are you right now?"

"Chet? How many ostriches do you own?"

"Nine. We just had us a blessed event." There was a pause. "Ooh, good test. It's really me."

"I'm at home in the kitchen getting Snake a beer."

"Tell him I said, 'Howdy.' Go into the family room and watch. I'm turning on the big screen. You need to see this." The events of the past year have convinced me to invest in some pretty sophisticated home security and since that's what Kandi's genius cousin did for a living I had top-of-the-line cameras and a home network that was professional quality. Chet had access and could check the cameras remotely, and he could send to any networked screen in the house.

I trotted into the family room and sat on the couch facing the wall with the big screen mounted on it. A minute later the Snake plopped down beside me. He's not much for trotting. There was a moment of static and then Chet was in a small window in one corner of the screen looking grim. Another window opened. It showed a video of Kandi standing in line at an airport check-in counter. The waiting area was crowded, full of people carrying coffee or bottles of water, and wheeling small suitcases. The windows behind the counter showed a 747's bulbous snout. Chet said, "Okay, now watch what happens." Kandi handed a sheet of paper, probably her boarding pass, to the woman behind the counter. The woman held it under the bar code reader, looked at the result and frowned. She punched some keys on her computer, looked puzzled, did it again, then shook her head and handed the paper back. Chet paused the playback. "We're not done. Watch this." As Kandi stood and talked to the check-in woman and the crowd behind her shifted and muttered, words appeared at the bottom of the screen.

We seem to be drifting into unknown places and unknown ways; into a whole world of dark and dreadful things.

"Mac, I haven't gotten into the airline system yet, but it looks like she was flying somewhere and her ticket, boarding pass actually, was denied at the gate."

"Cancelled. I bet somebody cancelled it."

"Yeah. Pard, that is some high-level hacking."

"You could do it."

Like I said, Chet is Kandi's cousin. He always calls her "Mary" because that's what he grew up with. He's a genius, a real, bona fide genius. If it's electronic he loves it, and he'd be a stereotypical geek if it weren't for the fact that he lives on a ranch outside of Las Vegas with a lovely showgirl named Katerina Kohl. He loves the Old West as it appears in movies; he's a crack shot with a six-shooter, speaks fluent Cantonese and fair Mandarin, and studied lock-picking on a whim. He used to be a hacker; now he's reformed, mostly, and owns a company that provides security for casinos all over the world. When he was still in school he designed a game called "Attack of the Space Floozies," which made him rich, and the sequel, "Revenge of the Space Floozies," that made him a multi-millionaire. I knew because I handled his investments.

"Sure, but there aren't many in my league. But why? And here's another thing I don't like -- this video was sent to me, not you."

"I got the still picture, you got the video. Somebody wants us to know they can get to both of us."

Next to me, Snake whispered, "*Dracula*. That quote is from the book, too."

My phone lit up with a text, but not from Kandi. The sender was a number I didn't recognize. The message set off more alarm bells. It said "Use," then listed four digits followed by a phone number.

I have a trick memory for numbers. I can tell you the license number of every car and motorcycle I've ever owned, the phone number of the pay phone on my floor of the dorm at Cal State Long Beach and lots of other fascinating stuff. What was on the little screen was the last four digits of the cell phone Chet Shaw had given me, the one he assured me was very difficult to tap. I had a feeling I knew who I would be talking to after I ran upstairs, dug the phone out of my sock drawer and dialed the number.

"T. R., oh my, am I glad to hear your voice."

My heart leapt. But first things first. "Kandi, where are you?"

"I'm at O'Hare. I want to come home."

"Are you at the gate?"

"Yes, and --"

"Your ticket was cancelled."

"Yes! I've been hacked. How did you know?"

"Kandi, listen carefully. Somebody recorded video of you at the check-in counter and sent it to Chet." There was a pause. "Kandi, I --"

"Wait. I am still trying to process this. You say they filmed me and sent it to Chet?"

"It gets better. Before that an unknown sender emailed me a still picture of you sitting in the terminal. By the way, smart of you to have me use a secure phone."

"Thanks. I was pretty sure I'd been hacked, but I didn't know about the picture and the video. Mac, if you're involved in something, now would be the time to tell me."

"Nothing, really. I went surfing this morning on the new board I sent you a picture of. That's it. I read about the killings, the murder-suicide. Is the clinic still closed?"

"No, not exactly. They're moving patients out."

"You haven't heard about Sigmund?"

I could hear her sharp intake of breath. There was a pause.

"Tell me."

I hated to tell her like this, but it would be worse for her to read about it. "I'm sorry, honey, but he's dead. Somebody tried to make it look like a hit-and-run, but he was murdered."

"Oh, my god."

"Yeah. Film at II when I know more. Chet and Tony are trying to get details."

"What is going on? What are you into now?"

"I have no idea what's going on, but we can figure it out. Tell me what happened."

"I was running late because I just decided to come home so I went to the gate to ask them if the flight would really be on time. When they checked my ticket they said I had cancelled it." She paused for breath. "So I said it was a mistake and that I really wanted to get on the flight and they looked on the computer and said, well, just buy another ticket, we have a seat left, but when I tried to do that my credit cards were all blocked. All of them! And at the gate they looked at me really funny and I think they were getting ready to call security so I moved away and found this pay phone. Mac, I have no credit and I only have twenty-three dollars and forty-eight cents in cash, you know I use plastic for everything and *why is this happening*?"

"I don't know, but the important thing is to get you home."

"Right. I don't have enough cash for a taxi, but I can have him wait outside my apartment. I've got some emergency cash."

"No! Stay where you are. Right now you are in one of the safest places on earth. Whoever did this probably wants you to go back to your apartment. Sit tight."

"Okay. Mac, I'll --" There was a beep and she was gone.

"I love you too."

February 18, 1934

Dearest Mama,

We have crossed the line and now are in New Mexico. The train rocks back and forth and one lady said it made her feel sick but it doesn't bother me, except Mrs. Petersen would not approve of my penmanship!

I want to tell you my plans so you will not worry. You know Lou Helen Hodges from the class ahead of me at Daniel Boone High, well, she went out to California and she wrote to me and said there was work. She is in the movies! Right now she is what they call an extra or sometimes a stuntwoman. She gets work because many of the girls there don't know how to ride a horse. She wrote me and said there was work if I wanted to come out. And we can share an apartment so it will cost less.

I know daddy will be hurt, but I have to do it and there isn't any work in Platteville. I know Grandpa Lamentations will not like it at all. Only show him my letters when you feel it is right.

I hope your cough is better.

Please include me in your Prayers as I pray for all of you. The Good Lord watch over everyone.

Your loving daughter,
Grace

Chapter Three

I tried to call Kandi back and got the message that says the number is not in service.

My Significant Other, the beautiful, smart, kind woman who has saved my life more than once, the woman who loved me and who I loved, is named Mary Shaw. In high school Mary was a nerd's nerd, staying home Friday night to study because she thought she liked it. And she *did* like it, but she felt pretty sure something was missing.

She was always the new girl because her college-professor parents moved every few years, chasing research grants and academic success. And she was bullied; bullies are everywhere in schools large and small. Mary was bullied everywhere she went. A lot.

Other girls' rooms had dolls and boy band posters. Mary's had a laptop, bookcases stuffed with textbooks, and a poster of the periodic table. But behind those books she had paperbacks describing the adventures of Xena: Warrior Princess and her sidekick, Gabrielle. When she got out of high school she created her own version of Xena, started calling herself Kandi (with a "K" as she always told people), studied martial arts, and got a job as a cocktail waitress at Hof's Hut in Long Beach. Oh, of course she went to college and was Dean's List every semester because she didn't know what else to do. After her BA, she stayed on at UCLA in the doctoral program in psychology.

Some issues at Hof's -- she dated a customer named Sly Staney who was very upset when she broke it off (she found out he had a wife) -- caused her to quit and get a job at Fred's Fine Mexican Food in Huntington Harbour, where I met her on her first day. A drunk guy -- Sly, who had followed her -- grabbed her butt; I made him stop, which made her really mad because she could have handled him. Sly didn't like it either. That afternoon we rolled him in the parking lot behind the restaurant. Well, what really happened was he assaulted her again, I knocked the wind out of him and we stuffed him in the back of his car after she took five bucks from his wallet, explaining that he stiffed her for the tip. However, what it came down to was we beat the snot out of him and stole money. The good news was nobody saw us and he didn't call the cops.

We spent that semi-stolen cash on ice cream. I could taste the berry flavor on her cold lips as we kissed. That's how it started. With Diana it was instant love, we both knew from day one that we were meant for each other. With Kandi it took longer and we have had our ups and downs but it's just as powerful as what my wife and I had. Maybe more.

There was a static chirp from Snake's backpack. He pulled out a bright yellow walkie-talkie that chirped again and then his wife's voice said, "Humı to Husı. Over."

He rolled his eyes and muttered, "I hate this shit." Then he pushed a button and said, "Cheryl—"

"Humı to Husı please follow radio protocol. Over."

He turned away from me and whispered, "Mac is with me and he can hear all this. This is embarrassing." No answer. Another eye roll. "Husı to Humı."

"Humı to Husı. Over, Husı, say 'Over.'"

"Bite me." No answer. "Over."

"Humı ETA six minutes."

He turned to me. "She's coming from a gun show, Anaheim Convention Center." Then, louder, into the walkie talkie, "Roger that. Synchronize watches. If captured will only give name, rank, and serial number. Wilco. Watch your six. Husı out. Over and out again."

"Will surveil once and then approach for pick-up. Humı out." There was a static click.

He yelled, "Bite me!" again. I stared at him. He sighed, dropped the walkie talkie into his backpack. "You don't want to know. But you will." We walked into the living room to wait.

I listened for the rattle of the air-cooled engine that powered Snake's restored antique VW van, but didn't hear it. Instead, from the front window I saw an enormous HumVee wagon lurch up, bounce one wheel over the curb, and settle into place blocking my driveway. The hood and passenger-side fender were painted camouflage; it had tires that looked like they would come up to my waist, deeply tinted glass, a row of lights and a black rack on the roof. Snake said, "You should come out and say hello." He gave me a look that said it was more than a suggestion.

"Maybe another time."

"Oh, you should really meet the new, improved Cheryl, particularly since it's your fault."

Snake's wife writes poetry, casts Celtic runes, and lies face-down in the dirt to get in touch with Gaia the Earth Mother. Or maybe she thinks she *is* the Earth Mother; with her it's sometimes hard to tell. I hadn't seen her since she'd been kidnapped by people she thought were saving the planet. When it turned out they weren't, I rescued her – rescued her and ended up driving a stolen forklift down Bolsa Boulevard in my underwear. No kidding. And at the time we were both soaking wet because I had set off the sprinkler system in the warehouse we were escaping from. It made the news. And YouTube. And Pinterest.

The Humvee grumbled at the curb. As we approached, the New Cheryl climbed out. Snake had told me there had been some changes but I wasn't sure what he meant and after I saw her, I still wasn't.

She pulled off a black knit cap and her dark glasses, tossing both onto the driver's seat, replaced the knit cap with a black ball cap that said "FBI." The last time I saw her, her hair had been waist-length and dark gray. Now it was about an inch long, sticking up all over her head in spikes, and dyed Elvis black. She was dressed in a khaki shirt, desert camo fatigues, a vest with pockets everywhere, and what looked like black paratrooper boots – shiny black and laced half-way up her calf. She adjusted a web belt, slipped a six-cell steel flashlight into its holder, adding enough weight that she actually stumbled as she stepped forward. I saw her check the street, sweeping her eyes north-south. A neighbor of mine drove by in her silver Mercedes convertible as Cheryl put something back in the car, sliding it under the seat, something that I was certain I didn't want to identify and something I really hoped my neighbor hadn't noticed. I offered a halfhearted wave and my neighbor waved back so I guessed she wasn't calling the police. But the little silver convertible accelerated down the quiet street.

Having finished securing her equipment, Cheryl was standing silently, thumbs hooked into her belt. After a moment I said, "Hey, Cheryl, uh, hey, you look different."

Her eyes were never still, moving from my face, to her husband's, then up the street then down. "Are you carrying?"

"What?"

"Strapped. Do you have a gun?"

"What? You mean right now? No, no. Yikes. Nice Bat-belt. Um, Cheryl, this is a new look for you."

"You consider that more important than the fact that two people were killed two nights ago in Chicago, people who worked at the nuthouse where Mary is interning?" I shouldn't have been surprised. News crawlers are common and the new Cheryl would have listed the names of everybody she knew. "And with that knowledge you are on the street unarmed?" She shook her head.

"Uh, well, I don't really know what to say to that, Cheryl, except that I don't see any threats right now." Well, except maybe for the kid planting a camera next to my garage door. I needed to tell Chet about that.

"I didn't either when I surveilled the immediate vicinity before arriving. However, don't look over your shoulder but there's a white Acura parked at the end of the street with one individual sitting inside. He was there when I made my first pass and he's still there." Okay, most people would laugh it off, call Cheryl paranoid, but I'm not most people, not anymore. I didn't turn, but I took out my cell phone, held it up with the lens pointing over my shoulder and snapped off three pictures.

I could see the white Acura in the reflection of the Humvee's windshield. It hadn't moved. Cheryl had gone to her version of parade rest, hands behind her back, feet spread. The black metal six-cell flashlight almost reached down to her knee.

Sometimes the universe or God or Cheryl's Gaia steps in to remind us what's important. I was looking at the pictures on my cell phone when the phone rang. Kandi was back.

"Hey, Kandi, glad you're back."

"I changed pay phones. So, any thoughts about who these people are or why they're after me?"

"Nothing. You passed the first TSA check and got to the gate."

"Tell me again that this is not a result of something you are involved in."

"It's not. TSA no problem?"

"Correct."

"Okay. So your ticket's bar code passed that check. What exactly did they say when you got to the gate?" Kandi is one of the smartest, most resourceful people I know, but there was a ragged edge of panic in her voice that I didn't like at all. She didn't answer. "All right, first things first. You're at O'Hare."

"Yes." I heard her suck in a deep breath. "Yes. O'Hare. The United terminal."

"Where in the terminal?"

"The gate and, yes, I printed a boarding pass last night and that got me through the first checkpoint."

"Did you check a bag?"

"No, I'm doing carry-on."

"Laptop?"

"In my purse. No internet access. Account cancelled, apparently by me, only I didn't."

Listing these details seemed to help. Or maybe I just wanted her to feel better. "Look around. Do you see a sign that says ATM?"

"No, but I saw one on the way to the TSA screening."

"No! Under no circumstances go back out through security! Wait one." I turned to Snake, and said, "My other cell phone is on the little table in the entryway. Get it. Call Chet." He took off running. My friend is overweight, an aging hippie, but in a tight spot there are few people I'd rather have at my back. "Cheryl, pull that monster forward so it doesn't block the driveway." She looked like she might say something, then climbed up into the Hummer and pulled it forward. I heard Kandi suck in another deep, ragged breath. "All right, honey, I'm back. Put your back to the phone and look around. Tell me what you see."

"With my back to the phone, clockwise starting at nine, I see windows looking out on the runway, the door to the jetway, kids with laptops sitting on the floor next to electrical outlets, people in line at Starbuck's, rows of plastic seats in some awful orange color, people in line to board the plane, the United counter—"

"Okay, they're boarding the flight. How long ago did they start?"

"They started fifteen minutes ago. They're boarding all rows now."

"All right. You won't be on that flight. Cameras?"

"Yes, I see three in the ceiling, covered in those little plastic half-globes."

"Is there a store or a newsstand?"

"Yes, but I can't see it from where I am. It's behind me on the other side of the wall."

"You're going to be fine."

"I have no credit cards. No computer access, and they stopped my cell phone."

"It's okay. You're in one of the safest places on earth right now. There's all kinds of security around you. What does your phone say when you turn it on?"

"It powers up and says No Service. And yes, I have walked all around the waiting area. It's not a dead spot. I have no cell service."

"All right, give me the number of the pay phone." She told me and even without my trick memory it would have been imprinted. "Now, just stay on the line." I moved the burner cell away from my ear and verified that I remembered its number. "Write down this number."

"Got it."

"Okay, now this one." I gave her a twelve-digit number. "That's my calling card number. Use it so you won't run out of quarters. It's old, but the account is still good. So, how are you doing, really?"

"I need Chet to fix my credit cards and phone. And internet access. I'm a little better now. I was really anxious until I talked to you."

"Back at you, honey. I'll get Chet on the credit issues. So, how's work?" Anything to keep her talking.

"The only outstanding event lately is, of course, the murder-suicide at the clinic. I knew both Jennifer and Harold, but not all that well. I can't think of a connection."

"Sit tight. Stay by the phone where you are. I'll call back in a few minutes."

"But, T. R., I just want to go back to my apartment. I have cash there. I can get a cab, tell him I need to get the money, I'll leave my bag as a guarantee, and --"

"No. Stay by this phone. Do not go back out through security."

"But -- okay, I get it. I'll take a look around this waiting area, see if anything jumps out at me. Poor choice of words but you know what I mean."

"No! Better if you stay by the phone so I can call you back."

"I don't do well with orders."

"Consider it a strong suggestion, please. I love you. Sit tight."

"For now." She hung up.

I needed to talk to Chet. He answered in the first ring. "Howdy, Mac, glad you called. I got me some info on that thing in Chi-town."

"Later, Chet. Mary's in trouble." I told him what was going on, at least what I knew, ending with, "And whoever is doing this is really, really good."

"Yep."

"Listen is it possible to disable credit and cancel tickets remotely?"

I could hear keys clacking as he typed. "The credit card hacking is not easy, neither is the cell phone. Her TRW profile shows everything cancelled."

"Would they have to be close? Like in the same waiting room?"

He said, "No, but it might make it easier. Okay, the immediate problem is how to get her out of there safely."

"No, the immediate problem is keeping her safe at the gate. We've bought a little time because she went off-script by not running back to her apartment, but whoever's doing this will take action probably sooner rather than later."

"They want her to run," he said.

I could almost feel his fine mind whirring, creating, then rejecting one idea after another

Finally, he said, "Okay, I gave my presentation last night. I can leave any time I want."

"I think I need you to stay there and work on the hacking."

"Right. Whoa, whoa just a sec here. She's at the gate?"

"Right. Gate G14 at O'Hare."

"Okay, I've got a map here. Concourse G, upper level. So she made it past the first layer of security."

I was afraid I knew where he was going and wished I had thought of it. "You mean where they check your boarding pass and ID?"

"Yeah."

"She got hacked between the time she passed that checkpoint and when she tried to board. Say half an hour, tops. That is very bad, very bad, Pard."

I said slowly, "Means they're good. Even better than I thought." I stopped for a moment, then shook my head. "Money first. There's a convenience store at the gate."

"U-Need-It Mini-Mart. I got it. I'm looking at a terminal map. And there's a kiosk with an ATM around the corner from where she is."

"No good. She needs a credit card to put in the machine."

"If I was there I could fix it."

"If wishes came true there would still be thousands of day traders. We have to fix it from here."

"I'm on it. I have all of her personal information. Mac, wait, does she have her laptop with her?"

"Yes."

"Tell her to power it down and keep it that way until I say to turn it on. Let's try to contain the damage."

Something else I hadn't thought of. "Got it." I needed to focus. When you're in the market, investing other people's money, you're going to make mistakes. There's a range of reactions from brooding uselessly to flailing wildly. The trick is to find the balance, the sweet spot between action and inaction.

I was reacting to events, not taking action.

That had to change.

Chapter Four

I walked out back. The tide was low so the ramp from the deck to the dock led down at a steep angle. This was like the moments after the Opening Bell, when information flooded in and the market started its daily gyrations. I forced myself to think.

Kandi is trapped in the Chicago airport.

Spears of light reflected off the still waters of the channel. I could hear traffic going by on Pacific Coast Highway, and the rhythmic clack-clack as some kid skateboarded by on the street. The air was full of the good, memory-laden smell of the sea. On my right a medium-sized SeaRay chugged by, the stern bristling with fishing poles. When the wake reached me the floating dock rocked gently side-to-side. I looked back at the house. Through the floor-to-ceiling windows I could see into the family room, where the screen showed the person I cared most about in the world, trapped, scared, and in trouble.

Kandi is trapped in the Chicago airport. Minimal cash, her credit's stopped, her ticket's cancelled.

Why?

She was coming home. Somebody doesn't want her to.

Could it be a prank, somebody hacking her accounts just for the hell of it? Maybe. Or maybe somebody's pissed. No way to tell with what we know. Act on the assumption that it's Door Number Two. Somebody wants to hurt her.

No. No, that's not it, not exactly. Wrong. There are better, simpler ways. Cheaper ways. This was complex and took skill to set up. They want to scare her. *See what I can do. I have power over you.* And they sent emails to me and to Chet, pictures of her. They want us to know. How do they expect us to react? Get her to safety as soon as possible. Home. Get her back to her apartment with the door locked. She can't get on a plane and she can't stay at the gate forever.

Did it matter? No. What mattered was getting Kandi to safety. The details could wait.

Who knew she was flying home? Everybody. Anybody who could hack her accounts could find the ticket purchase. No help there. Would they have left a trail on her laptop? Maybe. If they did leave a trail it would take somebody like Chet to find it. No help there, either, until we get our access to her computer, and that's not possible because her web provider thinks she's cancelled the account. Kandi unplugged.

What's the sequence? Kandi prints her boarding pass at home. She's not checking a bag so she goes straight to the gate. To do that first she shows ID and boarding pass, then she takes off her shoes. Her purse and bag are scanned and her laptop examined.

To quote Chet -- Whoa! It keeps coming back to the fact that this was done between the security scan and gate check-in

Now she wants to get back to her apartment in Chicago. They don't want her to. No, no, think it through. She gets thwarted, calls me. I send money and she's on the next flight. Delay? Keep her at O'Hare till they can pick her up? No. This was not spur of the moment. Again, it took planning and time to set up.

Airport police? TSA? Go up to them and explain that everything's cancelled but it's a mistake, and then what? *Why am I traveling? Oh, two people were killed where I work. Murder-suicide. How did I get through security in the first place? What do you mean, get down on the ground?*

She's coming home because the clinic is shut down after the murder-suicide. Wait, wait. The murder-suicide was at the clinic. They both worked there, but would it be shut down, patients moved to other facilities for this? I doubt it. There's something else, some piece of information the Chicago police are holding back. It can't be that Kandi's a suspect or they would never let her leave. I had an idea about that information and I didn't like it. It was of no help to the immediate problem so I shelved it.

Unless she is a suspect and she's running and that's why she can't get on a plane. No, that doesn't work.

They want to scare her.

What else do they want?

I got it, not all of it but a part at least. Enough to act.

This went through my head in the time it took the cabin cruiser to pass me. The guy at the wheel waved. I waved back and sprinted across the dock, with the planks swaying side-to-side under me, up the ramp, across the deck and into the kitchen, where I grabbed the scrap of paper with the pay phone number on it and dialed.

She answered on the first ring. "What?"

"Mary, listen to me. We'll get you out of there but it will take a while. Going back to your apartment is a very bad idea."

"Why?"

"What's the first thing you thought of when your ticket was no good and your credit cards were cancelled?"

"Get home, lock the door, call you. If I couldn't get you, call Chet. In that order."

"He's speaking at a conference in San Francisco."

"I want to go home. I don't want to be here."

"Yeah, I know, honey. It's a sure thing that whoever went to this much trouble wants you to do that. Right now you are in a secure area. It would be very hard for anybody to harm you."

"My chest is constricted, I'm having difficulty breathing, my heart is pounding, I'm perspiring. I'm suffering a panic attack." She laughed shrilly. "My first. Isn't that nice? It will help me relate to my patients." She laughed again.

"I need you to do something for me."

"Of course, certainly, certainly. I just have oodles of free time here."

"Put Kandi on. I want to talk to Kandi."

I met the persona, Kandi, before I found out about Mary, but I love them both.

There was silence for a minute, then, "Hey, Sailor." Even the voice was different.

"Hey."

"Hey. Mary's freaking out here and I gotta tell you I'm a little antsy myself."

"I know. Listen, I have an idea, but it means you have to hang out in the airport for a while, maybe several hours." I told her what I had in mind.

"So I go back to the apartment and they're waiting for me."

"Something like that, yeah, I think so."

"If I could pick up a piece on the way home . . ."

"No! Bad idea! No guns. Let's see if I can make this work."

She was slow to answer. "Yeah, okay. I don't have enough cash for a weapon anyway. Sailor, there's something else."

"Can you save it till I make these calls?"

There was a pause. I visualized her unwrapping a stick of watermelon gum and popping it into her mouth. "Look, I, uh, I may not be here when you call back. Mary's getting a teensy bit nervous about me. That's why she took this internship, well, one of the reasons. She wants to get rid of me."

Mary is trapped in the airport, alone and nearly broke. Scared. That's what they want. That's it. And if she goes back to her apartment the terror campaign will continue because that's the idea. And she wants to eliminate the part of her personality best suited to dealing with the situation.

"She won't. She won't get rid of you, at least not now. She needs you too much." I hope. "Tell me what you see. Put your back to the wall and go left to right."

"Sailor, you gettin' forgetful in your old age? I did that."

"Do it again." I might have missed something, and I wanted to keep her occupied while I thought.

"All right, Sailor. I see a crowded airport waiting room. Check-in counter. Rows of plastic chairs with people in them, a few people sitting on the floor because it's crowded, windows, planes on the other side, planes that I'm not on. There's a sort of standing thingie that lets you charge laptops and phones."

"What about a store, a convenience store?"

"Behind me."

"On your side of security, right?"

"Yes."

"Hold on." I covered the mouthpiece. "Snake, Chet sent a map of the terminal. Would you print it get it off the printer in my office upstairs?" I spoke into the burner cell. "Kandi, you still there?"

"No, I decided to take a walk, troll for cute guys."

"Does anybody look like they want to use this phone? The pay phone you're on now?"

"Nope."

Something beeped. When I looked at the display I saw that the battery on the cheap cell was not dead, but definitely on life support. "Kandi I have to hang up now --"

"No!"

"-- but I promise I will call back." There was another beep and she was gone.

I ran upstairs, threw my socks out of the drawer to find the charger, ran back downstairs and plugged it into a socket over the kitchen counter. Then I snatched my regular cell and called Chet.

"Mac, I've been poking at this from up here and I don't like what I see."

"Tell me."

"This was one slick criminal. They got around multiple passwords, firewalls and security systems, all for different accounts. I doubt that it was a prank; it's too well done. On the other hand, there's no evidence of theft."

"Bank accounts?"

"I'm watching them. No activity."

"No-fly list?"

"Yep."

"Can you fix it? And take the block off her credit cards?"

"Yes, to the credit cards. I have contacts at all the bureaus -- Equifax, Transunion, TRW, but it will take time. No-fly--yeah, I think so. That puppy's a lot harder."

"How long?"

"Twenty-four hours before I get the changes in place and the credit agencies update their records. Maybe a little less. Mac, about the flight Mary was supposed to be on . . ."

"Can it wait?"

"Sure, Pard, sure."

Snake was looking at me expectantly. Cheryl had posted herself in the living room, peering out a narrow crack in the drapes, one thumb hooked in her belt. "Time for Plan B." They continued looking at me. Clearly, they expected me to have a Plan B, when I wasn't even sure what Plan A had been. "All right. First things first. Chet, I need the number of the U-Need-It store where she is."

"I'm on it."

Five minutes later I had my wallet in my hand and the phone was ringing in the convenience store.

"Windy City U-Need-It, Penelope speaking."

"Hi, Penelope. My name is Macdonald and I have a favor to ask. My friend Mary needs to buy a cell phone. She's in the waiting area now, but her wallet was stolen, with her credit cards and most of her cash. If I give you --"

"Your card number. Yeah, sure, as long as you have the three-digit security code on the back."

"Got it right here." And the card I was holding was not connected to me. For somebody to hack it they'd have to be inside American Express and the credit bureau. Chet had set it up for me, just as a precaution. I thought it was overkill, but it turns out he was right.

Less than five minutes later I was calling Kandi back at her pay phone. This time she picked up before I even heard the first ring. "All right. Go into the U-Need-It and buy a phone. They'll charge my American Express. Pick up some snacks, too." I explained that the clerk believed her wallet had been stolen and was kind enough to help. "When you get the phone, call me with the number."

I broke the connection and called Chet. "Chet, can you get access to the cameras in O'Hare?"

"Way ahead of you, pard. An ex-student of mine owns the company that has the maintenance contract. He's giving me access to the public parts of the network. He was reluctant to give access to things like the cameras in the control tower, but I told him I didn't need it."

"Chet, you're awesome." There was no answer. I could imagine him turning bright red in his hotel room. "How soon?"

"Let's see, he's doing this the right way, creating a User ID for me, and . . .hmm. He says maybe five minutes."

"I'll call you back."

My next call was to Las Vegas. Coco Shirakawa answered on the second ring. "Mac, how nice to hear from you." She chuckled. "I assume you are calling to accept my job offer?"

It was a standing semi-joke between us. Kandi and I had helped Coco and her hotel, The Bromeliad Resort and Spa, out of a very difficult situation and as a result she had the mistaken idea that I would be a good addition to the hotel's security forces. No matter how often I told her she was nuts, she persisted.

"Kandi's in trouble." As a result we had comped rooms and anything else whenever we were in Vegas. I was about to abuse that kindness.

"What do you need?"

"I need to borrow the Lucky Lady IV."

The Lucky Lady IV was the hotel's Gulfstream G5, the $40-million- aircraft they used to fly in whales. Casinos love whales, with good reason. It was cost-effective because in Vegas terms a "whale" is somebody who makes minimum bets of $10,000 and who plays at least four hours a day. Send the jet across the country to pick them up? No problem.

"Hold, please." She came back five long minutes later. "Mac, she's in Atlanta right now, airborne in an hour." Coco didn't ask why I needed the aircraft until she found out where it was; I liked that because it made it more likely that she would help.

"Destination?"

"Home. Returning to the hotel before going on to Dubai to pick up a party. Tell me what this is about."

"Can they stop at O'Hare and pick up Kandi?"

"You want me to divert the company jet to Chicago to pick up Mary Shaw?"

"Yeah. It's important."

"Hold, please." This time she was gone longer. I realized that I was squeezing the phone hard enough to make the tendons in my arm stand out. I tried to relax. "All right. I have yet to make a final decision but the pilot is already filing an alternate flight plan. I assume this will be a good story."

"It will be," I told her.

"Call you back."

My phone rang, showing a number I'd never seen before.

"Kandi?"

"Yep. Sailor, it worked. And Penelope is a pal. She thinks it's an old boyfriend stalking me. Thank you. Listen, I have to keep the phone plugged in while the battery charges, but I found an outlet."

"Okay, good. I'm working on something to get you out of there but it will take a while." I promised I would call regularly.

I punched in Chet's number. "Tex, we got cameras yet?"

"Coming up now. I'm sending it to the big monitor in your family room."

My wall-mounted big-screen monitor changed from quadrants devoted to my security cameras to an image of a busy waiting area. Chet flicked through six other cameras before we saw Mary sitting on the floor, leaning against the wall with a Starbucks's Vente next to her and a pile of napkins in her lap. Smart, I thought. Back to the wall. Smart and scared. And there was an outlet next to her. I could see the cable leading to the phone in her lap.

"How long till her new phone is charged?"

"No way to tell, depends on how low the battery was. If it was down to zero then maybe two hours for a full charge. But it's usable as long as it's plugged in. Actually, lithium batteries need to be run down to nothing once in a while, because --"

"Great, thanks, Chet."

In the terminal, Mary picked up a brown paper napkin, folded it carefully along the crease before stacking it on top of the cup, on top of the other napkins. Pursing her lips and frowning a little she studied the tidy pile for a moment, then took one more and added it. There. That was right. Seven was the right number. Seated on the floor close to the outlet, she began to shred the napkins into pieces, carefully, doing each one exactly the same -- unfolding it, smoothing it along the crease, then starting with the edge and working around until what was left was the size of her thumbnail. Around and around. Exactly the same. Counterclockwise. Around and around. One of the napkins tore across the center, splitting the flimsy paper in half. She wadded it and the others up, stood and threw them all out. Then she hurried to the condiments counter and selected more. Seven more.

I grabbed my phone the moment it buzzed. Coco said, "All right, the flight plan is changed. They're taking off in about half an hour, so they'll land in Chicago in three hours."

Okay, maybe this would work. "Coco, thank you."

"Mac, I think it will help that we have security on the flight, someone you know, in fact. Bryant was on board to keep an eye on our whales."

"Armed?"

"Of course. But he will not be permitted to carry the weapon into O'Hare. I can probably arrange it, but it will take time."

"I don't think we'll need it. But good to know he's around." I got his cell number. At last we were catching a break. Bryant was a tall Chinese-American who had been a limo driver for the hotel. I liked what I saw when he helped get Kandi and me out of a carjacking and told management about it. Now he worked for Bromeliad Security, carried a sidearm and escorted high rollers.

As I worked at the details I kept my eye on the airport camera. And I didn't like what I saw.

"Chet, are you watching this?"

"Of course."

"Guy in the black hoodie, with the baseball cap. Two --"

"-- rows over, facing where Kandi's sitting. Dark glasses. I see him. Okay, I've been working on software for the -- never mind who -- to monitor crowd movements, people changing position in relation to one another. Modeled on herd behavior with a dash of queuing theory from Information Science." I knew better than to interrupt despite the fact that I had slightly less interest in queueing theory -- whatever that was -- than the names of the craters in the dark side of the moon. "I'm having it look at the last half-hour of that waiting area. Wait one." I could hear keys clicking and could almost see him in his hotel room in the Hyatt at Fisherman's Wharf, ignoring the view to watch the screens. No, he probably didn't even bother opening the drapes. Of course it would be multiple screens because Chet never traveled without at least two laptops, an iPad and an assortment of cell phones. Another window opened on my screen, showing the waiting area. This wasn't live; there was a time code running along the bottom. The recording showed people moving around, some dragging bags, some not. Each face was surrounded by a little red autofocus square with a number next to it. Along the right side of the screen numbers scrolled upward. The video went to fast forward and the people moved quickly, with their little squares keeping pace. "Scanning, scanning, c'mon. Right, got him. Y'all have a good eye. That hombre has changed position three times, each one facing Mary. And watch what he did when she got up fourteen minutes ago, when Mary went to buy the cell phone." My screen rearranged itself into two windows, one live and one with a time code in the past.

"He stands up and walks around."

"Yeah, but watch when I zoom on his hands."

The second time I watched I got it. "Sleeves. The sweatshirt has extra-long sleeves and he pulls them down to cover his hands when he touches the arms of the seat."

"Give that cowpoke a bottle of Jim Beam. Yep, he's tryin' not to leave prints."

I thought about it. "Which means he thinks somebody might look for them, and that means he plans on doing something to make people check his prints and we have to assume that it's something bad involving Kandi. But in the terminal that would be nearly impossible. I mean, say he drugs her somehow and pretends to be helping her. Airport security would still be there in minutes. They'd never let some guy just haul a semi-conscious woman away, not without some checking. They must have a protocol for situations like that."

I heard more keys being tapped. "I'm reading it now. Yep, if the person is non-responsive, airport medical staff has to either release them or order transport. Nobody leaves without being checked by airport EMTs."

"Okay, he's inside security at the gate, so that means he's passed the full-body scan and he's got a boarding pass. He's waiting for her to leave."

"Grab her outside, when she's waiting for a cab. But why go to all this trouble to kidnap her? Don't make sense. There's easier places to grab somebody."

I thought about it for a minute, then said, "It does if you want people to think they know why she's missing. Her credit is no good, cards maxed out, she bought a ticket and didn't use it and then she vanishes. Add that to the murder-suicide at the clinic and you have a reason for her to run. She's not abducted, she's a fugitive."

"Our boy's getting nervous." And Chet was right. On the live screen the hooded figure was shifting in the seat, then stood, once again using sleeves to cover the chair arms, and walked briskly toward the bathrooms, keeping his head down the whole way. He waited behind two children and got a quick drink of water. "Watching out he don't show in the cameras."

"Kandi was supposed to be freaked out; somebody's hacked her credit cards. One way or another she would call somebody, me, maybe, and get out of there."

"Police?"

"Maybe. But she might not want to, not after the killings." I got it. "And if she calls the cops they say, 'Come in and fill out a report' --"

"And he grabs her outside the terminal," Chet finished.

"And she's a fugitive, just one who called the cops and changed her mind."

"This boy's good."

"Yeah, but so are we. No way he could figure on you getting access to the airport cameras. Okay, Chet, keep watching. I'm going to talk to Kandi." But before I did I sat for a moment just watching. Our mystery figure was back in his seat, now looking at a cell phone. Mary was sitting next to the outlet, shredding another napkin. As I watched she picked up the cell phone, looked at the display and unplugged it.

"Mac, the motion-monitoring program picked out somebody else, but --" he paused. "Nope. Gone now. Wearing a hoodie."

I looked at the time on my phone. The Lucky Lady IV was in the air, en route to Chicago.

Something bothered me. "Chet, run the video back to ten minutes before she gets to the gate. "Look for --" I went silent as it became clear. He said it first. "There's two of them."

"Yep. They don't talk, don't look at each other."

"But they're together. One's female."

"Both in hoodies." I tried to figure it out, couldn't. "Okay, there's two. Our problem remains the same."

My phone lit up with Coco's number. "Mac, just a heads-up. To make our schedule the Lucky Lady has to land in Vegas, take on fuel and a new pilot, and then leave for Dubai. So I can get Kandi to Vegas, and she'll be safe because Bryant will be with her, but I can't get her to Orange County on the Lucky Lady. I can send a hotel limo for her."

"No need, Coco. I'll pick her up. When will they land?"

"The Captain says six, six-and-a-half hours total time Atlanta to Chicago to Las Vegas, depending on their takeoff priority in Chicago."

"Thanks, Coco. I appreciate this."

"Mac, just how bad is this trouble? I can let you have Bryant as long as you need him."

"At this point I just need him to make sure she gets on the plane in Chicago and to stay with her in Vegas." I almost said that I hoped that was all I needed, but held back.

"When you see Mary give her my love."

Through the windows in the family room I could see my dock and the channel. The fog had burned off and it was turning into a beautiful day. My new paddleboard was everything I'd hoped for. The ticker running along the bottom of the TV showed the market to be up and I'm certain that if I went outside I'd hear sparrows singing joyous songs. It was a perfect day, except for the fact that above the ticker the TV showed the person I cared about more than anything in the world, now sitting on the floor in an airport waiting area, shredding brown Starbucks's paper napkins because she was trapped with no credit cards and very little cash.

And she was close to losing it. I'd seen the napkin-shredding before.

Don't thrash, think.

Okay, so far Kandi is safe, and I have arranged a way for her to get to Vegas. Obviously, hotel security or no, I want to be there to meet that plane. It should land around 5 p.m. our time. To be safe I need to be on the road no later than noon. She won't be on the Lucky Lady IV by then, so I can't wait for that to leave for Vegas. What if worst comes to worst and I need to go to Chicago? Get a flight from McCarran. It was like the old days on the trading floor, watching five or six stocks moving closer to trigger points, with minutes, seconds, to decide your next move. Just like the old days except that now I knew what high stakes really were.

I ran up the stairs took a five-minute shower, dressed in jeans and a purple Polo shirt and a pair of old, battered Vans. I threw a change of clothes into a gym bag and then pushed my shirts aside to stand looking at the gun safe built into the wall of my closet. I have a permit, but it doesn't extend to carrying concealed and, although I have stretched that point on several occasions I don't like to if I can help it, and of course there was the little matter of crossing a state line. And I wasn't certain how bad this was.

I shook my head. Three dead people. That's how bad it was. I opened the safe and took out the gun and clip. Leaving the clip in an automatic like my .45 can damage the spring, so I always remove it. I checked the loads, inserted the clip and shoved it and the shoulder holster under the clothes in my bag. Kandi's tiny Raven .25 automatic was also in the safe. I repeated the load-checking and clip-inserting and it went into the bag next to the .45. I trotted into the family room and added my laptop and both phones to the bag.

Snake and Cheryl met me at the door from the entryway to the garage. Cheryl finished checking the loads in a matte-black automatic and slipped it into a shoulder holster. She pulled a black jacket on to hide the artillery. "I'm going with you."

"No, listen, thank you both, but --"

Snake said, "Cheryl, listen, really, there's not much we can do."

She said, "I think both vehicles. Backup."

Snake gave up. "Mac, you said it yourself. This guy is good. If he can hack credit accounts he can almost certainly look at flight plans. What are the odds he will figure out Kandi's planning to board the casino plane and have somebody waiting for her when she lands at McCarran?"

"I hope he does."

He muttered, "Oh, goody."

Cheryl pumped a fist and nodded. "Let's take my Hummer. It's better in a combat situation."

"It's not a --" I stopped. Yeah, it was combat. The shooting started three days ago in a Chicago clinic. "All right, you can come. And thanks. But we're taking my car." I opened the door and ushered my friends into the garage.

Cheryl said, "Honey, you have no weapons training. You don't need to come, really."

"Just move the war machine, okay?"

I pushed the button and the garage door rolled up. There were no feet on the other side. After checking sightlines for snipers, Cheryl pulled the H1 forward, snatched a black duffel bag from the back seat and we were ready.

One of the few inconvenient things about living in the Harbour is that it's not close to any freeway. Bolsa Chica to the 22 took ten minutes, then we connected to the 55. But then we were in the carpool lane blasting north to catch the 91. After we made the connection I called my friend Tony Genucci on his personal line. In the movies the hero or heroine never brings in the cops, usually for some stupid reason like, "This is personal, between me and Fu Manchu," or whatever villain they're up against. The reality is you're nuts if you don't tell somebody. It might make you feel good to pound your chest and say, "I'll deal with it." I didn't care about feeling good. I cared about Kandi. Tony is Huntington Beach police as well as a friend. When he answered I told him everything. By the time I'd finished I was guiding the Chevy around the sweeping left-hand curve that connects the 55 to the 91 and we were pointed at Sin City. I don't know if all roads lead to Vegas, but this one did.

February 20, 1934

Dear Diary

Well, here I am in California! And although it is February we went to Long Beach yesterday and went in the ocean. It was scary at first but Lou Helen was there and some other girls from the movie she is working on and we jumped waves and had a nice picnic lunch.

February 27, 1934

Dear Diary

The big news is I have a job! I am an extra -- that means you are in the movie but you don't get to say any lines -- in a movie called Mystery Riders of the Blazing Plains. The story is about a cowboy who comes to the rescue of a girl who might lose her ranch. Lou Helen and I got the jobs because we can ride horses. Many of the girls they interviewed said they could ride, but they fudged a little. Then they couldn't even get on the horse and it was funny to see them try. A lot of them fell off, but nobody got hurt, at least not very bad. When I stepped up and put the saddle on my horse and tightened the straps Mr. Heems, he is making the movie, said, "Girlie, you got yourself a job." We started work the next week in a place called Bronson Canyon where there is a real cave. The pay is good and Lou Helen and I have a room in a nice house.

Well, I have to go because we report to work early. A lot of the girls complain but on the farm we got up earlier, so I think it's funny. It is no problem for me. Mr.

Heems told me there would be more work for me when this movie is done. Oh, I forgot. Mystery Riders of the Blazing Plains is what they call a serial. It is made in short pieces that theaters show before the big movie. It will be funny if the first movie I see is one that I am in!

Lou Helen is out with her beau Willeford Freedman. This is the third time she has gone out with him. He seems nice and he always pays for my dinner when I go out with them. I know he has a job, but I am not sure exactly what it is, except Lou Helen says he works for important people.

I was scared when I got on that train, but now I am glad I am here. I want so bad to do something, I don't know what it is exactly, but I know it's not on a farm. Modern girls do all kinds of things that Grandfather Lamentations disapproves of.

Here's a secret, Diary. I hope I find a boyfriend. There, I said it. Willeford has promised to introduce me to a friend of his named Clyde Biggs.

Now I have to go. Lou Helen is back from her date and wants to turn the light off.

March 3, 1934

Dear Diary,

Today was hard work we rode and rode all over. Some of the girls were saddle-sore. Mr. Heems told me if any of those boys try to snap your garters you tell me. I will have to ask Lou Helen what he means.

Supper was at the studio canteen. It is okay to eat all your meals out, but I sure miss Mama's cooking, except the okra.

Now for bed. Lou Helen isn't back yet, but I am tired. I will leave the light on for her.

Chapter Five

After we were on the 91, Snake fumbled around with my phone and the Bluetooth connection hidden behind the radio to set up a conference call and I was able to talk to Chet and Kandi. My laptop, balanced between us on the bench seat, showed her in the same place. The two people wearing hooded sweatshirts who might be watching Kandi were not on any screen Chet could find.

"Okay, Kandi, we've got it under control. The Lucky Lady will land in Chicago in about two hours and once you're on it you're home free. I'll talk to Bryant, he's on the plane, and when they're in the landing pattern I want you to go quickly to the gate. They will land at an FBO."

"That's a Fixed Base Operator, sort of like a little private terminal," Chet interjected.

"But that means you'll have to go outside, on the other side of the security checkpoints, so stay put till then. Right now you're safe. You're behind multiple layers of security --"

"Actually three concentric layers of security."

"Thanks, Chet. And you're on camera at all times. So relax, and have a cup of tea, because help is on the way. Okay? And remember, this credit card thing could all be a prank. It's just better not to take chances."

She laughed. "I nodded 'yes' but I suppose you can't see it."

"Wrong, honey. The eye in the sky sees all."

"Yes, I'll wait. I don't have much choice. Mac, do you really think it's a prank?"

"Bryant is armed, but he can't bring the weapon into the airport, so I want you to stay in plain sight till he arrives and I call you with directions to the FBO."

And it hit me. Kandi was only one of the targets. I was the other one, and Chet. Whoever was taunting us wanted us to react. I said, "Snake, you don't email, right?"

"The university makes me, but, no, not much."

"I'll check," Cheryl said from the back seat and started tapping her phone. She was silent for a moment, then I heard, "Oh, my."

"What?" I was afraid I knew.

"Walter, look at this." She passed him the phone.

"It's Kandi. And I'm afraid it's live. She's drinking something from a Starbuck's cup."

Cheryl said, "I think it's a live feed attached to an email sent to Walter's university account."

From the dash speaker, Chet said, "I'll take a look."

"My password is –"

"Please. And I'd change it if I were you. Cheryl's birthday is so easy it's almost subtle."

"I remember privacy. I liked it."

"They're watching me, right now? Right this moment?" I had forgotten Kandi was part of the conversation.

"All right, honey. Wave to us."

Chet said, "Look at a camera and wave to us."

"But they'll – Oh. I get it. That tells them you're watching."

"Exactly. It's time for us to start sending messages." She waved, hesitantly at first, then exuberantly, like she was welcoming home a long lost boyfriend.

"This is not an airport security camera feed, so, yes, they're watching you on their own camera," I said.

"I hate this! All right, I'm done fooling around." She started to her feet. "I am going to check every person in this waiting area and when I find the person doing this I will confront them."

"No, no, that's what they want, maybe, and –"

The live feed went blank, replaced by text that read:

Don't miss the next exciting episode! See The Perils of Kandi, Chapter Two: Airport of Doom!

"I really don't like this," Chet said.

Kandi said, "Mac, what do you think?"

I told her the truth. "No. It's not a prank. Someone is out to scare you. Possibly harm you, but they haven't done that yet, and, like I said, you are in a very secure place. But sit tight for now. No confrontations."

"Don't sugarcoat it, Sailor. Yeah, that's what I think too." She laughed nervously. "They're doing a pretty good job."

"And they're organized and good at this sort of thing. They want us to know that."

She said, "And there are three dead people."

Best that she not think about that too much. "There may be no connection. Chet, tell her about your ex-student who works in airport security."

He did and she said, "Thanks, Cousin. How'd your presentation go?"

He laughed. "I think at least half of them understood at least thirty percent of what I was talking about."

"Did you tell them they were stupid?"

"No, ma'am, I did not."

"Chet, I'm proud of you. That's real personal growth."

"All right, you two scholars talk shop. It's getting windy so I'm gonna drive." I dropped out of the conversation.

After I hung up, Cheryl said, "I think we've picked up a tail."

"What?"

"A tail, a tail. Someone following us."

"I know what a tail is."

"They're in a silver minivan. It was with us when we got on the 55 and it's there now."

Snake said, "They could be going to Vegas. I imagine there are a few people on the freeway who aren't racing across the desert, armed to the teeth, on a desperate mission."

I thought about it. "Let's find out."

So we pulled into Barstow Station for gas and food. Time was not a problem and I had a hunch I wanted to check.

Barstow Station is famous as a stop for busses going to and from Las Vegas. It's built partly out of a passenger train car from the thirties, now with a huge McDonalds attached, a gift shop, and a part of the dining room roped off and labeled, "Bus Drivers Only." And it is always busy, packed at any hour of the day or night. I was sure there would be a line, and I was right. After telling Snake to get me two Double Cheeseburgers, a Coke, and a large fries, I left him in line and slipped out a side door to the parking lot. Staying low, I worked my way back to where I could see my Chevy.

The silver minivan was next to it, between my car and the building. I was not entirely surprised.

Keeping even lower, I worked my way over to the bus parking and cleverly trotted alongside one of the behemoths as it pulled out of the lot. When I stopped I was on the far side, looking at my Chevy, while a kid, so young he would be carded every time he ordered a beer, carefully unrolled something under the driver's side front tire, then scooted over and began dragging it toward the passenger side. I dropped back a couple of cars and then stepped out, strolling toward him with my hands in my pockets and whistling. When I got close enough I said, "Can I help you?" He jerked upright, took a step back and tried to speak. His friend appeared from the direction of the restaurant, but hadn't seen me yet.

"They're still in line and --" his friend said, and then, seeing me, continued, "Oh. Um, hey, cool car. We were just looking."

"Did you lose something under it?" I wanted to give the kid a way out, allay his fears, and, most of all, get him talking.

"Oh, uh, yeah, my keys." He stood up, dusted his baggy shorts.

"Here, let me back the car up."

"Oh, no, that's ok, I got 'em."

"Good." I knew they were lying; they thought I might know but they weren't sure. In a minute I'd stop the farce and see what happened. Too bad I didn't get that minute.

"Freeze, both of you, don't move! Drop your weapons! Down on the ground! Keep your hands where I can see them! Do it now! Do it, suckers!" It was Cheryl and she had actually pulled a gun in the middle of a crowded parking lot. She stood in a fair approximation of the Weaver shooting stance, legs spread, both hands wrapped around her Glock 9-mil, wide-eyed and crazed-looking. The only sounds were her panting and a bus engine starting up, followed by the whoosh of the door opening. Fortunately, the boarding passengers were too busy taking pictures to be looking our way.

The boys were freaked, and with good reason. "Holy shit!" one of them shouted. They dove into the van. Cheryl braced herself, and I was afraid she would fire so I lunged at her and grabbed the gun. The van burned rubber as it powered out of the lot. Cheryl was panting, wide-eyed, with sweat running down her face. She began to shake.

After they were gone and after it seemed unlikely that anyone was going to shoot at us and the police didn't show up, I got down and looked under the car. I reached in and pulled out a three-inch-wide metal ribbon with metal points sticking up all along the length.

Cheryl said, "It's a spike strip. LEOs—Law Enforcement Officers—use them to stop suspect vehicles. I learned about them in a class—" I looked at her. She blushed. "Okay, I saw it on one of my *CSI: Miami* DVDs. It would have punctured all four tires. We never would have made it out of the parking lot." I rolled it up and put it in the trunk. Never can tell when you'll need a good spike strip.

We stood for a minute and then got back in the car.

A few minutes later Snake got in muttering about having to carry all the bags of food and cardboard trays of drinks by himself. He started handing out food. It seemed no one had noticed our little weapons display; however, since it had undoubtedly been captured by the parking lot cameras, I decided it was time to get back on the road. Carefully obeying all the laws I could think of, signaling for every turn, I pulled out of the parking lot and got us back on the northbound 15. In minutes we were out of town and the desert was unreeling beside us, brown and flat and empty until it reached mountains.

I told Chet about the kids with the spike strip. He said he would get into the McDonald's security cameras but didn't hold out much hope of a license number because of all the busses blocking the view. In a few minutes he was back.

"No joy on the van's plates. Okay, Las Vegas, which means 'The Meadows by the way, was founded because it was a source of water in the middle of the desert.

And despite its location, it has a monsoon season often with torrential rains," Chet's voice sounded good despite coming from the tiny speaker in the dash. He had been rambling for the last five or ten minutes as we barreled across the desert, but I let him because, along with the trivia, I could hear his keyboard clicking as he worked on something and knew he was typing as he rambled. "And now y'all are entering the Mojave National Preserve. Then the clicking stopped and I could hear him suck in his breath. "BTW, Mac, we may have a problem beyond those rustlers messing with your ride at Barstow Station."

Snake said, "BTW?"

Chet said, "Snake, at least get with the last millennium. BTW is by the way."

"Hm. I thought maybe Bite the Weenie."

"Tell me about the problem, Chet."

"GPS shows you east of Barstow, approaching Baker. After that you'll hit the California-Nevada border."

Which we'll cross carrying all kinds of weapons. I chose not to mention that on the air. "Yeah."

"There's no checkpoint going into Nevada. Coming back there's an agricultural inspection. Okay, the Lucky Lady IV is ninety minutes out. They were delayed taking off."

"So we have plenty of time."

"You do, but the Lady doesn't because there's two rainstorms approaching. If they get together we may see training."

"Talk to me, Chet. What's 'training?'"

"Sure, pard, sure, only this is just now happening, you know? I'm doing about six things at once here."

"If anybody can, you can, Chet."

"Okay, you know the monsoon season in the Las Vegas Valley is July and August?"

"I do now."

"I did, I knew that," Snake piped up.

"It's when moist winds from the Gulf of California raise the humidity. Heavy rains, which are not unusual, can cause flooding."

Snake muttered, "I knew that, too."

I said, "Chet, it's February. We're not in this monsoon season."

"That was just background. You need to know that Vegas can experience flash floods. Training is like that, but different."

Snake looked at and mouthed, "Like that but different?" I shrugged. Chet was on a roll and it was best not to interrupt.

"It's when two storm systems combine and it can be very nasty, dump several inches of water in a short time. And it looks like it's developing now, over the mountains. There's rain building over Mount Charleston."

"Are you telling me they might close McCarran?"

"Mac, they might close Interstate 15. It's gonna rain like a cow pissing on a flat rock."

"Like what?"

Snake said smugly, "I got that one."

"Downpours like this are bad news."

"What about the plane?"

Next to me, Snake muttered, "Der plane, Boss, der plane."

I said, "Quiet."

Chet said, "What? I'm sorry, sometimes I give too much information. I know that."

"Talking to the loose nut next to me, not you. Go on. Downpours like this --"

Snake stared out the window at the miles of desert leading to mountains in the distance. Mountains with clouds. He was absently running fingers through his gray beard with one hand and shoving the last of a Big Mac into his mouth with the other. At least he had shut up. And at least it was his wife who had the gun.

"If they close McCarran the most likely places for the Lucky Lady to land are Ontario or Palm Springs." Now Snake had quit eating and was staring at me; Cheryl was purse-lipped, watching out the back for suspicious vehicles, ignoring the plastic container of salad and the soft plastic envelope of dressing on the seat next to her.

An hour went by with the only voice Chet's, giving us weather updates. Then ahead I could see the Stateline casinos -- Buffalo Bill's and Whiskey Pete's and the lonely liquor store that marked the exact edge of California, there to sell California lottery tickets that were illegal in Nevada. In the distance clouds were piling up on the horizon, dark gray masses that looked like you could walk on them.

Chet said, "Okay, before he took off from O'Hare the pilot filed an alternate flight plan listing Ontario. That's where he'll go if they close McCarran."

"Where will they close the highway?"

"The most likely spot is the Cajon Pass, right at the Summit Inn. It's the high point, four thousand one hundred and ninety feet."

"What's the current temperature there?"

"Forty-one degrees Fahrenheit. The expected low is thirty-eight."

"Chet, I was teasing you."

"Oh."

"All right. Keep monitoring the weather and --"

"Uh-oh, uh-oh. Wait one." There was a pause "I'm monitoring the air-to-ground from the Lucky Lady and the pilot is asking about closing the airport. He really wants to land in Vegas because, wait, wait --"

"What?"

"He wants to land because his fuel is low. Headwinds leaving Chicago made him burn more fuel."

My mouth went dry. Kandi was in that plane. Kandi was on that plane because I'd sent it for her. "You mean he might not make Ontario?"

"Wait, okay, yeah, he says he can but he doesn't like it."

"The hits just keep on coming. So, let me see if I get this. If these storms get together --"

"Train."

"Yeah. If they train, the Lucky Lady could be diverted to Ontario, and we could be stuck in Vegas if they close the interstate behind us."

There was a moment of silence. Then Chet said, "It's a possibility. Yeah."

Next to me Snake said, "If we turn around now we can beat the storm and be waiting at Ontario."

"Chet, is it raining at the Cajon Pass?"

"Not yet."

Without turning from her ceaseless scanning of the road behind, Cheryl said, "Normally I'd say go for it, go on to Vegas because that's the most likely place for them to land, but if we turn around it will make anybody following us show themselves."

"Anybody else. We already know we're being followed."

I had slowed and moved over to the right lane, maintaining a safe distance behind one of the hundreds of tractor-trailer rigs on the road. Another behemoth moved up behind us and Cheryl relaxed and ate some salad as the rear window filled with bug-spattered truck radiator. In my mind I built a grid of possibilities.

The storms would either train or not. If they did train, either McCarran would close or it wouldn't and that would be before or after the casino jet arrived. The storms were coming in from the north. McCarran is on the south end of Las Vegas, so we would get there before we hit the Strip and casinos.

Okay. I slid out from the line of big rigs and took the Chevy up to a steady eighty. The mountainous dark clouds in the distance looked closer.

One thing I have learned the hard way is you need to know the terrain, and if you're smart you map out escape routes just in case. "All right. How's the security going in to the airport?"

"The field for private planes has a separate entrance. It's a gate with an armed guard. The hotel has vouched for you so you're on the list."

"Thoughtful of them."

"Well, I knew they were busy so I sent the email for them, from Bromeliad Security."

Crossing a state line with weapons, gaining access to a secure airport by using a forged email; hell, we might as well stop and rob a convenience store. I groaned and said, "Thanks, I'm sure the hotel appreciates it. Exits other than the road in?"

"None, by design. If you try to approach the main terminal on foot you'll set off motion detectors and the road is guarded. You are going to terminal two, to the FBO. Are you expecting trouble? Never mind."

"Chet, send my laptop a map of the airport and the approaches. Where exactly will they land?"

"The private jets land on the west side. Lucky Lady will most likely be coming down on 24L. The FBO is a separate building, like a small terminal with private hangars, storage for service trucks like food and sanitation -- these folks do not dine with the common folks -- and a waiting room, a plush waiting room complete with full bar and gourmet snacks."

Snake said, "Got the map, got it. Okay, first off ramp, then take the first entrance, go past the parking structure and straight on." His last words were drowned in a rumble of thunder. Big drops splatted against the windshield. I could still make out the clouds farther away; this was a different weather event. Training. "Oh, man, I don't like this." Snake looked at the drops, at me, then went back to the laptop.

"Talk to me, Chet."

"Wind warnings on I-15. High-profile vehicles not advised east of the Cajon Pass. Possible closure." On the other side the lanes were already slowing as traffic built up but the rain had stopped almost as soon as it started. Behind us the big rig and the one behind it signaled then pulled off to the shoulder. I guess they got the news. The retro Chevy rocked on its springs as the first gust of wind hit us.

"What about the airport?"

"I'm trying, pard, I'm listening and, okay, so far so good. If they do close, it won't be for a half-hour unless something changes."

"And the Lucky Lady?"

"Wait one, wait, okay, forty-five minutes out. Must have hit another headwind."

Snake muttered, "Can you spell WC, 'worst case?'"

Chet said, "Mac, I don't know what to tell you."

"Not to worry, pal. We're committed." The wipers started; more gusts rocked us. I took the car up to ninety.

Twenty minutes later Snake said, "There's the sign for the exit. One mile." He pointed as the green sign flashed by on our right.

I said, "Welcome to Fabulous Las Vegas."

Chapter Six

Cheryl said, "The SUV behind us is slowing, too."

Lightning strobed down to the ground from the clouds ahead of us, clouds that had seemed off in the distance just a few minutes ago, but now appeared closer, much closer; as I opened my mouth to say something the first flash was followed by another jagged, blinding fork. Snake muttered, moving his lips. "Four seconds."

From the dash speaker Chet said, "Four seconds? Is that the time between the flash and the thunder?"

Snake said, "Yeah."

"Not good, pards. The speed of sound in dry air at 20 °C (68 °F), is 343 meters per second or 1,125 feet per second."

Snake grumbled, "Chet, quit showing off and get to the point."

"I'm sorry. That's 1,234 kilometers per hour or 767 miles per hour, or about a kilometer in three seconds or a mile in five seconds."

I said, "The storm is less than a mile away."

"Right. That part of it. Assume it's the leading edge."

Snake groaned, folded the laptop and put it down in the footwell. He powered his window down -- the car was retro but had all the modern electronics -- stuck his head out and sucked in air. "Carsick. I have a delicate stomach." He swiped the rain out of his beard, then let the rain coat his face and sighed with relief.

"I'm sure the Big Mac, Fish Filet, large fries and special St. Patrick's Day green malt have nothing to do with it. Come to think of it, your face is the same color as the malt."

He rubbed rainwater on the back of his neck. "Could be worse, could be raining. Name the movie that's from. Anybody? Anybody? That's from a movie, too."

He laughed and muttered something under his breath. Snake was still muttering under his breath as Chet said, "Okay, the pilot will make his final decision at ten miles out. They're going to bring them in at Terminal 2, the one for charter and international flights. North side of the airport. Go in off of Paradise Road. And be careful. The most dangerous time for driving in bad weather is right after it starts to rain, when the gas and oil that accumulate in the cracks of the asphalt float to the surface and make hydroplaning much more likely. You can lose traction and spin out before you even realize what's happening."

"Important safety tip from the boy genius," Snake muttered.

"Thanks, Chet. I'll remember." I braked as much as I could before the exit, then carefully piloted the Chevy around the looping offramp with my foot on the gas. Of course, my hot rod Chevy had modern disc brakes, but I couldn't remember if she had ABS. Anti-lock braking systems allowed the tires to maintain contact with the road without locking up, especially useful if the surface was slippery. I hoped the Chevy had it. Sure, we had it.

I heard Cheryl work the slide on her Glock as she said, "SUV is still with us." She sounded calm and that worried me.

This private part of the field was protected by a gate with an old-school striped crossbar blocking the road and a guardhouse next to it. I could see the uniform inside checking something on a clipboard. We stopped and the guard looked us over. He was in his late fifties, graying hair buzzed short, no facial hair, perfect creases in his shirt despite the humidity, eyes hidden behind aviator shades. He looked like ex-military, got out after twenty and supplemented his retirement with guard duty. He opened his little window. He looked me over, then looked at Snake and at Cheryl in the back seat and I had a very bad moment when I remembered that she had all sorts of weapons. Somehow she had squirmed out of the Batbelt with all its gadgets and covered it and the gun with her jacket. "Name, please?"

"Macdonald. T. R. Macdonald." I've always wanted to say that, and after all I was driving a fancy car and carrying heat.

He nodded and pushed a button that raised the bar. "Yes, sir. The rest of your party isn't here yet. Been here before?" I shook my head. "Okay. Sand-colored building across the way? That's Terminal 2. The FBO where the hotel jets load and unload is next to it. Follow this road alongside the runway. Watch the signs. Do not drive out onto the runway. Do not drive anywhere other than directly to the FBO. Park in marked spaces only. Got it?"

I said I got it. The SUV was not in sight. We rolled slowly onto what seemed like an endless plain of asphalt broken by strips of desert between the runways. A jackrabbit bounded out from behind a bush and vanished into its burrow. In the distance I could see the parking structure and low buildings that made up the main terminal.

We followed the signs and I backed the car into a spot in front of the FBO building, staying in the car with the engine running not only to stay dry but also to hear what Chet was saying. There was no sign of the SUV. With each passing minute the rain got harder, until it was pounding the roof of the car.

A jet, a huge 747, dropped down out of the clouds and landed. I liked that. If he could do it, so could the Lucky Lady IV. Or so I told myself. But the wind was still gusting hard enough to rock the car on its springs.

The minutes ticked by. I kept the wipers running. Cheryl took the opportunity to squirt dressing on her salad and eat. The rain slid across the runways in gray curtains. No other planes landed.

Snake said, "Okay, tell me about this stable and your dad."

It was better than watching rain move across the empty runways, so I said, "I read a little about it after my visit. Built in the twenties, by the grandfather of the current owners. There are three owners at present, Acey is the oldest. From what I read she seems to do most of the day-to-day managing and in her blog posts is pretty open about not liking it. Her brothers Deuce and Trey were out buying a horse when I was there."

Cheryl said, "Bad to carry resentments around like that. They can fester." We both turned and looked at her, sitting sideways in the back seat with her plastic salad container on her lap and a fork halfway to her mouth. "What? Just because my eyes have been opened to the way the world really is, doesn't mean I've forgotten everything about my previous life."

"Well, you're gonna love this. The grandfather, the guy who started the business, was murdered."

Snake choked. "Murdered? As in somebody killed him?"

"That's the definition. I found a newspaper article that said he was beaten severely and shot in 1935 by person or persons unknown."

"Wow."

"According to the web page, Jackie is Acey's nephew."

"The old guy?"

"Neville is the only name he has. He was an infant, left on the stable doorstep just before the owner was murdered. Asked me if I knew who his parents are. I guess he asks everybody."

"So he's like eighty, and still working?"

"I get the feeling he's never been anywhere else."

Since that was all I had to share we sat in silence, watching the rain. Lights came on in a warehouse next to the FBO waiting room and workers started doing things with equipment. I hoped they were getting ready for the Lucky Lady and not battening down for the typhoon. Off in the distance lightning flashed. I counted three seconds. 3,375 feet away. Cheryl finished her salad and put the container and fork in the paper bag.

Gusty winds picked up gravel and leaves and fast food wrappers and sent them scurrying across the runway up into the air and along as if they had somewhere to go and were late.

Chet said, "Twenty-five miles." The blowing leaves reminded me of a Vegas gimmick, a glass box the size of a phone booth with a layer of bills on the bottom, bills that were blown around when the fan was on and some lucky winner got to spend thirty seconds grabbing as many flying bills as she could.

"Fifteen miles. He's asking the tower about wind shear."

I gripped the steering wheel. "All right, they're bringing him in."

And as I tried to remember the name of the casino that had that particular prize suddenly the Lucky Lady IV dove down out of the clouds. All at once it moved sideways, just jerked left like a broken-field runner, before it corrected and lined up the approach again, dropping lower and I felt my heart start to beat again. Then I could hear the roar of the engines and it pulled up and banked right. In seconds it was lost in the clouds.

In his hotel room the keys stopped clacking and Chet's voice, tense, was the only sound from the speaker. "Pilot's going to circle once and try again. If there's more wind shear he'll divert."

"Thanks, Chet. Ontario?"

"Check."

"What about the I-15?"

"They anticipate closing at the Cajon Pass in five to ten minutes unless the storm lets up."

We waited. I managed not to chew on the steering wheel or my arm. When I'm nervous I like to count things, but there were no other parked cars or planes to count, so I counted twenty-three scraggly bushes between the runways.

Chet spoke up. "Okay, they're not going to a jetway. As soon as the plane's on the ground, they'll roll stairs out."

"When? How soon?"

"Now. Here they go."

And then the Lucky Lady appeared again, rocking side to side before it straightened and lined up. It touched down hard, spraying water and smoke from the tires, hopped up like a much smaller plane, touched down again in another burst of water and tire smoke and ran straight before slowly, gently, swerving sideways. It didn't seem to be losing speed at all, just heading inexorably for the weedy border of the runway at a 45-degree angle like a stock car cornering on a dirt track. The sound as the pilot reversed the engines was loud enough to hear over the storm, but somehow he got it under control. One tire crossed into the weeds before the plane turned and ponderously rolled to the spot where a man in a bright lime green rain slicker with the hood up was pointing with lighted batons. The engines began to wind down as if nothing was wrong. I started to breathe again and pried my fingers off the steering wheel.

"Okay, here come the stairs," Snake said as a pickup truck and the motorized ramp rolled up and the jet's door opened for Bryant to stick his head out and look around carefully, ignoring the rain. I got out of the car and started to walk toward the plane when, above the storm, I heard a car approaching.

I turned and saw a black Bromeliad limo, wipers frantically waving, rain spraying off the hood and the roof, forming a head-high v from the tires, barreling through the rain at about sixty. It swept past us and the driver aimed his missile toward the motorized ramp, now moving up to the jet's forward door. The truck positioned the ramp, stopped and the driver got out and ran for it. I turned back to the plane because I wanted to see her the moment she stepped out. I saw: Bryant with his left hand under his coat at the top of the stairs, looking out carefully, talking into a cell phone. Kandi in an unbuttoned black jacket over a white blouse and short denim skirt stepping out onto the platform holding her coat over a book bag and a medium-sized black purse. Kandi smiling, tugging at the collar of her jacket, and saying something to Bryant as he opened a black umbrella for her. A little spurt of water kicking up at the foot of the ramp. Kandi giving him a hug. Bryant frowning over her shoulder. A faint sound like some kid popping a paper bag. Kandi turning and seeing me, starting to wave. Two little spurts of water, spraying up.

It clicked into place. All at once it clicked into place and when I looked back a dark figure was standing up out of the sunroof of the speeding limo, shooting, and I was grabbing for my gun, my gun that was safely hidden under the seat of the Chevy. I wheeled around, slipping. As I sprinted for the car I snapped a look over my shoulder and saw Kandi, now halfway down the ramp, kick off her high heels, put one hand on the railing and vault smoothly over the side, vanishing out of sight, while at the top Bryant abandoned the umbrella to the next gust which immediately swept it away into the storm, before he dropped to one knee with a gun in his hand, trying to aim at something, hopefully the limo. That was the moment the storms chose to combine, to train, and I learned the real meaning of the word downpour. Downpour like nothing I had ever experienced, enough water that it seemed like if you fell and landed on your back it could fill your mouth and nose and drown you, Mother Nature's water boarding. My feet slid again and almost went out from under me; the old Vans I had on were nearly tredless, but to be fair I didn't have time to select an appropriate wardrobe for the trip and who knew it would rain like this?

That slip was only the beginning; I jerked in the other direction -- it was like I imagine ice skating to be -- and lost it. My bad shoulder hit the tarmac, shooting pain from neck to wrist, and I rolled, just a step or two from the car so I rolled again, like a bad ski fall on a steep slope where you keep sliding down the run and you think, "Well, the more I slide the closer to the bottom I'll be," before snatching the passenger-side door open and crawling in so I could fumble for the gun and finally pull the .45 out from under the seat on the driver's side. Somehow Snake had gotten into the back seat and now huddled on the floor. Next to him Cheryl sat, wide-eyed, with her gun in her lap. Sprawled on the bench seat, I jerked my head up for a quick glimpse out the window to see the limo, now stopped between my car and the plane, and now with two dark figures standing up through the sunroof with guns in their hands. For the moment they weren't shooting. Back down I got my Bluetooth ear bud out of the glove box and jammed it in and at once heard Chet yelling frantically, "Anybody! Is anybody there? Talk to me! C'mon, pards, somebody talk to me!"

"I'm here, Chet."

"Mac, what's happening?"

"No idea. The plane landed, the ramp rolled up and then two men stood up out of the hotel limo and started shooting and to answer your next question I don't know where Kandi is. She jumped off the stairs and is out there somewhere in the rain."

"T. R. where are you now?"

"In the car."

"Stay there! You've got to stay there. Do not get out of the car."

"Chet, what are you talking about?" Struggling with the wet laces to my shoes.

"Do not get out of the car! This is a big ol' thunderstorm, a real gullywasher, and that airport is going to see possible flooding and major lightning strikes --"

"One or two already."

"-- and believe me, you don't want to be out on the runway. If she's in the plane she's all right, pard, but if not, then both of you get to shelter."

The storm was so loud that if the guys in the limo were still shooting I couldn't hear it. I reached down and pulled off my shoes and socks, took a deep breath, kicked the passenger-side door open, and rolled out, staying low. The rain immediately drenched me, making it hard to see, and breathe. I shoved the gun under my shirt to keep it as dry as possible.

There was a splash and Snake was beside me, clutching the door handle uncertainly. "Visit beautiful Las Vegas, where the dry climate is good for all types of respiratory illnesses." He peered into the distance. "Which way, T. R.?" Then Cheryl was there, still wide-eyed, looking truly scary, with her black hair plastered to her head, black eyeliner running down both cheeks, naturally with her gun in hand. She waved it around uncertainly, looking for something to shoot, just as her husband let go of the handle, took a step, grabbed her elbow, slipped and pulled them both to their knees. Flopping around on the ground with a loaded weapon is not good. I reached down and gently took her gun, checked the safety and stuck it in my belt next to my 45. Watch out, it's two-gun Macdonald.

"Both of you, back in the car, now! And stay down!"

For once in her life Cheryl was reasonable. "Walter, T. R.'s right. We can't help." She got up and pulled him to his feet.

"No, no, . . ."

"Honey, get in the car."

I started sprinting toward the plane. Here's a tip: if the footing is really bad, slick and nasty, you're better off barefoot. My feet had gotten soft when I was in Manhattan, but a year of surfing nearly every day had toughened them up.

All at once a tanker truck, a small one painted bright pink with "Sano Pump Ltd." on the side over the cheerful slogan, "Always a straight flush with Sano Pump," appeared out of the rain on my right, turned and headed straight for me, lurching from side to side, blowing its horn and skidding as it came on. It had a cylindrical tank with a curved ladder going up the side, and all kinds of hoses attached to it. Lightning flashed again. One of the hoses was loose, dragging with the metal coupling on the end producing sparks. The driver, wearing a hot pink baseball cap backwards, was clearly visible, steering with one hand and waving frantically with the other, motioning for me to get out of the way, giving me just enough time to dart left, trip and do a total face plant before getting sprayed with water as the big tires skimmed past and Sano Pump vanished into the rain. I shook my head, spat out a mouthful of water and got to my knees.

Then it came back, just materializing out of the rain. The truck lost traction, spun in a complete 360, then continued around until it was pointing back the way it came, which was toward me, accelerating, swerving from side to side as the driver struggled to get it under control. The sky was split with two lighting flashes in quick succession. The hose had unrolled more and now was flopping wildly, swinging back and forth. The truck plowed on toward me; the hose swung out to chop me off at the ankles and I jumped.

I jumped right over that hose, landed without falling and was feeling pretty proud of myself until the metal fitting hit the side of the Chevy and bounced, causing the hose to slam across my shoulders, sending me sprawling again. At that I guess I was lucky -- I could have gotten clipped with the metal fitting on the end.

Sano Pump slid around in another turn and raced off into the rain. A moment later I heard a crash. Snake and Cheryl were peering out of the window, open-mouthed. I got to my feet again, slower this time, and waved to show that I was okay.

I started trotting toward the plane. The good news was that I didn't see any vehicles trying to run me down; the bad news was I couldn't see more than ten feet in any direction. While I was dodging Sano Pump, I moved and now the storm hid everything. I heard a voice and realized the phone bug was still in my ear. "Chet, you there?"

"Sure thing, pard. Are you okay? Are you under cover? Tell me you're not out on the runway."

Without thinking I had trotted in the direction I thought was right and now the car was lost, out of sight. "Um, yeah." It was wet and cold and loud with thunder and rain and I couldn't see a thing except gray walls of water.

"Yeah what? What's that noise?"

"Rain."

"Are you out in the runway?"

"I think I might be."

"You think you might be on the runway?"

"I can't see a thing. I may be on the runway or I may be on an access road. There's no planes landing." I hope.

"Are you okay?"

"Well, the toilet truck's not after me anymore."

"What?"

"Never mind." I was casting about, taking a few steps in one direction, then another, trying to catch sight of something. "Listen, I can't see, the storm has reduced visibility that much, and I'm lost. Have you got me on GPS?"

"Sure thing."

"Can you direct me to the plane?"

"Wait one. Yes. Tell me what you see."

"Nothing. It's like being inside a snow globe."

There was a pause, then, slowly, "Pard, that makes it harder and we really need to get you under cover." There was another pause when all I could hear was rain and static. Then Chet, but fainter now, buried under storm sounds. "Okay, the Lucky Lady is about a hundred yards east of you, but I don't know how to tell you which way to go. I don't know which way you're facing. Can you see anything at all?"

"Nope. How accurate is the positioning?"

"About eighteen inches."

I started walking. "I'm impressed. You can see in this weather?"

"I'm, uh, sort of piggybacking on an asynchronous Keyhole satellite that's passing over. We're good for another eight point six minutes, then it's back to civilian. That accuracy will be --"

"All right, I'm walking, tell me if I'm going in the right direction."

A minute later the tinny voice in my ear said, "Turn bzzzzzt ninety degrees."

I yelled, "Say again, Chet, say again."

"Right, right."

"Is that turn right?" No answer, so I turned to my right. "Okay, now --" I lost him again. All at once he was back. "And, Mac, run, don't walk. Get under cover fast."

"Wait, which way did you say before?"

"Run! I said 'run.' The main part of the lightning is coming. I've got almost continuous strikes zero point four miles northeast of your position and it's moving in your direction."

"You mean this isn't --" And, right on cue, at that moment there was a double strike, one bolt thrashing down followed by another in the space of a heartbeat. My feet tingled, that's how close it was. I flipped a mental coin and kept going in the direction I'd started.

The next one was closer. All at once I was flying through the air, then landing on my face and sliding -- look, Ma, I'm hydroplaning! When I finally stopped it was very quiet, the rain pounding on my head in complete silence. I got up and started running, hoping I wouldn't trip over something on the runway or that the limo gunmen wouldn't appear and shoot me or the Sano Pump truck run me down. And full disclosure requires me to confess that if my hot rod had appeared out of the rain I would have dived inside and been grateful. There was a flash and I could sort of hear the bang and I saw a dark shape angling up from the tarmac. There was another flash and I lost it, blinded. Yelling for Chet, running, but if he answered I couldn't hear it. I was completely turned around; I'd lost communication, and the visibility was, if anything, less than it had been. When in doubt, do something and see what happens. I sprinted on into the rain. After ten paces there was a yellow line, visible at my feet. Okay, center of the runway. Maybe. Probably. Sure it was. The Lucky Lady IV is waiting along this line, but which way? I shrugged and ran left, keeping that line in view. Watching the line I couldn't see where I was going until I stumbled forward and almost bumped into a huge wheel. I ducked under the fuselage, hoping that would serve as the cover Chet had wanted me to get under, but really having no idea -- maybe the plane would attract lightning and I'd be crispy-crittered, but at least it was drier. I wiped my face on my sleeve, grabbed the front of my jeans to see if the guns were still stuck down there -- they were -- and felt a little better. Whoever was shooting would be hampered by the weather as much as I was. I hoped. Although, as well organized as these people seemed to be, for all I knew they could be aiming a heat-seeking missile at me right now.

I ran from one end of the plane to the other, tail to nose, but somehow it didn't seem as big as it had when it landed, and there were no stairs.

March 20, 1934

Dearest Mama,

I am sorry it has been so long since my last letter. Much has happened out here in California.

First, how are you feeling? I surely hope that cough is better.

We are fine and the weather is real nice. I saw in the paper where you still haven't gotten much rain. Lou Helen and I are almost finished with our work on Mystery Riders of the Blazing Plains. Mr. Heems says there will be more work for us, he just has to decide what to do next.

We got yesterday off as some of the actors were not there and one of the girls said they were mad about not getting paid. I know Mr. Heems will pay us all as soon as he can, but, anyway it was real nice we went to the movies and had a nice picnic supper.

I have to go now we are going to have supper with some of the other girls from the movie.

You are all in my prayers.

Your loving daughter,
Grace

April 20, 1934

Dearest Mama,

How are you? We are fine out here.

Mystery Riders has ended. It was awful sudden. We just went in to work one day to do the last couple of scenes and the bus to take us out to Bronson Canyon wasn't there and then a man from the studio came and said that the movie was done. One girl said what about the last week of pay that we are owed and the man said he was sure it would all be taken care of.

Lou Helen says not to worry there are lots more movies and I am sure she is right and Mr. Heems said he would use us in his next western.

Your Loving Daughter,
Grace

Chapter Seven

"Chet, wrong plane, it's the wrong plane, can you see another one? Chet?" I have never felt so alone as those moments when I was huddling under that plane in the rain with a dead phone and no hearing.

Okay, no Chet. Think: What did the GPS show when you parked? What did the weather alert crawl across the bottom say? Couldn't remember. The storm came out of the mountains to the north, the wind is backing, moving counterclockwise, and the plane was almost due west when I last saw it from the car. Face into the wind.

I bought my first sailboat, a gaff-rigged Sunfish, when I was sixteen. Wind is something I know. I looked at my watch and was amazed to see that less than ten minutes had elapsed since I dove out of the car. Okay. The wind direction hasn't shifted that much. Face the wind. That's north. A quarter turn to my right should point me at the plane. Okay. Ten steps that way, if no plane, turn left, then do it again, keep it up till the right plane shows. I trotted out from under cover.

Hey, kids, here's something new. The runway was now a river, water rushing over the tops of my feet and rising, ankle deep now and pushing hard, really moving. I reflected on the fact and did you know that as little as six inches of rapidly flowing water can move a car and wondered if mine would get washed away and end up in Lake Mead. But, since there was nothing I could do about that I focused on my immediate problem, which was that a fall now could have serious consequences, like fatal, if I got knocked unconscious. I think I might have shaken my fist at the sky and screamed, "Can't I catch a break here?" but in my defense I was pretty loopy by then.

And the Universe answered. After one turn and ten-step walk I saw something, a dark shape on my left. Three more steps and in a lightning flash it was shown to be the stairs leading up to the plane and safety.

Flash. Flash. Another double, followed by a horizontal bolt slashing from cloud to cloud.

Lighting is one of our oldest, most primeval fears, rooted in that reptilian brain couched in the base of our skulls, gibbering and cowering with fear at loud noises in the dark. That brain was screaming at me, telling me to get up the stairs and inside where it was safe and dry and quiet and there were no terrifying, blinding flashes from the sky. And I almost listened to it. Almost. Instead I trotted forward to see that indeed the shape was a plane. I slogged under the stairs, noticing that my feet were numb, telling myself that being under the metal would protect me (later Chet explained that that was wrong, but what you don't know can't scare you, right?) and all at once it was quieter, just the rain pounding on the metal stairs instead of my head, and there she was, lying on her side with one arm outstretched, bare feet out in the rain, lying there as if she were asleep but of course she wasn't. Dark lashes against her cheeks had caught droplets of moisture; her lips were slightly parted. A tiny bubble formed in the corner of her mouth so I knew she was alive. Her head was resting on her outstretched arm; that's the only thing that kept her mouth and nose out of the flowing water.

The first-responder courses teach the three c's: check, call, and care. Check to make sure that going to the injured party won't add you to the casualty list (and the example they always use is a downed power line that electrocutes the first sucker who runs to help, can't tell you how glad I was to remember that); call for help; and then care for the victim. Check, call, and care.

I ignored all of that, ran, dropped to my knees, slid over to Kandi and felt for a pulse. The water was rising, almost to her mouth.

The moment I touched her, her eyes opened. She blinked and said, "Why do you keep doing this?" No doubt the poor thing was in shock. "Really, you must start thinking before you rush in to save people. It's insanity." Yes, definitely in shock. Didn't know what she was saying.

"You're welcome."

"Do you know how bad I'd feel if you got killed trying to save me? Oh, I do appreciate it, T. R., I really do, but I'm fine."

"Don't worry, if it will make you feel better I'll make sure you get killed, too. Can we have this conversation later?"

"Someone's shooting at us."

"Yeah." I struggled to my feet, bracing one hand against the ladder and reached down to help Kandi up. There was a moment when I wasn't sure if she was coming up or I was going down, but finally she stood on one foot, balancing against me. I got her up over my left shoulder, stood up straight and my feet went out from under me.

The next thing I knew I was lying on the tarmac with Kandi shaking my shoulder. "T. R., snap out of it, come on, you're right, we need to get out of here." She shook me again, harder. "If, if you're dead I don't know what I'll do. Wake up, dammit!"

"Unnh. Yeah. Yeah."

"How's your head?"

"Fine. It's still attached, right?"

"Now I know you're okay. But, repeated blows to the head can add up to serious damage."

"Come on," I shifted to help her up, thought better of it and stood.

She shook her head. "Turned my ankle when I jumped off the stairs. You go. I'll be fine."

I crouched down. "Lean over, get your waist on my shoulder, let your legs hang in front of me."

"T. R., I know what a fireman's carry is. How are you, really? Can you stay on your feet this time?"

"Yeah."

"I know you can. Ouch!"

"What?"

"That last tumble, my wrist."

I lifted her and got to my feet like an elderly, arthritic ape, but I made it.

Her head and arms dangling down my back, I staggered to the foot of the stairs. With one arm around her legs and the other clutching the railing I started up. One step at a time, my shoulder screaming at me, the rain hard enough to make breathing difficult and my bare feet numb. Another flash, another tingle in my hand that was gripping the rail, Chet saying something that was totally lost in the storm, but at least I was no longer deaf, and this time I was looking up to see where I was going. Step. The railing was slick with rain. Step. Get the other foot up. What must it be like for Kandi, hanging head down? Could she breathe? Step. Her hand, which had been clutching at my belt, fell away. She went limp. Step. Try to shift her so she could breathe? Step -- no, my big toe caught the lip of the stair riser and folded under, and it was a good thing because the pain snapped me out of it, the stumble narrowing my focus so that, while I kept going, I stopped thinking. I was falling forward; my hand on the rail slowed the fall and then came loose. I shoved my foot forward as hard as I could and it slammed into the step. My face followed, but it was a pretty gentle bump. We lay there for a minute, Kandi and I, gasping in the rain, until somehow I got one knee under us and was able to get to my feet. "Hang in there, honey, we're almost there." But there was no response. I grabbed that damn railing again. Step. Step.

We made it to the platform at the top of the stairs. The door was closed.

I pounded on it, still with Kandi draped over my shoulder, thinking if I lost my balance we'd go over backwards and land at the foot of the stairs where the lightning would electrocute us before we could drown, but of course we both would probably have broken necks by the time we hit bottom so it wouldn't matter. I think that was the reptile brain talking. I pounded some more, teetering now, mentally rehearsing how I would slide Kandi off my shoulder and onto the platform if I started to fall.

Then I felt a vibration in my feet. I stopped pounding and made sure. The big jet started rolling forward slowly. The good news was that it sort of dragged the stairs with it. I pounded and yelled until my fist hurt and I was hoarse.

All at once there was a face in the little circular window, gaping at me. A hand waved urgently, shooing me back. What the hell? At last I got it and stepped back. The engines cycled down, the door pushed out and slid to the side and Bryant was there, gently pulling Kandi away from me and saying something that I couldn't hear. I decided the rain must be letting up because it was much quieter.

Bryant cradled Kandi in his arms and vanished inside the plane. I slid to a sitting position on the top step and said to no one in particular, "You know, one of those trucks that pump sewage out of planes tried to run me over. It was pink and it said Always a Straight Flush on the side. Then I think I broke my big toe." There was a very bright flash, a loud thunderclap, and it was lights out for Mac-boy.

"You're going to be fine." A man with a stethoscope around his neck was bending over me.

"What?"

He shouted in my ear, "The hearing loss is temporary. You were very lucky."

"Kandi. Where's Kandi?"

He looked confused. "They'll bring you Jell-O if you want a snack."

I grabbed the front of his smock, jostling an IV line that led into somebody's arm, probably mine. "Mary Shaw, the woman with me."

He had no trouble pulling my hand off. "Ms. Shaw is in the next room. She's going to be fine. She's in better shape than you are."

The door opened. The doctor stepped toward it and started to say, "Visiting hours are --" as Bryant brushed past him and strode in, followed closely by two large men, all three in identical gray suits with their coats unbuttoned and suspicious bulges under their arms, all with discreet flesh-colored ear bugs. Bryant's left hand was bandaged and he held the arm awkwardly, as if it hurt to move it. Their eyes swept the room before he looked at me and grinned and nodded to the others, who stepped out. My guess was that they were taking up positions in the hall outside. The doctor threw up his hands -- I always thought that was a figure of speech but he really did it -- and huffed out. Bryant answered my question before I asked it. "Two more outside Kandi's room."

"Thanks." I started to say something else but he raised his hand, the one without the bandages.

"Here's what we know. The hotel limo was stopped and the driver tied up and put in the trunk. We don't have any idea who did it, but they were good. They remotely disabled the dash cam and all of the electronics, and the doors wouldn't open until there were people standing outside with guns pointing at the driver. This was all inside the hotel parking structure. But it looks like somebody's on your side because the sewage truck that almost ran you down drove straight into the limo, t-boned it, which discouraged the people inside from further shooting."

"Was it pink? The truck?"

He looked at me oddly. It was okay; I was used to it. "Yes, as a matter of fact it was. Why?"

"Oh, nothing. Go on."

"The truck was also stolen, taken from the storage yard at the north end of the runway. You ran through the storm, picked up Kandi and got her up the stairs. I carried her in, there was another strike, very close, that knocked you unconscious. All of the shooters and drivers got away before the police and ambulance arrived. We were afraid to take you down the stairs until the storm died. As soon as it did, they brought you here. Your friends Walter and Cheryl are fine – fine because they're lucky: They were both wandering on the runway, apparently looking for you. You were only out a few hours, Kandi even less. It's about midnight. And that's it. Coco sends her love and says she's billing you for damages to the limo."

"Tell her to put it on my tab."

He grinned. "She said you would say that, and that she would."

"How did you do that?" I nodded at his wrist.

"Came out to drag you in, slipped, went down a couple of stairs before I caught the railing."

"Thank you."

"I'll put it on your tab."

"Right. Those hotel limos are supposed to be secure."

"Question of the hour. The driver says all the electronics quit, he thinks he heard a click, like the doors locking, then there was a gun in his face. Then he was in the trunk with a cell phone minus the battery. The security control room assumed the car was off-grid because of the storm."

"Been there, done that," I muttered.

"Coco wants Chet, personally, to look at ways to modify the limo electronics so that won't happen again."

"Let me guess. His bill goes on my tab." Bryant just smiled.

A nurse came in and made shooing motions at Bryant. He grinned and nodded. Then he stepped over to the bed and raised his good hand. I caught it in mine. "Good job, man."

I said, "You, too."

I dozed. I talked to police, surprisingly brief conversations. I slept some more, the doctor came in and did things. A nurse came in and did other things, and then it was morning and Kandi was standing next to the bed with a metal crutch under her right shoulder and a fashionable black brace on that ankle. My room must have been on the south side of the hospital; the storm had passed and sunlight was streaming in the windows.

I opened my mouth to say something and managed only a croak until she poured water from a plastic pitcher and handed it to me. I sipped and said, "Good to see you."

She smiled and took my hand. "Hey, Sailor."

"Hey, Cutie."

"T. R., it's all crazy, my credit cards, my phone, Sly in the airport."

"Whoa, wait, Sly? Sly was there?"

"Yes, he came up to me while I was at the United gate, with a blonde named Cherri. She's his assistant. He said he was in Chicago on business and wanted to see me, then he heard about the shootings at the clinic and wanted to help. He offered to buy me a ticket home, said he was on the next flight."

"But you said no."

"Do I look dumb? C'mon, Sailor. I said 'Oh, thank you very much' and then ditched him. It was . . ."

"Way too convenient."

"He looked, no, his behavior was odd. He's lost weight, shaved his head. He would reach out like he wanted to touch my arm, then pull his hand back and put it in his pocket. He did that over and over and I don't think he was even aware of it."

"Weird."

"I have observed similar behavior in seriously disturbed individuals. And --"

"What?"

"I remembered he owned a chain of PC repair shops."

"I thought he was -- Never mind. He could have been responsible for your credit cards."

"I don't see how. Nobody knew I was flying out. I just decided, bought the ticket, and an hour later was on my way to O'Hare. Anyway, I don't know, but with the Lucky Lady coming I wasn't going to take that risk."

"How did you get away from him?"

"Said I had to go to the Ladies Room and instead ducked into the U-Need-It. My new friend Penelope was still working so I told her about Sly and tried to give her twenty bucks to let me go out the back door to a service corridor. She wouldn't take the money."

"Then you had to get to the FBO."

"And for that I had to go outside security, but I called the FBO -- thank god for that burner cell -- and they sent a car. Once I was inside their terminal I was okay."

"And Sly is probably still waiting for you to come back."

"Nope. That ol' boy was on the next flight." Chet stuck his head into the room, then came in carrying a laptop computer in one hand and a white Stetson in the other. He was in his usual uniform of faded jeans, western shirt, and ostrich-skin boots. Three dark lines on his belt marked where it used to enclose significantly more belly. "As soon as they called pre-boarding Sly got on. He must have been flying first class."

"Hey, Tex. You got here fast."

"Got lucky, got a flight out of San Francisco and landed right after they opened McCarran. Mary, your cards and phone are fixed. I talked to TRW, Transunion, and Equifax and they'll notify me if anybody tries it again." Kandi hugged him. "So, who is this Sly character and what does he have against my cousin?"

I looked at Kandi and decided to tell Chet everything I knew. "We met a little over a year ago."

Kandi sighed. "I'll tell it, Mac. I had a very short affair with him when I was working at Hof's Hut on Second Street in Long Beach. The restaurant is gone now, but I got my start serving drinks in their bar. Anyway, I found out he was married and broke it off, only he didn't take it well and followed me to Fred's. There was a scene, I dealt with him," I chose not to interrupt and point out that yours truly had something to do with dealing with him, "and I haven't seen him since."

I said, "That's how we met. First drunk I ever rolled in a parking lot." Neither of them laughed but I thought it was funny.

Chet closed his laptop. "Walter and Cheryl brought your car here; it's in the hospital parking lot. The only damage is a scratch in the paint."

"That would be from the loose hose on the back of the Sano Pump truck."

He shook his head. "I don't know how you do it."

"It's a gift. The doctor says if I can eat lunch and keep it down they'll release me this afternoon."

They looked at each other and Kandi made the little whirly-next-to-your-temple sign that meant I was nuts.

"I saw that," I said. "It's a long story but I am afraid it's true. Look, we all need to sit down and try to figure out what's happening here, but I don't think this is the place, and I feel like I should get home."

Kandi said, "Chet, would you wait outside? I want to talk to T. R." When your Significant Other says something like that it's never for her to invite you to go have wild sex and eat chocolate-covered strawberries. Why is that? I thought about asking Kandi since she was certain to appreciate my wit but decided not to. I was right.

"T. R., I want to thank you for saving me. With my ankle I couldn't have climbed the stairs and if you hadn't gotten me into the plane a close strike might have electrocuted me." She sat on the edge of the bed and took my hand. "But I can't do this anymore. I love you, you know I do, but things just, just happen around you. I've been shot at, kidnapped, nearly drowned . . ."

"But it wasn't boring."

"And then there's the You Tube video of my boyfriend driving a forklift down Bolsa Boulevard in his underwear."

"Why does everyone keep bringing that up?"

"T. R., it went viral."

"It seemed like a good idea at the time. Anyway, they took my clothes."

"Like your mother says, always wear clean underwear because you never know." She smiled and I thought I might be making progress. I was wrong.

"Not mine."

"T. R., I have to tell you --" She paused.

"The ticket that got cancelled was Chicago to Vegas. You weren't coming home."

"You figured it out." I shrugged, rattling the IV stuck into my hand. "You hadn't made any arrangements to be picked up at John Wayne. And you were fine with landing at McCarran because that's where you were going all along."

"It's just too scary and it's not how I want to spend my life. The time I spent in Chicago just reminded me of how much satisfaction I derive from working with the mentally ill, and, and they're releasing me in a little while and I – I've asked Bryant to take me to the Bromeliad. I'm going to stay there until I have to go back to Chicago. After that, well, after that I just don't know. But you know I love you. I just, I just have to think."

"You're staying here?"

"I am."

I wanted to say something that would make it all right, something romantic and tender and perceptive. You know what I thought about, what popped into my head? What if I played the 'I ran across a runway in the middle of a thunderstorm and saved your life' card and she changed her mind and threw herself into my arms? If that happened I'd never know for sure, and maybe she wouldn't either. She had asked for time to think. I had to let her have it.

"What about whoever it is hacking your accounts?"

"Chet has fixed that and the Bromeliad has world-class security. I feel that I need time to think. This seems like a good opportunity."

"Your Raven is in my bag over there," I said.

She shook her head. "Having it around makes you likely to use it. I'm staying here."

Our eyes met. I shrugged. "Sure."

Chapter Eight

After she left, the rage and pain bubbled in me, toxic bubbles seeping up from a poisoned swamp. Somebody hacks her credit cards and e-ticket; I arrange for transport, dash through the storm, drag her into the plane, wind up in the hospital -- again -- and her response is, "I can't do this anymore?" At that moment I felt every cut, sprain, and bruise that I'd picked up on my dash across the runway, and I wanted to blame her. A nurse came in and asked if I was all right, because the monitor showed my blood pressure spiking. I snapped that I was fine, just peachy and my compliments to the chef on the Jell-O. After a while she went away and there wasn't much of anything.

I wanted her to come back with me. But I wanted her to want it. I could not bring myself to ask because no matter what she said, I'd lose. She says no and I'm hurt even more. She says yes and I'm forever wondering did she really want to be with me? I wanted to say something tough and tender like "I love you but you're free," but while she was there I couldn't think of anything and after she left it was too late.

So that afternoon Kandi moved to a room at the Bromeliad, not a suite, but on one of the upper, secure floors. You had to show a room key on the ground floor before getting on the elevator, there was a concierge (read plainclothes security) manning a desk in the upper elevator lobby, and of course there were cameras everywhere -- inside the elevators, in the hall, over the desk where security sat, cameras watching other cameras.

The only clothes she had were the ones she had stuffed into her carry-on suitcase and her shoulder bag, so she'd have to go shopping. Bryant promised she would have hotel security with her when she did. Not that I'd asked.

You've got to stop doing this.

What if she was right? Something in me said she might be right.

Very early in my career as a broker-analyst I learned not to ignore information just because you didn't like it. That way lies poverty.

But I never could have left her out on the runway in the rain.

I never could have left her stranded at O'Hare.

You've got to stop doing this.

What if she was wrong, and I needed to be there for her?

Kandi loved me. Kandi couldn't be with me because it scared her.

Someone was playing with us. If Cheryl hadn't scared them off, maybe I could have learned something from the kids at Barstow Station.

This was like a carnival fun house -- nothing happens, then some guy in a hockey mask jumps out and yells, "Boo!"

Two LVPD detectives came to the hospital and questioned me again, but not for long. The sewage truck and the t-boned Bromeliad limo yielded no prints and nothing useful. After the rain stopped the cops took a careful look at the area around the Lucky Lady IV and found over a dozen marks in the tarmac, which might have come from bullet impacts, but the slugs had been washed away and were probably on their way to add to the pollution in Lake Mead. No one was wounded during the shooting, and it seemed like my up-close-and-personal lightning experience was the most serious injury. One of the detectives said, "Mr. Macdonald, we talked to Bromeliad security and to a detective Genucci of the Huntington Beach police. They vouch for you, so if you want to take a look around the area where the incident took place, it's okay with us." I said I was sure they had found everything worth finding, but thanks for the offer. I kept my lunch down -- bland spaghetti, bland cooked carrots, and tasty lime Jell-O -- so they said I was safe to leave the hospital or, as one witty MD said, "Be released on an unsuspecting world."

Bryant's pals rode down in the elevator with me, Snake, and Cheryl and escorted us to where the hot rod Chevy was parked. That was fine with me.

Nobody jumped out and yelled "Boo!" Nobody shot at us. The pink Sano Flush truck did not put in an appearance. On the ride back to Huntington, Cheryl and Snake took turns driving. I sat in the back. Nobody talked much and I didn't bother watching for cars that might be following us. It didn't seem to matter.

Finally, Snake said, "This is nuts, man. Nuts. What do these people want?"

"I think I know. They want Kandi. They want to split us up. And they got it, didn't they?"

Snake was silent for a moment. "Let's see if I get it. They scare her, make you do crazy shit, fight, whatever, and it freaks her out, drives her away."

"Yeah. And If I find these people and do what I need to in order to protect her, I risk losing her."

"What are you going to do?"

"What do you think?"

He sighed. "We need a plan."

"I don't know. I keep thinking about the first time we met. It was in Fred's, she was serving drinks and this drunk grabbed her. Other than taking my order, you know what the first thing she said to me was? After I dragged the drunk off her?"

"No."

"She said, 'I could have handled him.'"

"Who was the guy?"

"Businessman named Sly Staney."

Just past Baker, home of the world's tallest thermometer, I fell asleep. I woke up when Snake bumped two tires over the curb trying to get the car into my driveway.

There were no messages from Kandi. No messages from Kandi: This was where I came in. I said thanks for bringing me home, walked my friends out to the half-Camo-painted SUV. Cheryl said, "I'm painting it myself. Computer-generated camouflage pattern."

"Looks good."

She climbed up, got behind the wheel and after she put on a black CSI ball cap they rumbled off down the street. Around me the suburban Orange County neighborhood was quiet.

When I need to think it helps to get out, preferably on the water. I loaded my short tri-fin surfboard into the Chevy -- it was small enough to fit into the passenger compartment, angled from back seat to dashboard -- and headed for the pier. It was afternoon and high tide so the surf would probably suck, but I didn't care. Then I remembered they were building an arch across Pacific Coast Highway, setting up for the surf contest and stopped at Seventeenth Street. It didn't matter much where I went; the surf would be crummy.

I was right about the conditions. I was also right that it didn't matter. I set the car alarm, parked on PCH, fed the meter, pulled off my tank top, kicked off my sandals and pulled on my full suit. I punched the code into the alarm, stashed the car key on top of the driver's side front tire, grabbed the board and headed out, pulling up the suit's zipper as I trotted toward the ocean. Normally I prefer to surf a little farther north but today the break right in front of the traffic light at Seventeenth and Pacific Coast Highway looked marginally better. I ran into the water, threw the board down and flopped on top of it. Two strokes in I pushed through a small, mushy wave and got the ever-popular shot of cold water down the back of the wetsuit; I shook water out of my eyes and laughed. Okay, call me a man of simple pleasures: surf of almost any size and shape, a breakfast burrito at Fred's Fine Mexican Food, coffee made with freshly ground Kenya AA, my friends, and Kandi my love. I pushed that last part aside.

Outside the break line I turned the board around and watched the shore for a few minutes. To the south I could see the hotel where some very unpleasant people had tried their best to kill someone I cared about.

Back in the old days, a year ago, when I was a broker-analyst, I learned very quickly that the only thing you can count on is the unexpected. The slimy CFO who you are sure is embezzling millions turns state's evidence and saves the day; your friend the hedge fund manager who buys you a drink is fishing for privileged information. And so on.

After an hour my shoulder started to ache so I called it a day. I loaded the board, put a towel over the seat, cranked up AC/DC's "Highway to Hell" and punched it, just a little, getting onto PCH. I went home and did the ritual rinsing of the board and my wetsuit. Then I put on a pot of coffee.

I plopped down in the deck chair with the old, frayed webbing and tried to think. Thinking was hard and the afternoon sun was reflecting off the glassy water of the channel, so I closed my eyes.

I was in bed, asleep, and it was all right because there was a warm female body next to me; Kandi had come back. I opened my eyes and looked into dark brown eyes framed by glossy brown hair worn parted in the middle and down to her shoulders. Her bangs were a little longer than the last time I'd seen her, down to her eyebrows.

My dead wife Diana was lying next to me, wide awake, chin propped on her palm. She smiled. "Can I borrow a pen? And some paper?"

"Diana."

"Hey, grappler." She used to call me that, a reference to my wrestling exploits. "You love her, don't you?"

"Yes. I, I'm --"

"Shh. It's all right. So what are you gonna do?"

"What do you mean?"

She reached out and touched my cheek. I could feel it, I really could. Then she was gone.

So what are you gonna do? Highway to hell. And I'm goin' down.

I woke up, checked the lines holding the Whaler to the dock, went inside to get my phone and started making calls.

My first call was to Tony Genucci of the HBPD. "Tony, it's all too easy." I stretched out on the dock on my back in the sun. The warm planks felt good.

"Oh, rats. You have uncovered the nefarious plot." Tony thinks I'm funny, except that was supposed to be serious. "How are you feeling? You need anything?"

"Come on, Tony, shots were fired, two vehicles crashed, I nearly got fried and it's all going away? Answers, that's what I need."

"Mac, the Las Vegas police were -- and are -- sort of busy. In addition to over two dozen accidents caused by the rain, there were two convenience store robberies and three trick rolls where the girls used chloroform -- very old school -- to subdue the john before taking wallet, credit cards, jewelry, and dumping the poor sucker in a bathtub full of ice. And before you ask, yes, when they were found they had the usual internal organs"

"I always thought that was an urban legend."

"It is. It appears these young women and/or their friends have a sense of humor, except one of the johns was in the tub too long and got frostbite on his posterior. So your adventure, while spectacular, is not a top priority, in fact, it's not even up to your standards. Remember the time --"

"Please don't bring up the forklift."

"You know, around the station house when we're not eating donuts, all you have to do is say the word 'forklift' to get a laugh."

"I refuse to respond to that. Tony, listen, it's more what they didn't do, you know? At the airport, they had us cold. I got Kandi under the stairs but she'd twisted her ankle. If they had wanted to kill us they could have, same for a kidnap."

"And that supports the theory that nothing really happened. I repeat, no one was hurt, no slugs were ever located. Mac, it comes down to a traffic accident and possibly random shots. Spectacular, but a traffic accident and random shots just the same."

"What about Bryant? What does he say"

"Bryant might have seen muzzle flashes, but he never fired his weapon, which is a very good thing for him."

"Yeah. I saw what might have been chips of asphalt fly up where the alleged bullets might have struck the pavement. There might possibly have been holes in the tarmac."

"Do I detect a note of sarcasm? No holes could be positively identified as the result of bullet strikes. The entire runway was under water. The provable events come down to a traffic accident combined with a foolish person who ran out on a flat surface during a lightning storm."

I said slowly, "No bullet holes in the plane?"

"None."

"Or my car."

"They were terrible shots."

"They're worse than me and I could hit a G5 at that distance."

"LVPD attributes the lack of hits to the terrible conditions. And, before you ask, there is nothing on the computer hacking that started all of this. Mac, I want to add 'brave'. 'Foolish and brave.' Mary might have died, I am aware of that."

I wanted just one person to say that it was a good thing to do. I wanted to be sure of it myself. "Thanks, Tony. Listen --"

"If I hear anything I will let you know."

"Wait, hold it, Tony. The convenience stores that were robbed, where were they?"

"I think I have the addresses here. Wait one." A moment later he was back. "They were -- oh. North Las Vegas. All three."

"Opposite side of town from the airport."

"Yes."

"Tony, they were a distraction, designed to draw resources away from the airport. What about the times?"

"Possible. The final robbery was ten minutes before the Lucky Lady IV landed. You know, it's just possible. Maybe. I'll give it a maybe and pass the thought on to LVPD. Mac, if you are so concerned, why didn't you go out and look at the scene?"

"Honestly? I just wasn't up for it, and I hadn't figured all this out. You'll keep me posted?"

"Yes. Goodbye now."

I was sitting in my living room looking out at the street when a white 50th Anniversary Mustang fastback with wide blue stripes down the middle pulled up in front of my house, followed a moment later by a white Ford Econoline van. Both the Mustang and the van had the Space Floozy Enterprises logo -- a blonde Valkyrie with a brass brassiere and a ray gun -- on the doors. Kandi's cousin, Chet Shaw, got out of the passenger side of the Mustang and started for the house, tapping on his cellphone; the driver jumped out and hurried around to open the hatchback. He removed a small, wheeled suitcase, three laptop cases, and a shopping bag. He lugged all this stuff up to the porch before trotting to the Econoline and jumping in the sliding door. The van was rolling even before it slid shut. I pushed cancel and got rid of the text I was sending to Kandi. It was pretty lame anyway. I opened the door and let Chet in.

Inside, Chet pulled a Mountain Dew out of the shopping bag, popped the top and had a long slug before saying, "Ah, breakfast of champions."

"Breakfast of nerds who stayed up all night playing *Half Life*."

"That is so last millennium. I think I was about twelve when I beat that game the first time."

"Good to see you, Chet." I shook his hand and it turned into an almost-hug, sort of a back pat. Very manly.

He blurted. "You scared the crap out of me, pard, when your phone went dead and I lost the satellite feed." He blushed, had another swig of Mountain Dew. "Those boys who drove me over are some of my techies, large-system specialists, and they are in a hurry because they are going to Chicago. My friend at O'Hare -- the one who let us look over his shoulder so we could keep an eye on Mary -- wants to know how his security got cracked. He doesn't like it that someone got into the airline registration system. Doesn't like it at all. I should go with them; he expects me."

"Coco wants you, too. But you're here." He shrugged and took another long drink. "Thanks for coming."

I rolled his suitcase through the living room and into the family room, where he ignored unpacking clothes in favor of setting up his laptops. In five minutes there were cables stretching from computers to surge protectors to every available plug. "You gotta get this place rewired, pard. Need more outlets. How old is the panel?"

"Cut it some slack; the house was built in the sixties. Panel?"

He grunted and entered a password that had to be at least twenty-five characters. "Like a metal box on the side of the house where circuit breakers live? You do know about circuit breakers?" He shook his head. "Never mind."

"See what you can find out about Sly. I need to track him down, drag him out of wherever he's hiding, and have a serious conversation with him."

Chet looked at me oddly. "I like this better than Mr. 'It Doesn't Matter'. Sure, sure, we'll get to that. First you need to know something about him."

"I already do. He picked up Kandi when she worked at Hof's Hut on Second Street. When she found out he was married she broke it off, but he followed her to Fred's and that's where I met him. He's a nutcase."

"Yeah, I've heard that story."

"Right, in the hospital." Seemed like my brain was not running on all cylinders yet. "Snake and Cheryl are on their way and they're bringing pizza."

Sure enough, the Hummer rumbled up out front and Snake emerged carrying pizza boxes, and his wife, after checking sight lines, followed him in. She'd been busy; now I could see that the passenger-side door was also painted camo.

Chet looked up from his laptop. "Mac, I've been reviewing your security footage. This morning before we got here you had a kid hanging around. He knocked, then seemed to study the front door lock."

"The kid's name is Cracker and he needs some help with business arithmetic. I'll call him later."

"Oh, good. He's a student. Mac, he was looking at your lock pretty carefully."

"Cracker's hobby is breaking and entering."

I poured coffee for myself and Snake, Chet opened another Mountain Dew, and they all looked at me. Ever practical, I opened the pizza boxes, rummaged around under the sink and found a roll of paper towels that I put on the table next to the pizza. I am nothing if not a good host. "Right. Council of War. Here's where we are now. Somebody hacked Kandi's credit cards. No, wait, she was coming home because there was trouble at the Usher clinic, *then* she got hacked. Then we went to pick her up at McCarran and we got shot at." Chet looked at me oddly when I said that and I realized that he knew Kandi's ticket was not to Orange County. He let it go.

Chet said, "Roughly seventy-two hours from the murder-suicide to the airport shooting."

"Right. There's not much we can do about the hacking without Kandi's laptop. But at least she's safe." My friends were looking at me like I'd lost my mind. I'm perceptive about that sort of thing because it happens to me a lot. That is, everybody but the Snake. He looked grim. Snake's been around. More than forty years ago he spent some time running from the cops. "Chet, you've never had a ride in my new hot rod. I'll take you for a spin after we eat."

Snake said, "I'll go, too."

We ate pizza, cleaned up the empty boxes, put the few remaining slices in tin foil and stashed them in the fridge. We piled into the Chevy; I took us out of the Harbour and down Warner to the Bolsa Chica Interpretive Center. There was parking and a few minutes later we were walking along the trail, surrounded by wetland that had looked approximately the same for hundreds of years; shallow water, birds, marsh grass blowing in the gentle afternoon breeze. There were a few other people walking, two set up with tripods and huge telephoto lenses, and a group of kids being herded by two adults. Nobody seemed interested in us.

Snake said, "You think your house is bugged."

"I think we have to assume it is."

Chet said, "I'll scan as soon as we get back."

I shook my head. "Let it go. Maybe we can feed them some misinformation."

Cheryl slapped her leg. "Enemies! You have enemies and you are under attack. We need a strategy. We need to work out tactics. We need to take the fight to your enemies, and soon. I brought weapons." Snake pulled a Dos Equis dark out of his coat pocket and opened it with his Swiss Army knife. She pursed her lips and said, "I'm dropping back for a perimeter check." Her husband studied the bottle cap before depositing it in his jeans pocket.

"Don't shoot a heron! I think they're protected! Don't shoot anything." She waved, turned and trotted back the way we came, doing her best to look like a movie version of a Navy SEAL. We all stood for a moment, maybe waiting to hear gunshots and screams. I yelled, "We're not saving you any ice cream! If you're not back we're leaving without you and I'm going to eat it all."

Chet said, "Is there ice cream?"

"I thought I'd stop at the store on our way back."

Snake said, "Well, I'll say it if no one else will."

I said, "Cheryl's off the deep end?"

"No, Mac, I mean, well, yes, she sort of changed after those people kidnapped her, but I -- Shit. Mac, where's Kandi?"

Chet looked acutely uncomfortable, but he didn't start fiddling with his Gameboy. He looked at me. Snake looked at me. I started walking. A pair of blue herons standing in the water studied something we couldn't see. Suddenly one speared his beak down into the water and came up with a small, squirming fish. The heron tossed his head, deftly caught the fish head first and swallowed. Life in the food chain.

"Kandi stayed in Vegas."

"Why isn't she with you?" Snake wasn't going to let this go.

"She has some issues to work out. And that's all I'm going to say."

"Issues like wherever you go people seem to shoot at you?"

"It's not my fault, I just --" But it was my fault. I made decisions that resulted in violence, more than the average person ever sees. And it didn't look like it was going to stop anytime soon. "No. You're right. Bad shit happens around me. I don't like it, I want it to stop as much as anybody, but right now that doesn't seem to be an option." I took a deep breath. "Help me figure this out. Once this is done I wouldn't blame you if you didn't want to have anything to do with me. I understand. It's dangerous and it's scary. But help me with this, please."

Mary, the psychologist half of my Significant Other, would be proud of me for admitting that I needed help, but unfortunately I'd made this great breakthrough just as my closest friends might have decided I was too dangerous to be around. Except, of course, for the gun-totin' nutcase now prowling around behind us, looking for who knew what. Did I have a right to put them in danger to help Kandi? No. Would I do it? Ask them to take what might be very real risks? Without hesitation. Sometimes I'm not very nice.

Snake and Chet looked at each other. Snake looked over his shoulder at Cheryl, now striding back toward us. He said, "We better save her some ice cream. I think we'll need her."

Chet said, "Cheryl's right. We have to take the fight to your enemies." I sighed with relief.

Snake said, "This all goes back to the two dead people in Chicago."

"Farther."

Snake said, "The guy that got run over."

"Strangled with a belt and then run over. But maybe even farther than that." I told them about the stable and the anonymous grant that brought my father back to Surf City.

Snake whistled softly. "I should have brought another beer. I'm beginning to think Cheryl's paranoia is contagious. Okay, I'll bite. Why do you think the grant that brought your dad here is connected?"

"I think it was meant to keep me occupied."

We collected Cheryl and went home, stopping at the market in the Harbour center for a couple of six-packs and two half-gallons of ice cream, Rocky Road and chocolate. It pays to be prepared.

Back home Snake stowed the beer and ice cream, Cheryl went on another perimeter check, Chet did cryptic stuff at one of his laptops. I sat at the kitchen table and cleaned the guns, my .45 and Kandi's little Raven. It seemed like a good idea after getting them wet. As I put the Raven back together I wondered what she was doing at that moment. Cheryl came in and stood carefully to the side of the living room windows and watched sight lines. Just another typical afternoon around the Macdonald household. I finished cleaning the guns and pondered. A beer? Ice cream? Coffee?

Now Chet typed, fast keystroking on the largest of his laptops. "Wait, I remember now. You had me look up *LA Times* articles, some kind of hit-and-run."

"Except it wasn't. He was choked to death."

I looked at the clock over the stove, then stepped into the living room. It was empty. "Where's Cheryl?" They all stood. "No. You guys stay here. She's armed and nervous. Let me see what's going on."

I found her crouching by the side of the house, peering through a bush, watching the street. I knelt beside her. She whispered, "The same minivan has gone by twice."

"Silver?"

"No, this one's white." We watched for another minute or two and didn't see the suspicious van.

On the way back to the house, Cheryl said. "You haven't made some crack about me being paranoid."

"Don't take this wrong, but I'm afraid you're not."

May 29, 1934

Dearest Mother,

Thank you so much for the two dollars you sent me in your last letter. I know how hard things are at home and I want you to know that I will repay you as soon as I am able, but everything is so dear out here that it is hard to make ends meet.

I am working but Lou Helen is not yet and it is sometimes hard. She has a young man! Her beau's name is Willeford Freedman and he seems very nice and polite. He has a flivver and takes us for rides. He took us to a dance last Saturday. We met several girls he knew and he introduced me to a friend of his named Clyde Biggs.

It is nice here and my secretarial work is hard, but I like it. I have found a church like you asked about in your last letter and I attend Sunday as often as I can.

Your loving daughter,
Grace

Chapter Nine

After we ate ice cream, Snake and Cheryl went home. Chet settled in to look over the shoulders of teams he had working in Chicago and Las Vegas.

I decided I needed another shot at my father. The grant appearing out of nowhere could be unrelated to everything else, but I doubted it.

I could hear the chatter of air-hammers, the high whine of saws, the deeper rumble of heavy equipment. I followed it around the office building. In back, the old stable had been demolished. A bulldozer rolled toward the pile of broken, dusty lumber, lowered the blade, scooped up scrap, then backed around, made a reverse k-turn and deposited the debris in the trailer of a waiting tractor-trailer rig. Scoop, k-turn, deposit. Repeat.

I found him sitting on a stool, painting, and paused for a minute to look over his shoulder at the work. The watercolor on the easel was unfinished but he had captured the brute power and massive grace of the dusty white bulldozer.

I stepped closer for a better look.

"You're in my light."

"Hey, Dad."

Impatiently he waved an arm, pointing to my right. I took two steps that way. He cocked his head to one side, added a couple of brush-stokes, sighed and carefully placed the brush in a jar before he turned and looked at me over his shoulder. "You're back." He turned to face me and my first thought was: my god, he's old. His face was deeply lined and tan from a lifetime spent outdoors; his shoulders strained the "Endless Summer" T-shirt; his hair was the same: long, parted on the left and worn down over his ears. He looked all right. Then you saw his legs, how thin and wasted they were, scarred and jutting out from his board shorts. They looked like sticks with bumps on his shin under his knees, surf knots that had survived the wreck, the surgeries, and the rehab. Seeing them hurt more than anything else.

Try for the light touch, right? Maybe his feelings have changed. "Hey, you know, just thought I'd stop by." He didn't smile.

He gestured to the bulldozer. "Always liked this kind of job. Other guys wanted to drive the really big stuff, the D9s, but there's a lot of skill involved in moving this kind of scrap, and getting it in the trailer in as few trips as possible, keeps the drivers happy because they're paid by the load. Not like just driving back and forth, load the fill here, dump it there."

"I heard about the grant," I said.

"I thought for a minute you might have done it, you know, get me down here closer."

"No."

"Knew it."

"Dad, I know we have some issues --"

"Jesus! Issues! Psychobabble. You did bad things. Period. That ain't *issues*, that's your wife's dead. And that ain't right." He glared at me, blue eyes cold under shaggy brows.

I knew I shouldn't, but I simply couldn't help it. "So it doesn't count that I tracked down the guy who did it and he's locked up? And that killing her had nothing to do with me?" I guess my voice carried because Jerry was back in another tank top, pretending to pour coffee from a silver thermos while he kept an eye on us. Protecting the old guy. From his son.

"Why are you here?"

"I think you're in trouble."

"Some wacko's sending threatening notes. Wants me gone. I don't need saving." He glared at me. "Yeah, I read about you in the paper."

"There was vandalism."

"Kid stuff. None of this has anything to do with me."

"Who gave the stable the grant?"

"Anonymous. Went to the stable to bring me down and paint the demolition and new construction."

"Anonymous? Don't you think that's odd? And it specified you to do the painting?" He looked at me sourly. "That came out wrong. I understand you're really good and --"

Just like old times, old times a year ago when nothing either of us said came out right, so the obvious solution was to say nothing. Except I had a strong feeling that I couldn't do that this time. He was still looking at me. "Listen, please. Since I was here some things have happened and I'm pretty sure we need to take the threats seriously."

"I'm not stupid and I'm not taking chances. Hell, you think there weren't threats every time one of the unions went out on strike?"

"I think this might be different."

"Bathroom."

"Titanic." I grinned. He didn't respond, just draped a piece of cheesecloth over the painting to keep the dust off.

He reached out for the sticks, but one of them fell over and landed in the dirt. I reached for it but, bending over, he glared up at me through bushy gray eyebrows. Our eyes met for a moment, but there was no flash of understanding like in the movies, only resentment in his eyes and I guess in mine, too. He snatched up his crutches, slid his arms through the rings, and levered himself up off the stool. Stump, thud, stump, thud, muffled noises as he worked his way across the dirt. He passed out of sight and I heard a louder thud and a grunt. I held my breath, but I didn't move. After a moment the stump, thud resumed.

As soon as it was quiet I carefully opened his bag, memorizing the arrangement of the contents before I moved them. A letter had what I wanted: a Ventura address scratched out and a Huntington Beach address printed neatly next to it. I memorized the address and put everything back, as it turned out just in time.

"Yo, who the hell are you?"

The twenty-something hulk I'd seen before, Jackie, was standing behind me, looking unfriendly. He was even bigger than I remembered, huge, easily 6' 4" and 250 and not fat. He looked like a bouncer on his day off from an upscale club. Somehow I didn't think we'd get along. Stump, thud, stump, thud. My father returned, settled on his chair with a sigh. He leaned his crutches against a box and for a moment looked at them, his expression unreadable.

"Jack, this is --"

"Not talkin' to you, old man. Talkin' to him." Jack had an odd face, now that I looked at him more closely. His brow jutted out, burying his eyes in deep sockets, so buried that I couldn't be sure of their color, his chin receded sharply, making a serious overbite even more noticeable. "This area's closed for the construction. Beat it."

"Sure. When I'm finished talking to my father."

"You're done now." He took a step forward and you know what popped into my head, right after the fact that this guy was enormous? It was that I was about to get in a fight in front of my father. The giant would take a swing at me -- most guys his size never study the art of dirty fighting because they don't have to -- I'd step around behind him, reach up and get him in a choke hold. A wrist lock would be safer, but if he was too strong for me I would be in serious trouble. No, a choke hold was the way to go, bar arm across the throat; eleven pounds of pressure across the windpipe and he's unconscious; game over, and my dad would see me do something that didn't involve a spreadsheet. I really, really wanted to do it. I stepped away, my dad snorted and picked up his brush.

"Jackie! Stop it!" The giant instantly froze, unclenched his fists and took a step back.

A short, dark-haired woman dressed in dusty jeans, a western shirt and a blue bandanna around her throat stood behind us, hands on hips, glaring at us both. My Dad said, "Acey, this is my son, T. R. Macdonald."

She nodded. "Meetcha. Your father is doing good work." She shrugged. "Art's not my thing. We look forward to displaying it in the new office." This had the sound of a rehearsed speech. Jackie the giant was staring at his boots with his hands clasped in front of him like a school kid in the principal's office. I noticed strands of gray in her hair and revised up my estimate of her age. Fifties, maybe.

The older man, in his seventies, or older, marched by with a large, flat-bladed shovel over his shoulder. He stopped, grounded the shovel between his feet, and stared at us, smiling and nodding his shaggy gray head. He looked at me and smiled, revealing teeth so perfect they had to be dentures. "Neville. My name is Neville."

There was no sign he remembered me from our first meeting. "Hello, Neville. My name is Mac." He nodded again and stood patiently, still smiling and holding the shovel, as if waiting for something. I stuck out my hand and he put down the shovel and solemnly shook it.

"April's coming. April's coming and it's a mean month. Do you know who my people are?" He used his tongue to slide the dentures back and forth, "Mean. There's stuff I don't know, but I know that. Mean." He stared at a spot over my left shoulder and continued working the dentures and nodding.

"Sure. Tax season." I grinned. He smiled and his wrinkled face lit up.

The giant found his voice. "Beat it, dummy," he said. "Go shovel some horse shit."

"Sure Jackie, sure." Neville's smile vanished and he focused on Jack, and for a moment there was something in his eyes, just a flash of awareness. He picked up the shovel and his hands tightened on the handle.

With no hesitation whatsoever, the woman, Acey, reached up and backhanded the huge man across the face, hard. He staggered a little and rubbed his cheek. Neville hoisted his shovel and trudged off as if this were an everyday occurrence. She said, "Jackie, you forgot again."

The giant looked properly abashed and hurried off in the other direction, not before throwing me a look that was not abashed at all. She said, "That's Neville. He's been with the stables his whole life, he's mildly retarded, and I will not tolerate it when people, even my nephew, abuse him. Acey Decker." She stuck out her hand. "My brothers and I own the stable."

"T. R. Macdonald." We shook. Her hand was hard, calloused, and not something I would want to be smacked with. "I came to visit my father. Ms. Decker, I understand you've had some problems."

"Walk with me." Without waiting for me to say yes, she took my arm and led me back toward the parking lot. I looked back over my shoulder but my father did not look up from his painting.

We passed a small group of construction workers sitting in the shade, eating sandwiches and burritos out of battered lunch pails. They all nodded or waved to her. "My brothers Deuce and Trey and I own the stable but I'm the oldest so I do most of the work. They're in South Carolina looking at horses while I run the place and, yes, we have received threats. And there was a small fire."

"When did the threats start?"

"The day after your father arrived."

"What did they say?" Tony had sent copies of the notes to my cell phone, but I wanted to hear what she said.

"The first was a note under a truck's wiper blade. Said, "Get rid of the old painter if you know what's good for you.""

"Direct and to the point. Sounds like somebody doesn't want him painting here.""

She stopped next to my car, let go of my arm and stood facing me, hands on her hips. "I know about you." Construction had stopped for lunch. I could hear the clip-clop of hooves and the sound of children laughing.

"I deny everything." I grinned but, like my father, she wasn't having it. Seemed like nobody thought I was funny today. Being entertaining can be such a burden.

"You're some kind of vigilante, run around busting evildoers." Yeah, she actually said, "Evildoers." "Well, I won't have it, not at my stables. You think there's a problem and you're going to charge in here and fix it." She shook her head. "Not going to happen. One, I gave the threatening notes to the authorities and I made sure they investigated the small fire and they will handle it. Two, a new private security company offered us a deal, so we've got them, too."

"If my father is in any danger --"

"The authorities will handle it. Look, Mr. Macdonald, my nephew is big and mean, I understand that, but he was right. We don't want you here. You've seen your father and he's fine, so it's time for you to leave. And we would prefer it if you didn't come back." She paused, untied the bandanna and wiped her forehead, pushing strands of damp gray hair aside. "When I say 'we,' that includes your father. Don't come back."

No snappy comebacks to that one. "Ms. Decker, it should be obvious that I can't promise that."

"One, you're in a restricted area, and you are trespassing. Two, my nephew is ex-Special Forces." Oops. Well, it was an honest mistake; most guys his size don't study dirty fighting. I was trying to think of some advantage I'd have if it came to a confrontation and the only thing I could think of was maybe he would take it easy because he was afraid of killing me. Of course, he might want to kill me, so I decided that if it came to a showdown, running was my best option. My dad would think I was smart, maybe. The woman, flicking her eyes back and forth between me and the workers eating lunch, was still talking. "Jackie would cheerfully throw you out onto Goldenwest Street. He would like it. It would be legal. By that I mean Jack will pound you into jelly and laugh while he does it. Do I make myself clear?" The sounds of horses and children had stopped. Neville appeared from the stable pushing a wheelbarrow of horse poop. Acey looked at the construction crew and glanced at her watch. They got the hint and stood up, closing their lunch pails, chugging the last of their coffee.

"Gee, I'll have to work up a spreadsheet, but I think I can figure it out."

Without another word she turned and walked away, an attractive fifty-something woman who had promised that her semi-tame gorilla nephew would pound me into jelly and laugh while he did it. I decided my attempts at humor did not extend far enough to let him do it.

I could go home, get my .45 out of the gun safe, come back and wave it around, maybe shoot the big guy, but I wasn't clear what that would accomplish given the fact that no one, including my father, wanted me here. I decided to save that as a fallback position.

Following someone using only one vehicle is difficult even if you're skilled, and under the best conditions it can't be kept up for long. In this case the red crew cab pickup behind me obviously didn't care if I knew it was there.

Under most circumstances I like to think I'm pretty level-headed, not prone to picking fights, but this had been a day that had started poorly and gone steadily downhill and I had just about reached my limit. I pulled into the shopping center parking lot at the corner of Garfield and Goldenwest, jerked the sawed-off pool cue handle out of the clip that holds it under the dash, and got out to meet Jack. Special Forces, huge, mean, and somebody who didn't like me already, and I simply didn't care anymore. They asked me to leave and I left. I was tired of being ordered around and angry at just about everybody. It was the middle of a weekday and the lot was empty except right outside the supermarket doors, where seniors waited patiently for a close parking space to open up, patient because their grandkids had set up their DVR to capture "Days of Our Lives," and after that was over there was only

"House Hunters International" until "Dancing With the Stars" came on or bingo in the clubhouse started. If they saw me and Jack rolling around on the asphalt, kicking and punching, it would make their week. But the seniors were looking for parking and the only observers for the upcoming match were a flock of gray and white seagulls who stared beadily for a moment before returning to their main business -- pecking at half a slice of pizza. One would peck, hop up a little to tear off a tasty chunk, then fly off a short distance to dine. The only sound was the traffic, sparse at this time of day and the slow clip-clop of a horse and rider going by on the bridle path that bordered the parking lot.

I slipped the leather cord I'd added to the pool cue handle around my wrist and held the stick by the small end, folded up inside my forearm where it would not be visible. Many hours of practice had worn the varnish off; a coat of lemon oil kept the layers of laminated Canadian Maple from drying out. Kandi sometimes looked at me oddly when she observed the care I lavished on the weapon, but she hadn't said anything. As I felt the reassuring pressure against my forearm I realized that a thought was trying to work its way to the top of my mind, something that had come to me when I decided I was pissed at all the things that had been happening and wanted very much to hit somebody. But Jackie the Giant was on me before I could grab the thought.

He was good, one of the best I've come up against, but he'd been away from it too long and he'd been the victor in too many bar fights where the opponent was drunk and slow. I was neither. The fool actually took a roundhouse swing at me, his big fist passing so close that I could see the scar tissue on his large, dirty, knuckles, and he looked surprised when I hadn't obligingly left my face there to meet it. I stepped in and hit him on the bicep, hard, with the pool cue handle. The blow should have made his whole arm go numb, which gets most people's attention, but he just grunted, and flexed it. Then he did something strange -- he reached up and smacked himself on the side of his head, snorted, wiped his nose on his wrist, and came at me again. More cautiously, this time, shuffling now, not charging, feinting with the injured arm, all the time watching my midsection, not my eyes. Bad sign. Now I had a problem. I'd lost any chance of taking him by surprise with the pool cue handle. The shot to the bicep was supposed to end it -- after the initial numbness it hurts like hell -- but it had only made the giant madder and I didn't want to kill him, just put him down and send a message to his aunt. But that's the problem with fights. You can't go into a real one thinking that you wouldn't hurt your opponent seriously, because he might not see it that way. I had a pool cue handle, he was roughly the size of a rhinoceros, and there was no way to say, "Okay, look, fun is fun but we don't really want to hurt each other."

He head-faked again and I dodged another swing. I was glad he was still using his fists and not the edges of his hands. He caught me with a left. I slipped the punch enough to take it on my shoulder, nevertheless it spun me around. I sprawled across the hood of the Chevy, banging my head in the process, and slid to the ground.

Everything went away. My last thought was along the lines of "What happened?"

I was back in school. It was a rainy fall day at Cal State Long Beach and Diana and I were sitting in Lecture Hall 151, listening to a professor drone on about the historical causes of major conflicts. My wife Diana poked me in the ribs and showed me her Bic pen, which was out of ink. I dug a spare out of my backpack and gave it to her, thinking about the wrestling match I had just won. The other kid was bigger than me, right at the top end of the weight class, and I pinned him in the first period, slamming my leg out in a perfect sit-out and rolling over to jerk his wrist up to flip him on his back before dropping on him with all my weight. The ref counted and slapped the mat. The other kid pushed me off angrily and stalked away, only coming back for the obligatory handshake and arm-raising (mine) in the center of the blue mat. All of this took less time than it does to tell it, which was a very good thing for me because when I opened my eyes Jackie the rhinoceros was waiting patiently and from the look on his Neanderthal face he was not happy. And yes, there was a moment when I thought "Maybe if I lay real still he'll go away and stop hitting me." Jackie was unhappy? So was I. I got up, trying to look tough.

I got lucky. Jackie tried a foot sweep, and if his size thirteen boot had connected with my knee I would have gone down, seriously injured and well on my way to becoming strawberry jelly. I dodged it, barely, let the stick dangle by the wrist cord and caught the heel of his cowboy boot as he turned, off balance. Heaving with all my strength I was able to yank his leg up and slam him to the asphalt on his back. When he tried to get up I twisted the heel of the boot and said, "Don't or I'll break it." So much for not seriously injuring him. Suddenly he went limp and closed his eyes. There was no reason I could see; he just decided to take a nap.

As I was trying to decide what to do next, a black limousine coasted quietly to a stop next to us. A gray-haired woman in dark glasses and wearing a chauffeur uniform, complete with cap, hopped out from behind the wheel and leaned on the car door casually. She was followed by a man, also older, with the same color hair. He smiled at me and said, "I think you can let go now." I did and they both helped Jack to his feet. He was unsteady, bracing himself against the truck's door, weaving back and forth and shaking his head. This was worse than it should have been. He scrubbed at his face with both hands, looked at them, then at me, completely blank, no hostility, no recognition, shook his head again like a dog drying off, then got in his truck and drove away.

The woman looked at me, winked, and said, "See you around."

"Wait, wait, who are you? Do you know him?"

"No." She winked again, slid behind the wheel, and they left, heading south on Goldenwest while Jackie drove north and I stood there holding a stick, my mouth open.

Three possibilities presented themselves: follow the limo with the gray-haired couple, follow Jack, or try to figure out what Diana was trying to tell me.

My wife Diana was killed about a year ago, pushed down a flight of stairs by a sociopath who had broken into our house. She'd gotten out of rehab a day earlier than expected and thought she would surprise me. I wasn't home; I was with Kandi. Being dead doesn't prevent Diana from showing up now and then to talk to me.

Diana's visits would be a lot more fun if she brought good news, or just stopped in to chat, but she always wanted to deliver cryptic messages about bad things coming up. She could not give specifics, she says there are rules, but what she has to say is never good.

I jumped in my car and followed Jackie. I didn't like the confused head-shaking or the blank look. His actions didn't match our little scuffle. He might pass out or something. Two blocks from the entrance to the stable, the truck came into view on Edwards, weaving a little but staying in the lane for the most part. He turned the dusty pickup onto the dirt road beside the exercise area. Once he was on their property and less likely to wrap the truck around a light pole, I made a u-turn and headed back to the Harbour. I wanted to sit on the deck with a cold Dos Equis Dark and think about the day.

Who was I kidding? I wanted to think about Diana.

She never brought good news.

Chapter Ten

Mulling over what my dead wife might be trying to tell me would have to wait. I had what my dad used to call "a houseful" when he barbecued for the other heavy-equipment operators and their wives or girlfriends. Chet, Snake and Cheryl were standing around my kitchen table watching a video on Chet's laptop. I hoped it wasn't me doing something stupid. Chet was in his usual plaid shirt with the sleeves rolled up. Cheryl was all in black, and she'd added wide black leather bands around her wrists. The video turned out to be a shot of the pier as a crew set up grandstands, a huge arch across PCH, and a stage for the bikini contest.

A small window in the corner of the live feed showed an artist's conception of the completed "Arch of Bikinis." It started from the Mexican restaurant on the inland side to the stage set up in front of Duke's at the foot of the Pier. When it was completed it was to be covered in balloons. Text crawling along the bottom of the screen advertised Perq's Bar and Grill, Jack's Surf Shop, and Pierside Tacos.

I blurted, "I got really mad this afternoon, wanted to pound this guy into jelly."

Chet closed his computer. "Um, howdy."

Cheryl said, "Cool. You do it? Pound him?"

Snake said nothing, just looked out the windows.

"No!" I shrugged, not sure how to tell my friends about this latest violence. Instead I got beers for me and Snake, a Mountain Dew in the can for Chet, and Cheryl put on water for tea. She might have given up *Femme Poetry* for *Guns & Ammo*, but she still drank only organic, herbal tea. Then she and the Snake and I were sitting out on my deck, he and I sipping Dos Equis Dark from the bottle while she worked on a mug of raspberry-flavored herbal tea. Chet had taken a big swig from his can of soda and stayed in the family room, doing something on one of his laptops.

"Hey, Tex, c'mon out. You need to hear this, too." He waved, finished typing something and joined us. I was in the good old beach chair with frayed webbing, the others on redwood benches that went with my new patio set. Chet wiped off a spot on the table for his laptop, set it down and, once seated, looked at me expectantly. When I didn't speak, he said, "I swept the house again and you're clean, no bugs."

"So they're not here now. Interesting."

"I think you must have interrupted them. The hoodie guy at the garage door and his pal were probably setting more bugs," Chet said.

"I went out to the stable today to see my dad. I talked to Acey, the owner, an old man named Neville who is mildly mentally handicapped and Acey's nephew, this clown named Jackie. He ragged on Neville and his sister Acey smacked him a good one for it."

Snake muttered, "We're gonna need more beer."

Chet pursed his lips as he studied his laptop. "Right. You know, I keep thinking about Beachside Stables. This seems to have started with your father getting the grant to paint. Neville has been there his whole life. Remember, he was a foundling, literally left on the front porch in 1935. Acey's father, no, make that grandfather, took the baby in. He was murdered less than a year later. Six months later there's a follow-on article that says the search for papers to identify the baby is ongoing." He looked up. "My guess is they never found the papers and that's why Neville asks everyone if they know his people."

I had already found out most of that. "Thanks, Chet. We've been trying to figure out what's behind all of this -- the hacking, the airport, and so on. And this afternoon I got so mad I wanted to get in a fight." I told them about my experience at the stable, the almost-fight in the supermarket parking lot and the couple in the van.

Snake said, "Mac, you've got people coming out of the woodwork. I hate to say it, but I think it's time to talk to the cops. Call your pal Tony. Oh, wait, I'm getting something here." He held his head. "In fact, he got you into this when he asked you to check out the stable."

As usual, Snake was right. That had started everything, or seemed to. The sequence was: Beachside stable got the grant, my dad started painting, there were threats and a small fire, Tony called, I went to the stable, Kandi was trapped at O'Hare, we went to McCarran. If I was right the idea was to drive Kandi away from me. Or was it just hacking? In a world where kids release malware just because they can, it's hard to sort out evil with a purpose. But I had an idea, one I didn't much like.

"Forget about the stable for now. Somebody's pulling the strings."

"Wow," Snake said. "An evil genius. Fu Manchu goes to Surf City and kidnaps Annette. Bela Lugosi with a killer robot. Shit."

Without looking up from his laptop, Chet clicked a few keys and said, "*The Phantom Creeps,* a serial from 1939."

I said, "Chet, what does that have to do with our problems?"

"Nothing. Just holding up my end of the conversation." Since this represented personal growth for the boy genius, I let it go.

Cheryl, busy scanning the bushes and the channel for threats, said, "Get to the fight."

I said, "At least, I'm supposed to think that. Somebody's manipulating me. We had that part on the way home from McCarran. But there's more."

Snake muttered, "How much would you pay now?" and paced back and forth, looking out at the water.

Chet said, "What?"

"Two groups, working at cross-purposes."

Snake came back to the table and plopped in a chair. "The van that showed up at your fight with Jackie."

"Got it in one, Snake. Group One carjacked the Bromeliad limo and shot up the airport. Whether or not there was physical evidence, I know what I saw."

"And somebody else, call them Group Two, stole the sewage truck and rammed the limo."

"Snake, you are two for two. I think Group One's idea is to freak me out, make me do crazy things, like beat people up, things that force Kandi away."

"Possible." Chet had stopped working and was focused on the conversation. "But they couldn't know that Jackie would follow you today."

"I think that was a bonus, something they didn't plan, but hoped might happen."

Snake said, "This is where I came in. You said that, or, 'pound him into jelly,' if I remember right. There is no purpose behind the events themselves. Group One puts Kandi in jeopardy, you punch 'em out, and she bails because she doesn't want that kind of life."

"You have enemies." Cheryl sounded delighted. She probably wanted to shoot her gun. She was back to scanning the bushes for armed psychos. I couldn't blame her.

"They want me to do several things. The first is to convince Kandi to come home."

"But, but they tried to stop her. They, they did stop her." Chet was too nice, too straightforward to get it.

Snake did. He sounded grim. "Okay, so what are you going to do?"

"Give them what they want. Get Kandi back here."

"But," Chet was frowning. "If that's what they want you to do, why do it?" Then it clicked. Chet is really smart. "Oh, now I get it. Shoe's on the other foot, right?"

"I'm lost. Tell me." Cheryl sipped her tea. She held up her hand for silence and watched carefully as a neighbor putted by in his inflatable, fishing rods sticking out if the stern. I wasn't much of a fisherman but it looked better than what we were doing.

"Chet, go for it."

He paused for a moment, staring out over the channel, watching a small flock of seagulls trailing the inflatable. "Okay, sure, I think I got it. Whoever this is wants Kandi in Long Beach, or better yet, right here."

"Probably." I nodded.

Chet was frowning and thumbing his GameBoy as he put it together. "So they set up these incidents to scare Kandi, make her want to stay away. And Mac wants her close so he can protect her."

Snake said, "They want you to talk her into coming home and so they can take her away from you somehow."

All at once Chet blurted, "Am I the only one who sees the real problem here? Lord, what about Kandi? She's stuck in Las Vegas and somebody with some real mad skills hacked her, probably trying to get to you, and you're going to ask her to come back? That's the real problem, not this silly 'I almost had a fight in a parking lot' stuff." He paused for breath. "Sorry, T. R. But it's true. You're not addressing the real issue, you're just not. Sorry, I'm sorry, really." He bent over the GameBoy, furiously zapping aliens.

I got up and paced, counting the seagulls standing on my next-door-neighbor's dock. There were thirteen gray-and-white seabirds. As I watched another flew up and joined the others. And as the others sidestepped to make room for the newcomer, I made up my mind. I sprinted back to the table and snatched up my phone. "What?" Snake wanted to know. Chet did not look up from his game. I opened the texting application in my phone, then just as quickly closed it and grabbed Chet's phone. I held it up. "Secure?"

"Military-grade encryption, plus some things of my own. Yeah, secure."

I typed:

> Kandi, all this stuff is about u not me. Call this number from a new burner
> phone not yours. Love U. M

The others read over my shoulder. "OMG," Chet said. He worked the little joysticks for a minute, playing something that seemed to involve helicopters and explosions. That's what he does to think. There was a louder explosion from the little box, he muttered, "Gotcha." Then said, "It fits. Oh, boy, this is bad."

"Yeah. And if Kandi stays in Vegas they'll have to act again, something more drastic. And don't tell me Kandi can take care of herself. I know she's tough and a better shot than I am, but she's also by herself. Bromeliand security can't cover her all the time."

Chet nodded. "And obviously you think your phones are tapped."

"I'm assuming they are. Can you get me a new phone and install this security?"

"Got one in my bag."

"How about for Snake?"

The bearded one shook his head, then relented. "All right, I'll take one. But if I get brain cancer it's your fault."

Chet said, "Okay, suppose Kandi does come back. They -- whoever they are -- will try to take her away, or hurt her. What about that?"

"I won't let them."

At that moment Cheryl trotted out of my neighbor's yard. She was panting, out of breath. She had left so quietly that I hadn't noticed. "The white van I observed at 13:45 is back. I followed it and they're parked in the strip mall parking lot off of Algonquin. Two suspects inside." There are only two roads off the islands that make up Huntington Harbour and if the van was in the right spot they could surveil both of them. Now I was thinking like Cheryl.

Chet and Snake were showing dawning realization. Chet said, "It would explain the incidents--"

I added, "And why nobody was hurt at the airport. They were shooting to miss. And everywhere I go people say, 'I've heard about you.' And they go on to say I'm some kind of vigilante and not wanted. Somebody's sending people links to blogs about me."

"To your dad?" Snake said softly.

"Yeah. He knows a lot about the things I've been up to."

As always, Chet was tapping his keyboard. "Beachside Stables, right? I have some deeper background. They may say they're supporting him because he's a nice guy, but I'm looking at their financials and they need the grant money. The construction costs have escalated, they're in debt, and if they don't get the next grant payment Simon Legree could take the ranch." He looked up and grinned.

Snake shook his head. "There are three dead bodies. How do they fit in?"

I had no answer to that one, but a tall skinny kid carrying a book bag rode his skateboard down the cement walk by the side of the house and into the back yard so I was saved from displaying my ignorance. He stepped off, kicked up the end and caught the board as it flipped up and stood looking at us. He was tall, with buzzed hair, low-slung, tattered black jeans and a baggy Marina Basketball sweatshirt . Cheryl moved quickly, stepping over to her gym bag, never taking her eyes off the newcomer.

High school poets don't have much street cred, but fortunately for my buddy Cracker he was 6'2", still growing, and played basketball at Marina. It didn't hurt that his other passion was skateboarding. He said, "Mac, I was just gonna call you."

Behind me Cheryl said urgently, "White minivan, right now, in the strip mall parking lot."

"Whoa, I heard that, bro! Are you on a case? Can I help? I can skate by and check them out, they'll never catch me, and --"

"No! Cracker, stay away from the van."

"I can get some shots with my phone as I go by, I won't even have to stop."

"No. Tell me about business arithmetic."

"That's what I was calling about. I'm grounded, bro. Can't skate till I get my business arithmetic done. You said --"

"Could be worse."

"I have, um, sort of a lot."

"How much? And if you're grounded why are you here? Wait, you went out the window."

"Hey, I'm reading this poem called *The Wasteland*, and wow, it totally rocks. This guy Eliot . . ."

"How much homework do you have?"

"Um, like a couple days' worth, you know, I got busy and you know . . ." His voice trailed off.

"How much, really?" He looked down at his tennis shoes. "Speak up, you degenerate skate punk. How much arithmetic do you have?"

He mumbled, "A week. It's dumb stuff. And who cares? But, uh, well, coach says I need to pull my grade up or I get benched on Friday."

"Cracker, meet my friends the Snake, his wife Cheryl -- watch out, she's packing heat."

"Cool! Can I see your gun?"

"Sure. Which one?"

"No. No gun," I said. "Cheryl's bummed because she hasn't gotten to shoot anybody all day. And that's Kandi's cousin, Chet. Everybody, this is Cracker. He and I are working our way through business arithmetic."

Cracker said, "I bet it's a nine mil." He waited then said, "Bro, I gotta turn this shit in or I'm grounded and benched."

I had no idea how to deal with my overall problem, so I did what was in front of me, which was help Cracker work through his arithmetic problems and wait for a text or call from Kandi.

Cracker looked at a battered text he pulled out of his backpack. "Um, I got simple and compound interest, and basic mortgages."

Cheryl went off to surveil or sharpen knives or whatever; Snake got another beer and pulled a paperback book out of his backpack. Of course, Chet was tapping keys.

An hour later I had an idea. "Okay, Cracker, I think you've got it." I looked at my watch. Enough time had gone by.

He crammed the book and papers into his backpack, zipped it and said, "When you explain it, this shit makes sense. Thanks, man."

"Listen, I need a favor. You were going to look for the van anyway, weren't you?"

"Hey, you told me not to."

"I'll take that as a yes."

In Surf City, there are so many kids on skateboards – and adults for that matter – that there was no way he could be spotted. "Okay, if it's gone, text me and let me know. Otherwise send the picture. Under no circumstances get close to the van. Promise me that."

"Sure, yeah, no prob. This is one of your adventures, right? This is so cool! Oh, man, I love it. Later." A quick fist bump and he was rolling, book bag over his shoulder, cell phone in his hand.

Snake said, "Nice kid. What made you change your mind?"

"A couple of things. Cracker's pretty sneaky. Cracker likes three things: basketball, skateboarding, poetry, and breaking and entering. He's, uh, had a couple of brushes with police. I think he can get away with it."

The bearded one said, "That's four things. B and E?"

"The breaking and entering is more of a hobby. Loves locked buildings. Calls himself a building hacker. He used to be a thief but he's pretty much given that up."

"How did you meet this character and, by the way, where's my wallet? And the second reason you changed your mind?"

"If I'm right the people in the van are Group 2. Which means they're on our side, sort of. Maybe."

"That's a long string of ifs and maybes. How did you meet this young criminal?"

"Oh, I've known him a while." Snake raised an eyebrow. "All right. I saw an article in the *Independent* about how Marina High needed arithmetic tutors so I signed up."

"Oh."

"Cracker is very good at sneaking around. He got into Perq's, that dive bar on Main Street, and stole a handle off one of the beer taps, just to prove he could. If anybody can get close to the van it's him."

The next time my phone rang it showed me a picture of my teenage friend. He was standing next to the van's sliding door. His hands were behind him, out of sight. His eyes were wide. Silver duct tape covered his mouth.

At that time of afternoon the parking lot was relatively quiet. Five skater kids, delighted to be out of school, skimmed across the blacktop to Algonquin and out of sight. Two young women, probably nannys, pushed strollers along the sidewalk, heading to the small park on Pickwick Circle. For a moment I thought about checking for suspicious people, but since I already knew they were here, and they already knew I was coming, I skipped it. I backed the Bel Air into a spot three spaces from the van and walked over. Cracker was taped at wrists and ankles and leaned against the side of the van. Behind him the open sliding door revealed an older couple. The woman was sitting sideways on the middle seat, knitting. The man just stood next to Cracker, arms folded, and watched me approach.

I pulled the tape off the kid's mouth, turned him around and sliced his wrists and ankles free with my Swiss Army knife. Neither of his captors made a move to stop me. "Thanks, Cracker, you're done. I'm sorry this happened."

"Sorry, man, it just happened so fast. I was never even close and they weren't in the van and then they had me."

"It's okay. You did fine."

For a moment he just stood staring down at his scuffed Vans and I pretended not to notice the shaking. He shrugged, still not meeting my eyes, pulled a black knit cap out of his backpack and tugged it on.

I clapped him on the back. "Mortgages part two tomorrow, right?"

He nodded. Then in one fluid motion he ran three steps, dropped his skateboard and leapt on, slipping the straps of the backpack over his shoulders as he did. He casually jumped the board up onto a bus bench, back down and then off the curb to street level and was gone. I turned my attention to the elderly couple.

The nice lady, the one who I thought might be on my side, reached into her bag and pulled out a small matte-finish automatic. She kept it in her lap instead of shooting me, which I took as a good sign. She had on a velour warm-up suit, burgundy pants and jacket zipped up to her throat. Glasses dangled on her chest on a silver chain. She had white hair worn long, warm brown eyes in a face showing a network of wrinkles, mostly vertical lines above and below her thin lips. Her face looked like an early-stage apple doll before it starts looking like something from *Picnic With the Living Dead*. She looked like chocolate chip cookies made with Tollhouse chocolate bits, hot cocoa with a marshmallow floating on top, and iodine for a skinned knee. Except for the gun, of course.

She said, "Now you're going to tell us that we better leave your young friend alone, or else."

"Nope."

For a moment she drew back and slipped her index finger inside the trigger guard of the gun. "Get in the van, please."

"No."

The gun-toting grandma blinked at me. "Young man, have you noticed that I have a gun? And I am pointing it at you?"

I sighed. It happens a lot. People watch too much TV and as a result they think if you point a gun at somebody that person automatically has to do what you say. And I guess it works both ways. The people getting the weapon pointed at them think they are required to do as they are told. It's not true. "If you wanted to kill me you would have. You want me to do something and you assaulted a friend of mine to get me here."

The old guy grinned and held out his hand. "Ten bucks. I was right."

She sniffed. "Dumb luck." His hand was still out. She dug in her purse, removed a smaller purse and pulled out a ten.

He leaned over and kissed her cheek. She said, "Double or nothing they'll be here before we're finished."

"You're on. When you lose, I'll take it out in trade, honey." She smiled at him. She smiled but never took her eyes off me.

"You drove back and forth in the van until Cheryl noticed --"

She sniffed, "Took her long enough."

"Cheryl's new to this. Anyway, you wanted to be seen, wanted somebody to follow and check you out."

"You knew and sent your friend anyway."

I shrugged. "You wanted me here. Okay, I'm here."

"Get in the van."

"We're not off to a very good start, but, okay, I'll listen and I might even do it." Her eyes widened slightly. "Obviously you want something from me. But we'll talk out here. You parked the van to block the camera at the bank's ATM, but there are three others covering the parking lot. This is Huntington Harbour and we are very security conscious."

Some kind of communication passed between them, a flicker, a look, a blink almost too fast to see and I knew that they were deciding.

It's not the eyes you watch, it's the body. If her hand moved or she leaned forward to get a better shot I'd have to act. She was a pro, that was clear, but she thought of me as an amateur, I hoped. At least she was surprised, or pretended to be, when I refused to get in the van. So she would expect me to run. Instead I would lunge forward, turning sideways to present a smaller target, grab her partner and slam him into her gun arm. After that, assuming it worked and the bullet only grazed me—there was little hope of a complete miss—my plan was vague but it involved dragging them out of the vehicle and smashing their gray heads together, and if their old bones were brittle that was just too damn bad. I realized that Surf City Urgent Care (Body Ding? We'll Patch You Up!) was behind me at the end of the strip mall and liked my plan better. I hoped they had my blood type.

The man said, "I like this guy." He had a florid complexion, bushy brows and a full head of gray hair. In tan shorts and forest-green Polo shirt he looked like eighteen holes twice a week, Kiwanis or Rotary and he'd always help out with the pancake breakfast. He was big, still over six feet at a time of life when seniors start losing inches. Big hands with heavily scarred knuckles dangled beside his belt. The word that popped into my head was "boxer" but maybe "street brawler' would be closer. I needed to find smaller people to threaten me. Where are the Munchkins when you need one?

"If you decide you really want to tell me something, text me." I turned to go.

He said, "We're here to help you."

"I know."

"No, really. Someone is out to get you."

"They always are."

"I assume you heard about the unfortunate Mr. Sigmund?" Uh-oh. He nodded. "That was us. Oh, forgive me. Introductions. Call me Barney."

"And I'm Betty."

"Swell. Sigmund?"

Barney rubbed his thumb and index finger together. "We were paid."

She said, "And he was not a nice person. We didn't like him at all. We extended the hand of friendship and we were rebuffed."

Barney nodded. "True, so true. We tried to be friends but he rebuffed us."

"Gee, I'm glad I shook hands."

He said, "If Mr. Sigmund had been nicer we might not have done it. We never take an assignment until we are certain. That's important to us."

She stopped knitting for a moment and patted his arm, but she kept her eyes on me while she did it, watching my hands. "This was a bit outside our usual line of work, but things were slow. This dreadful business downturn affected us just like everyone else." She looked at Barney, then back at me. "I dislike having this conversation standing in the parking lot. Won't you please get in?"

"There's a Starbucks at the end of the mall."

Betty smiled, her warm brown eyes twinkled and she said, "Are you buying, young man?"

"Nope. You want me for something, you buy."

So, after she pulled out a large canvas bag into which she put the small gun and covered it with the knitting stuff, we walked over to the coffee shop and settled in with two coffees and a tea.

"Tell me about this assignment."

"It is our policy not to ask." He shifted uncomfortably. "But then --"

"The same client --"

"Gave us another assignment."

Betty sighed. "One we were not comfortable with."

"I don't suppose you'd care to tell me the name of your client?"

"We can't. No, we have confessed to a murder. That's not all. After we dealt with Mr. Sigmund we flew to Chicago." Suddenly I didn't want my coffee. Suddenly this was not so much fun. Suddenly I wasn't winning. He nodded. "First class, of course. The service was excellent."

She sniffed. "We always fly first class. If you must subject yourself to flying, first class at least makes it somewhat tolerable. Of course we add it to our expenses and bill our clients."

"I want to know about Chicago." I put my hands in my lap, and after a moment moved my forearms up under the table. It was not bolted down—I had checked before sitting down—and if it came to it I thought I had a good chance of upending it, sending scalding coffee into their faces and hopefully slamming the table edge down on her hand before she could shoot me. These were the people who had killed Kandi's friends. "Tell me about this assignment."

Barney took up the story. "Your obvious suspicions are partially correct. We accepted an assignment to deal with an individual at Mary Shaw's clinic. Unfortunately we were too late to prevent his killing his girlfriend." He was watching me; she kept her eyes on the parking lot and the people around us. Cheryl would have approved. "I appreciate your not bothering with the silly speeches which begin, 'If you hurt Kandi I'll --'. We have no intention of harming her. Quite the reverse in fact. The man we killed in Chicago was seriously disturbed, not a nice person at all, no, and if Ms. Shaw had not agreed to run away with him he planned to eliminate her next, eliminate her and then kill himself. So, we have helped you. Now we need your help."

"The doctor in Chicago was planning to kill Kandi?"

He nodded. "If she refused to run away with him, yes."

"That's nuts. Why did he shoot Jennifer Prewett?"

She said, "No one will ever know for certain. Mental illness is contagious. He caught it from his patients." She waited a moment. "That was a joke. Come on, we know you have a sense of humor."

"I suppose if it's true I should say thank you. Why are we having this conversation that you have so carefully arranged?"

They looked at each other, then she returned to watching the Starbucks, the parking lot, and their van. The stream of students released from school had tapered off and the seniors—except for the two who were sort of holding me captive—had settled in for an afternoon of soaps or shuffleboard. Two young mothers jogged by, pushing high-tech three-wheeled strollers. I gave up any idea of tipping over the table. Too many people around if the old couple started shooting. Betty sighed and took out her knitting. The needles flashed in the almost-horizontal light as the sun arced down behind the Urgent Care building. "We have developed certain reservations about the person who hired us."

"The check bounced?"

"No, but -- Barney."

Suddenly her voice was urgent and her hand was in her bag as she nodded toward the north entrance to the parking lot. We both turned to look. I decided I might have to do it anyway and shifted my feet to a better position and got ready to tip over the table and yell, "Earthquake!" An enormous white Escalade with deeply-tinted windows turned off Algonquin into the parking lot, cruised slowly down one aisle, turned the corner, then drove past Barney and Betty's van.

I said, "Friends of yours?"

Barney was punching something into his cell phone, then holding it up, trying to get a picture of the Escalade before it was blocked by a brown UPS truck.

They didn't bother answering me.

Betty said smugly, "We're even."

"They're good."

"We may need to—"

Seconds later flames were visible in the back of the van.

"—take drastic action," he finished.

"I guess they're not your friends."

"We are sorry, Mr. Macdonald, but we will have to continue this conversation at a later date." Barney got to his feet and trotted off into another part of the parking lot, moving surprisingly well for someone of his apparent age. Betty, thin lips pursed, alternated between watching me and the lot. A moment later Barney was back, behind the wheel of a dark gray Mustang fastback. Betty, still scanning the parking lot, took the time to pick up their paper cups. There's a special skill to running with hot beverages, and she had it. She climbed into the passenger seat and they pulled out onto Algonquin, turning right toward Warner and the beach. They drove sedately, obeying all laws, attracting no attention. People were running toward the burning van, two kids carrying fire extinguishers. About a dozen people had emerged from stores and offices to take pictures and send texts telling their friends what they were missing. I finished my coffee and decided it was a good time to be somewhere else.

June 15, 1934

Dear Diary,

Well, we are about settled in our new room. It is not as nice as the one in Los Angeles.

After Mystery Riders of the Blazing Plains ended, Lou Helen and I both thought we would have more work. The producer, Mr. Heems, said he would use us in his next movie which was another Western, but then he had some problems with the people who were putting up the money and now he may not make the movie after all. He owes us two weeks' salary. He says he will pay us as soon as he can and I believe him. Lou Helen has her doubts.

Lou Helen got a job waitressing at a diner on Wilshire Boulevard but it didn't last. I got a secretary job until the man who owned the company made advances and then fired me when I refused. He wouldn't give me a recommendation, either. Then Lou Helen's beau Willeford lost his job but I am not sure what it was.

So we moved down to a town called Huntington Beach. It is about thirty miles south of Hollywood. Lou Helen doesn't like it because she says it is too far from the movie industry and she still wants to be an actress. I don't mind. I have a good job as a secretary to a man who works for an oil company. There are oil wells everywhere, even on the beach. It is a nice town but many of the men you see on Main Street are quite rough because they work in the oil fields. He said sometimes I might have to work late. I said I didn't mind.

Being in the serial was all right, but many of the people were not very nice.

I plan to read the Bible and pray because I have missed a few days with the move and all.

Later —

Lou Helen got a job handing out towels at the Plunge. It is a big public pool on Pacific Coast Highway at the foot of the Pier.

July 1, 1934

Dear Diary,

    I don't know what is wrong with people. I had to quit my secretarial job at the oil company. The man I worked for came up yesterday and just grabbed me. We were in his office and I said, "You leave me alone or I will hit you." He grabbed me again, so I hit him and then I quit. And I was wearing Lou Helen's dress and the seam along the shoulder got ripped. It was just about pulled all the way apart but I can fix it.

    They tell me they have a big Fourth of July Parade here in Huntington Beach. I am looking forward to seeing it. I have never seen a real parade before.

Chapter Eleven

When I got home, I sent Kandi another text, to the disposable cell number.

> K. You need to come home. I know you have concerns but now is not
> the time. Bad things are happening. M.

Then I had Chet find video of the van fire and send it to Kandi. Cell phone
footage had already been posted by four people. That evening Chet, Snake, Cheryl,
and I brought in Chinese food from The Happy Fish and talked things over.

Waving my chopsticks dramatically, I said, "We need to locate Sly Staney. I want
to drag him out from whatever rock he's hiding under and get some answers."

Chet said, "Uh, Mac, I know where he is."

"It may take some digging, but when I find him --"

"He's in his office. He has a business called Gleaner Computing over by Ellis
and the 405 and he goes in to work every day."

Snake shrugged and shoveled in a giant forkful of fried rice.

I said, "You found him already?"

"Pard, it was easy. That ol' boy's not hiding."

"He's not hiding?" All of my noodles slid off my chopsticks and plopped down
on my paper plate. Snake looked in the noodle carton and, seeing it was empty,
scooped mine off my plate and ate them. Cheryl poked him in the ribs and Chet
laughed. It struck me that we were having a nice time. If Kandi had been sitting next
to me it would have been perfect.

Chet said, "Nope it's business as usual for our Mr. Staney. His schedule is easy
to get into. If fact, he'll be in the office tomorrow afternoon."

"You're sure this is the right guy? He's not hiding?"

"Yep and nope."

"Well," I paused. "He should be." It sounded pretty lame, even to me.

After dinner we moved out to the dock and arranged the chairs to look out over the water. Snake and I settled in with Dos Equis Darks, Chet had the ever-present Mountain Dew and, after a perimeter check, Cheryl brewed herself a cup of chamomile tea and sat next to her husband. We sat and watched as the sun went down and painted the undersides of the clouds pink.

After a while the color faded from the clouds and they turned gray, changing to an ever-deeper shade as the sun dropped and my friends disappeared into the gloom, each of us lost in our own thoughts. After a while Snake and Cheryl went home. Chet went inside to check on his staff working on the Bromeliad's security network. I went inside and sat next to him. After a while I moved to the couch and slept. I woke up at 1:00 am, restless and unsure of next steps, and decided to go for a drive past Gleaner Computing. The Chevy was very recognizable, so I got Chet's keys out of his laptop case and took the Mustang. Of course, it had the Space Floozies logo on the door, but it was dark. Better than the hot rod Chevy.

It was difficult to tell anything about the row of one-story offices. All the windows were dark, and none of the businesses had their signs lit. I parked on a side street and walked back.

In the rear I found additional parking, a larger lot than the one in front, also dark. The only vehicles were two vans, both at least ten years old and parked in back of what might be Gleaner.

After half an hour the two Dos Equis Darks were making their presence felt. That seemed to be a good indication that it was time to go home, but as I stood I saw lights move through the front parking lot. I decided to stay a little longer, despite my discomfort. On TV the detectives never have this problem.

Okay, I had suffered long enough. I slipped over to a bush, did what I had to and was just about ready to leave when a white Cadillac Escalade quietly rolled into the lot and stopped parallel to the back of the building. It sat. I watched. Then the passenger door opened for a moment. That was the side of the car away from me so I couldn't see who got out. A back door opened and closed. There were no lights inside the building so again I didn't see anybody. Then the Escalade slowly rolled back out to Ellis and turned left, toward the onramp for the 405 freeway. I waited another quarter-hour and then crept out of the parking lot and went home.

I opened my eyes again before dawn, but the now sun was painting the clouds a deep red. Red sky at morning.

There were no messages from Kandi. I got up and shuffled into the kitchen to get coffee started. Chet came down and opened a Mountain Dew. Then he went to work, watching code scroll by on one of his laptops.

So now I had a morning to kill. I microwaved some unidentifiable chunky stuff in brown sauce that I found in one of the Happy Fish cartons and choked it down. Then I actually did some chores. Time could be your friend or your enemy. So I filled it. I took out the trash, hosed down the deck, washed the Boston Whaler. I looked at the circular burned spot on the deck and thought about Diana and some of the parties she must have had. I had finally replaced the upstairs toilet that had had a bullet hole just above the waterline, but I found the burned spot on the deck somehow hard to get rid of.

I suppose I'd known what I was going to do when I snooped in my dad's bag and got his Huntington Beach address.

In the late morning I found myself cruising down Adams to Newland and driving into the mobile home community where my father lived. It was simple -- I wanted to see him. I wanted to talk about our life when I was in grade school and he drove heavy equipment. I wanted him to forgive me, and, if I do say so myself, I can be persuasive, very persuasive. So I pulled into his driveway and got out and he threw the door open and welcomed me with open arms and said he understood. He got out a six-pack and put on a Bruce Brown DVD and we had a great time.

Okay, the truth is I drove around for a while before I pulled into the development. I wanted to be sure nobody was tailing me. That's what I told myself. And, driving around, I had a chance to think.

We recovered when my mother ran away. We rebuilt our lives after his accident.

Could we do it again, after Diana?

Sure. But, doing that opened the door to getting hurt again. He was scared.

That made two of us.

So eventually I parked and rang the bell. When there was no answer I was relieved, but to be certain I walked around back and there he was, sitting on the small deck in a cheap aluminum beach chair, reading the *Huntington Beach Independent*.

His crutches leaned against the arm of the chair. A jar of sun tea was brewing next to him. He looked at me and grunted. "Still stubborn."

I took a deep breath and I thought about what Kandi—when she was Mary and providing therapy—would want me to say. "Dad, I hate the way things are between us. I want it to be better. What can I do to help make that happen?" There, I'd done it. Thanks, Mary/Kandi. I stood in front of him and waited.

"I need to get to Beachside. I gotta go in and call a taxi."

"C'mon, I'll drive you to the stable."

He grunted, "Damn taxis are ripoffs anyway."

He struggled out of the chair, got his arms into his sticks (I knew enough not to help) and we loaded his easel and paints into the Chevy. The stable was only a fifteen-minute drive from his manufactured home; I wished it was longer and at the same time I wished it was shorter. A couple of times I tried to talk, but when that failed I lied and told myself it was a comfortable silence. It wasn't. It was more like the silence sitting in front of the TV with a thick crust Número Uno pizza watching a tape of Harry Callahan shooting some poor fool, with me trying desperately to think of something I could tell him about school, but in the sixth grade there's not much that's worth sharing with a parent. So we drove in silence.

The afternoon onshore wind was picking up, blowing the palm trees and occasionally ripping off a frond and depositing it in the street.

"There are rats in those palms," I observed.

Nothing.

"Big ones."

Still nothing.

I swerved around one of the falling fronds and said, "I never figured you for art, you know? But what I saw of your work I liked, and you got this grant . . ." He turned to reach over the bench seat and steady his tackle box of paints where it was resting in the back.

"Take it easy, will you? Not one of your damn car chases." Still holding the paint box he said, "In Ventura I took some classes. Local JC. The prof hated everything I did, so I knew I was on the right track." I dodged another palm frond. He muttered something that sounded like "car chase." Then he said, "This teacher liked nonrepresentational, colors that speak to emotion and art that bypasses cognition, you know, and I was painting bulldozers." My jaw dropped and I missed the next palm frond, driving right over it. Was this my father talking? As it has so often in the past, my mouth ran off on its own. "So, how long you been a pod person?" I grinned. "That's a movie --"

"I saw the original *Bodysnatchers* in the theater when I was a kid. Scared the crap out of me. I took some other art classes and I read a lot. I don't get to many galleries with the sticks." I swerved around another palm frond; he swore and dragged the paintbox into the front seat and held it on his lap.

"Ever paint seascapes? I'd think . . ." I realized how bad a suggestion that was and shut up. He said nothing.

As I turned off Goldenwest onto the dirt road leading to the construction area, my phone buzzed with a message from Cracker. I decided to get to it later. Maybe my dad would say something, maybe ignoring Cracker's message would impress him with how important I thought this was.

That worked as well as my attempts at conversation.

On the way to the spot where my dad wanted to set up, him stumping along the dirt path on his crutches, hurrying a bit because the afternoon light was good, Jackie saw us and dropped the saddle he was carrying to stride in our direction, obviously intending to get in my face. I held up both hands, palm out, in the universal "I don't want to fight" gesture. "Yo, let's talk," he growled and jerked a thumb in the direction of the barn. He shook his head as if he was warding off flies and marched away without looking back. I followed him, figuring he was the kind who had to get worked up, so angry he couldn't see straight, before he was ready to fight. At least that's what I hoped. Trying to guess what he wanted to talk about was useless.

In the dim cool of the tack room he stood waiting next to, of all things, a large red-and-white Playmate ice chest. He had on grimy jeans and a black tank top advertising a Garden Grove topless bar. Dust motes and pieces of hay floated in the afternoon light slanting through the small, high windows; behind me a horse made a horse noise, sort of a soft whinny, and another one snorted and pawed at the straw covering the floor if its stall. The same scene could be reenacted across America, except we were in Surf City, three miles from the afternoon glass-off.

He bent down and reached into the cooler, pulled out a dripping can of Bud, and, without straightening, tossed it to me. I caught it, left-handed, too, and was pretty happy considering I wasn't expecting the toss and it seemed like a bad idea to take my eyes off him. The big man had probably given me a beer as sort of a last meal, a gesture of goodwill preparatory to beating the snot out of me. We both popped our cans open. All at once, for no reason that I knew of, he whipped his head around to the left and bashed it into one of the posts holding up the hayloft, hard enough that I heard the thunk clear across the room.

I guess my jaw dropped.

"Yo, Adrian! Ow!"

"Sometimes I forget stuff, you know?" I held back from pointing out that beating his head against posts might have something to do with that. "I had papers, you know? Found 'em in grand dad's stuff. Now I lost 'em. They were maybe important. I want you to find the box."

"What box? The one the papers were in?"

He grunted and drained his can and crumpled it against his forehead and all at once I thought of John Belushi doing exactly that in *Animal House*, a movie I'd watched on DVD with my dad about a million times, with him pointing at the screen and laughing, and declaring, "I knew guys that could do that!" My dad who was outside painting and no doubt wondering if I was in trouble. Come to think of it, *I* was wondering if I was in trouble

"Huh. You think that hurt? Yo, check this." He smacked his head into the post again and grinned. "Huh. Yeah." The post must have had a rough spot because now a trickle of blood was running down the side of his face.

He fished out another beer, popped the top and had a long drink; I had a sip of mine just to be polite and decided that Bud was just fine, but I would need my wits about me to get out of this alive, or at least with the majority of my bones unbroken. My host dug a huge finger into his ear, withdrew it in order to examine the results, and then flicked something away into the shadows. "Well?"

"Uh, thanks for the beer. Listen --"

He held up a dinner-plate size hand. His eyes darted around the room. "Yo, you hear it, too?"

"Yeah, I mean, no. Hear what?"

"Whaddaya want?"

"I just gave my father a lift over here so he could paint."

"You gonna look for the box?"

"I kind of have a full plate right now, but, if I can, sure, I'll look."

"You smell that?"

"Horses, yeah." Actually, I was downwind and could smell horse and Jackie but decided I didn't need to share that with my host. The horses smelled better.

"Huh. Whaddaya want?" Without waiting for an answer he slugged down the rest of his beer, some of it running down his chin and over the impossibly well-endowed young lady on his tank top. He crumpled the can in a huge fist and tossed it back into the cooler, then belched contentedly.

"Hey, Jackie, look-- uh, look, I gotta go. I'm glad things are cool between us, that we're okay."

"Huh. Yeah, sure. Why wouldn't they be?" He looked confused. "Yo, you gonna finish that?"

By way of answer I carefully set my can down on the straw-covered dirt floor and started backing out. He looked at me like I was nuts, but by the time I reached the door he had my beer and was finishing it. What does it mean when an obvious crazy thinks you're nuts?

"You're in one piece. Bitchin','" my dad said when I stepped up beside him, carefully positioning myself so I could keep an eye on the stable. "You punch him out? Use the famous pool cue handle on him?"

"No, I mean, yeah, we seem to be pals now. No, I didn't punch him out. I hardly ever get in fights. And somehow I don't think he remembers our fight and I want to keep it that way."

He did not look up from the easel. "You really waste that guy? Bash his head in with a rock?"

I was getting tired of people who weren't there, who had no idea what it was like to be flat on your back and see somebody swinging a shotgun toward your face, close enough that you could smell the gun oil, people who had never felt their insides turn to jelly, but who were perfectly willing to tell me what I should have done in the situation. But this was my father. I stalled, taking my cell phone out of my pocket and checking the text from Cracker.

Need to talk to u. Important. Call!

I put it back in my pocket. "Yes, dad, I did kill him. And I can't go back and change it, and if I could I wouldn't because he had every intention of blowing my head off. So, I had that rock and I hit him with it, his skull fractured and he died of a cerebral hemorrhage. He wanted me dead and I wanted to be alive."

"I don't like the idea of my son being a killer. I saw enough of that in Nam." He nodded. "I guess I have to live with it. But Diana . . . ."

And that was as close as we got to really talking out what had happened between me and my wife. I was aware vaguely of somebody running out of the barn and people yelling but, overwhelmed and at the same time lost for something to say, I paid no attention. I should have paid attention.

"I don't like it," he said again, and went back to painting. I went back to trying to think of something to say, to make it all right between us. But how could I when it wasn't all right with me? And of course there was Diana. That wasn't all right, either.

My dad's fingers were long and slim and his strokes were swift and sure, working from a snapshot of a small white Bobcat tractor tacked to the edge of the easel, blending it with the background, capturing the power contained within the small vehicle and the beauty of the setting. I was thinking of a way to tell him that I was impressed but I wanted to phrase it right, only I lost the chance because a fire truck, an ambulance, and a black-and-white patrol car wheeled into the space in front of the barn and slid to stops in clouds of dust and hay. Flashing lights on, sirens off. For a whole lot of very good reasons police and fire fighters don't like civilians getting in the way, so I just stood and watched. After one look over his shoulder my dad kept painting, capturing the morning light as it filtered through the trees. In the sudden quiet I could hear horses whinnying and stamping, upset by the noise and the strange people. And I clearly heard a voice say, "No rush." And it came to me that it was quiet; the construction noise had stopped.

Acey sprinted around the corner of the office, running flat out, a bridle in her hand, a cleaning rag over her shoulder, and disappeared into the barn, just ahead of two EMTs manhandling a stretcher over the rough ground. A moment later one of them came out and spoke to the policewoman standing by their car. There was some handwaving, followed by nodding. Then they all looked in my direction. Then they walked toward me, not in a line but next to each other and spreading out. I recognized the move—they were fanning out into a semi-circle meant to keep suspects from making a break for it. Now my dad was looking up, first at them, then at me as he groped for his sticks, slid his arms into them and struggled to his feet. Once he was up, grunting with the effort but wobbling only a little, he tugged his t-shirt straight and stood next to me as the police marched up. I will remember that forever. He got to his feet and stood next to me.

"T. R. Macdonald?"

I said yes and handed her my Driver's License. She handed it back after a glance and said, "Would you mind if we asked you some questions?"

"No, I wouldn't mind."

"You had an altercation with Mr. Decker last week?"

"Yes."

"And that day he followed you from the stable and there was another altercation, this one in a parking lot."

"How did you find out about the encounter in the parking lot?"

"YouTube video, anonymously sent to the sister. What did you discuss with him today?"

"What's wrong with Jackie?"

"Answer the question, please. What did you talk about?"

For a moment we just looked at each other, a thirty-something female cop facing down somebody who might be a suspect. "Actually, nothing much. He asked me to come into the stable, then he gave me a beer and that's it."

"There was no further altercation today? You are sure he didn't threaten you? Ask you to leave?"

"No. What's all this about?" But a sinking feeling in my stomach said it wasn't good. I asked again, "What's wrong with Jackie?"

The younger cop said, "Hey, buddy, how this works is real simple. We ask the questions and you answer. There's a large discoloration on the side of his face. You know anything about that?"

I decided not to point out that, after saying they'd ask the questions, he had volunteered information. "I'd like to see him." They stepped away from me and talked in low voices. She kept her eyes on me. Then they reached a decision and came back.

"Don't get close." The young guy took my elbow. I gently removed it from his grasp. Being grabbed is one of my pet peeves. He started to say something and the situation showed signs of going south. Then my dad gestured with his crutch and the cop looked at me and led me into the barn with my dad following.

Sudden death is rarely graceful. This was no exception.

Jackie lay sprawled on his back next to the Playmate cooler with his left arm resting across it protectively, the way you might rest an arm across a favorite dog that was snoozing with you after a great Frisbee session at Dog Beach. His legs were twisted under him and one boot looked like it had come partway off. He could have been napping with his favorite cooler except for the tiny piece of straw that lay across the cornea of a staring, blank eye. In death he looked smaller than he had when alive, smaller and less threatening. He seemed sad and lost.

I blurted, "I was just talking to him. And he --" I stopped, with behavioral clues assembling into maybe the beginning of a picture. Where was Mary the therapist when I needed her?

The female cop spoke. "What? He what, Mr. Macdonald?"

"He seemed a little off. You're not going to believe this."

"Try us," the younger one said. "We just love a good story."

The other one jerked her head. "Outside." We walked back to where my dad's stuff was.

"Well, he smacked his head into the post that holds up the hay loft. More than once. That's how he got the bruise."

The young one snorted. "You know, that's just what I was saying. He did it to himself. Yep, he was hangin' out, havin' a brewski or six and he thought, hey, why don't I smash my head into the post to see what it feels like?" He stared at me. "He didn't maybe have some help from you?"

"Interviews like this make me want to smash my head into a post," his partner said. Next this comedy team would give each other high fives. She quit smiling. "You can't do any better than that?"

"You've seen Jackie. You think I could smash his face into the post? I don't."

"One more time. You want to revise your story about what went on?"

I shook my head.

A third cop trotted up carrying a laptop. All three of them looked at it for a couple of minutes. Then she wordlessly turned and showed it to me. It was the security camera from the supermarket, showing me flattening Jackie and him struggling to get up. It stopped before the limo with Barney and Betty showed up.

My father looked at me and shook his head. As they took me away for what they claimed was routine questioning he was picking up supplies and putting them back in the tackle box. The light was gone.

After the newest episode of T. R. Macdonald's reality show, things got better. They took my statement in the cop car, told me not to leave town and cut me loose.

I stopped by my dad's to make sure he had gotten home all right. I found him sitting on his patio with another senior, this one older, well into his eighties.

"This is Pete. He lives next door. Pete, this is my son, T. R. Macdonald. He's the one you've read about."

Since there was a walker parked next to his chair, Pete and I shook hands with him sitting.

"Heard you had some excitement over at the stable. Mike was just telling me about it."

"Yeah, it was bad. A man who worked there was killed." Pete pulled a pill bottle out of the pouch on the side of his walker, took one out and slipped it under his tongue. He and my dad looked at each other and I felt out of place so I said, "Nice to meet you, Pete," and left.

Chet was waiting when I got home. "Let's see what Sly has to say."

"Coffee." Fortunately there was half a pot left from the morning. I microwaved a cup and sipped carefully.

"Uh, Mac, you know I got into the Gleaner Computing network? I could see his schedule?"

"And?"

"When I checked just now, we're on it."

"You and me? We're on Sly Staney's schedule?"

"We have a 3:30 appointment."

I picked up my old cell phone, the one without military-grade encryption. My calendar showed:

3:30pm Gleaner computing.

Clear the air.

Chet went through more emails as we drove to Gleaner Computing, LLC. He didn't find anything strange, but it kept him busy so he didn't talk. That was fine with me.

There are some really nice areas in Huntington Beach; the artificial islands that make up Huntington Harbour where I live is one of them. Sly's office was inland, almost in Fountain Valley, where Ellis runs into the 405 and it was not one of the nice areas. It occupied a middle spot in a single-story row of businesses across from the twelve-foot high cinderblock walls surrounding the Orange County Sanitation District.

Brick arches framed glass fronts to the small businesses. String 'Em Up Beads was next to George for Guns and Terri for Trains. The latter two had matching signs so I jumped to the wild conclusion that George and Terri were connected, perhaps husband and wife. The unit next to Sly's was vacant, the glass covered with brown butcher paper. Apparently it had been leased because there was a sign saying "New Home of Anybody Personal Security Services." It was easy to find a parking spot, but I avoided driving past Gleaner Computing and backed the Chevy into a space at the far end of the lot, out of sight of his office. We walked along the row of shops, all of them clean and well lit, and some even with customers. The only shop that featured obvious security was George for Guns, which sported a steel-barred door leading into a little entryway with another barred door at the end and a camera for examining prospective customers before you let them in. They call them man-traps. I guess if you sell weapons and ammunition that's prudent.

Chet and I were here to stir things up. We didn't really know how this would play out, but after the van got torched in the parking lot I went home and talked it over with my friends. After a review of events—murder-suicide in Chicago, Bernard Sigmund strangled and run down, Kandi getting hacked and stranded at O'Hare, and the senior citizens who captured a teenage jock with no difficulty at all—it was certain there was a plan and Sly was somehow involved.

From what Chet had told me, Sly was doing well, but you couldn't see that by the location. Gleaner Computing LLC had flyspecked, dusty vertical blinds that might have started life as taupe but now had sun-faded to dirty gray. The blinds were cranked partially open over the glass windows covering the front. I could see an empty desk in front of a gray cube wall, the tall kind that you have to stretch to see over. The door was unlocked so we went in. The front door closed behind us and we were in a short entryway, facing a second glass door. I looked at Chet and raised my eyebrows. He nodded as if he understood and when I pushed through door number two, I had an idea. It was cold. Sly must have had some serious air conditioning going and the double doors kept him from losing too much cold air when the outer door was opened.

A blonde young woman wearing a short denim skirt and a long-sleeved gray blouse over a blue-and-white striped crop top that could have come from Kandi's closet came out to greet us. She was tall, around 5' 9," and slim, but not skinny, more like no body fat, like a serious runner or triathlete. Her nails were short and unpainted. She said, "Hi! I'm Cherri, with an 'i'. You're T. R. Macdonald. And you must be Chet Shaw. You're Kandi's cousin."

Cherri had an unusual face, not so much in looks but rather in mobility. She was constantly scrunching her eyebrows together or blinking, and when she didn't like something it was odd: her lip curled up on the left side like a dog snarling. Just on the left side, an asymmetrical snarl.

Her eyes met mine and there was something in hers, a flash of what? Recognition? But I have worked at remembering names and faces and was sure I had never met "Cherri with an i" before. She looked down and hurried to the desk and tapped at the laptop. Studying it, she absently unwrapped a stick of watermelon gum and popped it into her mouth.

"We came to see Sly."

"I know, I know. How nice to meet you in person." She looked up and held out her hand and we shook, only she didn't let go. She just stood there holding my hand and staring into my eyes, long enough that it became awkward. Chet cleared his throat and slipped his backpack off his shoulders. "Chet, nice to meet you too. You spoke at the system security conference in San Francisco."

Chet turned pink and looked down at his boots. "Um, yeah. Were you there?"

"No, I had to work, but I watched the video. You were brilliant." She giggled. "But the shots of the audience, well, I don't think they got half of it."

"Thanks, I --" But she had turned back to her laptop.

She picked up her cell phone and tapped out a short text message. In a moment she said, "Mr. Staney will be right with you. May I get you anything? Coffee? Tea?" The whole time she was speaking she was staring at me, and smiling. At that moment Sly came out from behind the partition and I realized why it had been hard to identify him on the airport videos; Kandi was right, there had been some changes since I last saw him.

When we first met he had been a typical Orange County businessman, somewhat overweight, black suit, second-day white shirt that hung down below the coat. Now he was fit and trim, wearing stone-washed jeans and a muted plaid shirt unstuffed with the sleeves rolled up over his forearms. His head was shaved and he had a trendy mustache and goatee.

"Mr. Staney, this is --"

Sly grinned. "It's all right, Cherri, I know this guy. In fact the last time we met he rolled me in the parking lot of Fred's Fine Mexican Food, and took five dollars from my wallet."

He patted her shoulder. "If you've finished the preliminary on last night's take, you can go."

She scrunched her eyebrows together, looked at me and said, "I have a little more work. I'll stay." Her face twisted her lip lifted in the snarl. For a moment he looked like he might send her away, but then he nodded.

"C'mon back." He indicated that we should follow him around the cube wall. "Cherri, did you offer the gentlemen coffee?"

She looked at us expectantly. I grinned. "Sure. Cream and sugar in mine."

Chet said, "I'm fine."

"Coming up. Mr. Staney, remember you have a four o'clock and then the review of last night's findings."

"Right. Have you done the preliminary?"

She nodded energetically. "I have. I have. Some potentially good stuff."

"Come on back." The newly remodeled Sly waved and led us behind the partition.

The storefront office was three-quarters one big room. The cube wall split off a small reception area, then there was what seemed to be Sly's office, with a wall at the rear and a door in its middle. If my guess about the size of the space was right, there was a small room on the other side. The walls were covered with black and white pictures of Huntington Beach in the twenties and thirties, unframed, held up with push pins. Main Street with Model A's parked on both sides, a bandstand and a pool at the foot of the pier, beach covered with oil derricks and an archway across PCH. I recognized them as pages from calendars a few years back.

Sly's office contained a battered gray desk, a worktable pushed up against the left wall and covered with papers. A brown couch, and two chairs in front of the desk. On the right a small alcove held a sink and a coffee maker. "Sit, sit." He waved at the chairs. I sat in one of the chairs, Chet put his Stetson and backpack on the couch and sat in the other. Cherri bustled around, making coffee. "Flavored or regular? I've just gotten some hazelnut, you should try it." Without waiting for an answer she started brewing. It took a few minutes for both cups to finish, one at a time, but then we were settled around the desk. She set a tray with two mismatched mugs on the desk, casually resting her free hand on my shoulder as she did. Then she went back to the coffee maker and brewed a cup for herself. She curled up on the couch and sipped. She had a habit of reaching out with her tongue and touching the rim of the mug before she drank. Maybe she thought it was cute. Then she frowned, jumped to her feet and vanished into the back.

"So, the almost-famous T. R. Macdonald in the flesh. It's been a while."

"Look, Mr. Staney --"

He slapped the desk. "Forget it. I know why you're here."

Chet muttered, "The great and powerful Oz knows all."

"And you must be the faithful friend, Kandi's cousin, Chet." Before Chet could answer, Sly went on. "You want to know about Kandi and the airport, what went on at O'Hare." Cherri reappeared with a can of Mountain Dew, silently handed it to Chet and went back to the couch. He popped the top and silently thanked her by raising the can slightly and nodding at her.

"That's part of it," I said.

"I will explain everything to you, but to you alone. I'd like it to be just us, man to man." Chet shifted in his chair.

"My friend stays."

"Or what? Will you beat me up like you did before? Choke me and then perhaps take more money from my wallet? You might find it more difficult. I'm in much better shape, and when she isn't working for me, Cherri is a martial arts instructor." He chuckled. "That was really something. My very first fistfight, you know. When I woke up in the back seat of that awful rental car for a minute I had no idea where I was or how I had gotten there. I was completely disoriented. Really something, yes."

"Why were you at O'Hare? Were you following Kandi?"

"By the way, thank you for rolling the car window down. It was hot, but bearable. Oh, hell, I don't care, he can stay."

"O'Hare."

His smile vanished. "Please try your coffee. I would like your opinion."

I raised the mug to my lips and paused. The Keurig coffeemaker brewed one cup at a time, from little plastic containers. It would be easy to punch a hole in the top and add whatever you felt like. Sly was watching me expectantly. If he wanted us dead there were better ways. I drank some. I drank a little more, never breaking eye contact.

"Very nice. O'Hare."

"The world is full of coincidences, they happen all the time, it's called --"

Chet muttered, "Synchronicity."

"Exactly. Like you coming here today, why, it's great. Saves me having to set something up. The airport in Chicago? It was chance, simply a seized opportunity. I was not following Kandi, not exactly." He sipped his coffee and looked over my shoulder, staring off into space or maybe checking to make sure we hadn't stolen any of his historic prints. "I had business on the East Coast and chose to go through Chicago on my return. I knew she was there, completing her internship, and I had a vague idea of paying her a visit to, ah, clear the air so to speak."

"So you were stalking her."

"No, no, Mr. Macdonald. Not at all, not at all. And please quit reading into this situation, making it more dramatic than it is. I know we got off in the wrong foot, you and I, and I'm glad you're here so we can clear the air, let bygones be bygones. You and I have a great deal in common. I hope that we can be friends."

I have had a lot of practice in interviews so I didn't gape at him or ask him what universe he lived in. The most I thought I had in common with this guy was species. "So you weren't stalking her. It was coincidence that you both were at the same gate at the same time at one of the busiest airports in the country."

Chet spoke up. "Third busiest. Behind Hartsfield-Jackson Atlanta and LAX, by total passenger boarding." Blurting out odd facts, usually numbers, is Chet's idea of conversation. When I first met him he was fat, and antisocial and pretended to like it that way. Now he actually could relate to a few people outside of the programming community. For him this was progress. This time I was glad for the interruption. I needed a moment to think. And to see if Sly had poisoned me. No symptoms yet.

"As I said, I only had the vaguest of plans, but when I learned of the tragedy at her clinic I knew I was obligated to offer whatever assistance I could."

Chet started to speak, but Sly cut him off, still smiling. "It is my turn now. You two have come to my place of work, uninvited and you are demanding answers, and, hey, I'm glad to see you guys, I mean it. And I understand your concerns, really I do, and it's good that you're voicing them, but I assure you they are groundless. I was not stalking Kandi and I am not now."

"You hacked into her PC to cancel her ticket."

"Again, no. How could I? That morning I was in Teterboro, New Jersey or en route to Chicago. And I can prove that. Hey, I can have Cherri copy you my travel docs and my calendar for that day and she was with me. As I said, fortuitous. I made some calls on my way to the Windy City and learned that she was flying out, and from there it was easy to deduce which was the most likely flight for her to be on so I swapped my ticket, paying the extortionate fees, and tried to help. I never got to say what I had planned because she deceived me and vanished, choosing to accept transportation from you."

We all sat for a moment. This was not turning out the way I thought it would. "What do --"

"My business? Ah, Mr. Macdonald, to explain that I must tell you what happened to me after I woke up in the back seat of that hideous rental."

"Kandi said you drove a Corvette."

For a moment his face changed. "Sold." He held up his cup. Cherri uncoiled from the couch, took it over to the coffee machine and started another cup brewing.

"I sold the Vette and of course that is why I had the rental." He sighed. "I had one of those preplanned lives, one right out of a guidance counselor's handbook. I was a fairly good student in both high school and college, and from a very early age I understood that people are the most important part of any business, and I made sure I remembered people. After graduation I found employment without too much trouble. I worked the counter at Enterprise Rent-a-Car for eighteen months while I looked around for something better. At the end of that time I went to work for IBM and shortly after that I married the girl I had dated at Enterprise. IBM promoted me, sent us to Atlanta, then back to a facility in Cerritos. Smaller facility, but a more important job in the IBM world. Then one day I stopped for a drink in Long Beach and met a waitress named Kandi."

Cherri placed his mug on the desk, again resting her hand on my shoulder as she did.

"Life was still good. People have these little flings quite often, and I felt that it was nothing to be ashamed of."

"Then Kandi found out you were married."

"Yes, Mr. Macdonald, precisely."

I heard a door open and a moment later a young guy opened the back door and stuck his head in. I paused. Cherri jumped up and hurried to talk to him. I caught bits of conversation. "You're early" and "Put them right there." A minute later she came back to the couch.

"And she dumped you."

"She chose to end the relationship, yes. It was her right and of course I had not been forthcoming with her. My mistake. Honesty is the foundation of all relationships and I ignored that maxim to my detriment. But, hey, I survived, after all, and like I said, this sort of event is far from rare."

"You didn't care that she dumped you?"

He flicked his eyes to Cherri and back. "Of course I cared, but, so what? Life went on, it was not great, but it was all right. Then my wife found out about the affair. The irony of it still makes me chuckle, because, you see, by the time my wife found out, Kandi had ended it."

"How did she find out?"

"One of her book club friends saw me with Kandi in the parking lot of Hof's Hut. She took pictures with her cell phone. The bitch never liked me, anyway. She waited weeks before she sent the snapshots to my wife, who, to my surprise, took it very seriously, very seriously indeed." He looked over my shoulder, staring into space, seeing things made him compress his lips into a thin line. "There were no tearful scenes; she simply left. One day she was there, the next she wasn't, and then I received the first of a series of registered letters from her attorney. Then IBM had a restructuring and I was forced to lay off most of my staff, which I did in a forthright and honest manner, after all, business is business. They all took it very well, because I am a people person and a good boss, honest and forthcoming. When that was done I got a phone call one evening at the apartment I had rented while we -- no, that's inaccurate, while my wife's attorneys sold our house. We had a nice home, very nice, close to the college in Long Beach, did you know that? No, of course not. The assistant to the IBM vice president to whom I reported called that night and said, 'Your position has been eliminated. Your key card is deactivated, so you need to check in with security when you come to clean out your desk. Your severance package is the standard plus fifteen percent for quality work.' I was speechless, literally speechless, so the nasty little man, this assistant to my direct report, took that as a sign to continue. 'Oh, by the way, your username and log-in are deactivated as well. When you come in to box up your personal belongings a security officer will monitor you, but you will be allowed one more log-in to check your email. The vice president wants me to thank you for your years of service and I extend my thanks as well. Human resources will contact you for an exit interview.'"

For a moment, Sly paused and just stared. "He extended his thanks as well! Can you imagine? A glorified secretary, a, a twerp, yes, that's it, a twerp." He paused for breath, raised the coffee cup to his lips before he realized it was empty again, and did the thing where he stared over my shoulder again.

It happens. If you work for corporations, large or small, in the modern business world you will get laid off every now and then. I knew for a fact that if I had two bad quarters in a row the brokerage I worked for would cut me loose, without even bothering to say they were sorry. It's unpleasant, but most people deal with it and move on. Sly shook his head, blinked and gestured to Cherri who smiled at me before she disappeared into the back room and came back with a bottle of water for her boss.

Chet said, "That's corporate life for you."

"How would you know?" He snapped. "You've spent your life in complete safety, closeted at CalTech, or inventing that stupid game that made you millions. I was out there, in the trenches, fighting the corporate wars while you played with the Space Floozies. Don't you dare speak to me of corporate life." He got up and paced, visibly struggling to regain control of himself, before he sat, the old green cushion of his chair giving out a mighty wheeze as he did, and said, "I apologize. That was rude and uncalled for. I am in an anger management treatment program but sometimes I slip." Cherri jumped up, ran around behind him and started massaging his shoulders while she smiled at us.

Chet shrugged and said, "Accepted. Y'all asked me to leave and I chose to stay and take the consequences. Now I believe I will leave. I haven't gotten in my walk today and I don't want to miss it." He stood and walked out carrying his Mountain Dew can. A moment later the bell tinkled as the front door closed.

"So what happened after you got canned?"

"More coffee?" I shook my head. "Well, I had my severance, and I had assets that my wife was not aware of, mostly cash, but also some rare stamps and a half-interest in a purebred Arabian stallion. Beautiful animal, just beautiful."

"And?"

"And I started this business. We recycle computers."

The bell at the door tinkled again and Chet came in with the Mountain Dew can. He held it up and Cherri pointed at a blue recycling bin in the corner. He deposited the can and left.

I was pretty much out of questions so I thanked Sly for the coffee and stood up. Cherri stood and walked me out.

At the door I turned and looked back. Sly had rolled his chair out from behind his desk and was standing next to it, gripping the edge of his desk and watching me.

"You don't by any chance keep your horse at Beachside Stables in Huntington Beach, do you?"

"Hmm? Oh, no, the original owner did and we kept him there for a short while, but Prince Ali is a thoroughbred and somewhat high-strung and we were afraid the noise and tumult of the construction they were planning would upset him, so we moved him to Norco. He seems quite happy there. The whole city is built around horses so it's a good place for him."

"How long ago was this move?"

"Oh, I believe almost a year now." Cherri and I stopped at the door. "Any more questions? I want things to be all right between us. It's important."

"No. No more questions." I walked outside. Cherri watched from the office, arms crossed under her breasts. Chet stood two doors down next to the Chevy, tapping out something on his cell phone. I turned and Sly was behind me. He had moved so quietly I had no idea. He looked me in the eye.

"I see. Yes, well, I have something to say. I am learning to be even more forthright, even when it is difficult. Now that you and I have cleared the air and have a better relationship I am comfortable saying this." He took a deep breath. "Mr. Macdonald, I'm sorry, but I think you should stay away from Kandi. I know it is difficult for you because you obviously have feelings for her. However, you are involved in more unpleasantness – yes, I am aware of the incident at the Las Vegas airport. I do not think you should put her in any more danger. I do not think she wants you to." He raised a hand, palm toward me. "I am in no way making a threat, and if I were I would not have the ability to carry it out. I simply speak as a friend of yours and Ms. Shaw's, someone who still has feelings for her. Quite simply, I care about her, in fact,

I love her and I believe, given time, that she will love me in return. All I ask is that you do what is best for her." Another deep breath on his part. "And if I can help in any way, if you just want to talk, you know how to get in touch."

It was quite a speech. He turned and went back inside. Cherri, still watching from the window, had her face twisted into her snarl. Then looked at me for a moment, gave a small finger wave, then cranked the blinds shut.

When I turned away Chet was standing next to the Chevy, and three large guys were casually leaning against the car. I walked up, and said, "Get off my car."

They were all young, twentysomethings with the usual assortment of tats and piercings. They were all wearing black sleeveless muscle t-shirts that said Anybody Personal Security. Next to me Chet stood with both thumbs hooked into his wide cowboy belt. He lives in Las Vegas, where security is about as tough as it gets outside of Tel Aviv. These kids didn't bother him, or if they did he didn't show it.

"Or what?" the tallest one said. He had a shaved head, goatee, and those circular plugs that make a hole in your earlobe. With his bulging biceps, and a large silver ring on each hand I'm sure he was expecting a different response.

By way of answer I looked him in the eye, grabbed the guy next to him by the shirt front and threw him down. The oldest fake-out in the book and it worked on these guys. By the time they could react I had my pool cue handle out and ready. Chet had dropped his backpack and made fists, one of which was probably curled around a roll of quarters.

Cherri ran up, face red and contorted, and started yelling, "What's the matter with you? He came to see us and you're trying to push him around? What is *wrong* with you?" The one on the ground started to get up and she pushed him back down with a high-heeled foot. Just not his day. Then the biggest one reached out toward Cherri. I wasn't sure what he wanted to do so I started to move. Before I could even decide what body part to hit with the pool cue handle, she had grabbed his hand and twisted his wrist back, forcing him down to his knees.

He whined, "We're supposed to watch the parking lot, and this car was just sitting here." She let go of his wrist. He stayed down, rubbing his wrist and looking sullen.

Cherri turned to me and pressed her hand against my chest. "Are you all right?"

"Sure. Chet?"

"No problem."

Cherri kept her hand on my chest and giggled. "I got to see you in action. Impressive."

"Seemed like you did most of the work."

She turned and started to say something to the guys but they were gone. "See you later." With another little finger-wave she was gone, too.

Chet and I just looked at each other for a moment. Then he muttered, "Well, shit howdy." I wasn't sure what that meant but I agreed.

Chet slid into the Chevy. "This is an interesting place," he said without preamble. "In the back he's got a trash can full of old keyboards and a row of empty computer towers. Locked door leading into the back of the office, parking but no cars close, only one parked off to the side. But . . ." His voice trailed off. "The car, off by itself, weird, man, and there was something about it . . . White Acura, tinted windows." His voice trailed off again, rare for my friend. "Drive around back, I want to check it out."

"Weren't there cameras?"

"The usual number, yeah. But so what? I was just walking and they knew I was here anyway. C'mon, pard, saddle up. Let's check it out."

I did, but not directly. I pulled out of the lot onto Ellis, drove around and came back in at the other end, out of sight of the windows of Anybody Personal Security. I wasn't sure why, just paranoia. As it turned out, my cleverness was wasted because there was no sedan with tinted windows anywhere to be seen.

We sat for a few minutes, looking at the empty lot. The thugs from Anybody Personal Security didn't jump out and threaten us. Sly did not appear carrying a bazooka or dragging a dead body. In fact, nothing happened except the smell from the sewage processing plant wafted in through the Chevy's open windows. Chet snapped a few pictures with his phone, then took a Gameboy out of his backpack and fiddled with it, zapping aliens. I knew he was thinking and knew it was best to let him do it. He stopped and drummed his fingers on the dash.

"He made a mistake. He tried to cover it with the fake outburst but he screwed up."

I said, "I agree. What did you get?"

"How did he know I went to CalTech? Every bio on the net says I graduated from UCLA. The recent blogs were about you, hardly mentioned me at all, and they never talked about my college. So how did he know about me?" Chet was right. As somebody who worked in computer security, he was very careful about his online identity.

"He's been looking into us."

"You got it in one. And he's good. The Vegas hotels my company works for don't advertise it, you know? And it makes sense for him to gather information on you, you took Kandi away from him --"

"She was gone before I ever met her. That's why she came to work at Fred's, to get away from him."

"T. R., relationships are not my strong suit, but that's not how he sees it, trust me on this one. But why me?" He drummed his fingers in the dash some more. "And we didn't catch him when he did the research on me."

I thought about it. "And, oh, boy, he found Kandi on her first day at Fred's and showed up, drunk." When I met her she said it was her first day and I have, all false modesty aside, a good memory for conversations. "How did he do that? I bet if we looked we'd find an email or, more likely, a text she sent to a friend saying, 'Hey I have this new job.'"

"Uh, Mac, there is some good news."

"I'm ready."

"At least, I think you'll think it's good."

"Out with it, cowboy."

"At Sly's place Cherri left her cell phone in her purse under her desk."

"How do you know? Wait, I don't want to know."

"I have this gadget --"

"Of course you do."

"Well, anyway, I sort of watch for that sort of thing, you know, I mean I used to, but I don't anymore and -"

"Chet --"

"I bluesnarfed it. When I poked at her phone I found a vulnerability, it was discoverable, so I did it."

"Uh, Chet, you better tell me exactly what you've done."

"Bluesnarfing is copying the important data from a cell phone's SIM card. Um, I can see everything on her phone. Calendar, contact list, and so on. I think they figure they're a software company and too smart for anybody to do this."

"But you just walked by."

"I had to be close, with thirty meters. And um, well, this sort of thing is kind of what I do." He stared down at his boots and turned as red as this morning's sunrise. "I did the ID walking by, finished from the other side of the door. I pretended to fumble in my backpack. He's got cameras watching the door. Was it wrong?"

"Hell, yes, and I love it. Chet, you're a genius. Sneaky, but a genius."

He turned bright red again. "Um, well, I, um, I mean, thanks. Cherri with an 'i' what kind of a name is that?"

"One she made up herself, like Kandi with an 'i'"

"Crazy."

"Okay, what's she up to?"

Chapter Twelve

He studied his tablet. "Um, oooh, interesting. Tonight Cherri with an i and Sly are attending a little wing-ding at the Segerstrom Center for the Performing Arts. Let me look it up, get the details." He poked at the tablet surface for a few seconds, "Hoo-ee, I tell you what, this is some hoe-down. Orange County movers and shakers gathering to meet other movers and shakers and talk about funding a new addition to the Center. I mean, even I know who these folks are because there's streets named after them. If you put all of their land holdings together it would be a major chunk of the county." He looked up. "Some of them started with real orange groves." More tapping at the screen. "Except the Segerstroms themselves were into lima beans."

"I never eat 'em. And Sly is going? Our Sly with the low-rent office? How did he get invited?"

"No clue, about that, pard, but he and Cherri are on the guest list. She's got email confirmations. And it's formal. She's paid for tuxedo rental for two guys, neither of whom is Sly. Maybe security?"

"Good guess."

We stopped at the Ellis and Beach Boulevard light, which is one of the longest in the city, takes forever to cycle, and I turned it over in my mind. "Chet, can you get me in there? And Kandi?"

"I can't fake a donation or their books will never balance, but there's a special celebrity list. I'll get you on that and get you in."

"Do it. And Kandi." He looked at me and nodded.

I called Kandi on the secure cell. "Where are you?"

"Passing South Point." South Point is one of the newer Vegas casinos and as such it's on Interstate 15 close to Stateline, so she was maybe four hours out. It was a little after four. We could do it. "Coco lent me a hotel limo so I am traveling in style.

Bryant wanted to drive me but I said no, my ankle and wrist are fine. Wait till you hear the sound system."

Chet pumped a fist and mouthed, "Yee-haw!"

"Something to live for. Kandi, thank you. I know you didn't want to come back yet." The light changed but I didn't react until somebody tooted their horn. I crossed Beach and pulled into the Denny's parking lot.

"Mac, are you there?"

"Yes, I am. Oh, honey, I am so glad. What made you change your mind?"

"Save it, Sailor. I can't let you fumble around on your own."

"Do you happen to own a little black dress?"

"Mac, don't read more into this than I intend. I just couldn't see myself hanging out at the hotel much longer. We still have many issues to resolve. No, wait, that's not right. I am the one with issues. That's what I realized when I spent some time in Vegas. I rode the New York New York roller coaster and the Rio zip line. I put myself in scary situations, alone."

I didn't think there was any comparison between a roller coaster and a limo carrying guys with guns, but what do I know? And she was coming home. "Yeah, I understand, well, no, I really don't but that's --"

"Normal for you."

"Har de har har. So, do you own a little black dress? Something dressy and kind of formal?"

"Sure, who doesn't?"

Chet said, "Cheryl."

"Step on it, baby. We have a date." I told her about the Segerstrom and sent her a link to the descriptive page that she looked at when she pulled into the rest stop east of Baker.

She called as soon as she was back on the road. "Are you out of your mind?"

"Well, if I am, you're the one to diagnose it. Har de har har." Okay, it was silly, and yes, I really said har de har har, but I felt better than I had in a long time.

"An event like this, Mac, you don't just show up. OMG, there is so much to do! Dress, hair, nails, mine are just a wreck, shoes, oh, no, *shoes*! I need shoes!" This was a side of Kandi I'd never seen. Apparently there was more involved than I understood. "Get off the phone! Cheryl, I need to talk to Cheryl, quick!"

"Yeah, uh, sure." But she was gone.

The logistics were challenging, but ultimately they worked out. Snake and Cheryl met us at my place. Cheryl drove Kandi up to Long Beach for hair and nails, then dropped her at her apartment and came back for me. Time was tight because I wanted to arrive early. So I climbed into my best Armani, a souvenir of my days on Wall Street, and we drove the limo back to Long Beach to pick up Kandi.

Cheryl and I waited in the car while she finished whatever, neither of us feeling at all silly watching for suspicious activity.

Half an hour later she ran down the stairs in her robe, barefoot, carrying the dress in a garment bag, shoes and a tiny black purse in her other hand, and leapt into the back of the limo. I leaned over and dragged the door shut while she unzipped the garment bag. As Cheryl pulled away from the curb, Kandi slipped out of the robe, pulled pantyhose out of her bag and started struggling into them. She said, "I know, I know. I hope people will think it's retro."

"I was just thinking I was glad we have tinted windows. A fashion statement?"

"Nope. I got bruised, and no, it wasn't a fight, it was practice and, well, look. Martial arts is like piano, you have to stay in practice."

She showed me a large purple bruise on her left thigh. "Whoa, looks like it hurt."

"It did. Hence the fashion statement. And by the way, I wouldn't do this for just anybody. I hate pantyhose."

"Well, you're still breathtaking."

She squirmed around in the seat and slid into the dress. "Zip me up, Sailor. We'll talk later."

"I love to talk." I tugged at the zipper. Unfortunately, it slid up smoothly.

She was rummaging in her bag. "Tell me again why we want to be one of the first to arrive?"

"Two reasons. One, I want to get a feel for the layout --"

"Exits, sight lines, choke points. Good." From the front seat, Cheryl pumped a fist in approval.

"-- and two, I want to beat Sly and Cherri. I want them to walk in and see us."

She removed her shoes from the bag and held them up for me to admire. "Speaking of Sly and this woman he's with, I want you to promise me something."

"Wear those shoes and you've got it." But I could see she was serious. "Okay, okay. What?"

"Did you bring my gun?"

"Boy Scout Macdonald, always prepared." I reached into the gym bag at my feet, got the little Raven .25 out and handed it to her. She opened the hidden compartment under the wet bar and put it in. "Now yours." The .45 made her hand look tiny, but she expertly slipped out the clip and locked it up. "You're pretty sure Sly is behind this?"

"Yeah. Maybe not all, maybe not killing Sigmund, but the airport hacking, yeah. He thinks he loves you and this is his way of proving it."

"Understood. And I agree. But, Mac, he needs help."

"Can't argue with that."

"And you are deliberately provoking him, setting up a possible confrontation."

I sighed. "It's what I do. Kandi, I'm not a subtle person. He wants to create situations where I react with violence. He wants you. And, so far, we have reacted to his moves. Even when Chet and I dropped in on him at Gleaner Computing, he knew we were coming and put it on his calendar. It's time to go on the offensive."

"I want you to keep him alive." I guess I stared at her. "I mean it. He's dangerous, yes, but he can be helped."

"Kandi, of course I have no intention of killing him, but, right now he thinks you love him, or will learn to. What happens if you reject him and it sinks in? He figures out you don't love him? What happens to his feelings then?"

"It's hard to say, it's—no. Strike that. I will not mislead you. If I reject Sly and he believes it, the most probable outcome is that those feelings of love turn to hate." There was a moment when we just looked at each other in the back of the limo as it hissed along Seventh Street to the 405. I wasn't bothering to check for cars that might be following us. The moment stretched. "Keep him alive. It's important to me. I do not want to be responsible for his death."

"I'll do my best." She took my hand and held it all the way until we got off the 405 at Bristol and joined the other limos heading for the event.

So that night at eight o' clock we were stepping out of the Bromeliad limo in front of the Segerstrom Center for the Performing Arts, onto a red carpet bordered by velvet ropes to hold back lesser mortals. Since the real celebrities hadn't showed up yet, the press settled for us.

I my ear Chet said, "This much press is unusual, unless, ah, yes."

I said, "What?"

Kandi pretended to adjust her dangly Lunch at the Ritz earrings and slipped her ear bud in.

"Ziggy Z, Jason Eleven, and Ramona. Plus their respective entourages."

I guess I looked blank, because Kandi said, "The first two are aging gangsta rappers looking to be respectable. Ramona is born-again metal."

Chet said, "Whoa, cowgirl, I'm impressed."

"You two are both hopeless."

Flashes popped, people yelled questions, one of them a reporter who screamed, "Mr. Macdonald, Mr. Macdonald, any comment on the suspicious death you were involved in at Beachside Stables?"

Chet had done his job. After Cheryl drove away in the limo I gave our names to the tuxedoed muscle at the door, who spoke briefly into his lapel mike before nodding and passing us on to an elderly docent who gave us a program and welcomed us.

The Henry and Renee Segerstrom Concert Hall for the Performing Arts is one of the showpieces of Orange County. It's part of a spectacular cluster of buildings on Anton, off Bristol and just across from the city-sized shopping center called South Coast Plaza. The Segerstrom is white, with glass and curving lines so graceful is hardly seems like a building at all, with tiny sparkling lights spiraling up over the four-story lobby and the three levels of seating. Tonight's event was big enough that the entire lobby and balcony above were in use. We were among the first to arrive, so most people were in the entry level sipping champagne and listening to a string quartet.

Chet murmured into my earbug. "How you doin'?"

"So far, so good." Mary had slipped into the Kandi persona along with the little black dress, so she was doing fine, chatting with a gray-haired guy who looked like he wanted her to sit on his lap, until his wife, who looked a lot like a carp, came up and dragged him away.

Kandi strolled over to me and said, "Vivaldi."

"Oh, yeah, sure."

"Cultural illiterate. My parents loved his string quartet compositions when I was growing up."

"Name Bruce Brown's first surf movie."

"Hah. *Endless Summer.*"

"*Slippery When Wet.*"

She sniffed and moved away.

We have done gigs like this before, so it was second nature to split up, circle the room in different directions, always staying in sight of the other person, marking cameras, security, and of course exits. We met again at the bar where Kandi got a glass of white wine and I got a club soda with a twist. It's only in the movies that the good guy knocks back shots and then shoots straight, and I thought I had my .45 stuck in the back of my slacks. Then I remembered.

Chet said, "Mac, I've been trolling the guest list and there's somebody on it you know."

"Thanks, Chet. She's seen me and is heading this way."

Before Acey got to me there was a change in a good portion of the crowd, their attention focusing on the entrance.

Sly and Cherri stepped past the security and stood for a moment, taking in the scene. He had on a brown suit, coat unbuttoned, with his thumbs hooked into his belt. She was in a sleeveless black gown that even I recognized as spectacular. There was a great deal of hugs, handshaking and backslapping as they moved into the room.

Kandi said, "What a dork. Everybody's in formal black and Sly's in a brown suit."

"My dear, that suit is pure Vicuña. It cost upwards of twenty thousand dollars. Vicuña doesn't tolerate dyes, so all the suits are the natural color." She gaped at me.

I shrugged. "At Fields, Smith, and Barkman we catered to very wealthy clients. I had two who owned Vicuña suits."

"Well, I'm impressed with your fashion knowledge. But it's still a brown suit at a black-tie event. Mr. Staney is sending two messages. One, he doesn't care that it's black-tie, he'll wear what he wants. Two, he can afford a very expensive suit."

"Now I'm impressed."

"Mac, clothes are communication. I guarantee he knows exactly what he's doing. But, look, check it out. Look at how the other people relate to Sly."

"Hmm. He seems to know everybody. They're practically lining up to speak to him."

"Watch the body language. Watch how the people move around him."

I said, "Chet, you getting this?"

"I'm in the security network, yes. Okay, yeah, people all around him, but," he paused. "I wish I had my crowd mapping program running. There's something funny."

Kandi snorted. "You guys! Really! You don't need software for this. Watch, just watch." It took me a minute but then I saw it.

"One at a time."

She said, "Right. There's never more than one person talking to him at a time. And the blonde in the tacky dress is always close, but not within earshot. And she's always playing with her phone. She is so tacky I can hardly stand it."

"Private conversations."

"That's what they think," Chet interrupted. "Cherri -- she's the hot blonde, Mary -- is making notes, sending texts back to the office server."

"Okay, let's file that away and mingle. Chet, if you see anything odd on the security feeds, call me at once."

"Got it, pard."

"Chet, you will pay for that 'hot blonde' comment."

"Mac will protect me, won't you, Mac. Mac? You there?"

I said, "Let's mingle."

Kandi's mingling had to be better than mine since Acey stalked up and stared moodily at me. She looked uncomfortable in a strapless, tight red gown that trailed behind her on the floor. "All right. I owe you an apology. I'm sorry. He was mean and big and liked to push people around but he was family." Irritably she tugged the top of her gown up.

"Jackie?"

"Who else? He had anomic aphasia. He got shot in Iraq and his brain was deprived of oxygen long enough to cause it. He had a hard time remembering names, sometimes places."

"I'm sorry."

"It drove him nuts, literally. You didn't kill him." I already knew that, so I said nothing. "The Medical Examiner said it was a cumulative effect from many small blows to the head."

"I'm sorry, really." There didn't seem to be much else to say.

"You know the story about how Neville came to live at the stable?" Another irritated tug at the gown.

"Found on the doorstep as an infant.."

"By my grandfather. The story is there were papers with him, a box with letters or something. Nobody ever found them."

"Jackie was talking about that, just before he died. Box of papers."

"Did he ask you to find them?"

"Yeah, he did. And your grandfather was killed."

"Murdered. Yeah. And they never found who did it, or why. The man had no enemies, he was never involved in rum running, and somebody beat him to death."

"What about these papers?"

"I always hoped we'd find them and learn who Neville is. He really wants to know and now, now --" She paused and cleared her throat. "Now that he's getting old --"

"The clock is ticking."

"Yeah. My grandfather told his oldest son about a cigar box with papers, and he told the story to his son, who was Jackie's father."

"Acey, what brought you here tonight?"

"You mean I don't fit with the big wheels?" She laughed. "You're right. But our new security company got the tickets and invited me. Maybe some of these people will notice the stable and move their horses to us."

Something clicked into place. "So Anybody Personal Security gave you the tickets?"

"That's what I said. All right, I'm gonna mingle. You're not rich enough to help us." She paused. "No offense." She looked like she might give me a hug, thought better of it, patted my arm and left to look for wealthy patrons.

A whiff of perfume and a warm female body pressed against my side told me Cherri had decided to chat. She whispered, "We *must* talk."

"Cherri, I'm not so sure that's a good idea."

"I know, I know. Now that she's back she'll be watching. But we can manage. I know you'll think of something." She saw Kandi moving in our direction and whispered, "Send me a message." Then the two women were face to face, and Cherri was smiling and saying, "I just love your shoes! I wore some just like them to my senior prom."

"Thank you."

"And pantyhose! How retro; it's just *darling*."

Sly came up and draped an arm over Cherri's shoulders, which probably saved us from two women down on the floor biting and kicking. Then I remembered they both had martial arts training and decided their fight would turn serious, possibly lethal, very quickly. Sly must have sensed the same thing because I could see his fingers gripping Cherri's shoulder. He said, "Mary, I'm very glad you decided to come back. It's good to see you. After Chicago I was a bit concerned until I knew you were on the flight to Las Vegas."

"I'm sorry if I worried you. I couldn't find you and the flight was leaving so I had to scramble to make it."

"All's well that ends well, my dear. All's well that ends well. So, how do you like tonight's event? Spectacular, isn't it?"

"Yes, it is. You seem to know just about everybody."

"Business acquaintances."

They moved off, circulating and chatting with the power elite. "That gown!" Kandi said. "It's a Vera Wang—and don't say it."

"Who me?"

"Your specialty is junior-high humor."

"It's a gift. So it's a designer gown. A Vera Wang."

"Mac, that's a ten thousand dollar gown and, much as I hate to say it, she wears it well." She paused, then her eyes widened. "Got it, at least I might. Chet, you there?"

"Of course."

"I need you to find who in the OC sells Vera Wang. Then match that list to Gleaner Computing's customers."

I said, "That's good. That's very good. You think she got the dress in some sort of barter or something."

"Or something, yeah."

In less than a minute Chet was back. "Cousin, you scored. Gowns by Archibald, Newport Beach. Gleaner recycles their PCs on a regular basis. But what does it mean?"

She sighed. "No idea, except it's a connection."

The rappers arrived, complete with assistants, their own photographers, and bodyguards who took up positions by the doors and looked bored. So we ate little shrimp and caviar on bits of flatbread, sipped club soda, and worked the room. Three celebrity chefs had set up around the perimeter of the room and were busily chopping, grilling, and stirring things in woks. It all smelled wonderful.

An hour later I was ready to pack it in, go home, lock up the artillery and talk to Kandi. Well, I wouldn't lock up all the artillery. I made a note to make sure and share that witticism with her. Time to have Cheryl bring up the limo. Go home and talk to Kandi.

Chet spoke in my ear. "Uh-oh, Mac, I got something here." Chet sounded shaken, rattled. "Mac, it's, it's bad, if it's real, it's bad. I think it's real. I'm afraid it's real."

"What is it?"

"A video."

I stepped to the side of the room caught Kandi's eye and signaled her to come over to me. She smiled at the gentleman who was leering at her and strolled casually toward me. She was at my side in seconds. "Okay, Chet, Kandi's here. Show us." We both looked at the little screen on my phone. I was sorry we looked.

It was a video, hand-held, looked like maybe shot with a cell phone. The room was poorly-lit and shabby. It showed a man I didn't recognize sitting in a battered recliner, sagging against the arms of the chair, mumbling. At least his lips were moving but there was no audio. The man picked up a glass of milky fluid, then set it down. Then a figure in a hoodie entered and all at once I thought I knew what was coming and why Chet was so freaked.

There was no sound, but the hooded figure appeared to be talking to the person in the chair. A moment later hoodie left. The guy in the chair picked up the glass of milky fluid and downed it. He immediately began to gag and clutch at his throat. Suddenly his back arched, he vomited explosively, an enormous amount of fluid spewing from his mouth and nostrils. He tried to stand, fell back, tried again, made it to his feet and turned in a circle as if in some weird dance before staggering around behind the chair, scrabbling at his throat. The frothy liquid dribbling from his mouth was streaked with red. He clutched the chair back and then fell across it and lay still, head down, hands on the chair arms.

I said, "Chet, where did you get this?"

Chet's voice was unsteady as he answered. "Sly has an email account tied to a page in the dark net. This was sent to that address."

"So somebody sent what looks like a snuff video to Sly?"

"Not exactly. There's no way to connect that email address to him. I only tied them together when he opened that inbox. So whoever sent this may not know who's reading the message, that is, the real identity of the person owning the email account."

"Tell me about this web account."

"W-e-ll, Pard, I don't know much. I tell you, the boys running this thing are scary good."

"All right. Don't go back to that site unless you are absolutely certain you are anonymous."

"Yep."

Kandi looked up, wide-eyed. "Somebody sent this to Sly?"

"Chet, you want to take this?"

"Sure. Sly has an email address on a website that's not part of the normal internet. It's on the dark net, a hidden network that's used mostly for illegal purposes. Sly set this email up, but without any personal information. He can read messages, but the senders can't identify him."

"If I were him, I'd want to keep it that way. Whoever sent that video is terrifying."

I had a pretty good idea of who the senders were, and why they had sent it to Sly.

July 20, 1934

Dear Diary,

I am tired and my feet hurt, but I have a job. What happened was Clyde and I would go to the dance hall down by the pier when Lou Helen was working there and it was nice. I would have my limit (one glass) of whiskey and sometimes other fellas would ask me to dance. Clyde said it was okay just don't get fresh with my girl and they would laugh and then I would dance with them. So last night Clyde said to me, "Hey you are doing that for free why don't you get paid?" I didn't know what he meant. Clyde explained the dance hall hired girls to dance with the men. Most of the men work in the oil fields. There is at least one fight every night.

The owner of the dance hall said, "Well I might give her a try she's real pretty," and he said how I should show him my legs and he and Clyde laughed, so I lifted up my skirt, but just a little, not even to my garters. And now I get a quarter a dance and the hall keeps half and I made five dollars my first night. Lou Helen was glad and said now I could pay her the money I owed, but I don't remember owing her.

Some of the men are rough and don't smell good but I put perfume under my nose so it's all right. I don't have any other opportunities so I guess this is it for now. Maybe Mr. Heems will get another movie. He said he would wire us as soon as he had work because we were good workers and could ride horses and came to work on time.

It's good because I work at night and Clyde is usually there playing dominos in the back anyway. He and his friends can play forty-two all night long.

I know Mama wouldn't like it, but the money Aunt Mildred sent didn't last long because last week Clyde needed to pay Willeford for gas when we used his flivver and he had lost playing dominos so he didn't have any extra. He said, well you were in the car too so you should pony up some money, but I know he didn't mean to be spiteful. Later he said he was real sorry and we went to the little café at the end of the pier and he bought me apple pie with a slice of cheese melted on it. It was just like back home except my mother's pie crust is better.

The Fourth of July parade was just wonderful! There were floats and marching bands and we just had a nice time.

Lou Helen has taken up with a man from the new stable off Goldenwest Street. He seems nice but he is older. His wife died a year ago of consumption or something. I don't think Willeford knows.

And I can't find any work and anyway it's just temporary until Mr. Heems starts his new movie. And Clyde is out of work. I love him so much, Diary. I'll do it for him.

I just have to remember that I want to <u>do</u> something. I sure don't want to go back to Platteville because there's nothing there for me and I really don't mind my new job much.

August 23, 1934

Dear Diary,

I don't feel so good today. Last night at the dance hall I drank too much whiskey and I can just imagine what that old goat Grandpa Lamentations would say about that, but I don't care a fig. All the girls at the dance hall drink and it was only a little. I made seven dollars so we can pay the old hag that owns the house the rent we owe and maybe go to a movie. Willeford and Clyde are in Los Angeles on business so we can do what we want this afternoon and I am sick of this fleabag room. If the boys get back in time, we may take the red car trolley down to Newport Beach and have dinner. Clyde said one of the things they were going to do in Los Angeles was get some money from a man who owed them.

Last week I took the bus up to the studio in Hollywood and tried to talk to Mr. Heems, but they wouldn't let me on the lot without a pass and when they called his office he told them he didn't know me. I don't like it, but people out here just lie whenever they feel like it. And that skunk Heems is like all the rest.

I thought I might save up enough money to visit back home but I can't do it. And if Mama saw me smoking she would just die.

Later—

No movie. No red car to Newport. The hag said we owed extra for something I forget what and Lou Helen is off at the stable. I don't know what would happen if Willeford found out. He can be awful mean. Last night at the dance hall one of Willeford's friends had a pistol shoved into his belt. I saw it but I was afraid to say anything. Maybe I will tell Clyde.

Nothing in the afternoon post from Aunt Mildred. She probably told my mother. I never should have written to her again and I have a job now anyway.

Willeford came in while I was getting ready for work and I was in my slip and he didn't even knock. I was borrowing Lou Helen's sleeveless green dress. I had it laid out nice on the bed and he sat right on it. I think I will tell Clyde and let Clyde punch him. Willeford said, "Woo-woo, baby." What do I care what a stupid rum runner thinks anyway?

Midnight—

Not much business tonight. Came home early. When Clyde came back I told him about Willeford walking in on me and he said, "So what?" If he doesn't care, I don't. I am about sick of Clyde anyway. Where's this good job he was supposed to get so we can get married? And when I asked him about the money he and Willeford were supposed to get, he told me to shut up in a real mean voice. Later he said he was sorry. No pie this time.

Must remember to write to Mama. Her last letter said Daddy was sick with a bad cough. I hope it isn't that dust pneumonia they talk about.

Chapter Thirteen

If you try something and it doesn't work because it's a dumb idea, why, the obvious thing to do is try it again. Playing blackjack, the time to double your bet is just after you've lost, right?

At the Segerstrom Gala after viewing the horrific video I looked up to see Sly across the room, beckoning to Cherri. They both looked down at his cell. There was a brief conversation. They both made phone calls; then a moment later they hurried out. Next to me Kandi said, "There's a camera pointing at them. Chet might be able to look at their expressions. But I don't think we need to."

"They saw the video and it freaked them out."

She nodded. "They're not the only ones. I found it quite disturbing."

"I think we're done here."

In my ear Chet said, "I got the video of Sly and Cherri but they're both looking down, I can't see faces."

We worked our way toward the door. I ate a few more little shrimp on flatbread. Then we stepped into the limo and headed home. There was no need to bring Cheryl up to speed on recent events; she had been listening to everything we said. We rode in grim silence.

About one in the morning it was time to act on my dumb idea.

I slipped out of bed and drove the limo to Gleaner Computing. I parked on a quiet residential street a quarter-mile away and, keeping to shadows as much as possible, slipped into the parking lot at the rear of the strip of businesses.

I crouched behind a bush at the southeast corner of the lot, close to the building, watching and waiting to break into Sly's office. Staking it out seemed like a good idea.

He had been pretty freaked by the video; and if he was going to do anything, tonight would be it. And if he didn't put in an appearance I had another plan. The back door would be locked but I had studied lock-picking on the internet and how tough could it be, right? I could always break the glass front door. I had a roll of duct tape to make that easier. That's what they do in the movies. The only sound was the metallic click-click of a skateboard along the walk in front. After a moment it quit. I decided to wait a little while longer to make sure the midnight tuber had gone home, and there was always hope that sanity would prevail and I'd go home, too.

There were several possible outcomes to tonight's adventure, and most of them had me learning something, so I stayed behind my bush. This time I'd made sure there would be no Dos Equis issues. I was prepared to wait.

The skateboarder came back, hopped the curb into the parking lot and did a couple of one-eighties before stopping about ten feet from my hiding place and bending to examine one of the board's wheels. He whispered, "Don't do it, man. Abort. Abort. Go home." It was my friend Cracker, the basketball-playing reformed thief.

"Cracker? What are you doing here?"

"They're watching you, bro. You make a move and they're on you. They have two low-light cameras on the roof, and one in that tree, and the security car is parked around the corner with two guys sitting in it. This place is serious, man, serious."

In stocks one thing you learn if you want to continue employment is when to cut your losses. "How did you get here?" We were at least five miles from the Harbour.

"This guy I know from the team dropped me at Ward and Ellis. I skated the rest of the way."

"All right. Get out of here. Skate straight down Ellis and I'll pick you up." He didn't say a word, just plopped the board down, took three running steps and jumped on.

They were on him before he made it out if the parking lot.

He gave it his best shot, pretending not to see the car with the bubble flasher on the dashboard, picking up speed with the practiced leg swing of a truly good boarder, when a second anonymous sedan with a bubble flasher on the dash cut him off. Two men in uniform held him while a third patted him down. I stood up and walked toward them.

"Let the kid go. He's got nothing to do with this." They jerked his hands behind his back and put plastic cuffs on him. Then they shoved him into the back seat. His black knit cap got knocked off and fell on the asphalt and one of the guys from Anybody Security picked it up and tossed it into the back seat. That made me nervous. There wasn't a thing I could do against four thugs with only my pool cue, and they had my friend. They cuffed me and pushed me into the back of the other car. Nobody said, "Watch your head." Cops say that on TV; I had the feeling these guys didn't care.

They didn't take us to a police station. We went to the offices of Anybody Personal Security, a small storefront next to Sly's, with a steel front door, blacked-out windows and a front room filled with screens and people watching them. Some showed Sly's parking lot – and Cracker was right, the cameras were excellent, providing clear images in the low light, while other cameras showed buildings, parking lots, and hallways that meant nothing to me. Sure enough, one of the screens showed the parking lot and my bushes, the one I'd hidden behind and the one I'd used for other purposes the night before. Perfect. The video of me taking a leak was probably already viral.

I was not surprised to see Sly in the APS office, sitting in a swivel chair, still dressed in his $20,000 Vicuna suit, a tablet computer on the desk in front of him. One of the uniforms set Cracker's board on the desk, wheels up. It was a land ski, almost three feet long, with sharply pointed ends, made for long distance skating. Not so great on ramps, but good for covering miles. I noticed it was so new there were hardly any chips out of the ends.

"Let the kid go and I'll tell you what you want to know."

Sly laughed, rich, rolling, good humor. "Tell me what? There's nothing you know that I need. All right, tell me something and if I don't know it I will release your young boarder friend. Come on, speak up."

He idly flapped a hand in my direction. Cherri was nowhere to be seen, and that worried me.

When your bluff gets called, you grin and ride it out, ride that strange torpedo to the end, as Hunter Thompson once said. Snake quotes him all the time. "I know you hacked Kandi's e-ticket and her credit cards and stranded her at O'Hare. You wanted to show up and save her. And I can't prove it yet, but I know it was you."

"Bzzzzzt! Honk!" He made game show noises, slapped the desk, and laughed again. "Sorry, Mr. Macdonald, you should have used your Lifeline. Nope, I know you think you know that. Too bad! Let's see what you would have won, oh, sorry, Vanna's not with us tonight. You lose. Nice try, though, yes, a noble effort."

"Where's Cherri with an 'I'? She wouldn't want to miss all this."

He smiled, then shook his head. "It would be best if you didn't find that out. Let's hope that is not required."

I had no idea what he meant, but I knew I didn't like it. Next to me Cracker shifted uncomfortably, staring down at the toes of his ratty tennis shoes. I didn't blame him; I was not feeling too good myself. Part of my uneasiness was my friends. I had tried to leave them behind, but my track record at that is not too good, okay, I've never been successful at ditching them. If they were outside, having followed me, there was a real possibility that Cheryl might kick down a door and jump in, guns blazing. And it looked like I might actually learn something about what was going on, so I was sort of hoping that wouldn't happen.

"All right. I think we can dispense with the cuffs. We're all friends here." He slapped his hand and one of his guys pulled a knife out of his boot top and cut the plastic cuffs. He made sure we got a good look at the blade before he put it away.

Sly turned to my teenage friend. "Cracker, may I call you Cracker? Of course, I can. You have been a busy boy, busy and naughty. Nothing serious, at least lately. You have two B&Es on your record, nothing serious. You were just learning your craft, weren't you? You didn't quit, you just got good at it. Now you play basketball, write poetry, and skate. Everyone thinks you are rehabilitated, but we know better, don't we? Never mind."

He looked at his tablet again, pursed his lips and shook his head sadly before looking up.

"Two years ago you were caught stealing money from a local store. You told the police that your father had left and your sister needed money for food. My goodness, it says here that your story was probably true. My, my, sad, so sad. And now she, your sister, AnnaBeth, isn't it? Yes, of course. AnnaBeth lives with her mother in Reno now and you are here. My, my. Soap opera time. And it says here -- I'm reading some of her Facebook posts -- she hates it."

He looked at me, mock sad, whispered, "The mother drinks."

Cracker lunged at him. I caught his shirt collar before Sly's thugs got him. He turned away and I pretended not to see as he swiped tears from his eyes. Unperturbed, Sly went on. "Did you know AnnaBeth has started cutting again?" Another lunge. This time there was no hiding the tears and one of the unis snickered. He was maybe an inch taller than me, buzzed blond hair, soul patch under his lip. I marked him, memorized his face. I smiled at him and he took a step back. Then he realized what he had done and moved forward again, deliberately moving into my personal space.

"What do you want, Sly?" I said.

He leaned back in the chair, nodded to the thugs. "Turn the young master loose. Oh, drive one of the SUVs over his new skateboard. Then turn him loose. A nice walk home will be good for him." Cracker didn't look at me as they dragged him out the back door.

When we were alone Sly studied me closely. "Good. Very good. You resist the impulse to attack me, perhaps use your famous pool cue handle on me. You notice my friends did not take it from you?"

"Yeah." Of course, that was why I hadn't jumped him. "What do you want?"

"My, my. You surprise me, but I suppose you shouldn't. You live up to your reputation. No threats, no speeches that begin, 'If you hurt that kid I'll'. . .'"

I shrugged. "You want a speech? Okay, how about this. There's no if. You've already done it. And you know it."

His eyes narrowed and flicked to the partition on the left so I knew where the reinforcements were hiding. "Here is what will happen. You will convince Kandi to leave you. You will do that by agreeing that you are bad for her and her life needs to move in other directions. It happens to be true. My indirect efforts to demonstrate this truth have only met with mixed success, so I will be direct. Leave her."

"If you think I'm going to tell her to hook up with you you're nuts."

"Unnecessary. I will handle that. She cared for me once and she will again. You will do this because you have already lost her almost completely, and because if you do not, Fountain Valley police will receive video of your young friend in my parking lot and then opening the back door. The first part will show his face clearly, the second we will create. Two iPads and a large amount of cash will be reported missing. While he may not be convicted, the accusation will be enough to force his removal from his beloved basketball team. Sad, so sad. And he was doing so well."

"I understand."

He stood and his thugs started to herd me in the direction of the back door. "Oh, one more thing." And then here it came, what he really wanted. "There are two individuals who wish to do me harm. When they contact you, you will eliminate them, or you will incapacitate them and call this office. I will send people to deal with them."

Add one more name to the list of those who thought I went around killing people. "So you're worried about Barney and Betty, are you? In my humble opinion, you should be. It's possible, though unlikely, that they're even crazier then you are."

"You will do what I tell you. There is also your father to consider. The vandalism at Beachside could be only the beginning. There could be an unprovoked attack. You understand?"

"Yeah."

For a moment he studied my face. "I'm not so sure. I fact, I'm not sure at all. I think you need a demonstration." He picked up his cellphone. "You were right, my dear, the demonstration is required." There was a moment of silence. "Just a little humor on my part. Now do as you're told." He pointed at the largest screen, wall-mounted above the partitions. In a moment it lit up with a green, night-vision video stream of a driveway. My father's. I think my heart almost stopped.

The camera was mounted on a pair of goggles. Once the door was opened the screen was a sick green as the person, most likely Cherri, moved through the living room and down short hall to where my father slept, on his back, snoring. A hand came into view and touched his crutches where they leaned against the nightstand. Then the camera moved into the bathroom and the owner faced the full-length mirror on the door so I could get a good look at a person wearing goggles and a jumpsuit that was probably dark gray. They waved at the camera.

Then my dad was on the intruder, bracing against the door jamb so he could swing a crutch at their head while leaning on the other. I saw him first in the reflection and then as the person turned. I guess he wasn't really asleep, after all. It was utterly hopeless, he stood no chance, and he did it anyway. Intruder in the house? Fight back. The scene was jerky as the goggle-wearer blocked the crutch easily and simply kicked the other one out from under the old man. He went down hard, flat on his back, useless legs splayed out at odd angles. A large, booted foot appeared on his chest and the intruder turned to the mirror again and raised an arm, posing like a big-game hunter with a dead lion. When the camera moved down and looked at the trophy I could see that my father was trying to pull himself free, scrabbling with his arms. The crutch was pulled off his arm and the rubber tip pushed against his throat. Sly keyed his mike. "No." The camera moved up and down, nod, and the other crutch was picked up. The camera showed the hallway and door.

Sly said. "Now do you understand?"

In my old line of work, giving in to emotion can cost your clients money. In this new whatever it was, emotion can cost you your life, or, worse, the lives of people you care about. "I understand."

"Good. I have no wish to hurt anyone, but I am threatened and you will help me."

"I said I understand."

He looked at me speculatively. "Isn't she wonderful? I just point her in the direction I want and off she goes."

I really didn't have an answer for that. But I was thinking about the large boot on my father's chest.

On the screen the camera showed the side door to my dad's closing. Then there was a sudden jerk and another elderly man was there, face filling the screen. It was Pete, the ninety-something neighbor. His mouth was moving and he looked angry, but there was no sound. He reached up and seemed to grab the shoulder of the intruder. A gloved hand lashed out and all at once the old man was clutching his throat, going to his knees, gagging. The camera followed him as he toppled over and lay still.

We all stared at the screen, frozen. Clearly killing my dad's neighbor was not part of Sly's plan. He took a deep breath, muttered, "Accidents happen," and turned off the video.

The really humiliating thing was how they just let me go. They walked me back to the limo -- driving it hadn't fooled anybody -- and stood while I got in. Sly followed us and stood by the driver's side window. "It was an accident. I never meant to hurt anyone. He was in the wrong place." I just looked at him.

I picked up Cracker as he was crossing Ward Street, shuffling along, carrying the two pieces of his skateboard. A moment later Cheryl's HumVee pulled out of a Shell station and fell in behind me.

I pulled into the Ralph's Supermarket parking lot. The HumVee parked next to me and we all got out and stood silently in the night for a moment.

I said, "Chet, 911, send cops to my father's address."

"Somebody else, I think your dad, already made the call."

"Any word on the old man?"

For a moment Chet looked down at his boots. "Pronounced dead at the scene. Cardiac arrest."

"Cracker, they'll give you a ride home. Can you get inside without getting in trouble?

"Easy-peasy. My dad's out of town somewhere on business, so yeah, I can get in." His eyes were wide. "Somebody got killed?"

"Looks that way," I took two hundreds—the new ones with the blue hologram strip—out of my wallet and tried to give them to Cracker. He shook his head and opened the car door. "Take the damn money, Cracker. Please. You need a new board and it's my fault." At last he grabbed the bills and got into the car.

I went to check on my dad.

The crime scene tape was up, but the ambulance was gone. For once Tony Genucci was off-duty so I got to talk to another detective. I told him everything. I was confident Sly would have a solid alibi for himself and everybody around him. He did. He didn't turn in the fake video of Cracker breaking in to Gleaner Computing. That didn't surprise me—he still needed me to deal with Kandi and the homicidal couple.

Everybody assumed, as usual, that the attack was because of something I was involved in. This time they were right.

It was getting light in the East by the time I made it back to my kitchen to be confronted by my friends. The only good news was that Kandi, exhausted by the drive from Vegas, the Segerstrom evening, and our after-party talk, was still asleep.

"And you didn't tell us about this harebrained scheme, because . . . ? I can't believe it." Snake sounded pissed. Chet just looked at me and shook his head. "You're a jerk sometimes, has anybody ever told you that? If not, they should have and let me correct that now. You're a jerk."

All at once Snake's eyes widened. "Bathroom. Back in a minute." Instead he closed his book not bothering with a bookmark because he always remembers where he left off, and went into Chet's wheelie suitcase and removed a cellphone-sized device with a stubby antenna that he extended all the way, and handed it to Chet.

The latter looked confused but went along with the gag, walking around the kitchen, then the dining room, using the device. "Walter, by any chance is your wife outside lurking in the bushes?" Snake nodded. "Okay, we got no electronic bugs here and if she's out there there's probably nobody doing physical surveillance or we'd have heard shots." He grinned, having made another joke. "Okay, Walter thinks somebody's spying on us, but they're not." He put the device on the table and straddled his chair.

Snake picked up his paperback copy of *The Wasteland* and noticed me looking at it. "Saw the kid writing lines from it on his skateboard." He put the book down and said, "I should let Cheryl shoot you. You planned it. Except for your father, you knew what would happen." I had forgotten just how smart my librarian friend was.

"Wha-a?" Chet's voice trailed off and he looked like he might be getting it.

Snake slapped his book down on the table. "Damn. *Damn!* T. R. This better be something you can explain. I mean, I get it, I think I do, but -- damn. Talk! Say something." Before I could start he looked at Chet and said, "He knew he'd get caught. That's why he didn't tell us."

"I either would get caught or I wouldn't, but, yes, it seemed like it was a pretty strong possibility. Chet and I visited Sly's office and I spent a little time that night watching it . . ."

"Yeah, your half-assed stakeout." Snake sucked at his beer.

Chet said, "I could have planted a camera. Much easier and safer."

"-- and it was just too simple, it was wrong. The place is low-rent, yet Sly's flying to New Jersey on business and he knows about the problems at the clinic, and he can afford to buy Kandi a ticket home, in other words he's got resources he's not showing."

Snake said, "Don't forget he bought tickets to the Segerstrom gala. Okay, you tried to break in, hoping he'd show his hand."

"Right. If I got away with it, well, maybe Sly is just what he seems, somebody getting by with a small business. On the other hand --"

Chet took it up. "If he has security and you get caught then he's more sophisticated than he seems. And he fell for it."

"Does it seem a little too easy?" Snake's voice was muffled because he was rooting in the refrigerator for another beer.

"The way he dealt with Cracker settled it. But my dad, he's something different."

He tried to pull the cap off a Dos Equis and said, "Ow! He's come out of hiding now, hasn't he? Told you what he wants. Buy some damn beer with twist-off caps." He pulled out a Swiss Army knife and popped off the cap. He picked it up from the table and looked at it thoughtfully. "Yeah, the kid tears it."

Chet had been working at his laptop. "Whoa, now this is interesting. Gleaner Computing's books are easy to break into, too easy, in fact."

I said, "Like the calendar on Sly's computer."

"Right. And I'm looking at file sizes that are too big."

"Okay, sorry for the interruption, Chet. Can you get into the files?"

He waved for silence. A moment later he said, "No. The files I can see on his network are simple, which leads me to believe he's got a standalone, a drive that's never connected to the internet. I can crack the encryption on the documents, but I need to have physical access to that drive."

"So we need to get to the computer." Snake sighed. "Back to burglary. People my age don't do well in prison."

Chet shook his head. "Not that easy. What we're looking for, incriminating data, could be on an outboard drive, a portable. Hell, you can get a two-terabyte drive that will fit in your shirt pocket. That's what I'd do. And that drive never leaves my possession."

"What about backups?"

"Mac, if this guy's as serious as I am beginning to think he is, there won't be any. He probably runs daily diagnostics on the drive, and as soon as he sees something he doesn't like, maybe a corrupted sector, he copies the data into a new drive and smashes the old drive, literally takes a sledgehammer to it."

Snake said, "He can't just erase it?"

"You know how a hard drive works, right?"

Snake mumbled something that sounded like "Just shoot me," but that didn't slow Chet down.

"When you store a document on a hard drive, the read-write head changes the direction of magnetization of a tiny spot on the disc." He saw the looks on our faces and hurried on. "Okay, okay. Here's what matters. When you erase a hard drive, the data may not be gone. Computer forensics programs can sometimes recover all or part of that data. That's how they caught the BTK killer, from a document that had been deleted on a disk he sent to the police. No, trust me, pard, he destroys that hard drive completely. Computer forensics..." His voice trailed off and his eyes got vague. Absently he pulled a Gameboy out of his backpack, looked at it, then set it on the table.

"If you could get to the drive, what would you need to do?"

"Hmm? Oh, well, when the drive is inside a PC it's easier. You just image the disk, copy everything onto a new drive, then remove the first one and replace it with the one you made. That gives you access to documents even if they've been erased and overwritten. The user never knows the difference." He drummed his fingers on the table. "For an outboard drive, it can't be replaced, just the data copied and that won't capture erased documents."

"How long would it take?"

"Can't tell until I see the drive. Maybe half an hour, probably less." He paused. "Mac, I think it get it. I need to have Cracker get something for me."

"No! Absolutely not! We can't get that kid in any more trouble."

"I'm giving him a ride to school." And the sun was up and Chet was gone.

He was back in an hour. Snake was sleeping on the couch, Cheryl had her head down on folded arms on the kitchen table. I could hear Kandi moving around upstairs. Snake and Cheryl woke up and we gathered around the table.

Pulling two hard drives from his backpack, Chet said, "I know how Sly makes his money. It was right in front of me. Gleaner Computing used to be called Calico Computers -- his little joke. Calico is a famous mining town. And Sly mines data off the drives people give him to recycle."

Kandi came in, incredibly cute in one of my t-shirts, yawning, and heard what Chet said. She said, "But they're erased. It's a requirement, says so on their website. 'You must erase your drives before we pick them up.'"

"Forensics. His customers erase their drives, then he brings back the erased documents. He sifts through massive amounts of data, looking for nuggets he can use."

"This is fascinating, but I need a shower." She took her coffee upstairs. A moment later the shower started.

"Blackmail?"

"And insider trading, and a wagonload of other stuff. He reads people's lives. I didn't see them in the trash, but I bet he does old cell phones, too. Same idea."

"You got these drives out of his trash?"

"We were in and out in less than a minute, and I jammed his wireless network so the cameras couldn't see us. They'll think it was a glitch. And there were so many drives in the trash they'll never miss these two."

"Chet, I wish --"

"That I'd told you." He looked me in the eye. "Sound familiar?" We were all silent for a moment. "The only way to get that drive, assuming it exists, is to take it off Sly. We have to grab him."

Snake nervously used his finger to make patterns in the condensation on his beer bottle. "We have no real evidence that Sly is behind this. I mean, I know you saw the video and I will take your word on it, but it's not provable. He made sure Cracker was out of the room before he said anything incriminating and damn! I can take early retirement in two years."

My feelings at that moment are difficult to describe. Chet was nodding, too, and he had closed the laptop. My friends would do it, if I asked them to. They would help me kidnap Sly to steal his portable hard drive, if it existed, and extract the information from it that would implicate him in criminal activity. I cleared my throat. "As much fun as it might be, we're not going to kidnap Sly. Snake's right, we don't know anything for sure. But, you guys, wow, uh --"

Snake slugged down the rest of his beer. "Good. I'm going to find whatever bush my wife is hiding under and take her home."

"She's in the living room," I said. "I started all of this, you know. Kandi -- no, Mary -- *Mary* went to Chicago because being around me scared her. Maybe Sly's right, maybe I am bad for her." Like I was bad for my wife Diana and my dad.

Snake looked at me, hoisting one strap of his battered backpack over his shoulder. "Get off the pity pot, Mac. You want the truth? Okay, here it is, the World According to Walter. Personally, I don't believe you are, but for the sake of the discussion let's say maybe you are bad for Kandi, but she loves you and you love her, and whatever else is true, there's somebody out there, probably Sly, who is manipulating her. They're scaring her to make her do something –leave you is probable – and you got her to do it, double bluff. Well, tag, man, you're it. People are dying. Kandi's scared and she's right to be scared. Whether you like it or not, it's you. Her other friends can try to help out, but you're the one with the, the --"

"Mad skills," Cheryl was standing in the door to the living room. They all looked at me.

Snake went on. "Yeah. She's in trouble and she needs you. You want to walk away, fine, but walk away after this is over."

It was quite a speech, and it was the truth. Too bad I wasn't paying attention at the end. "You're right, Snake, of course. First things first. But why is Sly coming out in the open now?"

Snake paused. "Good question. And he certainly has changed his approach. And I'm guessing you have figured something out. Most likely the video."

"He found Barney and Betty on the dark net and hired them to do his dirty work, part of which was eliminating people who he perceived as a threat to her. He might not have known for sure that the way they would fix his problem involved killing people, but it did. And now he's afraid they're after him, and he might be right. That's why he sent some guys from Anybody Security to torch their van. He wanted to warn them off."

Chet was flipping through screens on his tablet. "Probably the Rubbles, Fred and Wilma Flintstone's neighbors. Modeled on The Honeymooners, the Jackie Gleason series that ran –"

"Thanks, Chet." I shot Snake a significant glance. "Okay, they've shown up three times, when Jackie wanted to punch me out, when they grabbed Cracker, and I'll bet they were in the truck that t-boned the limo at McCarran."

Snake said, "They're looking out for you. They're the other players." He paused, then said softly, "The enemy of my enemy . . ."

"Right."

"The video at the Segerstrom. The guy drinking poison. If it was real."

Chet said, "What about it?"

"Barney and Betty sent it to him."

"So, where did they get it? And why send it to Sly?"

Snake sighed. "I'd be nervous, too. But in a way it solves our problems. We just let the old couple do their thing."

I shook my head. "I don't think Kandi would like that." Upstairs the shower quit.

Snake and Cheryl went home. Chet said he had a client on the East Coast who would be in her office soon and could he set up for the consultation in the family room?

I went upstairs intending to go to bed, but recent events weighed on me. Based on experience, I was half expecting my deceased ex-wife Diana to show up in my dreams – or in reality, take your pick – but it didn't happen. I woke up with afternoon sun pushing in through the drapes. I could hear Chet snoring from the guest room. There was a note in the pillow next to me saying Kandi had called a taxi and was going back to her apartment.

Surfline.com said the 17th Street was breaking nicely, three to four feet with fair shape, and despite the hour, the afternoon breeze hadn't come up. Minutes later I had my short tri-fin loaded into the Chevy, my wetsuit in the back seat and I was tooling down Warner to Pacific Coast Highway.

By the time I dropped into my first wave I had an idea. I hoped it was better than the one that got me grabbed by Sly's security people and Cracker's new skateboard crushed.

I wanted to put my plan into action as soon as I could so I only stayed until the wind came up.

At home I got cleaned up and opened my Facebook page. Some of what I said in my post was true, enough to clearly identify me as the T. R. Macdonald who had been in the blogs in stories about some extremely violent incidents. Then I answered their ever-present question: what's on your mind?

Meet the Rubbles. Today. Where M.S. works.

If I was right, my new friends would see it. What would happen after that was up in the air.

For a while I watched my page, thinking maybe they would write, but when nothing happened I drove over to Fred's for an early dinner, taking the laptop with me. And while I was there I did get a reply:

Tomorrow. After lunch.

Chapter Fourteen

I got to Fred's early and made some arrangements. Then I ordered a late lunch.

The breakfast burrito -- thin strips of prime rib, eggs, and jalapeños, not on the menu but they'll make it for me -- was delicious. I was just chasing the last bit of scrambled egg with a chip when I felt a hand on my shoulder. Since I make it a practice to always sit facing the door, preferably with my back to a wall, I was surprised.

"Well, here I am!" Cherri chirped happily. "I just knew you'd find a way." She moved around and stood in front of the table, blocking my view of the entrance, smiling and happy.

"Uh, right, here you are. Cherri? What are you doing here?"

"I got your message, you big silly." She playfully poked my shoulder.

"Message?" I leaned to the side to watch the door, but it was difficult to ignore her outfit. She was wearing a black leather vest over a silver long-sleeved blouse unbuttoned enough to show the top of a black lacy bra, a very short black leather skirt with a chain belt, black knee-high boots with chains around the ankles and silver spike heels. Her nails and lipstick were bright red. With her blonde hair and blue eyes she looked like Leather Girl Barbie. Three guys in suits at the bar were openly staring. She sat down across from me, giant silver hoop earrings clanking.

She looked over her shoulder, scanning the room. I was trying to watch her and the door since Barney and Betty could show up at any moment and I was not sure how they would react to another guest. Actually, I was pretty sure Cherri would blow everything. "I know you have to be careful, but *she's* not here, *she's* at UCLA meeting with her primary advisor. Oh, honey, I know how hard it is for you, pretending all the time, but don't worry, I'm working on it and I know we can be together."

"Cherri, this is not a good time . . ."

"I know, I know." She patted my hand. "I can see it in your eyes, how worried you are."

"Yes, yes, talk, good. Just not now. There are people coming I need to speak to, really, and I'm worried." I could see the tiny bartender, Mama, and two servers giving us the eye and knew this story would get back to Kandi the next time she came in to serve drinks. "I can explain everything."

"What?"

"Oh, nothing, just thinking out loud."

"Oh, that is so *sweet*! Honey, you don't have to worry about me. I can handle Sly. Oh, I knew the moment I saw you and I could see it in your eyes, too. You knew."

"Cherri, you have to go, please!"

She scrawled something on a Fred's coaster. Then she kissed it, leaving a bright red impression. "My place. You have no idea how much this means to me, to us."

The door opened, letting bright sunlight into the dim restaurant. Not the Rubbles. "Right, right."

She slipped the coaster inside my shirt, reached under the table and gave my thigh a playful squeeze, and stood. Then she leaned over and whispered in my ear. "Tonight. I'll be waiting. No, no, I understand how hard it is for you but not here. *She* has friends watching us and if you kiss me she'll know. I know she does. And besides, we might not be able to stop." Another leg squeeze. "This is so hard. You say goodbye first."

"Goodbye."

"I can't say it either."

"I did. I said it. Goodbye. Goodbye, Cherri. You have to go now."

"You are so strong! You are my rock. Until tonight, honey mine." She lifted my hand and kissed it, leaving another perfect lip print.

Heads at the bar swiveled to follow her as she strode out. Okay, I watched, too. So sue me.

A moment later the door opened and it was Barney and Betty. Both wore hats, hers a big, floppy-brimmed straw hat with a wide pink ribbon dangling down her back, his a baseball cap with those flaps that hang down to keep the sun off your neck. His said Huntington Beach and had a representation of the pier; hers said Disneyland on the ribbon in fancy script over the magic castle.

The guys at the bar swiveled when the door opened, probably hoping Cherri would come back and walk around some more. Their faces fell when they saw the Rubbles.

They came straight to my table. Barney held the chair for Betty and slid her in. Then he casually pulled a red plaid handkerchief out of his jeans and wiped the back of her chair where he had touched it. She fussed with a large tote bag and her dark glasses while he gripped the table and lowered himself into a chair. From a few injuries I've had I recognized the symptoms of a knee that was giving him trouble. He finally sat and sighed. Then he wiped the tabletop and pocketed the handkerchief.

"You are probably wondering why I called you here," I said and this time it got a response, she smiled, at least I think it was a smile. "Okay, what's going on?" She took a little gadget like a dwarf TV remote out of her purse and waved it at me, then looked at the results. "No, Betty, I'm not wired."

Barney said, "Is that lipstick on your hand?"

"Nothing, nothing, a spill, that's all."

Betty nudged him and stage-whispered, "I think our little boy has a new friend."

She laid the gadget on the table and watched its little lights for a moment. "We have to be very careful. You understand, in our line of work we cannot take unnecessary risks."

"And your line of work is what?"

She smiled. "We will get to that in due time."

He said, "Suicide. We assist with suicides. We like older houses with no G. F. I. in the bathroom. Run a tub of water, drop in a hair dryer and blammo!" He clapped his hands and chuckled. "We like that one because death by bathtub electrocution is hard to establish. See, there's ventricular fibrillation, so it looks like a heart attack."

"I'm sorry I asked."

"G. F. I. is Ground Fault Insulation. Now it is required wherever the electrical outlet is close to a water source. Made things more difficult. We are also fond of neuromuscular agents like succinylcholine or vecuronium. They are paralytics that act quickly, and they leave no trace except an injection mark that most autopsies never find."

She said, "Barney, we're not here to talk shop." Her warm, friendly brown eyes lit up. "Do you remember that crooked politician?" Of course, any chocolate chip cookies she baked could be laced with a neuromuscular agent. Or rat poison.

He laughed. "How could I forget? Oh, that was fun!"

They held hands while she said, "We dressed him in ladies foundation garments and strung him up."

"That assignment included a bonus if we discredited him. Do you know how difficult it can be to dispose of a body properly? My goodness, even if some poor soul stumbles across it years later, if it's thought to be murder there's an investigation."

He nodded. "And science just keeps getting better."

"So you make it look like suicide."

"We stumbled on the idea, really. We were both quite young and there was this terrible man. He was bothering Betty."

"Barney knew what had to be done and then we had the idea. Make it look like he killed himself!"

"So, what really happened to Jimmy Hoffa?"

"We could tell you, but then we'd have to kill you." He grinned. "That's a joke, son, we're kidding."

"All right, Barney. Enough of the good old days."

"It's important he understand us."

"Nonsense, Barney. You just like showing off. Get on with it."

I believed them. They meant every word they said. If you think it made me nervous, sitting talking to two confessed psycho killers, you'd be wrong. Terrified, not nervous. I had the .45 stuffed into the back of my board shorts next to the pool cue, covered by a sweatshirt, but I had a strong feeling that they could take me out before I could shoot them. But I have spent a fair amount of time talking to business executives, and co-workers for that matter, where it was important not to show any emotion, so I said, "When you need investment advice call me. I can refer you."

He said, "Thank you, but no, we like -- need -- extreme liquidity."

I nodded. "Gold bars, rare stamps."

"And good, old-fashioned cash."

Keep the sucker talking as long as possible. You never know what you'll learn. "Storage would be a problem. You have to decide between centralizing or distributing your assets."

"Barney, if you won't tell him I will."

"All right, all right --"

"Why have you been protecting me?"

Candice brought us glasses of water. Normally in California during a drought like the one we're in now, you have to ask for water, but I had arranged it in advance. It didn't work. Barney looked at the glass and used his napkin to pick it up. He sipped and said, "All right. The man in Chicago was a terrible person. We were brought in to correct the situation. We did, but not before he shot his girlfriend,"

"Ex-girlfriend." Betty had her knitting out. We were back to a normal weather pattern so the light was subdued and gray. The click-click of her needles was audible over the conversations.

"Darling, do you want to tell this?"

"No, no, I'm sure you'll eventually get to the point."

They were glaring at each other and, given their line of work, that was scary. "You, ah, arrange for people to have accidents."

"Why, yes, we do." Flash flash. Deft fingers, flying needles. She must be able to do it without looking because she never took her eyes off me. Maybe it was a sweater they'd put on their next victim as a kind of trademark. "And now we have a new assignment that we need your help with."

"No! And why does everybody assume I go around killing people?"

She went on quickly, "No, no, we don't need you to help us kill anyone. Quite the reverse, in fact."

"Kandi?" They must have thought they were safe, in a public place where anything I did could land me in jail. Of course, they thought I cared about jail, or worse consequences.. If I thought Kandi was their target they would not leave Fred's under their own power. I was pretty sure I could lunge across the table and crack their heads together before I got shot. I would take a knitting needle, maybe in the eye if I was unlucky, but I could do it. My friend Mario, the cook and a Mixed Martial Arts coach when he wasn't cooking, had moved out from the kitchen and was standing behind the bar next to Mama the bartender, drying his hands on a towel and watching us.

Barney and Betty must have read my mind because Betty shook her head and Barney lifted the napkin off his lap to show me a taser. I asked again. "Is Kandi—Mary Shaw—your assignment?"

Now it was their turn to be surprised. "Heaven's sakes, no, no, why would you think that? Your friend Mary? My goodness, she's such a nice young lady, no, no, you just forget that thought right now, young man." I believed her. I believed her. "No, you see, in our line of work there are numerous, well, call them security precautions. One of them is we never meet with our clients in person. We establish identity and, my, hasn't the internet made that easier! My, yes, we know who they are, and they know how to deliver the money."

"And they never know who we are." He finished his water.

"How do you make the initial contact?"

Barney said, "There are different methods. What matters now is that we have been deceived."

"You see, we only accept as assignments those individuals who deserve it. Truly unpleasant people who are doing no one any good and who pose a threat to others." She looked at me intently.

"Oxygen-wasters," Barney explained, then returned to watching the room. But his hand was still under the napkin.

She nodded. "Precisely. And we were given a new assignment, but we always evaluate first, making sure they are truly --"

"Oxygen-wasters," I said.

"This new assignment -- we never should have taken it. As I said, we were deceived and my husband and I do not take kindly to being deceived. We must end the assignment, end it with a degree of finality."

They looked at each other. He gave a fractional nod, slipped her the taser and stood. After he left, she said, "Poor Barney. Ever since his prostate trouble he just has to go more often."

"And he'll cruise around to make sure there's no cops waiting."

"I just knew you were a smart young man." Click-click. The knitting started again.

"So, who were the people shooting at the plane? You were the people driving the Sano Pump truck."

"Goodness, I have no idea. At first we thought they were other contractors brought in to complete our assignment, but now that seems unlikely. We're really not very interested in them."

"It doesn't seem like you would want to complete the assignment." I wondered what she was knitting. "So, what are you not telling me?"

"Correct. We have canceled that particular assignment."

"And you need me for what? I'm not a detective and even if I were I wouldn't help you. And you haven't answered my question."

"Oh, T. R., you really must help us. It's very important."

Barney came back and sat down. He looked at her and nodded again.. He said, "We were deceived about the real character of our assignment, but we were also deceived about the identity of our client."

"You don't know who hired you?"

"I believe I explained that." He gripped the side of the table and slid back. She followed suit. "Time's up."

A little light went on in my head. "You were deceived; you don't know who hired you, but that's not the part that worries you. Your client knows who you are, don't they?" Their lack of expression was all the answer I needed. "Okay, let me see if I understand. An unknown individual hired you to kill someone, but you have changed your mind. You want me to help identify your client." I admit it was tempting. Point these lethal old folks at Sly and friends and sit back to wait for results. Reluctantly, I decided I didn't have it in me.

She smiled, looking up from fussing in her knitting bag. Probably covering the guns, knives, hand grenades, poison, whatever. "They said you were quick."

"Okay, I'll bite. Who were you supposed to kill?"

They stared at me for a moment. Then Barney said, "Why, we thought you knew. You. You are, I mean, were, you were our assignment."

September 1, 1934

Dear Diary,

Well, I am not a little girl anymore. Somehow I thought I'd feel different after it happened, but I don't. I told Lou Helen and she just shrugged and said, "It's about time."

Got up this morning, well, it was about noon and wouldn't that old goat Grandfather Lamentations have something to say about that! My goodness he would. So I got up and Lou Helen was still sleeping so I went for a walk on the beach. I took my shoes off and got my feet wet and it was very pleasant. However, it is strange to live in a place that does not have seasons like we do back home.

Lou Helen has been concerned lately. I think Willeford has fallen in with some bad folks. I have never cared for him much and I think he would Take Advantage of me if he got a chance.

October 3, 1934

Dear Diary,

After I write this I am going to hide you. I'm not sure just exactly where I will hide you yet.

Clyde and Willeford have a lot of money now. Clyde had me quit my job at the dance hall. I told him I should get to decide where I worked, or what I did. He said women should be in the home. He just kept talking and wore me down so I gave in.

We have rented a sweet little beach cottage on Seventh Street here in Huntington Beach. It is close enough to walk to the beach and I will have a garden in the back yard in the spring.

I got up early this morning and went into Lou Helen and Willeford's room looking for cigarettes. They smoked all of mine playing Canasta and I didn't feel like getting dressed.

Willeford had two revolvers hidden under his coat.

Back home, of course we all had guns. I learned to shoot almost as soon as I could read. But these were pistols. And when I looked in Clyde's coat he had one, too.

I am scared of what they might be doing. I am scared of some of the things I have said to you, Diary.

Chapter Fifteen

I stayed by the table at Fred's, fending off wait staff until one of the HBPD's techs showed up to collect the prints. She was young, Hispanic, in her early twenties, with clever dark eyes and bangs and black hair pulled back into a short ponytail. Once in a while the edge of a tat would peek out from under her short sleeve. Her name tag said, C. Martinez. "Call me Connie, okay?" I introduced myself. She grinned and I could see her thinking about the forklift. But she restrained herself and didn't ask. I explained what was going on, that the person whose prints she was trying to capture had admitted to two murders and was planning another. I left out the part about me being a possible target. I said that I had carefully wiped down the table before Barney and Betty showed up so the only prints should be theirs and mine. Oh, and maybe a woman who works for Gleaner Computing, named Cherri.

"Detective Genucci sent your description of the old couple out and got interest from the Feds. They were more than willing to send me out to get prints." She walked around the table and looked at it carefully. "Give me a hand." We slid another table over next to mine. "So who are these people?" She briskly opened her small metal suitcase and took out a camera and other equipment I didn't recognize.

"No idea. But they seem to turn up at unusual places."

"Hmm. Smooth surface, looks clean."

"I wiped it down before they got here."

She didn't answer, crouching and looking at the table from different angles.

The customers gaped and took pictures with cell phones while she dusted, took pictures, then used powder and clear tape to bring up a single print from the underside of the table. I wasn't too worried about the Rubbles seeing the pictures. They would assume there were no prints to find, and anyway they said they didn't want to kill me. "Hmm. That's all, just a thumb. They were lucky or clever." She held a piece of tape up and looked at it critically, then set it on top of the cell phone-sized scanner. When it was finished she carefully folded the tape and placed it in her bag. "So, you going to the bikini contest?"

"I hadn't thought about it. Why, are you entered?" It just popped out, I don't know why I said it.

"As a matter of fact, I am. I have a totally killer bikini." She grinned at me, then looked back at the table.

I was sort of stuck for something to say so I came up with, "He was careful. He had a napkin in his hand."

"Ah. But his thumb slipped out."

"Will it be enough?"

"To ID the person? Maybe. Tony says you're okay, you're not a cop but you're not exactly a civilian, either. He says we should run the print, that you may be on to something. So they'll send it on."

Her cell phone buzzed. She listened for a moment, then her face went blank. Cop face. "Yes, sir." She paused and listened. "Yes, sir. Of course I'll stay with it."

I mouthed, "What?" She ignored me, said, "Yes, sir," one more time, then pocketed the phone.

"Step away from the table, please. And please keep your hands where I can see them. Please."

"What's going on?"

"Mr. Macdonald, step away from the table. Do it now." I moved back. And I kept my hands in plain sight.

"Tell me."

"Because I don't want you to touch anything. They're sending a van for the table. And I need to collect any surveillance video."

"The Huntington Beach Police want the whole table?"

"Don't touch it! And I need to check for more prints but I need to stay with the table and get the video."

I waved, and Mama, the ancient bartender, trundled over, drying her hands. She's, five feet tall, an indeterminate age, old enough for retirement but working because she likes it. And she carries a mean, leather-covered sap for use on patrons who get out of line. I've seen it. Obviously this was great gossip material. She patted her face with the bar rag and said, "What's going on?"

"No one touches this table."

"And we need the surveillance footage." Mama looked at the officer, then at me, still standing a careful distance from the table.

I said, "I think your people should collect it." The lab tech looked at me gratefully. "Okay, Mama, just don't touch the cameras or the hard drives."

She opened her mouth, looked at me and then at the uniformed officer, nodded, and trotted back behind the bar.

Connie said, "Thanks. This is my first big one. I would have messed up."

When the lab van arrived I gave another statement, acutely aware of the gun and pool cue handle stuck into my shorts. I talked fast.

I had driven over to Fred's in my Boston Whaler, because it's a pleasant short boat ride and because I hadn't used the outboard in a while. That meant the closest exit was through the kitchen and out to the dock. Instead, I strolled out the front doors propped open for two techs to dust and print. A large white van, bristling with antennae, was parked in the red, right in front of the door. I was not surprised to see that it had no identification.

Driving home I got a text from Sly Staney.

Video conf. Call.

When I was settled in my family room with a cup of fresh coffee I dialed and he was on the screen. He said, "You kept your side of the bargain. I really didn't think you would, but people frequently surprise me." He paused. "You don't have anything to say?"

I sipped some coffee. "You wanted to talk."

"Your friend the skate punk has been exonerated and has his spot on the basketball team back. And I have no further interest in you."

"I have an interest in you. And in Cherri with an 'i.'"

"We are both sorry about your father's neighbor."

"His name was Pete. He was ninety-one and a World War Two vet. Flew eighteen missions over Germany."

"I have said I am sorry. There's not much else I can do."

"Sure there is. Tell the person who killed him to turn themselves in."

"I can't do that. I need her. And it will not bring Pete back. He was just in the wrong place at the wrong time. And he died of natural causes. Heart attack." Once again, Sly's sources of information were better than mine.

"Maybe he saw somebody breaking into his neighbor's house and felt like he should help. But you're right, you may need the psycho Cherri."

"The people who want to harm me? I'll deal with them. I suggest that you and I declare a truce." He licked his lips. "It is in both our interests to focus our attention elsewhere."

"Sly, you hired people to kill me."

"I was desperate. And I changed my mind. And you can't prove that. Their name might be Subere." He paused. "What am I going to do?"

I shrugged. "They're your problem, not mine. What about Kandi? You can't believe you'll hook up with her."

"Of course, I will. She loves me." He smiled, utterly convinced. Naturally, at that moment Kandi came downstairs wearing one of my dress shirts. Okay, I'm human; for a moment had a good time wondering what else, if anything, she was wearing. I waved her back, urgently, keeping her out of sight and, being Kandi and very quick she got it and froze, standing in the short passage that connects the living room to the family room. "What was that waving all about? Is someone else there?"

"Nothing. Flies. Are we done?"

"So, who were the people you had lunch with at Fred's?"

I realized he had hired the killers, but had never seen them; they couldn't exactly put their pictures on their Facebook page. But when he discovered that I had called the cops to get prints, he'd figured it out. I knew what they looked like and might have a print. It was like a birthday party with a piñata and a blindfolded kid trying to smash it with a stick, only there were two kids at once and I was the piñata.

In response, I reached out and broke the connection.

I brought Kandi up to speed on my latest conversation with the odd Mr. Staney.

She nodded thoughtfully. Then she got a cup of coffee and settled next to me. "Tell me about your father and you."

And you know what? I did. Every bit of it. How I came home from school one day and my mother wasn't home and she never came back. How my dad and I got by. How he felt about my wife Diana, how he felt when she was killed on my watch, how I figured he was feeling now that his neighbor has been killed. Kandi watched intently while I told the story. Toward the end she held my hand. She said, "We'll talk."

I managed a grin, "I can hardly wait." And you know what? I felt better than I had since the first email showing Kandi at O'Hare.

"I mean talk," and went upstairs to get dressed. Then she left to run errands. She still had not established a schedule at Fred's Fine Mexican Food, and that was one of the errands she listed.

Surfline.com said the surf was awful, small and blown out, and therefore no fun with the short board, and I didn't feel like dragging the stand-up board down to the beach, so I stayed home that day and did stuff around the house. Kandi called around four and said she had checked in at the restaurant and not only was her job still available, one server had called in sick and she was going to work the six to closing shift.

That night, she came to where I was dozing on the couch and put both hands in my shoulders. "We need to talk. But not now. I had forgotten just how much work serving is. I am beat, beat, beat. We'll talk later, but in the meantime don't worry, for once it's not about us,"

"Thank you for coming back."

She squeezed my hand and we went upstairs and crashed.

The next morning it got interesting. I was actually considering going out and bringing in breakfast. When I opened the front door there was an immaculate silver BMW Z5 parked blocking my driveway. I walked over to the little two-seater.

"Well, Detective Genucci. What a surprise."

He was dressed in a charcoal suit, lightweight wool, white shirt and red power tie. I'd slept in the Duke's tank top I had on and there was some evidence of pepperoni, but my board shorts were classic Kanvas by Katin.

"Get in. We need to talk."

That reminded me of what Kandi said last night. Was I wearing a sign that said, "Want somebody to talk to? I'm available."

"Gee, Tony, I'd really like to but --"

"Mac, just get in the car."

For a moment I considered more witty banter but Tony G. didn't seem amused. "I need to lock the house."

I trotted up the walk and through the entryway, picking up wallet, keys and my cell phone from the kitchen counter before hustling up the stairs. Kandi was sleeping peacefully in the master bedroom; Chet was flat on his back, snoring in the guest room. Cheryl and Snake were spending the day at their tiny Seal Beach bungalow, where he would be reading and she would either be working in the garden or sharpening Bowie knives. I locked the front door and got in the little silver sports car.

"Well, here's one fantasy I can cross off the list. Being kidnapped by the police. Oh, wait, that fantasy was being kidnapped by a beautiful woman."

He didn't smile much, but there was a tiny uplifting at the corners of his mouth. "How do you do it? How do you stumble into these things?"

"It's a gift." Again, Tony was not amused.

"That print you sent in set off rockets."

"Rockets?"

"By the way, that was good thinking, using the whole table."

"Thanks. I got lucky. When he stood up he pushed back from the table and wiped the top, but he missed the underside. By the way, Mama says the owner wants his table back.

"That may take a while."

"Great. I suppose I'll end up paying for it."

"It was a smart move on your part." Here's a tip: when people try to butter you up, be afraid, especially if they carry guns.

"Rockets?"

"Describe the couple you spoke to. And, to be clear, this was the same couple you spoke to before their van caught on fire."

"I think I'd rather hear about these rockets."

"All in good time."

I sighed. "The first time I saw them they were in the van that caught on fire at the Harbour Mall. Older, maybe in their sixties. Gray hair. Hers was long, in a braid down her back. He had on a baseball cap, gray hair down over his collar. Dark glasses, both of them. Both times she's showed me a gun, and I'm pretty sure he had one, too. Hers was an automatic, looked like maybe a Raven 25. She kept it in her lap next to her knitting. His ball cap had those flaps that cover your neck. It said Huntington Beach. She had on a canvas beach hat with a wide brim. At Starbucks put lids on their tea and took it with them. After their van caught on fire, they weren't freaked at all. He just got their backup car and they drove away before the fire trucks got there."

"Go through the sequence for me, everything."

I had a lot of questions, but Tony was a friend and he was very intense. Also, he had a gun and I'd left mine in the house.

"You are going to explain all this, right?" I asked. "Right?"

He looked me in the eye and said, "Yes, of course."

The most sincere CFO I ever met during my investing career looted the small-cap company he was responsible for, sucked it dry and got away with it. He is now living someplace with no extradition. He looked me in the eye, too.

"What names did they give you?"

"He was Barney and she was Betty. They acted like it should mean something to me."

"Ever hear of Bedrock?"

"Sure, for a few months I was interested in mining equities." No smile. "All right. Yeah, they're the Rubbles. Fred and Wilma Flintstone's neighbors."

"Correct."

It was time to level with Tony. "Okay, here's what I know and what I think. I know they're armed, and they're following me around." He started to speak, but I rolled on. "I think, and this I can't prove, that a local businessman named Sly Staney, who thinks he's in love with Kandi, found them on the black internet and hired them to kill people who might compete with him for her attention, or who might harm her. Specifically, the hit-and-run that was supposed to have killed Bernard Sigmund, and the murder-suicide at the Usher Clinic in Chicago. I was supposed to be on the list but they investigated me and decided not to kill me because I'm such a nice guy. Like I said, they like me, and they don't like Mr. Staney. They have decided their client is someone they don't like. They don't have his identity because he was able to trick them, but he knows who they are. Not what they look like, but enough to maybe locate them."

"What about the airports?"

"Sly thinks Kandi loves me because I rescue her. So he wants to put her in jeopardy and save her. Or, because he knows she has doubts about the stuff that seems to happen around me --"

"Your gift."

"Yeah. He thinks he can freak her out, get her to ditch me for him. And Sly told me their last name is Subere. Sounds French."

At that he sat up straight and reached for his phone. "Interpol says their last name is Subere. If they are who we think they are, they are without a doubt the most successful team of assassins in recent history. Their specialty is making murder look like suicide."

Uh-oh.

"I see that means something to you."

Okay, so maybe my poker face wasn't as good as I thought, but I wasn't expecting to need it with a friend.

"We're uncertain about the exact number of kills, but we know it's double-digit. They've been around forever, and they're not keeping up with forensics, and that's how we began to put it together. First, they are probably younger than they looked, most likely mid-fifties. We think they have been killing for money since their teens, that is, the FBI agents working the case think so and Interpol agrees. I think they're giving them too much credit, but I could be wrong."

"I see what you mean by rockets. The people in Chicago."

He nodded. "We missed it at first because it looks like the Suberes only killed the man. He killed Jennifer Prewett."

"And of course they told me they did it."

"They seem to work on a contract basis, half up front, half after a successful kill."

"Pretty trusting."

"The agent who briefed me thinks one client tried to stiff them for the second half of the payment. The gentleman in question wrote a very remorseful note, drank a quart of vodka followed by twelve ounces of Draino. It was ruled a suicide."

I didn't feel well. I looked away for a moment. A convertible Miata went by with golf clubs in the passenger seat. In another universe that was me, and Kandi and I were married and she worked for a prestigious clinic, and I raised money for a battered womens' shelter. Neither of us owned a gun.

But you play the hand you are dealt.

"Draino?"

Tony nodded. "Dissolved his stomach and other parts. He bled out internally."

"Too much information. But I'll send you the video." That got his attention. "Chet intercepted it. It's not something you want to watch while you're eating."

"Who was the video sent to?"

"Sly, maybe. Tony, look, I really don't want to speculate. Let me see what I can find out and pass it on to you."

"Twenty-four hours. Then I want everything, speculation included. That supposed suicide -- the Draino one -- was where we got the partial that we matched to the one from the restaurant. They must have been rushed. The video from the restaurant where you met them may help."

I thought about it. "How do prospective clients find them? Was I right about the dark Net?"

"Yes. Private sites on offshore servers that are not reachable with a normal URL. Here's the odd thing: most of the people they killed, or who we think they killed, won't be missed."

I nodded. "I may have some insight about that."

"Mob guys, wife beaters, two Mexican cartel soldiers, and so on."

"Crooked politician?"

"You'll have to be more specific."

"Dressed in woman's underwear, hung himself."

"London, six years ago."

"One of their favorites."

"Lucky you." He reached into the side pocket, brought out a cloth and started wiping down the dash.

"Oh, yeah."

"I mean it. If they didn't like you, you probably would have killed yourself. *Point Break*, the guy paddles out in giant surf."

"Never saw it."

"Dude, it's a surf movie."

"So, what do you want from me?"

"Stay alert. Don't hang out at the Senior Center."

"Thanks. Good safety tip. Tony, this is what you've been waiting for isn't it? An important, high-profile case. A chance to play in the big leagues."

He grinned. "I've already started filling out the transfer papers. But, Mac, listen. These assassins are incredibly efficient. If they decide they don't like you, it could be serious. You watch yourself."

I slid out and closed the door. He reached for the key to start the engine. I stopped him.

"Here's what I think. That print found its way to the FBI. You are very interested in this couple. It's too much of a coincidence for you to be on that particular case, so you must be attached to my file somehow. And you showed up because I'd be more receptive to questioning from you, but . . . No, you were sent as a first attempt. If I'd been uncooperative I'd be in an interrogation room somewhere. Which car? Which one is FBI?"

"The gray SUV three houses down." He started the BMW.

"I'm going to go inside and check on Kandi now. I will be very unhappy if she's not there."

"She's fine. She has had no contact with these people. None of the agencies involved have any interest in her."

"I know, Tony, and I appreciate you making the approach. But those other agencies are involved and they may decide they need to have a serious conversation with Kandi."

"What made Barney and Betty approach you?"

"I think they wanted to make sure I was a nice guy so they didn't need to offer me a Draino cocktail. After that they wanted me to give them Staney."

"And you didn't."

"Right."

He shook his head. "About the Draino--they never use the same method twice."

I couldn't think of any witty repartee -- thoughts of drinking Daino will do that -- and I found myself wondering what else my friends the homicidal seniors would come up with. Tony drove away and after a moment the SUV followed.

After coffee -- going out to a restaurant seemed like a poor idea until we had taken some precautions -- I told Kandi we needed to take a ride. I drove us down to the beach parking lot at PCH and Warner. This early on a weekday I got a spot on the first row, facing the bike path, sand, and the Pacific. I killed the 327 and turned to face her.

I reached out and put my hand on her shoulder. Great sex did not equal any kind of resolution to our tangled relationship, especially not in the light of morning. She reached up and for a moment I thought she was going to remove my hand, but instead she put hers over mine and laced her fingers through. We both sighed at the same time, looked at each other and laughed.

"We're a fine pair," she said.

"But it's not boring."

It seemed like a safe place to talk. We sat quietly for a few moments, watching a lifeguard cruise by on a four-wheel ATV. The windows were down and a breeze carried the good ocean smell into the car. Her hand squeezed mine. "The party at the Segerstrom was nice."

"I liked it, too."

"But you were carrying a gun."

"Strapped, according to Cheryl."

"That's what I mean."

"Kandi, I know it bothers you."

She shook her head. Her French hairdo had not survived the evening and now blonde curls bounced as she shook her head again. "No! That's what I mean. It *didn't* bother me. I'm getting used to the idea of being in danger, of always checking exits as soon as I walk into a strange room. And that's not how I want to live."

"It's worse than we thought." I told her about my conversation with Tony G. and brought her up to speed on other current events.

"How are things with you and your father?" Trust my Significant Other to get to matters I'd rather not discuss. "That's what I wanted to talk about."

"We're making progress." I can't lie to her. Can't do it. "Okay, we were making progress until he saw the cops haul me away because they thought I'd bashed Jack's head in."

"He doesn't really think you did it, I mean, how could he?"

"Well, I seem to be involved in more bad stuff, and --"

"And he blames you for Diana's death." I took a deep breath, but before I could speak she went on. "And deep inside, you do too."

"No, no, honest, I know --"

"Mac, I do this for a living."

"It's a small part of me. Really."

"Look, you don't want to hear this, but I'm going to say it anyway --"

I love Kandi more than anything but she has a real jerk-your-covers attitude. She won't let people hide from unpleasant truths. In this case I was saved.

I heard an engine approaching and the lifeguard ATV was back, heading north on the return route. Out of the corner of my eye I noticed the rider as he reached over his shoulder and pulled a dull gray metal cylinder out of his backpack.

Then the ATV jumped the curb from bike path to parking lot and slid to a stop next to us. The rider twisted the cap on the cylinder and lobbed it through my window.

It landed squarely in my lap and we later decided that's what saved us, because it gave me a chance to grab it. There was an instant when I looked down and thought *holy shit, that thing's on fire*, but there were no flames, just intense cold, burning cold, if that makes any sense. So, instinctively I snatched it up, feeling like the tips of my fingers were being burned off, and tried to toss it out of the car, only it bounced off the glass because somehow the window had rolled itself up – we can laugh about this now, about the relationship between throwing accuracy and a metal cylinder doing its best to freeze your crotch off – and it landed in the back seat, where the contents spilled and a cloud filled the space and all at once it was cold, really cold. The windows misted over and why were they up, all of them? And why wouldn't they go down when I pushed the button?

Kandi was frantically trying to open her door, yanking on the handle, ramming her shoulder against it, but it was locked. And her window was up, too. They all were. When I tried to get out I discovered that my door was locked. She pushed, then pounded on, the switch and I tried my key, I guess thinking that if I could start the car maybe the door locks would work. The car didn't start and the doors stayed locked. I grabbed her and pulled her across me to the window on my side. Hers was still up and I had a strong feeling that it would stay that way, and we were out of time because by now the fumes in the back seat filled the entire rear of the car. We were both choking and frantically trying anything to get out.

I reached under the dash for my sawed-off pool cue handle and my fingers touched nothing except metal. Where was it? Had I left it behind? I pushed Kandi closer to the window and twisted down behind her, groped, groped again, stretching my arm to get as far under the dash as I possibly could. My eyes were burning now, on fire; I buried them in the crook of my elbow and groped again while Kandi pounded on the glass and yanked at the door handle. There was a very bad moment when I thought it really wasn't there, that it had fallen out and rolled over to the passenger side, or was at home safely lying on my nightstand next to my paperback copy of *The Count of Monte Cristo*. Finally I touched the small end but it wasn't easy with 110 pounds of squirming, screaming Kandi in my lap. Take a note: get the tool out from under the dash before dragging the woman over on top of you.

I smashed the handle into the window and the damn thing didn't break. Safety glass. Didn't even crack. Great. I hit it again and first it dented and there were little cracks spidering and suddenly it gave and bulged out like glass glued to cloth, the adhesive between the layers holding it until finally I pushed the whole thing out and used the handle to scrape out broken shards. The fumes were unbearable as I grabbed Kandi around the waist and shoved her head and shoulders out. Somehow she had grabbed her shoulderbag but it didn't catch in the windowsill. The belt on her denim skirt jammed but a good push on her butt forced her the rest of the way out. I was pretty motivated since the back of the Chevy's bench seat was starting to dissolve -- I know because I put my hand back there and touched nasty, sticky, goo that burned -- and I could smell chemicals, really unpleasant ones, and the car was completely full of fumes that were undoubtedly full of all kinds of toxic crap. Finally her hips and legs popped through the window. I saw a pair of red high heels vanishing into the haze pouring out of the car. She hit the asphalt and rolled, drawing her tiny Raven .25 automatic from a holster in the small of her back as she did. I put one hand on each side of the window, feeling the skin burn and smelling it over the chemical odor, like one of the pork roasts my dad cooked on the backyard grill. It's funny what your brain does at times like that. And I lunged out. In my mind I was going to roll gracefully like Kandi, jump to my feet, find the ATV driver and rearrange his face, but I sort of flopped on my stomach with both feet hung up inside the car and despite scrabbling with my fingernails at the asphalt I was not making any progress. Kandi holstered her gun, stumbled over, got both hands under my arms and pulled me free; behind me white clouds of who-knows-what billowed out of the broken window. The momentum of her yanking me out carried us both backward so we ended up lying on the pavement, gasping and choking.

She rubbed the wrist that she'd sprained at McCarran, pushed me off and panted, "Sailor, I can't imagine why Mary wants to do counseling when she could have fun dates like this." Then she leaned over and threw up on my leg. All things considered, I didn't mind. It made a nice warm spot. I flopped over on my back and stared at gray sky while my heart slowed to a non-fibrillation pace.

Kandi wiped her mouth, got to her feet and staggered around, coughing, moving the crowd back from the vehicle, the interior of which was now beginning to show as the fumes dissipated. The rear window developed a rapidly expanding pattern of jagged cracks, then sort of exploded, showering the trunk lid and the asphalt/ parking lot behind the car with glass. I probably should have been looking for the ATV rider, but that had become a lower priority because I was too busy coughing, trying not to pass out, and pulling off my new Reef sandals because something had gotten on them and they had started to melt. If the driver wanted to come back and shoot me, there was part of me that was okay with that.

I got to my feet, thinking that somebody, probably the young thugs from Anybody Personal Security, really had it in for me. Then I realized that they were playing with me, showing off, just like Kandi in the airport. *Look what I can do to you.*

And that really pissed me off.

Kandi stumbled over to me and rested her head on my shoulder. "Your three o'clock. Hoodie with a camera." An ATV pulled up behind the camera-person. Gender indeterminate, gray hooded sweatshirt, ball cap, dark glasses. Just like O'Hare.

I said, "I see him."

"Her. On three. My count. One, two --"

And we were splitting up, Kandi going left, me right, then turning in toward the hooded figure. If we were wrong it would be embarrassing, but I could live with that. The camera-weirder turned and jumped on the back of the ATV, yelling, "Go, go!"

But I had been thinking that might happen and changed course to cut off the ATV before it could get on the bike path/access road that runs between the parking lot and the water. I shoved through the crowd and as the driver pulled the little vehicle up over the curb I stuck out an arm and clothes-lined him, a solid forearm just under the helmet. They both went flying off the back, the driver landing flat on his back, the other figure doing a neat back roll to come to her feet. I dove at the driver -- he was closer -- but found that I was held by about six guys, all saying things like. "Hey, man, be cool," "Calm down," and, "Hey, man, leave the lifeguard alone."

"No, no, you don't understand, they did it."

"Take it easy, pal." The good Samaritans didn't let go. "It's cool to take pictures." Three others held Kandi. It was useless. The driver got to his feet, dusted himself off, the photographer hadn't even lost her glasses and was now driving. He climbed on and they both waved cheerily as they drive away.

They gave us oxygen in the ambulance and took us to Hoag hospital in Newport where we were treated for cuts and abrasions and breathed into tubes so they could check our lungs. They bandaged my hands where I'd frozen them on the metal surrounding the window and my leg where the liquid had burned it. Since my hands were covered in bandages Kandi sort of held my forearm while they worked on my leg. It was comforting.

"I'm a little freaked. The next time I have some frozen shit cocktail tossed in my lap I'll be more prepared."

She looked deep into my eyes, and when Kandi does that with her magnificent hazel eyes it is really something. "I hope you didn't sustain any serious injuries."

Suddenly we were both laughing like loons, howling and holding on to each other, coughing and gagging and laughing. And crying. She gasped, "No serious injuries, right?"

"Doctor, I think I will need an exam." That started us laughing again. My throat was sore and I'm sure hers was, too, but it was good to laugh. Good to hold each other and laugh. The nurse looked concerned and offered us more oxygen.

The EMT who had driven us to the hospital came in and got our autographs, and the little girl across the hall had Kandi sign her cast. Then the doctor came back in, shooed the kid out and said, "Okay we're releasing you. Ms. Shaw, you're fine except for a few bruises. Out of curiosity, how did you get the one on your leg? It's older than the others."

"I study martial arts. My practice partner got carried away."

"Ah. I see. Mr. Macdonald, this prescription is for a cream that I want you to apply to the places that were exposed to the liquid. I must say, yours is a more interesting case. The first instance of frostnip I've treated here in Orange County."

"Yeah, it was really cold. Wait, frostnip? Not frostbite?" Kandi was choking back laughter.

"That's what its called. Not as severe. You should recover completely."

"Oh, good."

Chet wanted to come and get us at the hospital, but all things considered, it seemed better for him to stay in my house with the doors locked. The FBI dropped us off after we were bandaged. I was not surprised to find Tony G. waiting for us in my kitchen. He finished measuring out coffee, pushed the Brew button and just looked at us, shaking his head. Then he hugged Kandi.

We sat at my kitchen table looking out the windows at the channel, Tony with coffee, me with a Dos Equis Dark that was the only thing that was standing between me and a nervous breakdown, Kandi with a glass of white wine. Chet had his ever-present can of Mountain Dew. I was fashionably attired in jeans with one leg cut off where the nice folks had removed it so they could put a dressing on my frozen spot. Frostnip. At least Tony and Chet thought it was more serious. Kandi waved her glass in the direction of my leg. "Frostnip. That's what he's got."

Cracker showed up on his new skateboard. Of course he had seen the videos. I discovered my bottle was empty and got another out of the refrigerator, thankful that whoever had done the grocery shopping hadn't missed the essentials. "You first."

To my surprise, my cop friend nodded. "The metal canister was full of liquid nitrogen, which is why the ATV driver wore gloves. He opened the valve on the top and lobbed it into the vehicle."

"What about the car doors?"

"Chet, you want to take this one?" Tony added a tiny dollop of cream to his coffee and sipped.

Chet said, "Probably the girl in the hoodie."

"Cherri."

He nodded. "Yep. She's the most likely candidate. She had a gadget that captured the car's lock/unlock code. Once the canister goes in, she pushes the button again. The car locks, and you're trapped. It's harder now because some of the manufacturers have modified the system so that the code changes every time you push the button—but not impossible. Shoot, there's always a brute force attack. You just use a gadget that tries all trillion possible combinations one after another."

"That would take forever."

"Yeah, pretty long. Sometimes a whole second." Chet went on. "He tossed in the thermos, then she used the gadget to roll up the windows and lock the doors. They wouldn't open because she initiated a childproofing protocol. Not that hard."

Tony said, "They found the real lifeguard bound and gagged in the Men's Room closest to the pier. No harm except to his pride."

I said, "How come it got so cold?"

Once again, Chet answered, "Adiabatic cooling. The gas gets cold as it expands. And you have the frostnip to prove it." Everybody laughed.

"Well, that's what it is," I said. "Hey, anybody can get frostbite. This is special."

"Your turn," Tony said. "You told the FBI you didn't recognize the driver or the girl."

"Full helmet. Could have been male or female. The girl had on a hoodie, a ball cap, big dark glasses, and a bandanna over her lower face."

"But you think it's Cherri." Tony mused.

"She's my candidate, but there's no proof."

"What else, Mac?"

"That's it."

Tony frowned. "You have been known to withhold information when you think it necessary."

"Well, only when I had to."

"I believe that's what I said. What are your thoughts on this latest incident?"

"The videos have gone viral already. You are averaging almost a thousand hits an hour."

"Thanks, Chet. What videos?"

"Are you kidding? At least six people had cell phones capturing the whole thing. Four of them posted the videos before the cops showed up and took the phones. You're famous, again. Well, Kandi is."

"I am? She is?"

"Ahem, ah, most of the comments are variations on 'Great legs!' Or 'What a hottie!' They seem to be referring to her flying out of the car."

"How about the heroic T. R. Macdonald?"

"One post, from the bartender at Fred's that says she's glad you're okay because you need to pay your tab."

"That's an attempt at humor. I don't have a tab." They looked at me. "Really, I don't. Okay, show us the video."

He did and it was interesting. For a cell phone video the quality was good. The video started when the car was rocking on its springs. The windows were solid gray. Then the driver's-side window was pushed out. Kandi squeezed out and rolled to a sitting position. Her purse flew off into the crowd. The cameraman zoomed in on her legs so he missed the beginning of my exit. Kandi got to her feet. I dragged myself halfway out, she got her hands under my arms and pulled me the rest of the way, then we flopped on the pavement. She got up a second time and a young woman wearing a hoodie stepped out of the crowd and handed Kandi her purse.

"Here's a new post," Chet said. "Some woman wants to know where you got your shoes."

I watched the fumes dissipate, the back window explode, and the EMTs arrive. And I thought about what happened. Then I watched it again.

Kandi started cleaning out her purse. "You know that proves my belief that the vast majority of humans are basically decent. Some girl gave this back to me after it got kicked into the crowd."

"Yeah, well, the only part of the movie *Wall Street* that isn't true is where the good guy wins. Wait, hold on." I froze the picture of the girl. Hoodie with the hood up, baseball cap, dark glasses. "She's the one who got away on the ATV." Kandi looked at the screen on Chet's laptop, looked at me, and then at her purse.

"Nothing's missing."

"Let's see if anything has been added." I examined the purse carefully, found nothing suspicious, but then in the bottom, in a crease of the lining, I pulled out a tiny object, about the size of a grain of rice.

My Swiss Army knife has a tiny magnifying glass built in. It revealed a chip inside the tiny plastic cylinder. "They use gadgets like this to track pets, right?"

"Right," Chet took it and examined it closely. "Inserted subdermally it lets you find a lost dog or cat. It's time for Mr. Identification Microchip to meet Mr. Boot Heel." Chet picked up the chip.

"Wait! Cracker, how's the new plank?"

He was sitting on the floor in the corner, his back against the wall, long legs sticking out. He had a Sharpie and was carefully printing something on the bottom of his skateboard. "It rocks, man, totally and completely rocks." He quit printing and hugged the board to his chest. "There's no refunds, man, I, like, rode it, you know, they won't take it back."

"Hey, Cracker, I'm not going to take it away from you." He looked relieved but still uncertain. Like those lab rats Kandi told me about that sometimes get food and sometimes get shocked. "It's yours. Lord, man, you earned it."

"Uh, I know I didn't give you the change, but I figured it was payoff for, you know, pain and suffering, shit like that." He started digging in his back pocket.

"You earned it all and more. There is no change."

He relaxed a little. "Hey, check this out." On the board he had printed:

That corpse you planted last year in your garden. Has it begun to sprout?

He spun one of the wheels and stared at it thoughtfully. "Is that awesome or what?" he murmured. "Whoa!" He started sketching a skull next to the words.

"Cracker, I worry about you sometimes."

He capped the Sharpie, slipped it into his backpack. "Sound like my dad. I missed a free throw Saturday and he made me shoot a hundred of them in our driveway before I could go to bed. And there was this killer party I didn't get to go to." In one fluid motion he was on his feet, backpack slung over one shoulder, tugging up his jeans so only an inch of plaid boxer shorts was visible, skateboard in hand. "What?"

"Take the chip, skate over to the RV parking lot at Warner and PCH. Look for an RV waiting in line to exit and stick this to the bumper. If you can find it, pick one with out-of-state license plates."

He grinned, wide, wider, widest. "Oh, bro, you are so *evil*! I love it, man. He'll chase that thing all over."

"That, my young friend, is the idea."

We stuck a small piece of duct tape to the chip and Cracker was gone, the rhythmic, train-like clack-clack of his new board fading as he rode off down the sidewalk.

Except somehow I knew that it wouldn't work. And that was the point.

Chapter Sixteen

"Chet, I'm going to set up a video conference with Sly. I want you to monitor it. I want to get an idea of what he's planning now."

I set the stage for the video chat carefully, in the family room in front of the wall-mounted flat-screen with my .45 on the coffee table in front of me, the spare clip next to it. I wanted him to see it. Chet had added a camera to the wall above the TV and cabled the feed to my laptop.

Sly answered on the first ring. The screen showed him sitting in front of a blank gray wall, impossible to identify. It didn't matter; I wasn't interested in where he was at the moment, only where he would be. I thought I heard a bong-bong in the background, like a clock chiming the hour.

I said, "Okay, here's what I know and what I think."

"Oooh, cards on the table time. I like it."

"First a question. What happened to 'I have no further interest in you?'"

"What do you mean?"

"Liquid nitrogen tossed into my car while Kandi and I were at the beach."

"I am always honest and above-board. My employees love me for it. It's possible some of them got carried away."

"You wanted Kandi back; after your wife left you it became an obsession. So you figured she was attracted to heroic types, you wanted to rescue her, so you set up the cancelled ticket and stranded her at O'Hare."

"Believe it or not I told the truth. That was improvised. I wanted to see her, I read about the killings, hacked her laptop and saw that she was flying home. Then I just cancelled everything."

Out of his line of sight Chet's jaw dropped. He scribbled on a notepad and held up a note for me to see-- "He can't be that good! Connection already in place. He was spying on her already."

Another puzzle, but not one I cared about very much at the moment.

"So you could rescue her."

"You do it all the time!"

I chose to ignore that. "You didn't improvise the bit with my father. You needed me out of the way, so you created the grant that brought him to Huntington Beach and then sent the threatening notes to make sure I would be involved. The idea was that I'd stay here to help him. The only problem at that point was my father refused my help. You got worried about Bernard Sigmund --"

"He was dangerous! A psychopath! I - I think he was planning to kill her so he could take over the internship. You heard her talk about him. You know that."

"Sure he was. So you hired two killers to take him out permanently, and once that was done, why not eliminate the guy in Chicago? He wanted Kandi, too."

"He was a psychopath, too. He murdered his girlfriend! I tried to stop it!"

And did I say something like, "It takes one to know one?" I did not, exhibiting remarkable self-control.

Kandi took the notepad from Chet and wrote "sociopaths" on it. As far as I was concerned the distinction was academic, like all the professors who quibble about whether or not the stock market is a true chaotic system.

"But things got seriously out of hand. Your security guys shot up the McCarran airport to scare Kandi, but Barney and Betty thought it was for real and drove the Sano Pump truck into their car. Now they've decided I am not a bad person so they won't kill me. They want the person who hired them, namely you. And I don't think they want to decline the job and return your money. And there's the liquid nitrogen attack. You seemed to hint that they did it without your knowledge or approval."

"Cherri is sometimes hard to control."

"Yeah. But it wasn't her who broke into my dad's place, was it? You tried to pin it on her. I bet she'd like to know that."

"I told them to stop, really, well not in so many words, but I indicated that we were finished with this part of the operation. A good manager doesn't micromanage."

He looked around nervously. Wherever he was, he wasn't completely comfortable.

"What's wrong, Sly?"

"Nothing, nothing."

"Okay, don't tell me." Yeah I could tell him we'd seen the video of the guy drinking drain cleaner, but then he would know we'd hacked his phone and at this stage of the game there was no advantage in letting him know that.

He blurted. "One -- one of my employees seems to be ah, well, he seems to be missing. His apartment is untouched, but he failed to arrive at the office and no one knows where he is." He looked around again.

"Is he the one who ran over Cracker's skateboard?"

"Yes. Will you help me find him?"

"No. My guess is you won't find him. My guess is the Suberes have figured out you're the one who hired them."

"All right, all right. I understand. We won't worry about him. Please, I need your help. Yes, I'm afraid they have identified me." He gave up on his employee pretty quickly. "Please. Protect me from the Suberes. I'll pay you."

"A lot of other people are looking for them. That should be enough."

"I know, and that was really smart, getting that fingerprint, you're really good, even better than I thought, but it won't be enough and you know it. They'll never find those two."

"My advice is hire some really good protection, somebody like Blackwater, and have them cover you while you take a vacation. I know you own Anybody Personal Security. Forget them. If those clowns go up against the Suberes, they'll end up like your missing employee. Make it a long vacation, something like backpacking along the scenic shores of the Amazon."

"You know you won't let them kill me. You don't have it in you."

You know the next-to-worst thing about getting mentioned in blogs and talked about in the press? Everybody thinks that tiny bit of adulterated, slanted information is true and they think they understand you. And the worst thing is sometimes they're right.

"Okay, here's what I can do. If I find Barney and Betty I'll do my best to talk them out of killing you."

"I'll gladly pay the other half of the money. Tell them that. Tell them I'll pay. I always honor debts."

"In return we never see or hear from you again. No setting Kandi up to be rescued. No crazy limos shooting at us. Nothing. No contact whatsoever. You give it up, Sly, for real."

His face changed.

"T. R., you know I can't do that. She loves me. It's time for you to understand that and to give her up. She, she, loves me and she doesn't know how to tell you, so I wanted to help. I'm sorry, I know this must be really hard for you."

Then we went off-script and things went downhill. Kandi strolled in and sat on my lap, giving me a warm, comfortable lap full of beautiful woman. A lesser man than I might have forgotten about the reason behind the call. She said, "Sly, you need to face reality. I don't love you, truly, I don't. You need to seek professional help. This obsession is not healthy. We have talked about this on several occasions." Her voice was calm, professional. Of course, when your therapist is sitting on some guy's lap it sort of detracts from the effectiveness. But she was detached and professional, and I think that's what sent him over the edge.

He said, "Kandi, oh, Kandi. I am so sorry I got you into this." So far, so good.

"My name is Mary Shaw. I am completing a doctoral program at the University of California, Los Angeles. As part of that program I went to the Usher Clinic in Chicago." She took a deep breath. "Sly, it's called erotomania and it can be treated. It's when one person believes another is in love with them. You have an erotomanic fixation on me. You need help; I want you to get help. Please."

He said, "I understand." Okay, good, maybe this would work after all. I felt a surge of hope. Boy, I can be dumb sometimes.

"I'm glad, Sly, really. That is the first step. I'll text you some names, people who can help you."

"He's threatening your family, isn't he? That's why you're with him." I guess my jaw dropped. "Macdonald, I withdraw my request for you to help me with the Suberes."

Kandi said, "Sly, no."

"Don't worry, my beautiful one."

"He's not threatening my family! Sly, listen to what I'm saying."

"He's making you say that. I see it now. Don't worry, darling, I'll --"

"Do you remember our conversations? How I said your mind, your need for love, is causing you to see things that aren't there?"

"No! No, it's not true. You better tell me the truth, you better tell me right this instant or, or there will be consequences. Say you love me and I will save you. Say it or there will be consequences, serious consequences."

"I left you in O'Hare. I ran! How about that?"

"Well, you were afraid of him and --" His voice trailed off.

"How about this?" She grabbed my shoulders and kissed me, and the kiss, accompanied her hand up under my shirt, was everything I had ever wanted, and more. "Sly, I can't say it's over, because it never was. Get help."

He got it. He understood at last.

His face, his face, it was like nothing I have ever seen. His mouth dropped open and he scoured at his cheeks with his nails, drawing blood. He didn't cry. He swallowed convulsively three or four times, maybe trying to speak. I was stunned, utterly stunned, but my lovely Kandi had been in serious counseling situations and had seen it all before. She was remorseless. "Sly, this is a good thing. You are starting to face reality; good for you. I know it's painful, truly I do, but this is good. The next step is for you to find professional help. Like I said, I will text you some names, any of them will be able to guide you through this and at the other end you will be better, please believe me. You have made the first step. And, Sly, I want you to know that --"

I whispered, "Don't say you'll always be friends."

Too late. "We will always be friends. Erotomania can be treated, really, it's like --" He smiled. He wiped the blood from his cheeks and blood was smeared on his teeth, and he smiled and smiled and it was terrible to see.

"I understand," he said softly. "I understand. I've been a fool, a fool to allow you to do this to me. How could you? How could you?" He screamed and broke the connection.

"-- stalking. Erotomania is like stalking." I looked at her. She said, "Well, I was going to phrase it differently." She took a deep breath. "That is without a doubt the most unprofessional thing I have ever done."

"It needed to be done."

"All at once I wasn't his therapist, I was a woman, a woman he was stalking, and vulnerable despite everything either of us could do. It was terrifying. And Kandi came out. The persona I created for difficult situations told him."

"Told him the truth."

I was moving before the screen reverted to my security cameras, unceremoniously dumping Kandi off my lap, yelling for Chet. "Chet, did you get it? Where is he, did you get a location?"

The cowboy came in from the kitchen and said, "Do you know that, right now, over two hundred thousand people are being stalked?"

"Why, no, I didn't know that. Location?"

"He's good, but this ol' cowpoke's better. I can't give you an address, but he's close."

"Define 'close.'"

"Best ping was from the cell tower south on PCH. He's in the neighborhood."

"Mac, what's wrong? He understands. I believe he had a real breakthrough." Kandi put her arms around me from behind and rested her chin in my shoulder. "Look, I get this stuff, okay? Sly may be miserable right now, but he will be all right after he reads my text, if he gets under the care of any of those names. And remember, he's not violent. He's willing to hire people to commit violent acts but he's cut off from them and on the run from the Suberes. If anything, we need to protect him from them."

"He wasn't surprised to see you. When you walked in he didn't look surprised. How did he know?" I had an idea, one I didn't like much. "Give me your purse."

"What?"

"Your purse, quick." Kandi had her phone out and was tapping the screen. "Do not send that text!"

She turned around to face me. "I don't like orders. Repeat: I don't like orders. I promised to send him the names."

"Look this is no time to --"

"And I already sent it."

"Chet, can it be called back?"

"The text? Well, this soon after sending, maybe."

"Do it."

"Stop! Stop this, this instant!" She paused, glaring. "My God, I sounded like my mother." She took a breath. "Chet, do not call back my text." He looked acutely uncomfortable, looking at her, at me, and at his Gameboy on the table. "Mac, I know what I am doing. And I will not take orders, not from you or anyone, unless I agree to it. I know it's a parent thing and I'm working on it but you need to understand." We looked at each other for a long moment. "I can handle Sly. I will get him the help he needs."

"Kandi, listen to me. Remember your patient, the cannibal?"

"Of course, and I see where you are going with this and I do not appreciate it. There are no parallels. And I might as well tell you that I've called your father and he's agreed to see me this afternoon. I feel a need to at least be acquainted with him."

"I'll –"

"No. Better if you're not there."

"Okay but the cannibal and Sly are both nuts. The difference is that Sly has resources the other guy didn't. He's got that security company."

Kandi said, "Why won't you understand? I know what I'm doing."

Kandi was right. I did need to understand, only I was focused and oblivious to anything else going on. She snatched her purse off the table and ran out the front door. A moment later I heard the sound of the limo starting up.

"What just happened?"

"Chet, I just made a mistake, maybe a serious one."

"Talk to me, pard."

"Sly's crazy, I mean really around the bend, and she doesn't understand. He will try to hurt, maybe kill her."

"I thought he loved her."

"He did, maybe he still does in some way, but she rejected him and that love turned to hate. Oh, boy, I should have kept her here, should have tied her up, something, I don't know what."

"Uh, pard, my cousin is pretty tough. You might have a hard time tying her up."

He was right. But I was bigger. And I had a sawed-off pool cue. Somehow I couldn't see myself saying, "Kandi, I love you and want to protect you so I have to hit you over the head." No, wouldn't work.

"And have you considered that she might be right? She has a lot of experience. Maybe she can handle him."

"She may be willing to bet her life on it, but I'm not. Sly's phone, can you find it now?"

"I can get close."

"Do it. I mean, please, try to find him. Thank you." See? I'm trainable.

"Sure. But how big a threat can he be? I mean, those senior citizen killers, the Suberes, they're after him, right?"

"Which means he has nothing to lose." Chet's eyes widened, but even as they did he was working at his laptop. "I'm afraid this is his endgame."

We watched the video of Sly again. There was nothing new. "Chet, can you isolate the background noise? Cut out what he says?"

"Sure."

So we listened to that. It was crowd noise, probably a bar. Stereo blaring, people yelling drink orders for Red Bull with a shot, beer, wine, and tequila. Nobody yelled, "Hey, we're having a great time here at this place," followed by the name of the establishment.

Despite Chet's best efforts we got no leads on either of them all night. Around three a.m. I took the Chevy out and cruised – it was breezy with the missing windows, but I didn't want to have the car in the shop. I looked for the hotel limo Kandi was driving, I looked for Sly, I looked for anybody following me that I could trap and beat up. I went home and sat in the family room and made some notes; sometimes that helps when I'm stuck, but nothing jumped out at me. I wrote Sly in big letters, underlined it, circled it, and tried to think where he might be. There was hope that Barney and Betty had found him. I could think that, but is it something I really wanted to happen to him?

I stretched out on the couch and dozed for a while. Sometimes that helps when I'm trying to figure things out. When I woke up the sun was peeking over Santiago

Peak, the taller of the two Saddleback Mountain. I took out my cell phone and looked at it. Just for laughs I called Kandi. Straight to voicemail. I sent a text.

> Kandi I'm sorry I didn't mean it please come back S is dangerous he wants to hurt U

A few minutes later I sent another one.

> Please.

Where could she have gone? And why? I called my dad's and got no answer, not even an offer to record a message.

I got a text from Sly.

> U think I can't find her? I won't have to.

Perfect. I declined to answer.

She'd want to help Sly; didn't matter that he wanted her help about as much as a nice glass of Draino. I really wished I would quit thinking about that. I called Tony and checked on the progress they were making toward finding the Suberes. It didn't take long because there was none. I asked him to put out a BOLO -- Be On the Look Out -- on Sly and he said I'd been watching too much TV but it was impressive that I knew what the letters stood for. I couldn't convince him that Sly was dangerous any more than I could Kandi, but I had seen Sly's face and I knew. I brewed some coffee and went to sit in the living room, but I wanted to be outside, so I went and sat in my Whaler and felt sorry for myself.

Out over the ocean a biplane trundled by towing a banner that said Surf Contest Tomorrow. The surf contest. She could blend in with the crowds. No, that's close but not right. Mike. She and my father had a common bond -- they both thought I was a jerk. I called him again with the same results. Chet came out and stood on the dock.

I showed Chet the text from Sly. "Why is he so sure he knows where Kandi will be? Wait, you gave Kandi a new cell phone, right?"

"Yep."

"Same number?"

"Yep. Told her to change it but she can be stubborn."

"Can you get in and look at her messages? Texts."

"Sure."

And we saw it. The most recent text thread was between me and Kandi.

> Mac, I know you are concerned, but I have experience in this area and will take precautions.

Followed by a reply.

> I know you have talked to my dad and I think it helped. Can you give him a ride to the contest? It's by the pier on Main Street.

"But I never got that text."

"Yeah, he's into your phone. We better switch you to another."

"He's directing her to the surf contest."

Chet said, "Okay, I get it. But she'll be hard, impossible, to find, like one steer in a stampede."

"Yeah. I think she'll try to let him find her at the surfing contest. That starts tomorrow morning so we have a little time to locate him, or the Suberes, or -- What? I've seen that look before."

"The bikini contest."

"I thought they banned that after the riot."

"Where have you been, Pard? They got two sponsorships and hired mucho extra security. It's tonight. Starts at sunset."

Right on cue another biplane chugged overhead. Its banner read, "Bikini Contest Tonight!"

"Perfect. I wonder. I wonder how he expects to find her among thousands of people. The one thing we can't do is start a panic. People could get trampled. And I wish you hadn't said 'stampede'." I got up and stepped onto the dock, which almost caused Chet to lose his balance when it rocked from side to side.

So Kandi and my father were both somewhere out of touch; Sly was maybe planning something once the crowd built up; and the Suberes were ready to end their assignment from him, end it permanently. The Bikini Contest kicked off at 8:00 pm. I needed to be downtown an hour or so ahead of that.

"Chet, try to nail down Sly's location if and when he turns his phone on."

"He's too savvy for that."

"Yeah. Look, I need to do something, so I'll be gone an hour, maybe a little more. When I get back we'll pick up Cracker and the others and finalize the plan."

"Mac, tell me you're not going off on your own again."

"No. No, not this time."

I stopped at the U-Need-It Minimart at the gas station on Pacific Coast Highway, made my purchase and drove north.

"I'm not much for speeches, so I thought we might just talk."

I stood on the hillside overlooking the Long Beach Harbor, in front of her grave and waited for inspiration. It never came.

Finally, I said, "Diana, I know why you haven't had anything to say lately. You want me to figure it out. I guess I have. I'm sorry, more than I can say. But --" Here I needed a deep breath. "I'm not responsible. I always knew that, you know, like Mary would say, on an intellectual level, but deep down, no, I didn't get it. And other people well, they thought I should have done better. Maybe so. But I get it at last. And you know what? It still hurts that you're gone. But that's okay. I can live with that. You said I was never very sentimental and I guess you're right. I'm, uh, in kind of a bad spot and may not get a chance to do this later so, hey, here's a sappy gesture. And I, I probably should have brought you some notebook paper, too."

I ran out of words. So I put the box of brand-new Bic pens on her headstone and stood for a moment, my heart full.

Driving south, I punched up my playlist, told it to be random and it gave me AC/DC. Here we go.

Rock and roll damnation.

Part Two: Contents Under Pressure

No man chooses evil because it is evil.
He mistakes it for happiness.
                    - Mary Wollstonecraft

I have a plan.
                    - T. R. Macdonald

Dec. 12, '34

Dear Diary,

Oh, Sweet Lord, how far I have fallen from Your Grace and I don't know what to do. I have committed a Sin, one that I repent of most heartily, Lord.

Clyde says Willeford knows a doctor in Tijuana, but I cannot do that. I cannot go home. I know what Grandfather Lamentations would say and Mother would take me in, but her face, oh, Lord I cannot bear to think what would be in her poor tired eyes. And she was so sick the last time I heard from her. I don't know what to do.

Chapter Seventeen

I drove home, told Chet we needed some B&E skills and I knew just the person.

In the Chevy on the way to pick up Cracker, Chet and I watched various video feeds on his laptop as the crowds grew around the pier.

Then, with Cracker in the back seat, excited at being involved in "a case" it was back to my place to find Snake and Cheryl waiting.

As we walked up the driveway, Chet balancing his laptop on one arm and typing with the other, he said, "Mac, you asked me to examine Sly's recent purchases."

"Yeah. Nothing suspicious, right?"

"Right. But that woman from his office, Cherri, bought a rifle and registered it. Small caliber, a .223. She passed the background check, no problem." That stopped me. A rifle? Sly's plans were usually complex, devious and to be perfectly honest, non-lethal. Maybe the game had changed. "And, wait, uh-oh, she bought a scope to go with it." He looked up at me.

"Chet, he's got another Identification Microchip on Kandi. So he can follow her. Tell me about the gizmo that will show him where she is."

"A chip? How on earth did you figure that?"

"It makes sense. He had Cherri plant one in her purse after the attack on the beach. He knew we'd find it and get rid of it. So, he's probably got another one on her somehow. Maybe when we were at Hoag being treated. It doesn't matter how he did it; I'm certain it's there. That's the only way he can be sure he'll find her. So, how will he read the signal?"

"Well, there are different kinds. The Power Tracker II looks kind of like an oversized remote control with a bigger screen."

"Does it give off a signal?"

"The Tracker? Um, yes, weak, but there's a signal, yes. Why?"

"Because I think he's up in the clock tower overlooking Main Street with a rifle and the tracker. I heard it chime on the video chat. If I can pick up a signal from his tracker I'll know for sure. This is his endgame. His love for Kandi has turned to hate and he wants to kill her." Great, now I sound like her all the time. "He also knows about Barney and Betty, so he figures, correctly, that he's got nothing to lose. At least she's not going to be there." But there was a thought in the back of my head, trying to force its way to the front. Something about the video chat.

"That's a big jump, but if you're right . . . Oh, pard, this is bad."

"But wait, there's more. If he can't find Kandi either with the tracker or by getting lucky and seeing her, I think he'll just open fire, kill as many as he can. People will get shot, be trampled, hell, die of heart attacks like Pete."

Once again we were gathered in my kitchen. "Cracker, can you get me into that tower?"

"Sure, bro, no prob. We need to go at night, but not too late. We need all the bars on Main Street to be full, and use the crowds for cover. There's this closet at the back of Perq's next to the men's and in it there's a trap door in the ceiling that leads up to a crawl space. You go along that to a ventilation shaft that runs up to the top of the clock tower. You'll come in the front; I'll come in from the alley in back."

"Now. Tonight."

Chet and Snake looked at each other. Snake said, "You think Sly's going to be up there with a rifle?"

Cracker shook his head. "You want to cowboy it -- just crash in. It won't work, man, no way. You'll attract attention, and Perq's hires some pretty tough bouncers."

"Okay, I go quiet. But you cannot come with me."

"I thought you might say that." He handed me a can that looked like it held hairspray. "Freon. Back in the day I got some use out of this stuff. Spray this in and it disrupts the lock. Works on older locks like the ones in Perq's. A good spray and a solid whap with a hammer and it opens."

Oh, boy, decision time. Calling the cops was a good idea -- I have never believed those TV shows where the good guy doesn't call for help because, "This is between me and him." Nuts. Something I realized when I visited Diana's grave was how much

I cared about Kandi. I didn't care about Sly. Oh, sure pounding his face would be great fun, but not if it meant Kandi got hurt.

On the other hand, if I called them they would surely capture or kill Sly. He was in the tower or would be, but he was trapped up there, probably barricaded since he'd had all night. How many people could he kill before the cops got him? If I called it in could they convince the mob to evacuate without causing a panic? There were close to a hundred thousand people in the downtown neighborhood. Would they clear the area in an orderly fashion? And what would Sly do when he saw the evacuation starting?

He knew me. He hated me, but I was a familiar face. I had to try.

As this and other silly questions went through my mind I was pulling on boots and a dark sweatshirt. I checked the loads in the .45 and slipped it into the back of my jeans. The pool cue handle went up my sleeve. I considered my sawed-off shotgun and almost decided against it, then I checked the safety and carefully loaded it into my backpack. Then I stopped. Outside I could hear laughter as a group of kids rode by on their beach cruisers, the bikes decorated with flags and red-white-and-blue ribbons no doubt left over from the last Fourth of July. They were on their way downtown where they would lock their bikes to a rack and mingle with thousands of other people out for beer and bikinis. When I checked my monitors they showed the crowd swelling so it filled the intersection of Pacific Coast Highway and Main Street, pressing in around the temporary stage set up in front of Duke's, where the Plunge had been in the Thirties.

"All right, listen, I'm going downtown. The contest starts at 8:00 p.m. If I haven't stopped Sly by 7:30, call Tony, tell him everything."

"You're going after him by yourself? Mac, that's nuts. Why?" Snake sounded more disappointed than angry.

"I know why. I didn't mean to eavesdrop, really, but I heard what Mary asked and what you said you'd do." Chet was looking down at his boots, couldn't meet my eyes

"What? What? Hello, Walter here. Remember me?"

Chet said, "Keep Staney alive. Mac promised Mary he wouldn't kill Sly."

Before Snake could speak—I had a pretty good idea of what he'd say—I said, "You, of all people, know the police. If Sly makes one false move they will take him down. They have to, they can't risk a crowd panic." Slowly, reluctantly, Snake nodded.

Chet put his hand on my arm. "What do you need?"

"I need Kandi to be here, safe. And my father. And you and …" My voice trailed off. The list of people I cared about was long, in fact, it didn't have an end. I said, "Dirty Harry." Chet looked at me oddly. Snake frowned. "The school bus full of kids." Snake sucked in a breath. He got it.

Chet stared as I unloaded the weapons. Pistol, extra clip, shotgun and box of shells went back on the table. He said, "Pard, you sure? You know Sly will have weapons."

"Well, hell, I'll just have to take them away."

Pacific Coast Highway was blocked off from Goldenwest in the north to Brookhurst in the south. There would be checkpoints for pedestrians as well as vehicles. Police would allow only residents with ID to drive into the area.

There was no parking within a mile of the event so I had Chet drop me off at Ninth Street and Orange.

Cheryl said, "Be sensible. Let's go back and get your weapons. Or at least take my Glock." She held it out.

"I promised. I told Kandi I'd keep him alive."

Ten minutes later I strolled into Perq's, picked up an empty mug from a corner of the long wooden bar and wandered toward the rear, and the men's room, and the closet. All at once I could hear an imaginary conversation. "So, how did he die?" "He walked into a bar with a loaded shotgun taped to his spine, somebody clapped him on the back and blew his butt off." The brain does funny things when you're under stress. But I was glad I'd left the guns at home.

Of all things, Chet had given me an old transistor radio and an earplug. He said to twist the dial until I heard a squeal; that would be the transmission from the hard drive in the Power Tracker, broadcasting on the am band.

Sly almost fooled me, again. Then I remembered the microchip in Kandi's purse, the one I was supposed to find. I was working on that thought, hesitating because once I was in the ventilator shaft there was no turning back, when someone tapped me on the shoulder.

Barney, dapper in a red Kanvas by Katin sweatshirt and matching baseball cap, smiled benignly. "We'll take it from here."

Betty, wearing an identical sweatshirt and cap, came up on my other side. "But we thank you for your help. Our conventional methods failed to identify our client."

"I led you to him."

"Yes, but it will work to your benefit. He does want to eliminate the young woman you are so attached to. And you as well." She smiled. "Young love. You children deserve happiness."

"But --"

"We have very little time." She opened her purse and showed me a bomb. Yeah, that's right, a bomb and I knew what it was immediately. I think it was the timer with red numbers currently all reading zero that gave it away.

"You'll kill so many people, and that's what I am trying to prevent."

"Far fewer casualties than if he starts shooting into a crowd. We believe he has fortified the floor of the clock tower, so we must resort to this. Otherwise, if we could get to him, poor Mr. Staney would have an attack of remorse and shoot himself." Barney smiled. It was as if he was saying, "I'm going to bingo tonight at the Senior Center."

"But --" I changed my mind. "This is a bad idea. Let me deal with him."

"No, no. You see, we can detonate this and get away. You would undoubtedly be captured and your life ruined. Remember, we have been doing this for a long time."

A group of laughing hotties all wearing cut-offs and bikini tops squeezed by us, trailing a mingled scent composed of equal parts Budweiser and Bain de Soleil. "Do me a favor. Try to talk to him before you trigger the bomb."

Betty said, "Why? We want to kill him. He is not a nice person."

Barney chimed in, "Not a nice person at all. We don't like him."

"Yes, but you don't like murdering innocent bystanders. If he surrenders, you can always kill him later."

"He's not going to give up."

Betty said, "And we have things to do."

Her husband chimed in, "That's right. Our godson has a soccer game."

Her lined face lit up. "A championship!"

"Well, sure, you're probably right, but why not try it? You've got the bomb and he's trapped. What's a few minutes trying to talk?"

"And you agree he is in the clock tower?"

"I heard the chime. On a video call from him I heard it in the background." I turned to go.

"Too easy," Barney said. "Young man, I am afraid we need some proof that we are not stepping into a trap of some kind. We know you have close relations with the local police."

"Can't help you, and time is running out. If you don't believe me, just leave and let me deal with him like I want to."

"Proof." She nudged me with her purse. The explosives inside made it heavy.

"Wait, okay, yeah. Kandi is bringing my father down to the bikini contest. I want to avoid a shoot-out, and if the cops corner you that's what will happen. I wouldn't put them at risk."

She said, "I want to believe you, but I just can't."

"How about this?" I opened my phone and showed them the text that Sly sent, pretending to be me.

The gray-haired assassins did that "look at each other and communicate" thing and she nodded. "Now we believe you. With your father in the crowd, with his disability, you cannot afford a panic. All right, we'll talk first if it will make you feel better."

He said, "If it works, we'll kill him later. After the soccer game. But it won't work."

Betty closed her purse. I liked that because I couldn't see the bomb anymore. "All right. But if his team wins there will be another game. And that will make it very late."

He clucked his tongue. "You're right. Can we kill him tomorrow?"

"No, it will have to be next week if we don't do it tonight. You know I hate putting things off."

Barney said, "Young man, we can kill him later tonight if it would help. But, for your purposes, he needs to be away from the crowd."

I said, "I understand."

Betty lifted her glasses up and looked at her watch. "We will go up and see what we can do." She turned to Barney. "Maybe he left a way in and we can slip the bomb in. When he tries to get away we can shoot him."

I was moving before they had started for the ventilator shaft.

Because I had finally gotten it. He wasn't up there at all. He was across the street, somewhere above the Mexican restaurant. The chime was another false lead.

Chapter Eighteen

I found Sly, all right, and it was just about as I expected. Actually, it could have been worse. Across the street from the clock tower there's another restaurant with a crawl space above the drop ceiling. I'd had Chet pull blueprints for as many buildings as possible and this one also had a permit for renovation. And I remembered the tracking chip I was meant to find. Sly meant for me to locate him. The freon worked as advertised and got me through the lock and into the closet-like room. I closed the metal door behind me and was in a small room with an electrical panel on one wall and a ladder bolted to the wall opposite the door. The ladder led to a closed trapdoor with an unlocked padlock dangling from a metal loop. The only thing missing was a note saying, "This way." There was no hope of sneaking up on him. If he wanted to he could blow my head off as soon as I stuck it up out of the trap, or, if he wanted to be quiet, he could just bash my head in, like that bar game called Whack-a-Mole where a cute, furry little animal sticks his head up and you smack him with a wooden mallet. I climbed up anyway. The crawl space led to a larger area, one with almost enough room to stand up in.

This attic extended over the restaurant and at least two of the shops next to it on the ground level. Dim light from the street filtered in from a row of small, dusty windows. One of the glass panes had been removed. Below us, the afternoon bar crowd was whooping it up, listening to a really awful DJ and loving it. I couldn't quite stand straight, but she could. Cherri was leaning against the wall. Next to her Sly was lying on the floor like a sausage in a casing. He was wrapped in clear plastic from toe to chin, held by bungee cords and plastic ties around his wrists and ankles. She had a rifle in one hand and a one-gallon food storage bag in the other. Naturally, the rifle was pointed at me.

She smiled, all happy like a puppy with a stick. "See, Mac, I got him for you."

"You've also got the business end of a .223 pointed at me. How about we talk?."

She scrunched her face into a truly nasty snarl. "I know what it means when your Significant Other says, 'We need to talk.' It's never good, it's never, "Let's have gorilla sex.'"

I murmured, "Chocolate-covered strawberries."

She smiled. "What? I know what you're going to say before you say it. We think alike." She nodded. "That's how I was able to interpret your messages. I got him for you."

"Yes, yes, you sure did. And that's good but we need to let the po- other people take it from here." The rifle barrel swung back and forth between me, Sly, and some unknown target that only she could see. I took a step forward. Sly was on her right, so, assuming I could get close enough I'd have to slap the rifle aside with my left hand. I told myself that was good because she wouldn't be expecting it. I almost believed it. Then she made up her mind.

"Okay, turn around, Mac my love."

I took a deep breath. "No."

She frowned. "That makes me *so* sad. I know you love me, but all this stuff, these other people, keep getting in the way. Okay, don't turn around. I got him for you, I tricked him when he loved me and I used to love him, but now I love you and love is *good,* it is. Caring is good. The bitch Kandi says so. Now I have to shoot him. You know what he was going to do."

"Tell me."

She pointed it at him. "This rifle. He made me buy it. I knew I loved you by then, but I had to do it or he would have been suspicious. That's how I got him for you. Love is worth fighting for."

"And the text from you sent Kandi and my dad down to Main Street."

"You believe love is worth fighting for, don't you?"

"Yes, I do, but not like this. What about the text you sent?"

"Sly thought it was for him. They get in trouble and he shows up and rescues her. And I take the blame! After everything I did for him, I take the blame! Everyone will think I'm crazy! You know better."

Well, yes, Cherri, they'll think that because you are, but I didn't say that. Self-preservation over honesty. So I stayed quiet.

She scrunched her face again and said. "This is so messed up! But I can fix it."

Keep her talking, right? "What do you mean?"

"Sly loves Kandi-the-Bitch, so I tried to be like her for him. I even took a psychology class at Orange Coast College." I restrained myself, in the interest of continued life, and said nothing. "Then I realized that was crazy." More restraint on my part.

"Cherri, that's great. You're doing better all the time. Real progress." Now if she'd only quit pointing the loaded rifle at me.

"Because it was you all along. I had to be like her for you – not for him."

I gaped at her. "What?"

She kicked Sly without taking her eyes off me. "You have to turn around now or I'll have to shoot you in the leg. I love you, darling, but I'll do it."

Well, I couldn't expect the bit about saying "no" to work every time. Sometimes you have to do what people expect so you can keep them thinking they're in control. I turned around. When she got close, I whirled and tried to knock the rifle out of her hands. Except she wasn't there and as I turned she stepped up and hit me, three hard shots to the body, pop-pop-pop, left-handed and I decided I never wanted to feel a right-hand pop.

I went to my knees, seeing spots, knowing I couldn't let myself pass out. She moved in back of me so she could put her foot in my back and kick me down on my face before slipping plastic flexi-cuffs around my wrists, saying over and over, "I'm sorry, I'm sorry. It will be all right. I'm sorry."

"You don't have to do this, you know that, right?" She finished with the plastic cuff and stepped around in front of me. I struggled to my feet. It's harder than it looks when your hands are tied behind you.

She shrugged. "Yes, darling, but I want to do it. I've had it with feeling like shit. I love you and you are going to see that and love me back, or else."

"Cherri, uh, tell me, what exactly is it that you're going to do?"

"I'm sorry, my love, but I know you will understand. We will be together."

"You can't possibly think this will make you feel better."

"Think it will make me feel better? I *know* it will. Hell, just thinking about it makes me feel better already. The only way it would be any better would be if the bitch herself was here." The rifle was lying comfortably in the crook of her arm, casual, but always pointed in my direction. "Pathetic, isn't it? Sly loves Kandi and I loved him. His love turned to hate, I made sure that happened, but now he doesn't have it in him to kill the bitch. I loved him and then he didn't love me back, so now I hate him. I am so glad you found me and sent the messages. You saved my life, you know that?"

"So you're going to kill him."

"Well, of course I'm going to kill him. We can't be together until they're both out of the way, you know that. I know you'd do it, but I'll do it for you. So I'm going to shoot him. Trust me, this fool is better off dead. And no, there won't be any stupid TV thing where I leave him with a canister of poison gas or a hungry alligator so he can escape. No, I put a bullet in his head. Like this --" and she held the barrel next to his temple. Eyes wide, shaking his head frantically, he tried to squirm away, not that it would have done him any good, but I suppose it was instinctual. Anyway, he scooted around the attic and she laughed and followed him with the rifle, teasing, letting him get a few feet away, then closing in. I tested the plastic tie and felt a little give, not enough to matter. But she noticed and came over and checked it. Sly huddled in the corner where he had squirmed and closed his eyes. I didn't blame him; I felt like closing mine, too. Cherri looked at the plastic tie closely, then jerked on it, hard, to make sure I hadn't somehow freed myself.

"Well, now what?"

"Oh, honey, I know this is hard for you. Let's see, I'll do him. Then I'll find the bitch and deal with her. She left you! I never would have stayed in Las Vegas, not me. I accept the violence in your life; in fact I embrace it, but not her, oh, no. She hurt you and she deserves to die just for that." She actually licked her lips at the prospect.

"Then we can be together, okay? You and me. You and me against the world." She looked closely at me. "That's the way it was meant to be."

"If you kill them we can't be together. You know that."

"Blaze of glory. No turning back now. Blaze of glory."

I didn't like the sound of that.

For a moment she looked confused. "No, that was the old plan. Dipshit here," she glared at Sly, "lost track of her. So there's a new plan." She held up the food storage bag. "I put this over dipshit's head and watch him turn blue and croak. Maybe I shoot him a little bit first. Then --" She kicked over a Mason jar full of liquid. The small space filled with the hot smell of gasoline. "Then there's a terrible accident. There's a fire, and people are getting shot, the crowd panics, people get trampled. Bummer, man." The restaurant below us was filled to Fire Department capacity with happy folks getting ready to start the weekend with a lot of beer, food, and a view of the bikini contest. With a fire in the attic they had no chance.

And I had thoughtfully arranged for the only people who might help to be across the street looking for somebody who wasn't there. And they had their own bomb. I love it when a plan comes together. In the corner, a tiny pair of beady eyes above a twitching nose studied me. I smelled like food, and I wasn't moving around. Then Cherri moved and the rat hunkered down and crept across the floor, dragging its belly. Then it vanished down a hole, slipping under the floorboards.

All at once the tracker on the floor next to her beeped. Her eyes lit up and she said, "Well, well, the bitch is close. Ha ha. The bitch is back. I like that. Let's just wait until I shoot her a little bit and then you can watch while the crowd tramples her. Hell, we might even get away with this."

"Cherri, listen, untie me and we can make this all right. Truly." I swallowed. "Darling, really, it will be okay." And I'll visit you wherever you are locked up, on Christmas and all major holidays. Maybe.

"Dipshit's business, which I started by the way, handy, isn't it? I have new identities waiting. That was in case you really did love me, we could escape, okay? Otherwise, blaze of glory." That didn't make a lot of sense, except I understood the "blaze of glory" part.

"Cherri, I, wait, we go out --"

"Together. Blaze of glory. Beautiful."

"And if I don't love you --"

"I have been disappointed before, okay? I have a back-up."

Let's see. Crack-brained Cherri is going to put a plastic bag over Sly's head and watch him turn blue and croak, then shoot him and then me, that's after she shoots Kandi, or, if she can't find her real target, just open up on the packed crowd of drunk bikini fans and cause a panic. After that she sets the restaurant on fire to cover her escape. And somewhere in there Barney and Betty have a bomb of undetermined size that they might detonate because they're crazy, too.

Never think things can't get worse.

"Hey, look, oh, sorry, you're all tied up." She giggled and pointed out the window. "Some old guy is gimping along on crutches. Hey, guess what? It's your dad! Wow, isn't that great? Oh, wait, when the crowd panics and runs he'll have a hard time on those sticks, won't he? No handicapped access during a stampede." Another giggle. You know how you read about villains who laugh insanely? Well, it's real and it's not a sound I ever want to hear again. It was like ice water dumped directly into my stomach. It was horrible. In my head I could hear Mary, saying, "The delusional live in worlds of their own making. If they believe some famous person loves them and is sending coded messages in press conferences, telling them it's not true won't help."

"Look, there's a guy in a cowboy hat, and he's with a short guy with a beard! Your friends are here. You know, I don't really have anything against them, except that they will take up your time. Anyway, if they get trampled that's too bad."

"Cherri, listen, this is the truth. Your quarrel is with Sly and me. You don't need to make this any worse."

"I think I liked you better down on the floor. Sit down, my love. Sit down or fall down when I shoot you." She pointed the rifle at my knee. I sat down. Call me chicken. She came over and squatted in front of me, stopping on the way to kick Sly in the ribs. "Make this any worse,'" she mused, stroking her cheek with the rifle barrel. She wasn't pointing the gun at me. Maybe I could lunge forward and bite her. "Hmm. Do you know how many hours I have spent thinking about this moment? You cannot imagine. No one knows me. Actually, I do need to make it worse, or, for me, better. I would rather be remembered for horror and carnage than not be remembered at all." She seemed to alternate between planning to escape and going out in a blaze of glory.

What do you say to that? "I'm going to stop you."

She closed her eyes and rubbed her cheek along the barrel. I thought about biting her again and to be honest it was looking like my best option. Maybe I could hit a vein or something and she'd bleed out before she started the fire. Then she pushed the rifle barrel into my ear. "Say you love me."

Where I come from -- Wall Street -- puts a great value on honesty and full disclosure. That's the truth. They do because the government holds a gun to their head and makes them, and they still get away with a lot. Cherri was delusional; she might even believe me if I said yes. But I'd left that all behind when my wife was murdered. I knew what Diana would want me to do.

She poked again. "Say it."

"Cherri, we can't control who we love. It just happens. But you and I, we can't even get to know each other unless you walk away from this."

"Right answer. You get to live for a while. Any lies and I would have shot you."

"Will you stop this? I know you didn't kill Pete. Sly wanted me to believe it, but I know it wasn't you. When Chet and I studied the video, the person wearing the camera was at least five inches taller than you."

"Stop this? Don't you get it? I'm having a good time, okay? Who's Pete?"

I couldn't decide if I was making progress or not, but I was still alive. All I needed to do was get loose from the plastic tie around my wrists, take the rifle away from a martial-arts-instructor, render her unconscious -- club her down, shoot her if I had to, but Kandi had made me promise not to kill anybody -- then use the rifle to shoot out the window and wound, not kill, the Suberes before they set off their bomb in an attempt to kill Sly, get out of the attic and find my father and Kandi among the ten or twenty thousand people filling Main Street or the eighty thousand down on the beach, convince the former that I was a good son and carry the latter away so we could live happily ever after in a vine-covered cottage with a vegetable garden.

I didn't like my chances. I'm not a very good shot with a rifle and I don't know anything about gardening.

On the other hand, I had nothing to lose. Not a damn thing.

When you're in good physical condition you tend to sweat a lot and, if I do say so myself, I was in pretty good shape. I had spent a year running, lifting, surfing, and skateboarding, so I was in better shape than at any time since I'd quit wrestling. And Crazy Cherri had actually stretched the plastic tie a bit when she tugged on it, checking it.

Getting out of a tight knot requires concentration. You have to relax, let your muscles contract, let your skin get slick with sweat so you can work free of the restraint a little bit at a time. I exhaled and tried to quit thinking about the woman with the gun staring out the window and licking her lips, tried to quit thinking at all. Blank. Blank out my mind. Inhale. Quiet, quiet.

The crowd noise fades. Exhale. The music fades, fades, replaced by waves. My eyes see the woman with the rifle but they don't, they really see a deserted beach. Gentle surf, tiny translucent waves lapping at the pure white sand, now make the sound fade, make it slowly fade. The tiny wave rolls in, slows, then pauses as some of it seeps into the sand, creating tiny bubbles before it recedes, slipping back into the sea to gather itself for another roll in. In, pause, out, and again, gentle, quiet, relax your toes, no, don't think about the plastic, that's not what's important now. No. Lost it. The woman with the rifle is back. Start over. Inhale, blank, blank, exhale, the wavelet rolls back, relax your toes, inhale, then relax your calves, the wavelet gathers itself, don't hurry, relax your thighs, your stomach muscles, and finally your arms, the wavelet rolls in over damp sand. Loose, loose biceps, limp, quiet, loose muscles in your forearms, your hand now slippery with sweat, visualize the plastic slipping a tiny bit, see it moving in your mind, moving toward the bump that is your thumb joint. There is nothing else in the world except the plastic tie and your slippery wrist and it is moving just a bit. Then it snaps back. No, no, don't tense up, relax, let the wavelet roll back out, slippery, wet, it goes back to the sea, and the tie moves a bit, then a bit more and Cherri is turning from the window, turning slowly, looking first at Sly, then at me and her eyes are narrowing, suspicious. Don't tense, let the plastic slip, let it move, relax, it is moving, moving over the joint of your thumb and it doesn't want to go, don't force it, no, relax, and she is looking back out the window and it tries to move back up. Just relax. It slips down. It slips over the thumb joint and time returns to a real pace. Things start happening fast.

"Oh, look, it's the bitch and she's found the old man. Oh, how sweet, he's buying her a churro. I hope she chokes!" She stuck her head out the window and screamed, "Choke and die, bitch!" Of course it was lost in the crowd noise. She pulled her head back in and said, "They're all together now. Come here Sly, you need to watch while I put a slug in her sweet little head. Blood and brains everywhere. That's what she gets for ruining our love." She set the rifle down and, puffing a little, she dragged Sly up to the window, just like he was already dead. "What's that, my love? Are you trying to say something? Here," she peeled the tape off his mouth. "Now, what's that?"

"Please," he gasped, "we can be together, it's not too late, I just didn't understand, but now I do. I didn't understand how much you loved me and she, she seduced me away from you, but now I see the truth."

"Then you won't mind if I put a bullet through her pretty little head?"

"Go ahead! Anything! Kill her! Kill them both! Just let me go so we can be together." This from the guy I had promised to keep alive. Perfect.

She laughed and leaned him against the wall. "Watch closely, now, this will be good." She twisted her face, pursed her lips. "I wish I had a video camera. I'd really like to post this on YouTube, you know, her head exploding, the old guy turns and then I put one in him, too. And then the crowd goes wild!" She was looking out the window while she delivered this charming rant. She raised both arms over her head and danced around in a circle. Then she shrugged. "Oh, well. Can't think of everything." I could see Sly working frantically at the plastic around his arms.

"I didn't understand! I didn't know how you felt, really, I -- I thought you were too good for me! Yes, that's it! You're young and beautiful and smart, no way I could think you'd go for me." Sly was right in there pitching, I'll give him that.

She raised the rifle. She pointed it out the window and peered through the telescopic sight. I could feel her slowing her heartbeat, exhaling, waiting for the perfect shot. I gathered my feet under me and lunged.

Sly yelled, "Look out!"

Cherri turned toward me with the rifle already raised and fired, no hesitation, just pulled the trigger, but by the time she did I was moving and the shot passed over my shoulder. She leapt at me as I launched myself at her. My left hand came loose and I punched her as hard as I could, feeling ribs crack. Martial arts are great, but I outweighed her by eighty pounds and I was pretty motivated. Chet once told me that force equals mass times acceleration. I took that to mean that I could hit a lot harder than she could. She staggered back and aimed the rifle at me again and Sly swung both plastic-wrapped legs, tripped her and she went down, gasping as the pain from her broken ribs grating together hit her. I guess he'd had another change of heart. She started trying to club him with the rifle butt. They landed with her on top, her smashing at his head with the rifle stock and him squirming like a man-sized worm. He got his arms loose and swung at her but missed. They rolled; she lost the rifle. I kicked it aside, grabbed her and threw her against the wall as hard as I could. Her shoulders hit first, then her head snapped back into the metal frame around the window and she went down.

When I turned, Sly had the rifle. He'd gotten his arms loose and wriggled over to where the rifle lay on the floor and now held it pointed at me as he struggled to his knees. The lower half of his body was still wrapped in plastic. He pointed it at me and fired but I jumped and behind me I heard Cherri gasp. A kinder person might have turned to see that she was hit but I had other problems. I slapped the gun out of Sly's hands. But he was surprisingly quick, scuttling across the floor and getting to it before me. I felt a sharp pain and looked down to see that Cherri had crawled across the floor, leaving a trail of blood, and was now biting my ankle. Sly had the gun and was getting to his feet. Growling, Cherri started pulling herself up my leg. It didn't hurt as much through my jeans. Sly levered a shell into the rifle's chamber and grinned.

At that moment Kandi levitated herself out of the trapdoor like a blonde Jack-in-the-Box and he turned the rifle on her and fired. She turned sideways to present a smaller target and he missed, hitting the wall and sending shards of wood flying. Then she was on him, grabbing the barrel of the rifle and pointing it skyward while she kicked his feet out from under him. Kandi screamed at him, "Hostile! You are so hostile! And you refuse therapy. How about this?" She kicked him in the ribs. "I'll teach you to be so hostile!" I took the opportunity to pull Cherri off my leg. I took my shirt off and made an impromptu dressing for her flesh wound. "Hold that in place and push on it. You'll be okay." To be honest, I had no idea how serious her wound was, but it sounded good. I heaved a huge sigh of relief. There was a moment when we all just looked at each other. I think we all were surprised that it was over.

Kandi had the rifle, Sly was nursing ribs that were probably broken, and Cherri was bleeding. Kandi smiled and stepped over to me, still keeping an eye on our captives.

Then the trapdoor slammed open and Barney stuck his head up into the room. He stared around at all of us for a moment -- I guess we were gaping back at him -- and reached down for the bomb. He shoved it up into the attic and said, "Sorry, Mr. Macdonald. Keeping you alive was always a secondary priority, second to taking care of Mr. Staney. And you deceived us! We don't like that, not at all." Before we could react he had disappeared, closing the trapdoor behind him. I could hear the bolt as it slammed shut.

The red numbers that had previously been zeros were now counting down. 9.99 and counting.

Sly said, "Shit."

That summed it up.

The window Cherri had removed was small, but it might be big enough. I grabbed the bomb and the plastic bag that had been over Sly's head. Shoving the bomb into it, I rushed over to the window. There was a narrow ledge just outside. "Kandi, when I get out, hand this to me."

"Mac, don't be crazy."

"This will work."

"You have a plan." But she was picking up the bomb bag. I squirmed out the window feet first. There was a bad moment when I didn't think I'd fit but a hard shove got me through. I hadn't figured on the drop from the window to the ledge below. When I stretched I could just touch it with the toe of my shoe. I would have to let go of the windowsill, drop, and trust that I could catch myself to balance on the ledge. Full disclosure: I hesitated. I didn't want to do it. But I probably couldn't pull myself back up, and if I did there was the bomb.

I let go.

There was a bad moment when my fingertips and toes were sliding down the wall. Then my toes touched, my heels slapped down and I was standing on the ledge, pressing my face to the rough surface of the wall. I looked up and saw Kandi above me, dangling the bag with the bomb in it. She stretched out as far as she could before letting it slip from her hand. And then I bobbled it – bounced it from hand to hand while feeling certain I was starting to fall backward onto the sidewalk 20 feet below – and then, clawing at the featureless wall, used my crotch to trap the bomb bag against the building like a citrus fruit in a cocktail-party game.

I put the lip of the bomb bag between my teeth and leaned against the cold face of the building. The sidewalk below me would just as surely kill me from a drop at this height as the bomb. Deep breath. Then Neville occurred to me. And the box that Jackie lost, that came too. And the rat disappearing into a tiny hole in the floor. Of course, Jackie had hidden the box, and the box held Neville's secret. Jackie had hidden it and then forgotten. And I had an idea of where.

Everything outside receded – everything but the seemingly impossible distance between me and the decorative arch suspended from the building to the beach side of Pacific Coast Highway. Just beyond that was the pier. I started working my way along the ledge toward the highway.

Cherri screamed, "My hero! I'll always love you!"

Kandi said, "Shut up before I smash your teeth in." That's my girl.

At the edge of my vision, the red numbers of the bomb blinked. I was sorry I'd looked. I looked down where partiers had started to notice the crazy drunk on the building above them, and I was sorry I'd done that too. I edged along the ledge, but that was too slow so I took a deep breath and began hurrying, scooting one foot along after the other as fast as I dared.

Then I heard a muffled grunt behind me and saw Kandi lever herself out onto the ledge.

"No, go back!"

Of course she didn't stop. I couldn't wait to see what happened and went back to working my way along the ledge. But I was listening for a scream. Then I chanced a look back over my shoulder just as she dropped and got to her feet smoothly. I hurried. She came right along behind me.

Now the crowd was interested, getting into it, cheering, yelling, egging us on. In the distance I heard sirens and the urgent whoop-whoop of a police car. None of the crowd moved away from the free show.

We made it across the decorative arch set up for the contest – crabwalking through blue and white balloons high over PCH. I shimmied down the pole on the opposite side and sprinted out onto the pier, with Kandi right behind me. But the crowd was dense, bovine, pie-eyed. Even shoving I could not make enough progress. Then Kandi was ahead of me, kicking, yelling. "Gun! Gun! Gun!!" People scrambled out of our path.

And suddenly a white Stetson appeared and Chet was yelling, shoving, with Snake by his side and Cheryl leaping in the air and making Kung Fu noises. It was nuts. It was wonderful. People stared, and then got out of the way.

4:26 and we were only to the kite store. We weren't going to make it. I had only succeeded in moving the bomb into a bigger crowd. Then two bicycle cops forced their way to us. Before they could dismount Kandi had leveled one. I clotheslined the other as he turned to look at his friend. As mine went down I got on his bike and started moving through the crowd, with Kandi once again ahead of me on the other bike. Now people sensed something was up and started to get out of the way. Ten yards from the end of the pier some drunk guy dragged Kandi off her bike. I kept pedaling.

The seaward end of the pier is devoted to a burger place called Ruby's, but there's a space on the ocean side of the restaurant that's used mostly for fishing. Several people had poles leaning against the waist-high railing.

I whirled the bomb sack around my head like a hammer-throw athlete, and threw it as far from the end of the pier as I could, still running, slamming into the railing as I let go and saw it arch out over the water. Then my velocity was carrying me over the rail, off-balance, slipping. I twisted and tried to grab something, anything, and got a hand as a Vietnamese fisherman caught my wrist and I was dangling. My hand slipped down and I was gripping his hand. He had me but then he was coming, too, getting pulled over. His belt caught and he had his free hand scrabbling for a grip, but it wasn't enough. He must have weighed at most 120 and he couldn't hold me. A younger face appeared, reaching for me, but the old man was half-off and falling, eyes wide, cigarette dangling from his lips.

I let go.

I saw understanding in his eyes as I dropped and I thought I saw hands clutching at his shoulders.

As I fell I got my feet together and clenched my butt muscles. Going into water from a height can drive a piston of water up inside you, doing all kinds of damage to internal organs. The very end of the pier sticks out several feet past the pilings that hold it up, so I wasn't worried about hitting one on my way down. (Okay, okay, at the moment all I could think of was *I'm falling!* But later I was sure I had thought about the pier sticking out.) I hit the water—impact and *cold!* followed by sharp pain as water pressure pushed at my eardrums—and exhaled sharply. I wanted to be as far down as possible when the bomb went off. I thought I had made it when an enormous force slammed into me, I tumbled over and over and everything went dark.

The next thing I knew somebody had me around the neck. They were pulling me up. Kandi had my neck in the crook of her elbow and she was flailing, trying to keep us afloat without much success. We sank again, pulled down by the weight of our clothes. I tried to kick for the surface and in my mind I was doing it, but the reality was I simply couldn't do it, still stunned from the explosion and disoriented. I was feebly trying to push her away—she'd have a better chance without my dead weight—when there were two splashes and two lifeguards had us. They had us hold onto floats while they maneuvered first Kandi, then me, into a device sort of like a Bosun's Chair that hauled us up to the pier, swiveled, and lowered us down into waiting arms.

Chet, Cheryl, and Snake staggered up, bruised from multiple pushes and shoves, and slumped down to lean against the wall. Chet had lost his Stetson. Cheryl and Snake sank down, with her leaning on her husband. Snake looked at Chet and said, "BMC."

Chet pulled a blue bandanna out of his hip pocket, wiped his face and said, "I don't think I know that one."

"Bite my crank." They both started laughing.

Kandi crawled over to me, held my head and yelled, "Stay awake! You may have a concussion!" Then she kissed me and you know what? I was wide awake. And grinning like a fool.

Huntington Beach Independent - April 19, 1935

Tragic Fire Claims Life

The body of Lou Helen Hodges, formerly of Platteville, Texas, was found this morning in the burned-out bedroom of a house she was renting. Miss Hodges apparently fell asleep with a lighted cigarette. There were no other casualties. Miss Hodges had been employed as a hostess at the Sand 'n Songs Dance Hall, but had recently lost her job. She had no family in the area. A friend, Grace Stillwater, is being sought, however neighbors say she may have returned to Texas.

Chapter Nineteen

The police took up most of the rest of the day, and what they didn't want we gladly gave to the lifeguards and paramedics who patched us up. They handcuffed Sly and Cherri to beds in the police ward of Hoag Hospital. Sly's portable hard drive was indeed in his pocket but it was filled with pictures of Kandi. Chet was brought in to see if data was hidden inside the pictures but he could find none. That was fine with me.

I called my dad to let him know I was all right and to tell him where I thought he should look for Neville's missing papers. He found them in what used to be Jackie's room when he was growing up. It was a cigar box, hidden under a loose floorboard. It was easy to speculate from there: What with time and the war and his subsequent headbanging, Jackie had likely forgotten where he put it. Jackie's father had probably gotten the papers from his father, who was apparently involved with some underworld characters. When the family had searched after the grandfather's murder, everybody assumed the box couldn't be in Jackie's room because he was the one who lost it and of course he'd searched there first.

We sat around my kitchen table again and I answered as many questions as I could.

Chet asked, "Okay, Sly wants to put Mary in jeopardy so he can be like T. R. and save her, right? So why send the pictures of her in the airport to T. R.?"

I said, "I think in his mind he was making me choose. He wanted me to know Kandi was in danger, and arrange it so I'd have to look after my dad. Remember, when he sent the first picture, I didn't know she was trapped. And he was pretty sure I'd stay here with my father. And Sly was already in Chicago, so he was close by and ready to help."

Chet shook his head. "Wow. Talk about a tangled web. Okay, so you get Mary back here and now he wants you to get out of the way. So, why have Cherri and one of his thugs throw liquid nitrogen in the car?"

"I think Cherri did that on her own. She wanted to force Kandi away."

Kandi herself took up the story. "At that point, she had switched her obsessive love from Sly to T. R., and wanted me to give up on him. And, I think, part of her just wanted to see him in action. She knew we'd get out of the car safely, she just wanted to watch, and record a video."

The Suberes vanished without a trace.

There were some chocolate-covered strawberries for Kandi and me, accompanied by late-night Jacuzzis. She never once said, "We need to talk."

Then she went back to Chicago to provide a deposition about the events at the clinic.

May 1, 1935

My Dear Little One —

Your name is Neville Stillwater. I hope that someday you get to read this so you will know the truth about who you are and who your people are.

I have to leave you for a while and I want you to know it's not because I don't love you, because I love you very much. You are my Little One and I would do anything for you, even give you up at least for a while. I want you to understand. If everything works I will come back and get you and I will be able to tell you this myself, but just in case I want it written down.

We came out to California from Texas when we was just girls. In no time she was in love and I thought I was. We met some real nice folks and we worked in the Movie Industry. We thought we was real grown-up but we weren't. Your people are all from a little town there used to be more Stillwaters but they are mostly all Gone To Their Rewards one way or the other. There is so much I want to tell you, Little Neville, but I don't have much time.

There were some very bad men who wanted to hurt us and she was wearing my dress and my bracelet with the little dog charm so they killed her and set fire to our room. The Good Lord protected me along with you. I had you out in the stroller and all the people thought the dead girl was me. So I pretended.

The bad men found out that I wasn't dead and now they are looking for me, so I have to leave you with my friend the man who owns the stable. I don't think they know about him.

I have nothing to leave you except my love and the Diary, and this packet of letters. What happened was Grandfather Lamentations who would be your great grandfather mailed them to the old address and they just now got to me. He was a hard man and he didn't like it when we came out West so when your grandparents Passed he sent the letters back. He could be mean sometimes. The man at the stable says he will hide them along with the Diary and this letter and give them to you when you are older.

Grace Harmony Stillwater was your Mama's name. Your father was a man named Clyde.

I am called Grace Harmony Stillwater, but Stillwater is not the name I was born with. It is the name you were born with.

It was me the bad men were after and they killed her instead so I pretended to be her because people always said we could be sisters and she had on my bracelet, the one with the little dog that Willeford gave me, and everybody thought it was me and I never told and I wish it hadn't happened but there it is.

She loved you very much and so do I.

Yours Truly,
Lou Helen Hodges

Epilogue

My hands stung from the nitrogen, my ribs ached where I'd been punched, and my leg was still bandaged. The leg wasn't even close to being healed but it was time to surf. Besides, salt water helps. I read that somewhere.

I put the roof rack on the Chevy—it had new windows and upholstery where the nitrogen had ruined it—loaded the stand-up board on it, and went to pick up dad at his mobile home. He wasn't ready, was in fact in his robe sitting in the kitchen spooning crystals from a jar of Taster's Choice into a cup of steaming water, with a microwaved breakfast sandwich on a paper napkin next to it. Two unframed watercolors hung in the wall of the dining alcove, and the refrigerator was covered with pencil sketches held in place with magnets. His crutches leaned against the table next to him.

He gave the coffee another stir and picked up his sandwich. Some of the cheese had melted and run down onto the napkin. He yanked it off and slapped the paper down on the table. "Mary put you up to this?"

"Good morning to you, too."

"Take the old guy out, make him feel better? All that happy horseshit?"

"My advice is get into your wetsuit because the water's cold. Mid-fifties." For a moment we glared at each other.

"It's crummy today, almost flat. Let's pick a better day." So he'd checked Surfline.

I handed him his crutches. "Wetsuit."

"This won't work, you know."

"If you have a full suit I'd wear it, but a shortie will be better than nothing"

"Are you kidding? When I had my nine-six Jacobs we never wore wetsuits. Cold? You don't know cold."

I grinned. "I know, and the boards weighed thirty pounds. And leashes hadn't been invented and I bet the surf was bigger then, too. And you got surf knots on your knees." I wished to hell I had that last back. There was a moment where I tried not to look at his destroyed legs. "Anyway, if you don't go --"

"You'll tell Mary." I just looked at him. "She did put you up to this, Mary did. Okay, once, for her, and I guarantee it will suck."

It took him a long time in the bedroom with his wetsuit, but he did it with no help, came out and clumped by me to the carport.

I let the valet at Duke's, the restaurant at the foot of the Huntington Pier, park the car. Their lot is really not for beach parking but I'm a regular and all the guys who park cars love the hot rod Chevy.

About a hundred yards north of the pier there's this asphalt strip running toward the water at a right angle to the bike path. It allows the disabled to get close to the surf. He slung his beach bag over his shoulder and clumped along ahead of me as I struggled with the stand-up board and paddle.

He was actually not too bad getting across the small amount of sand before he dropped the beach bag and clumsily got down.

The water was chilly on my hands and feet as I pushed the board in. Then I had a problem I hadn't thought of -- how to get my dad from the sand to the board.

I let the board drift, hurried back with the paddle and let him use it on his left side while I got on his right side. The board had turned and started to float away, but it was easy to straighten out and to my surprise he grabbed the rails and pulled himself on the bow easily. With a little struggle he managed to get to a seated position, legs dangling on each side of the board. I handed him the paddle, hopped on and knee-paddled.

It was gray and chilly, one of those foggy mornings when sounds are muffled and the world is gloomy. The end of the pier was lost in the mist. After a few strokes out the only sound was the splashing of my hands as I paddled. Then I took the paddle from him and stood. I'd been a little uncertain about standing on the board with another person on it, so I took a few tentative strokes, trying to master the changes in balance and the sluggishness of the board. I stood in back of him and paddled us out through the small break -- fortunately the surf was just a foot or two -- and there were few people out.

He slipped off the board once, but I knew better than to help him drag himself back on. He did it, and made it look easy.

And once we were outside, with him in his antique wetsuit with the rip along the zipper, I thought it would be okay, or at least better, but it wasn't. When I turned and pointed the board up the coast the shore was gone, covered by the mist, and it was as if we were all alone, in a strange silent world, just the two of us and the glassy sea beneath, with only the slow, gentle swells to point us toward the beach. Twenty-four hours ago the surf had been big and as a result the water was churned up, cloudy and brown. Big chunks of kelp drifted past, huge orange-brown leaves moving down the coast, occasionally brushing the bow. My dad irritably pushed them away.

I stroked us north, against the current, not sure how far we had traveled, and then turned and let us drift back south.

He was straddling the bow, useless legs dangling in the murky water, and his shoulders were shaking. "Thought I'd never see it again, not like this," he muttered, so faintly I could barely hear it. I'm not sure he knew he spoke aloud. Suddenly he reached down, cupped a handful of water and splashed his face. "Gimme the damn paddle. Let's go. Seventeenth Street light and back."

"Kind of --" I started to say it was a long way. He turned and looked at me over his shoulder, long sixties surfer hair dangling in his face, powerful hands gripping the board's rails. "Kind of cool. Let's do it." I handed him the paddle. His upper-body strength was incredible; he paddled like a machine, first on one side of the board, then the other, not even breathing hard as he stroked and we glided north. I stood for a while, then sat and enjoyed the ride.

We made it. We spotted the stoplight through the haze and he let us coast for a moment before he turned the big board. Seventeenth Street and back to the pier, just under a three-mile paddle. My dad was tireless. When the pier loomed out of the fog he hoisted the paddle over his head and hooted. Pure joy.

He tried to hand me the paddle but I shook my head. "Go for it, old man. Take us in. Let's see that famous wave sense."

I unfastened my leash when he was looking out to sea, checking the break. If this didn't work and he fell off I wanted to be able to grab him. The board was on its own. But I didn't need to. He timing was perfect, and on a new board, one he'd never been on before, using a paddle instead of his arms, he caught the first wave he went for, shifted his weight back to keep the nose up, and we rode it all the way in.

I left him holding on to the paddle, sitting in shallow water while I dragged the board up onto the sand, then went back and got an arm around his shoulders and helped him back to the towel.

Just to make the day perfect, a seagull had striped a huge present across the handle of one crutch. I took it down to the shore and rinsed it off in the shallows while he sat. When I came back, he took it and stood, gripping the handles. We said nothing. It should have been a bonding moment, a chance to let go of past pain and get back to a real relationship. Neither of us knew how to do that – or maybe we did, and were doing it.

I unzipped and peeled my wetsuit down to my waist just as another seagull flew over and unloaded, striping my stomach, my wetsuit leg, and, just for good measure, the center of my towel. We looked at this newest contribution, looked at each other and started laughing. He plopped down, lost his balance and fell on his back, pounded his fists into the sand and howled, just roared. I was in the shallows, scrubbing with handfuls of wet sand, rolling in the shore break and laughing.

It was one of the best days surfing ever, for either of us.

At home there was no text from Kandi. I felt okay anyway.

I sat on the deck, in the good old chair with the frayed webbing, next to the burned spot, and watched the sun slide toward the sea.

I don't have a job. I have a career, maybe a calling. Whether I found it or it found me is moot, or maybe it depends on whether you take your predestination straight or with a dash of free will.

The pay is nonexistent, many of the people I encounter are sociopaths, and, instead of a bad performance review, you can get your head blown off. Who am I?

I'm T. R. Macdonald.

. . . At the violet hour, the evening hour that strives Homeward, and brings the sailor home from sea . . .

- T. S. Eliot, The Waste Land

Mac and Kandi will return in *Remains To Be Seen*

About the author

James R. Preston spends most of his time at the keyboard, writing the award-winning Surf City Mysteries—think "beach noir." *Sailor Home From Sea* is the fifth novel in this series and was preceded by *Leave A Good-Looking Corpse, Read 'Em And Weep, The Road To Hell,* and *Pennies For Her Eyes.*

The Surf City Mysteries have been selected for inclusion in the California Detective Fiction collection of the Bancroft Library, one of the libraries at the University of California, Berkeley. You can read the opening chapter of each book at JamesRPreston.com.

Away from the keyboard, James likes reading, films (especially 1950's SF like Them and The Crawling Eye), sailing, bodyboarding, and Texas Hold'Em Poker. James played in one of the 2011 World Series tournaments and sadly busted out early. This year will be different.

Other Surf City Mysteries

Leave A Good-Looking Corpse

From the journals of T. R. Macdonald:

It isn't every night that a wet, bleeding man leads the hostess into her party at gunpoint . . . not even in Hollywood and this Orange County, home of Disneyland, Knott's Berry Farm and the Crystal Cathedral. Hell, even our baseball team is the Angels. A drop of blood ran down the side of my face. I let it drip off my chin, figuring it made me look tough.

That wet, bleeding gun-waver is me, T. R. Macdonald, and I'm a broker/analyst based in NYNY, or I was until I got a phone call about my wife. I walked off the trading floor, packed a bag and started driving for the left coast. After I got there things turned weird, then weirder. Some the weirdness was okay, but a lot of it was very nasty; for example, right after the party I had to shoot a kid.

Read 'Em And Weep

From the journals of T. R. Macdonald:

I was sort of hiding from two guys who either thought we were in business together or who wanted to kill me.

"Sort of hiding" because I could have left town and been relatively safe, but Las Vegas, NV, has so many wonderful things to see and do that I decided to go to a topless rollerskating show instead.

"Sort of hiding" because I was fairly sure that the guys in question would take Door Number Two and try to shoot me, a lot.

Why me? I'm T. R. Macdonald, a sort-of unemployed broker/ analyst from the boutique—we handle a small number of very rich clients—firm of Fields, Smith, and Barkman. My sort-of girlfriend, Kandi, had asked me to go to Vegas to see if we could talk to her cousin Chet, because she thinks his adoptive father, Dr. Woodrow Shaw, may be nuts. Are you getting all this? There will be a quiz. Dr. Shaw asked me to go, too, and he offered to pay.

It sounded like easy money.

I must be nuts.

The Road To Hell

From the journals of T. R. Macdonald:

I was standing in the desert, in the sun, outside of a semi-abandoned church, and I had a gun. My girlfriend, the lovely blonde Kandi Shaw, and I were registered in the Maiden's Blush Suite, one of the finest in Las Vegas' lavish Bromeliad Resort and Spa. Unfortunately, I wasn't in the suite. I was standing in the sun, waiting for my brains to finish boiling.

I'm T. R. Macdonald, a semi-unemployed broker-anaylst from Huntington Beach, California—Surf City, USA. And I was here instead of sitting on my short tri-fin outside the break line at the Huntington Pier because the casino offered me money to assist in security for WillieFest One, the richest slot tournament in history.

But so far I'd been mainly a moving target or punching bag—I was run off the road, chased by pit bulls, mixed it up with a vicious pimp, and was nearly trampled in a club stampede. Not to mention the part where I was poked in the nose. With a sawed-off shotgun. All of that led to the church, and my gun, and Kandi standing next to me with her gun in her hand—and she wanted to shoot somebody.

And if the two men inside the church didn't listen to reason, I was very much afraid she was right—I'd have to shoot them.

Pennies For Her Eyes

From the journals of T. R. Macdonald

I was sitting on a wet bike in frigid water, watching waves the size of three-story buildings slide toward me, hump up, then hump up again getting even taller before crashing down with a sound like a Las Vegas casino imploding. I could be in one of those casinos, a fancy one, too, because they liked me and wanted me to work for them, or I could be on Wall Street moving around billion-dollar chunks of money.

But instead I was here, cold and anxious and very soon I'd have to drive the wet bike in front of one of these waves, dragging a beautiful redhead behind me on the end of a towline, and if -- when--she fell I'd have to go get her. Or die trying. That was the part I didn't like, the "die trying."

My name is T. R. Macdonald and believe it or not this was the good part. People hadn't started stuffing me in the trunks of cars or shooting at me. Yet.